LOST in the CITY of FLOWERS

Lost in the City of Flowers

The Histories of Idan
Book I

MARIA C. TRUJILLO

HISTART PRESS
Boulder, CO

2020 Histart Press Paperback Edition

Cover & Artwork by Kate Forrester.

Originally published in paperback in the United States by Histart Press in 2014.

Library of Congress Control Number: 2020910324

ISBN 978-0-9915597-4-9 | ISBN 978-0-9915597-5-6

HISTART PRESS : Boulder, CO

histartpress.com

To my family, the old and the new.

Note from the Author

"HISTORY IS A GREAT adventure and art is just one of the many paths that can take your hand and lead you through it."

In the second chapter, Mrs. Reed says these words to the heroine to help her realize how important history is to the present and how enlightening art can be. This book is a quest, but it is also a tool to navigate the spirit of the Florence Renaissance. Before writing *Lost in the City of Flowers*, I spent half a year researching the social circumstances, architecture, and artwork of the time period. Through visual analysis and reading copious materials such as diaries and writings by distinguished historians, I wrote a story that brings this time period to life for the readers. The glossary located at the back of the book gives the reader more information about historical characters and defines art history terminology. In addition, the glossary points out which characters are actually real. A map is also included to help you follow Viola on her adventures through the City of Flowers.

"What is real and what is not?" is an indispensable question that comes up frequently in historical fiction. This story is based on real people and conditions of the time period. Most of the pivotal characters in this book actually co-existed. The descriptions of the artists and other historical figures are based on portraits or descriptions of them.

Information regarding artwork is also accurate, although some of the dates of the artwork have a wide range of possible completion. Therefore, for a few of the pieces, such as the *Baptism of Christ* by Andrea Verrocchio's workshop, it is difficult to determine when exactly they were finished.

Acknowledgments

AT SOME POINT IN a person's life they lose their way. Like many, I experienced that oh-so-familiar feeling of uncertainty and fear. But without that momentary anxiety, I would not have created the first novel of the Histories of Idan. The idea of Viola and her nostalgic travels started as a bud in my mind, but under the nurture of loved ones, friends, and strangers, it blossomed.

My parents, Sila and Alex, always encouraged me to explore my passions and helped me follow my dreams. I want to thank them for not holding me back when I went on to study something I loved. To my Uncle Tony and Aunt Gitta, I am eternally grateful for their constant support and for shedding light on my path when all was dark. Jorge, my husband, to whom I am most indebted for the hundreds of sacrifices he has undertaken and encouragement he has given—without which, this book or my sanity wouldn't be possible.

As so many know, when you move to another place, especially as a young child, your existence twists upside down and spins out of control. It is an incredible experience that is both precious and daunting. I was fortunate to find my balance with the help of my three siblings: Tommie, Teresa, and John. If it were not for the challenges we faced or the laughter we shared together, I would not be who I am today.

I not only owe my eternal gratitude to my family but also to my dear friends. It is my belief that friendship is the purest example of all that is wonderful about humanity. This bond is based on sharing joys and sorrows with kindred souls in a transient world. It is about caring, giving, and taking. I am thankful to Cristina for healing my wounds, fostering my confidence, and for being a constant source of inspiration. Denise, I am so appreciative of you for being my pillar in the calm and the storms. Thank you to the McGrail family, for always being so constant and for having faith in my vision. My brimming gratitude also goes out to the Soldo family. They made me fall in love with Italy. Moreover, I will never forget the extraordinary kindness they have shown me throughout the years. I asked for a helping hand, and you gave me shelter and strength.

I would like to extend another hearty thank you to the Beta Readers, especially to Alyssa Abraham. Lastly, I would like to tip my hat to all those who contributed to the crowdfunding campaign. Your trust and willingness has touched me. More importantly, you have brought these words and pages to life. All these individuals have collectively enabled me to realize my dream.

CHAPTER ONE

Happy Birthday

THE DESPAIR I FELT that night is as real now as it was on December 19, 1469. When you go through something so traumatic, the most frightening memory hides itself in an obscure corner of the mind. That memory likes to visit when you are most vulnerable. For me, it comes when it is cold outside—the wet kind that dampens your hair and makes your skin feel soggy. When I am lying on my bed exhausted but cannot sleep. If I close my eyes and let my thoughts drift, it comes.

I can feel the straw and linen beneath my bare neck. The smells of wood, rosemary, and sheep smother me. Slivers poke through my hair and cotton dress. I scratch at the phantom itch that comes from wearing rough wool stockings. The weight in my chest grows and expands until I feel like all the anxiety will burst from my body.

On that memorable night, the shock of losing myself 544 years in the past had finally worn off, and all the repercussions of it hit me in a single instant. Fears of never seeing my family, the bright lights of New York City, or realizing my dream of becoming an artist flooded my mind. By the time I finally fell asleep, I had drowned in terror.

Prior to lying on a mattress of straw, that morning I had woken up in my very own bed. The sound of someone whistling an offbeat "happy birthday" melody in a volume that was much too loud for 7:00 a.m. forced my eyelids open.

"Happy birthday, Vivi!" my dad sang from the kitchen. "It's time to get up for your first breakfast as a fifteen-year-old."

Grudgingly, I managed to get my legs and arms out from beneath the warm nest of sheets I had worked so hard on all night. In one clumsy motion, I rolled out of bed and walked to the foot of the window. The day was struggling to decide whether it would be sunny or overcast.

While the clouds were rushing across the skyline, the garden atop the building opposite mine was in danger of being swept away by the wind.

It was the perfect weather for my birthday, an indecisive day for an indecisive girl. Since the beginning of my birthdays I've always had a terrible time making decisions, especially in tight situations and where time was short. My appearance echoed my indecisive attitude. After only a few months in high school, I wasn't the tallest or the shortest. The hair that fell past my shoulders was a color somewhere in between red and brown and was not curly or straight. For an extra boost of confidence, my dad liked to say that my hair looked cast from a Greek sculpture because of its wavy strands and bronze color. The parts of me I liked best were my mismatched eyes. My left blue eye was slightly bigger than the right brown eye.

Resigned to the idea that the day might be a stormy one, I changed for my first day as a "fifteen-year-old." After slipping a green sweater over my head, I secured my jeans with a neon orange belt I had bought in Chinatown. With a quick glance at the mirror, I pulled my braided hair over my shoulder.

"Violet ... your breakfast is getting cold!" hollered my dad as I snatched my silver locket from the dresser and walked down the hallway to the kitchen.

My mom had been orphaned at only a few weeks old with nothing but a sad letter and a locket. She had given me the only clue to her past as a birthday present three years ago, and the locket was definitely my most prized possession.

My dad was reading some archaeological magazine when I sat down at our breakfast table. An assortment of French pastries from the bakery across the street waited on the table. My dad, Professor Menet, was tall and almost as skinny as me. Even though I jokingly asked him to let his hair grow, he kept his red hair and beard closely trimmed. He was sipping his probably fifth cup of coffee when he looked up at me from his large bifocal glasses.

"It's about time, Violet. Your tea is cold now, but I can warm it up for you on the stove," he said as he walked over with my favorite Amelia Earhart mug.

"It's okay," was all I could manage as I stuffed a strawberry-filled pastry into my mouth. I wiped the pastry flakes off my lips with the back of my hand.

My dad sat back down and placed my tea on the placemat. From underneath the table, he pulled out two parcels neatly wrapped in newspaper.

"Happy birthday, Vivi," he said as he leaned over and kissed the top of my head. I beamed.

Hiding behind the sports section of the *New York Times* was an assortment of new drawing pencils in a soft leather case.

"Oh, Dad, thanks! I needed new ones."

The second package was larger and contained a pair of purple Converse sneakers. I realized I could use the new pair, but it was so hard to part with my old ones. They had endured many charcoal and paint stains, not to mention the grime of the city's subway, sidewalks, and buses. My old ones almost felt like old friends. I didn't know what it felt like to have old friends, but if I did I was sure they would feel something like my faithful sneakers. It was kind of hard for me to make friends. It might have been a combination of how shy I was and plain luck. When I did make a friend, they moved away or changed schools.

The phone in the hallway rang loudly. "I think I know who that is." My dad stood and walked out of the kitchen.

As I polished off the rest of the pastry and gulped my tea, I could hear my dad speaking in hushed Italian. Immediately, I knew who he was speaking to. Minutes later, my dad returned.

"It's Clara," he whispered as he held out the phone. I extended my long fingers to receive it.

"Hi, Clara," I said, pressing the receiver to my ear.

"Happy birthday, Vivi!"

"Thanks, sissy." I smiled, letting stray pastry flakes fall on my sweater.

"How many pastries have you had already?" she asked. I could almost see her grinning all the way in California.

"One and counting."

"Amateur."

"I just woke up!"

"That's a sad start to your birthday," she teased.

"Hey! Vacation's just started ... I deserve some rest after exams."

"True ... Well save some of the chocolate ones for me."

"I can't make any promises when it comes to anything with chocolate."

"That's my sister." She laughed.

"You were supposed to be here for my birthday," I complained before taking a sip of my breakfast tea.

"I know, love, I'm sorry. The twelve-hour shifts at the hospital have me dead on my feet. I can barely put a whole sentence together. I just need to hibernate for a while before I can get back to my old self."

"You still haven't answered my question."

"I get there Christmas Eve."

"Lame," I protested, grabbing a chocolate croissant from the stack. "You are going to ruin the few traditions we have left!"

"Come on, Vivi, don't be hard—" She was interrupted by a beeping sound.

"Clara, can I call you back?" I asked, pulling apart the buttery crust. "Someone else is calling."

"Fine. But don't forget like you always do."

"I won't," I assured her before I pressed a button to receive the incoming call.

"Ciao, sweet Viola!" cheered my mom. "Happy birthday, beautiful!" The sound of her voice stirred an overwhelming mixture of excitement and resentment, which were both competing fiercely with the strawberry pastry in my stomach.

"Hi, Mom ... Thanks," I said, frowning at the sudden loss of my appetite.

"Are you having a good day so far?"

In that moment I realized how much I really missed her. If only she could be here with us now. She would have been quick to point out that Italian pastries were much better than French ones, and she would be jabbering about the birthday traditions of ancient Romans. Instead, she had to call me on the phone from Naples, Italy. This must have been the fourth time she had missed my birthday. My mom was an Italian art conservator; she fixed art that was broken or falling apart. Dad was the best, but it had been hard not to have Mom around. I couldn't tell my dad everything and my much older sister, Clara, was all the way in California, so it was hard to find someone to relate to.

"Oh, it's been good. Dad got me some nice pencils and sneakers. We still haven't talked about what we are doing today, but I think Dad already has a plan."

"He told me about it already, and it sounds fantastic! You must tell me every detail about it!"

"About what?"

"You will see! I don't want to give it away because then it will ruin your Dad's surprise." She paused for a moment. "Viola?"

"Yes, Mama?"

"Dad and I were talking about another birthday present for you." She paused again. "How would you like to come visit me at my work site?"

"You mean, come to Italy?" I asked, trying not to sound too excited.

"Well, to Herculaneum, Italy, to be more exact. You can read all about it in an article I sent to Dad.   I hope you've been practicing your Italian?" she asked with an inquisitive tone.

All I could manage was a lame "Uh ..." I glanced at my dad for help but he had reburied himself in a stack of papers. "Well, a little," I said with a twinge of guilt. Not wanting to ruin my chances at visiting Italy, I added, "I would love to visit you, Mama, and I'll read your article at least twice before I do."

"Viola, I think this will be great for both of us, because I can show you what I do away from home, and you can learn more about your heritage. Language is an important part of preserving your culture, so you need to practice your Italian. You never know when it will come in handy. Plus, it would make your grandmother happy."

"Okay, Mama, I understand." She was really laying the guilt on thick. I mean, my Italian's pretty good considering I've never been to Italy. Plus, I had been too busy with other things, like drawing or staring at Louis Martin in AP English class.

"Well then, I'll book your flight for after Christmas. Take care of your dad, and I hope you both have a special day. I wish I could be there, Viola ..." Her voice quivered. Sensing that she might cry, I told her that I loved her and not to worry. Once I hung up the phone, I noticed my dad had cleared his plate from the table. "Dad, I'm off the phone!" I hollered.

"Don't shout, Vivi," he answered. "Get ready to go. We are leaving in five minutes."

In my room I put on my new sneakers and my entire winter gear, hat, gloves, and scarf included. Before leaving I grabbed my mom's tan leather satchel and placed my sketchbook and pencils inside.

While we descended the flight of stairs to the street, Dad explained our plans for the day. "First, we have a surprise visit, and then I thought we could get some movie tickets for this evening," he said as he opened the building's brownstone door. I felt the cold air immediately begin to press against my nose and search for crevices beneath the layers of clothing.

"Vivi, don't you feel so alive when the air is this cold?" my dad asked. Trying to conserve my dad's good spirits and my own body warmth, I nodded in agreement as my dad fumbled for the keys to open up Charlemagne. That was his pet name for his beloved 1967 pale blue Volvo. Every time I suggested we buy a new car, he would launch into a long tale. It usually started with my grandparents, climaxed with a road trip to the Panama Canal, and ended with him driving my newborn-self home from the hospital. In short, Charlemagne was definitely a soft spot for Professor Menet.

The muddled sunlight and dust shined through the front window as we drove out onto Seventh Avenue. It was 9:30 a.m. and the car chugged along while the speakers hummed one of dad's obscure jazz tapes in the background. My curiosity got the better of me.

"Where are we going?"

"We're heading to the swinging golden coast of Long Island," my dad responded with a side glance and a wink.

His answer left me confused. What was there to do on Long Island? The only time I had been to Long Island was for a boring fourth-grade field trip to English gardens outside a deserted mansion.

"Oh ... what's in Long Island?" I said, trying not to sound too skeptical. He gave me a sly look.

"It has something to do with your sketchbook. Other than that, you'll just have to wait and see."

"My sketchbook?" No one, apart from my immediate family, had seen my drawings. Instantly I felt disappointed about the "surprise visit." Honestly, I'm not sure why I was so protective and private about it. Mostly, I didn't know if the drawings were any good. What if they were terrible, and I'm doing everything wrong? What if my drawings were mediocre, and it might soon spread around the world that Violet Menet has no talent for art? It would crush me. My family only had words of kindness and encouragement. That was their job though, wasn't it? I could make stick figures or handprints and they would still say, "Why, Vivi, that's wonderful!" They just wanted to make me happy, and they knew that drawing made me happy. Shouldn't that have been enough for me too?

I decided not to ask any more questions. The tape had stopped, and I turned it over. The low rumble of jazz continued as we passed inlets of frozen water and towering trees. Charlemagne swept by long expanses of naked forests and occasional stretches of houses built close together.

As the car ride wound down, the houses grew farther apart. Most of the time all we could see of the great mansions were their endless metal fences.

"It should be here somewhere," my dad mumbled as he consulted a small, crumpled paper. He made a slight left onto a gravel road. After about a minute, we were at a colossal gate entrance.

"So! What do you think?" asked my dad with a curious look.

Gravity seemed to pry my lips apart. The gate was a masterpiece all by itself. The magnificent entrance was at least twenty feet high. Twisting bars made intricate flowers and vines that sprouted from the ground. It had a large triangular shape at its pinnacle, where two golden horse heads faced each other. Some of the flowers were crowned with blue stones.

Behind the web of vines and flowers was a long and curvy driveway that hid the house from view. He rolled down the window and was about to press the button when an authoritative, but kind voice spoke out. "Professor Menet! Is that you?"

"Yes, Mrs. Reed! And I'm here with my daughter, Viola- I mean Violet!"

"Of course you are! I've been looking forward to seeing her all week! Mrs. Crawly will greet you at the main door, and I'll be in your delightful company shortly."

Once the gate opened, Charlemagne slowly chugged up the curvy road. The building and gardens that came into view were so grand that they made my fourth-grade field trip look ridiculous. The red brick house was three stories high, and I counted twenty-three windows on its facade. The third floor had five beautiful gables and a tower that poked out from the top. Broad sandy fields of manicured grass and barren rose bushes wrapped around the mansion. We parked at the front entrance. A balcony hung over the entryway supported by white columns on either side of the dark-paneled door.

"You do the honors," said my dad, pointing to the gold knocker in the shape of a running horse. Nervous, I reached for the handle and knocked twice.

CHAPTER TWO

Sketchbook

THE ELEGANT DOOR SWUNG open to reveal an elderly woman who must have been Mrs. Crawly. She had pulled back her gray hair tightly, showing a good-hearted face with heavy lines at the corners of her mouth and eyes. A mole hung on her upper lip.

"Good morning, Professor Menet. So good of you to visit."

"It's nice to finally meet you in person, Mrs. Crawly." There was a pause and Mrs. Crawly turned to examine me. My dad followed her gaze and said, "This is my daughter—"

"Violet," she finished with a soft smile.

"Mrs. Reed will meet you both in the library. Please follow me," she said as she briskly led the way under tall painted ceilings and across the black and white marble floor.

The library was bright. Three French windows on one side of the lofty room allowed light to warm the spines of thousands of books tucked into the dark cases covering the walls. On the opposite side of the room, a burning fire cast a glow onto two large green sofas and a caramel leather armchair. A woman was standing in front of the fire with her hands clasped behind her.

"Mrs. Reed, Professor Menet and Violet have arrived," Mrs. Crawly announced.

The woman looked up from the mantelpiece. To my surprise, her dark eyes were glassy with tears. When she smiled, several drops broke free. "Ah, you must excuse me," she said grabbing a handkerchief from her dress pocket. "The price to pay for staring at a fire too long." She dabbed her face. "You are both quite welcome. I hope you had a pleasant trip from the city?"

"Oh, there were some nice views, and we didn't meet any traffic," answered Dad. "Thank you again, Mrs. Reed, for inviting Violet here today."

While my eyes searched the room's lavish furnishings, they met Mrs. Reed's. Thick brows curved around her big brown eyes. They looked at me as if they had never seen a girl close up. When she smiled, her sun-kissed cheeks almost touched her eyes.

"Please, call me Annie. It's kind of you to let me share in your sweet Viola's special day ... happy birthday." The elegant woman had a slight accent. From where, I wasn't sure and thought it might be rude to ask. The way she spoke with her hands reminded me of my mom. Except my mom would never wear red nail polish. Gray streaks ran through dark, curly hair pinned into a labyrinth of twists. The black color of her satin dress complimented her olive skin. Even at the age of sixty or so, Mrs. Reed was beautiful.

"She actually prefers Violet. The name on her birth certificate is Viola, but I guess she thinks it's *weird*," he explained, using finger quotations for the last word. Feeling thoroughly embarrassed at being talked about in the third person, I fought an extreme urge to roll my eyes. "Teenagers," he added.

"Well, both names are lovely, but I do like the sound of Viola," said Mrs. Reed.

"Now that I have thoroughly embarrassed her, I'll be back to pick up Violet in two hours. Is that all right with you?"

"Of course, take your time. Will you not have some tea or coffee before you go?"

"Thank you, but I think I'll just leave you two to it! I have an appointment." Knowing my dad, that probably meant he was going to sneak into a bar to watch a soccer match.

"Very well, Mrs. Crawly, please see Professor Menet out."

My dad kissed me on the cheek. "Be on your best behavior please … and stand up straight," he whispered. I arched my back upwards.

When he left the room, I looked at Mrs. Reed with my bravest smile.

"Please come and sit with me by the fire, Violet. Mrs. Crawly will be here shortly with tea and cake. I told her to surprise us with anything but birthday cake, as I'm sure your dad has that planned for later." She gracefully sat in the leather armchair.

Following her example, I stepped quietly and lowered myself onto the green sofa. It was extremely comfortable. Between the fire, the chair, and Mrs. Reed's soothing voice, it was hard to stay awake.

"How is your mother, Violet?" Her question caught me off guard, so I stammered something about Italy and her work at Herculaneum. "I've read her latest article … quite impressive, the work she is doing over there. You must be proud."

"I am," I murmured, feeling even guiltier that I had not read the article.

"Will she be back any time soon?"

"I'm not sure. She wants me to go visit her in Italy before she comes back. That way I can also visit my grandmother."

At hearing this her face drooped into sad wrinkles. "Violet, do you know who I am?"

"Not exactly, ma'am." She paused and took out her handkerchief again.

"Your father and I met because I'm a donor of art and archaeological objects to the university he works at. He might not have told you, but I'm also an avid historian and art collector. When I was young, I married a brilliant inventor and explorer, Mr. John Reed. Until recently we have made it our life mission to uncover lost histories. Mr. Reed died two years ago. I must admit it's been hard for me, and I'm still in mourning, as you can see." She smoothed out the creases in her black dress.

"I'm sorry for your loss," I said.

"Which is why I so appreciate your company!" She continued, "Your father tells me that you are quite the artist. When he told me, I said, 'how lucky you are!' That's when I extended an invitation for you to visit my home so that I may see some of your drawings, and here we are!" She finished with her arms open as if to embrace me.

"Thank you again for inviting me," I replied, trying to avoid her stare.

"It's no trouble. In fact, it is a pleasure. I rarely get to spend time with any young people. It is refreshing! My son Peter is all grown up and very busy." The light from the fire made her brooch of fine red and white stones twinkle. "I hope you brought your sketchbook. Your father told me you bring it with you wherever you go." Her eyes searched mine as if to uncover my thoughts. How could I come up with an excuse now? There seemed to be no way out.

"Well, I did bring it, Mrs. Reed, but I'm not sure if you really want to see it. You are probably used to better artwork." I hesitated with the silent hope she would forget the idea completely.

She responded with a concerned look, which was interrupted by the sound of swirling skirts and ringing silver.

"Teatime!" rang Mrs. Crawly, swiftly putting the tray on a neighboring table and leaving the library.

"Do you take sugar or milk in your tea?" asked Mrs. Reed as she busied herself with the contents of the silver tray.

"Both, please," I said.

She handed me a gold-rimmed teacup laced with flower drawings and a generous slice of fruitcake. Trying not to spill it all over my jeans and the beautiful sofa, I balanced the cake on my lap and sipped my tea.

"Violet, do you consider yourself an artist?" she asked, preparing her own tea.

In all honesty, I didn't. I mean, how could I be? After all, I was only fifteen years old, and I barely knew anything about art. Living in New York City, I had plenty of opportunities to go to any of the hundreds of galleries or museums, but it was always so intimidating. Every time I walked out, I felt so defeated. There were so many artists, how could I have something great or unique to share with the world of art?

"Not really, Mrs. Reed."

"Why is that?"

"Well, I guess it's because I am only fifteen years old, and I don't really have enough experience." I piled the moist, nutty fruitcake into my mouth.

"I beg to differ," she said, cutting a slice of fruitcake for herself. "Of course, you know who the artist Leonardo da Vinci is?"

Although I knew of him, I couldn't point out any of his artwork or a picture of him. "I've heard of him, but I don't think I've seen his art in person," I said, feeling more and more embarrassed.

"Well, he was the definition of a Renaissance man... He was an extraordinary draftsman, painter, sculptor, scientist, architect, musician, and even inventor. He was only seventeen years old and was already very accomplished when he was an apprentice under another famous artist's workshop by the name of Andrea de Verrocchio..." She sipped her tea. "How much do you know about art history?"

"A little, but that's not really anyone's fault except my own." It was good my dad was not there as I was starting to sound dumb.

"It's important because it can tell you quite a bit about the present ... Much of what we know about past kings, battles, laws, and ways of life comes from art. I like to think that history is a great adventure, and art history is just one of the many paths that takes your hand and leads you through it ... I think it's important to know about where you, the artist, comes from. To know what has brought art to this unique moment in time. Many people think, like you do, that experience is most important for an artist, but don't let age define your limits, Violet." She paused and took a bite of her cake.

"You should be proud of your work! One of the survival skills of an artist is to have supreme confidence in yourself and in your art." The room was quiet save for the soft drip of the rain sliding down the windowpanes. "Dear, life will bring you opportunities disguised as obstacles or problems, but it is from these challenges and moments of adversity that you learn to trust and discover yourself." Mrs. Reed placed her free hand on my knee. "Only then will you find the confidence you need to be a supreme artist and person. If that is what you want, of course." A brief smile crossed her face before she pulled her hand back.

"I won't ask to see your sketchbook again until you're ready to show it to me, but I do think it's important that you broaden your horizons and build your self-confidence." She shot up from her seat and walked over to the fire.

It was strange to be lectured by an almost complete stranger. Although I knew it was mostly good advice, part of me jolted at being told what to do. While I contemplated her words, she raised her left arm and consulted her slender wristwatch. Then she pulled a second object from her gown. It looked like a pocket watch but it was diamond-shaped. It had a hard gold shell and a long chain that grazed the lush carpet. She glanced back at me. "Would you be interested in seeing my art gallery? I think you might find it enlightening."

"Oh ... yes please!" I said placing my teacup and plate on the tray.

Mrs. Reed wound several knobs on the pocket watch and closed its metal case.

"After you, dear Violet," she said, pointing at the entrance. I stood up and retraced my steps towards the doorway. When I turned around, Mrs. Reed was right behind me holding my satchel.

"Oh, thank you! Sorry, I'm sort of forgetful."

"I leave my purse in a room and often forget all about it until weeks later," she said, guiding me back towards the main entrance and up the maroon carpeted staircase.

On the walk up, I could see several exotic paintings of landscapes and portraits hanging on the wall. We continued up a second and third staircase. Mrs. Reed turned down a long hallway and opened a door to her left with a key. After turning on a light switch, she beckoned me to follow her. The room's lofty ceilings hovered above hundreds of paintings, sculptures, and objects. My dad would have loved to catalog even the dust mites.

Mrs. Reed drew back the thick navy curtains blocking the sunlight. "Violet, I'll come back and get you when I feel you're ready. May I suggest you spend some extra time looking at the painting at the end with the red curtain hanging over it. It happens to be the masterpiece of the whole collection. I think you could learn from the work here. And remember, leave no corner unturned." She was almost at the door when she paused. "Take extra care of yourself." The faint sound of a lock turning caused goosebumps to sprout on my arms.

Something about Mrs. Reed's words made me feel that something wasn't right. Maybe this was a test? She must have meant to be careful with the artwork, right? My dad probably told her how clumsy I was and not to let me within a hundred feet of anything valuable.

With some hesitation, I walked down rows crammed with delicate sculptures, dusty paintings, and jammed cabinets. Several glass cases held corroded coins and glittering jewelry. Farther down, gleaming in the low light, was an Egyptian sarcophagus encrusted with gold and precious stones. Two eyes made of shell and some sort of black stone looked up at the Heavens. Close to its belly was a latch that looked like it was easy to open. With my luck, it would probably topple over and a mummy would roll out.

Resisting the urge to open the sarcophagus, I walked past mannequins wearing antique costumes exploding with lace and soft tulle.

On the walls hung several rolls of fabric with scenes of people dancing, eating, and praying. Some of the sculptures were realistic and were
probably the faces of famous or important people. They looked like they
might come to life and walk down the art gallery with me.

After about half an hour of wandering, I thought Mrs. Reed might
be back soon, and I decided to take a shortcut to the painting she had
encouraged me to look at. I pulled back the velvet curtains, tied them in
place, and stood back. The painting underneath was at least five feet tall
and four feet wide. Even though my family wasn't religious, I could tell
it was a story about Christ's baptism. The blue sky in the background
changed from dark to light and two hands with a dove were coming
down from the top of the painting. In the center was a man dressed
in a loincloth. His eyes were cast down and his hands folded in prayer.
There was another man on the right who was dressed in flowing robes
of blue and brown. He held a crucifix staff and was pouring a bowl of
water on the praying man's head. Both of the men's bare feet were sub-
merged in a stream of clear water. The water seemed to be spreading
life to the surrounding oasis full of palm trees and rocks.

On the left were two angels dressed in soft blue garments. The folds
of the fabric were so lifelike I wanted to crinkle them with my fingertips.
Both angels were kneeling with their hands clasped together while gazing
up at Jesus, and one held what might have been Jesus' clothing. The angel-
ic face looked as if light was coming from it and that it might turn to look
at me. All four of the figures had golden halos floating above their heads.

Thinking that I might be quizzed on the painting later, I decided
to take an extra-long look at Mrs. Reed's masterpiece. The vibrant colors and creamy texture of the panel called for my fingertips. I looked
around. I knew there was a general rule about touching artwork, but
now I was alone in a private art gallery. No alarm would ring, and no
guard would come out if I touched it, just this once. The angels reached
out to me. I extended my right hand, expecting to graze the surface of
paint, but my fingers went beyond.

I felt nothing but cold air. My eyes squinted, struggling to believe what was happening. Color swirled around my hand. I dared another glance around the gallery before moving closer to the painting. I took a deep breath and stepped into the painting. My stomach churned with excitement and disbelief. There was a tunnel behind the painting and what looked like a dim light at the end.

"Is this what Mrs. Reed meant by leave no corner unturned?" I asked the angels. "She must have wanted me to go in. If not, why would she point at the painting to start with?"

With my mind made up, I pulled myself up into the tunnel and started to crawl on my knees.

The tunnel was dead silent. As I crawled, the light at the end grew brighter. The temperature dropped. It was impossible to crane my head around to look back. In order to go back, I had to go forward. Telling myself it would be easier to turn around at the end of the tunnel, I continued. What if I got stuck in here? Hopefully, Mrs. Reed would know to look behind the painting. Regret started to creep up my stiff limbs. All I could see was the illuminated outline of a door, but I could feel the mist of my breath against my face. My palms started to hurt from the frosty stone surface below.

Eventually, the tunnel became large enough for me to stand up straight. I walked, but my steps felt strangely heavy. Maybe this path led to the rose garden I saw coming up the driveway? When I reached the end of the tunnel, my chest was thumping, and I no longer felt I could stand up straight. The illuminated doorframe belonged to a metal door. There was a lot of noise coming from the other side. That couldn't be the garden! I turned the knob but nothing happened. Using my shoulder, I pushed against the door but it didn't budge. Taking a few paces back,

I broke out into a run. Before I reached the door, it flew open, and I stumbled hard onto a dirty cobblestone street.

CHAPTER THREE

Lost

MY HANDS FLEW OUT to break my fall. The cacophony of sound that surrounded me was overwhelming. Trying to get up was impossible as several feet walked around or on me. A fresh surge of pain seized me. Blood leaked from my palms onto the smooth stones. My knees stung, and the side of my face pressed against the muck of the street.

The sounds of a clock's ticking, tongues wagging, hooves beating, and wheels rolling echoed in my ears. Fumes of smoke and manure smothered me. Trying to protect my head, I propped my elbows up and covered it with my arms. Although I shut my eyes tight, there was a steady salty stream dripping down my face and under my chin. Suddenly, I felt hands grasp my shoulder, struggling to lift me to my feet. When I opened my eyes a part of me wished my head was still wedged between shoes and the ground.

The first thought that crossed my mind was that Mrs. Reed had slipped something in that Earl Gray tea or spiked the fruitcake. Bodies pushed against me from all directions, yelling in a language I could not yet comprehend. Dirt-covered hands and ringed fingers pointed in the direction of a wooden platform. A young woman stood with her knees bent and hands tied behind her back. Brown curls, cut off in clumps, clung to her linen smock. Sobs drenched her round face. People had begun to throw whatever they had at the platform.

My mind throbbed. "Stop that!" I yelled.

In an effort to wake myself from my hallucination, I pinched the skin on my forearm. Nothing happened. Cool air hit the exposed wounds on my knees, making my limbs shiver. Turning in circles, I tried to find an outlet, but I was stuck. Waves of people surrounded me, and beyond that were foreign-looking antiquated buildings. The stench made it difficult for me to breathe so I cupped a bloody hand over my nose. Focusing once again on the platform, I saw a strong, T- shaped wooden post with a noose dangling from it.

Oh my God ... This is a nightmare.

The crowd quieted as three men approached the wooden platform. The first man was short and heavyset. Each one of his facial features was unnaturally curvy but his expression severe. The two tall men directly behind him were dressed in elegant black costumes. The one at the rear had a crooked nose and wore a red cap, but he soon trailed off into the crowd followed by an escort of guards. The remaining two men mounted the stairs to the wooden platform. The woman was shaking violently in the midst of the rotten food surrounding her. Pity filled my heart.

It was at this particular moment that I realized the crowd around me was shouting in Italian. "Murderer!" screamed a chorus of voices. The round man was on a stool adjusting the rope while the taller man unwound a scroll. His long features and tailored mustache gave him an austere appearance as he read aloud to the crowd. It was impossible to catch every word because of the noise around me. The only words I heard were "trial...Silvia...drowned...children...guilty." The cheers of the crowd were deafening as he rolled up theparchment.

A shrill scream penetrated the poisoned air and their revelry. Two guards dressed in purple tunics had forced the woman to the stool and were tightening the noose around her pale neck. She no longer seemed human, but sprite-like. Her irises and pupils merged into one while her lips parted, screaming silently. The limber man's shaved head disappeared into the mob while the stout one placed his foot against the knobby stool. His boot swung back and then all went black.

While I regained consciousness, fear kept my eyes shut tight. My body slowly left the ground. My face felt dry as the sweat and tears began to crystallize. Lying there limp in anonymous arms, my heart beat so fast I thought he might feel it. The only thing I could hear was the faint voice of an elderly woman.

"Oh! Thank you, Signore Medici! You are kindness and greatness itself. I would not have been able to lift her out of there with these old tired arms. It is so good of you to help a poor woman and this odd girl. What a terrible place to faint, right in the middle of the Piazza della Signoria! She could have died there, and the hooded men would have had to carry her body off with the rest of those poor sick souls."

"It is nothing," replied the voice of the young man carrying me. "She is heavy! Where should I set her down?"

"My home is just a little ways on Via dei Benci," answered the older woman.

After walking a bit, I felt the stranger strengthen his grip around my shoulders and knees, his fatigue setting in. He stopped, and I could hear the sounds of keys jangling and wood creaking. The stranger walked up a step and gently set me down on a wooden table. It was too short, so my feet dangled off the end.

"You are too gracious, Signore Medici, please sit and rest! I must apologize because I have not gone to get water or milk yet ... I have only table wine and my gratitude to offer you." Sprawled across the table, I could hear the woman speak while she fumbled around the room. The sound of a chair scraping the tiled ground approached me.

"No, thank you," he said politely. "You have the privilege of knowing my name, but I do not yet know yours."

"Signora Caterina de Cioni, but everyone calls me Zia Cioni."

"Then I insist you call me Giuliano."

"Are you sure, my young lord? Would that not be unwise?"

"Not at present. You will call me Giuliano, and I will call you Zia Cioni."

"Yes, my lord."

"Giuliano, Zia!" he said cheerfully. "Giuliano!"

"Now then, do you know this young woman? Is she your relative?"

"Upon my word, I do not know her, but she does seem familiar. There was such a crowd about the Piazza today. I was on my way to Mercato Vecchio when I got caught up in the mob and almost tripped over this poor thing. I tried to pull her up but could not. That is when you came and helped me. So you see, I know just as much as you, good sir ... I do hope she is not too badly hurt." She walked over to the table and felt my forehead. "First, I will try my smelling salts," she said, her voice uneasy.

"What funny dress she has! It is not in my manner to go about alone or enter homes of those I do not know, but this peculiar girl has captured my curiosity," observed Giuliano.

"Indeed!" answered Zia Cioni. "Aha! Found them. For a moment, I thought I had lent them to Signora Rossi. My mind these days is not what it once was."

Two pairs of footsteps approached the table. Seconds later I felt glass press against my lips and an alarming scent consumed my nose. I began to cough hoarsely. Rolling onto my side, I opened my eyes that were brimming with water again. They focused on the brown tiled floor, mossy wool, and soft leather shoes.

A hand rubbed my back, "You are all right, girl! These are powerful salts. I get them from the best apothecary," clucked Zia Cioni.

I saw the pale face of an elderly woman. She had a constellation of dark moles scattered across her face. Concern was written across the wrinkles of her forehead. The light sifting through the room highlighted a large white scar under her left eye, and a gray shawl concealed her hair, giving her a holy air.

"There you are," she said as she peeled the locks of hair from my face. "Good gracious, look at those eyes! In all my days I have never seen such eyes." I made a move to sit up, but she pushed me on my back again. "Do not sit up just yet, child."

"Some of that table wine might do her some good, no?" suggested Giuliano.

He had been standing on the other side of the table silently observing. I turned towards his voice. A tingly feeling propelled through my veins. Giuliano Medici, who had referred to me as "heavy," had the most charming face. Black curly hair surrounded his square chin and shoulders. He had a slender nose that turned down. Spirited brown eyes framed by long eyelashes looked down at me. He had a cleft in his chin and his lips naturally curved into a smile. From my position on the table, it was hard to tell how tall he was, but he did have an athletic build. Unfortunately, his outfit looked ridiculous, especially considering the meager surroundings of the room. Giuliano wore a short mustard tunic trimmed with dark fur. Underneath was a brown suede coat that buttoned up to the nape of his neck.

"Yes... one blue, one brown, astonishing." My cheeks felt hot when I realized I had been staring at him.

"What is your name child?" asked Zia Cioni.

"Violet."

"Excuse me? Vi–what?" questioned Giuliano.

"I mean Viola," I said in Italian, suddenly grateful that my mom had bugged me to practice all these years.

"Viola, what is your full name?" pressed Zia Cioni.

"Oh ... Viola ..." I tried to buy time. Thinking it probably would not be wise to give them my real name, I settled for my mother's last name. "Viola Orofino," I finished, trying to make it sound natural.

"You have a foreign accent ... You are not from here?" asked Giuliano suspiciously.

"I am not sure where here is. I sort of stumbled here. It is probably best if I go back to that plaza. Can you show me where it is?" I asked, pulling myself up.

"You are in my home and you are not leaving quite yet," said Zia Cioni in a pacifying tone.

"Where is your home?" I implored.

"On Via dei Benci."

"And where is that?"

"Firenze, of course," said Giuliano with a concerned expression. There was a long bout of silence before he spoke again. "Were you kidnapped, Viola?" His question did seem like the most reasonable explanation. Firenze ... how did I travel to Florence, Italy? I needed to talk to someone I knew.

"Do you have a phone, Zia Cioni?"

"I am sorry, a what? I have never heard of such a thing," She shrugged. My heart sank. Extending my legs, I slid off the table and walked to the entrance.

"Viola! Wait! You must rest," pleaded Signora Cioni. Unlike the door in the tunnel, this door opened at my slightest touch. The street scene that flooded my eyes caused my knees to buckle. The early morning light was just reaching the narrow street of Via dei Benci. The path was crowded with men dressed in clothing similar to Giuliano's, though less fine. Shuffling past the door was an old man in somber garb and fur cap carrying a sack full of threadbare books. Further along a veiled woman held the hand of a small boy of five or so and tried to keep up with his skip. The boy was tossing a lemon in his other hand.

Three men argued loudly about money. The air was heavy with the stink of garbage and discarded matter decaying on the road. Wanderers huddled near houses with bowls attached to their starving fingers.

"What's wrong, Viola?" asked a distant voice.

"I'm lost."

CHAPTER FOUR

Locket

WITH THE HELP OF curiosity, clumsiness, and a tunnel, I had lost myself in Italy and in time. I closed the door and dropped to my knees. Covering my face with my hands, dry blood and all, I wept until I gasped for air.

Zia Cioni muttered inaudible words to Giuliano. He answered the elderly woman by swiftly leaving the house. Zia Cioni grabbed my hand and beckoned me to stand. Sniveling, I forced myself to my feet.

I saw the long wooden table I had been lying on and three chairs surrounding it. An array of dried herbs and flowers hung from the ceiling with packing string. On the east side of the room, two small windows gave the homely kitchen the optimism that only early light offers. On the opposite wall was a wooden staircase. Zia Cioni led me up the stairs and into a room.

The chamber was small, but it had a straw bed with clean linen draped over it. She urged me to sit on the only other piece of furniture in the room—a heavy chest—and assured me she would return shortly. I was completely alone. *How did I end up in this dreadful mess?* My mind frantically searched for shreds of hope while my body shook. *Will*

I ever see my parents or Clara again? My stomach growled. The fruitcake seemed like centuries ago.

While I waited for Zia, I took off my satchel spotted with muck and made sure nothing had fallen out. My sketchbook, birthday pencils, pens, strawberry lip gloss, and empty wallet fell onto the bed. I knew that was everything I had brought, but the satchel didn't feel empty.

I saw the zipper pocket looked heavy. After unzipping it, I felt my fingers close around cool metal. When I pulled the object out, its long, glittery chain fell across my lap. Hours earlier I had seen the diamond-shaped object in Mrs. Reed's hands! She must have put it in my satchel before I went into the gallery, but why? Why had she pushed me into this? With my head buzzing with questions, I looked for my answers in the angular contraption.

It fit comfortably into my palm, but the four knobs at each angle gave it an awkward look. On the back, I could see hundreds of engraved lines encircling an inscription that read "Idan." Adding the letters to the long list of things I was confused about; I opened its case. The gold metal framed a diamond face that did not tell time. Instead, a sheet of glass protected four round miniatures of a rising sun, bright sun, setting sun, and a moon made from precious stones at each corner. There was only one golden hand, and at that moment it was in between the rising and bright sun. Framing the clock's face were rectangular windows under which different things were inscribed. The rectangle at the top had the number twelve and the one to the right had nineteen. In the bottom peepholes of the clock were the numbers 1469 and thirty. *What did this thing mean, and why was it in my bag?*

Zia Cioni's approach interrupted my investigation. I thrust Idan, along with my other belongings, back into the satchel. When Zia opened the door, I was staring absently at a small but delicate painting of the Virgin Mary caressing baby Jesus. She returned with a basin of water and a sponge. She motioned for me to take off my clothes. Feeling weak and embarrassed, I shrugged them off.

She gave me a startled look and said, "What strange underclothes! You will freeze in such rubbish. Start to clean yourself; I will be back with some proper clothing ... You are lucky as I think you might be the same size my daughter was before she left home. I still have some of her dresses."

I washed my face and hands then moved onto my bloody knees until the water was a murky mauve. She returned with a pile of clothes and another pitcher of water. After dressing me in stockings, a white cotton dress, and a woolen indigo dress, she was content that I had on a sufficient number of warm layers. She then opened the window, looked down, and threw the dirty water onto the street.

After refilling the basin, she insisted I soak my hair. Her dry hands rubbed the edges of my face and hair with coarse soap. Drops of freezing water rolled down my back. During this process of clothing and primping, my mind had fallen into a meditative state. My eyes were parched but my heart wanted to grieve. Zia Cioni brushed and pulled my hair into arrangements. I must have looked like a sad zombie to her. My skin felt clammy against her warm touch.

"Why does your soul cry now that your eyes cannot, sweet child?"

"The public execution is still on my mind ... and you have been so kind, Zia Cioni," I answered, my eyes fixed on the painting.

"I am but a lonely Christian widow and my only living child is in the country far away from me. So you see, your company, however brief, gives me strength. You are lovely and burdened. Sorrow should cringe in the presence of your youth." She paused a moment. "Tell me what troubles you, Viola."

"I am not sure if I can explain, but I think I may be lost forever. I have zero hope of seeing my family again, and I don't have any money or way to repay you. All I have is this locket ..." I took off my locket. Delicate lines caressed its silver case and the embellished pearl at its center.

Sure of its value, I held out the locket to her. She stared at me, grasping for words.

"How did you get that?" She picked up the locket to inspect it.

"It was my grandmother's. My mom gave it to me on my twelfth birthday. She was..."

Zia gave me an incredulous look. She pulled out a locket from her dress. It was identical. "How is this possible? My ailing husband gave this to me before he passed away, and you have the same one."

Realizing that I was possibly in the presence of a very great grandmother, I thought about movies I had watched about time travel. *Would confessing have repercussions on my future?* Opting for silence, I sat staring stupidly at both lockets. Suddenly I felt less alone, and my foreign surroundings seemed more welcoming.

Zia's mouth quivered. "Surely this is a sign from God that I was meant to find you. You have been sent by the good Lord himself, and I will make sure you lack for nothing." With these reassuring words, she fastened the locket around my neck and kissed my forehead. "You must not worry, child. You are with family now. Do not grieve for the past. There is a plan for all those willing."

She grabbed my hands and examined them. "I can see you have not worked a day in your life. Your hands look like those of young Medici!" She laughed. "We will have to change that. What are your skills? Can you sew?"

"No, but I can learn," I said.

"Hmm ... Can you cook?

"A little," I confessed.

"Pray! What have you been doing with your youth?"

"I've learned other things though! I read and write. I'm pretty good at math. But mostly, I have been drawing and painting."

"*Allora*? That is most unusual. Those are all male professions. This makes things difficult." She paused. "Do you have proof you can do such things?"

"I do."

"Show me."

I took my sketchbook out of the satchel and passed it to her. She looked curiously at the doodles, quotes, and stickers covering it. As Zia started to flip through the pages, she passed some sketches of school children, bedroom sheets, strangers in Central Park, a garbage can full of protest posters, and my dad. She closed it and handed it back to me.

"I will speak to my nephew, Andrea, tomorrow. He is very famous here and owns a workshop. There might be some work for you there, but do not show your notebook to anyone." I nodded in agreement. "Speaking of Andrea, I must make my goat cannelloni! They are his favorite, and he could use the rest of the goat to make glue." She stood up and signaled for me to do the same.

"Glue from a goat?" I asked.

"Of course, child! How do you think that paper sticks to your book?" Remembering where and when I was, I stopped myself.

"Come, Viola, idleness is for the Devil and we have been idle indeed! Let us finish the day's tasks and we might roughen those delicate hands of yours." She stood in the doorway and waited for me to follow her.

When I stood up, my stomach made a loud gurgling sound. "Oh, Viola! You must be hungry. Why did you not say so? It is nearly two in the afternoon, and I am starting to get hungry as well. Shall we eat something before our errands?" she asked.

Nodding in agreement, I followed her down the staircase. Zia went into a room tucked behind the kitchen and carried out a wooden platter laden with cheese, fruit, and bread.

Apart from the table and its chairs, there were two large ceramic barrels in one corner of the room and next to the table was a shelving closet. The shelves held glass jars and had painted vine detailing around the edges. There was a stove with a fire pit below it and several pots waiting to be useful.

"The bread is dry, but you see I was going to go to the Mercato Vec-chio, but God thankfully put you in my way," she said, placing the wood-en block on the table. "We will go as soon as we are well fed. Oh, Viola, could you please get a knife from the cupboard?"

In reply, I walked over to the shelves, where there were knives with leather handles.

Zia cut some slices of goat cheese, small green apples, and dry bread. Also on the block was a small bowl with olive oil. "The oil will soften the bread ... eat!" she encouraged.

Although eager, I took little bites. While we ate in silence, my mind started to wander. When was the last time I ate? It was the fruitcake with Mrs. Reed and before that the pastries with my dad ... My stomach lurched and my appetite left. I missed my dad already, and it had been less than four hours since I went through the tun-nel. Where in the past was I exactly? A knock at the door stirred me from my thoughts. Zia peered out the window and then opened the door.

A woman in her early twenties with a baby in her arms stepped through the entrance. The baby had rolls at his ankles and neck.

"Was that the young Medici in front of your house?" she asked as the baby grabbed her long red hair.

"It was," added Zia, wringing her wrists. It was then the visitor no-ticed me.

"I beg your pardon. I had no idea you had guests," she said but made no move to leave. Tied around her tiny waist was an apron with scalloped edges and the white dress underneath stretched across her shapely hips.

"Oh, this is not a guest. This is my niece, Viola. She is visiting from the country."

"How wonderful! Have you come to spend time with our dear Zia or to find a husband?" she asked.

"At least, for now, to keep me company," interrupted Zia. "This is Giulia Bianchi and this is young Luca. Giulia, this is Viola Orofino."

"How lovely she is! Are you feeding her? She looks like she's been frightened half to death," observed Giulia. Baby Luca was growing restless in her arms.

"We were just getting to that," said Zia. "Who is looking after the other baby?"

"My husband, I just ran over to see what on earth that handsome young man was doing in your house."

"My niece fainted at the execution this morning in Piazza della Signoria. I tried to lift her up but could not, so the young Medici helped me as he was near us."

"How romantic," said Giulia, her green eyes sparkling. "Well, I will leave you to your meal as it's time for feedings anyway."

"Does Giulia have many children?" I asked a few moments after she left.

"Just one, the prettiest little girl you ever saw."

"And Luca?"

"Oh, she is a wet nurse."

Since when do people have wet nurses? My thoughts drifted to the pocket watch and its inscription. Did the diamond face give me any clues about where I was in time? It said the number twelve. Did that mean that today was still my birthday, December 19th? What about the other numbers thirty and 1469?

Judging from the clothes, the wet nurse, as well as bits and pieces of history class, I decided that I must be somewhere in the Middle Ages.

All I knew about the period was that there was a lot of war, sickness, and people were really dirty. After looking around the room, I decided everything looked clean. But what if I got sick? When was that terrible plague again? Cursing myself for not being a better listener in history class, I decided to take a risk.

"Zia ... do people here get sick often?" I asked trying not to sound too concerned.

"Well, that depends. I suppose you mean the Moria?" She frowned. "Well, the city has strict rules about who they let into the city and where our dead can be buried so as to avoid sickness. Much of my family was killed by the terrible disease you speak of. But it has been about fifty years or so since we have had an outbreak. The best thing to do is to avoid any sick person and bad airs." She finished nibbling on a dried fig. It might be difficult because so far everything except for Zia's home smelled bad.

"I'm sorry to hear about your family. That must have been painful. I hope my question did not upset you."

"Of course not, but it is sad to think of loved ones lost. Although we must all meet our maker someday." She cleared the table. "There is a shawl on the chair. Why don't you wrap it around your face so we may finish our errands for the day?"

Picking up the creamy shawl, I pulled it over and tucked the corners into the heavy dress. While Zia finished clearing the table, I went upstairs to grab my satchel.

"Take care to hold that satchel close to you. Do not speak to anyone unless I say otherwise, and do not let go of my arm, Viola," she said with a stern voice as she unfastened the lock of the door.

Zia stepped out and I followed close behind.

CHAPTER FIVE

Silk

WHEN I LOOKED OUT the door for the second time, all of Florence had awakened, and an icy chill blew through the street. The hungry scavengers had not left their posts but were now lost among the many people going about their business. Men dressed in dark monochromatic capes, tights, and fur hats flooded the street. After warning me to watch for the front step, Zia grabbed my hand and guided me to one of the doors across the street.

"We'd best get this over with," she said, shaking her head. A hefty middle-aged woman opened the door. She had light eyes with pillows of skin cushioning them. "I was just on my way to call on you. I saw the strangest thing ... It looked like Giuliano de' Medici was carrying a young girl in fr—"

"Yes, that is why I stopped by. This is my niece, Viola. She is ... well, what I mean to say is Viola has come from the country to stay with me."

"I am Signora Rossi," she said with a curt nod. "I had no idea you had a niece named Viola." Her eyebrows arched as she rubbed her thick fingers on the spotted dishcloth slung about her belt. "I would've remembered as it is my favorite name," she said, crossing her arms.

Zia shifted her weight from side to side, letting her eyes settle on the ground. "It is a nice name," she said.

"Well, what happened?"

"When?"

"With the young Medici?" insisted Rossi.

"Oh yes ... well, Viola fainted at the execution of that poor girl, and—"

"Poor girl indeed! She was accused of drowning her babe in the Arno," interrupted Signora Rossi. They both crossed themselves.

"Well the young Medici was nearby, and he graciously helped carry her to my house."

"What a strapping young man," said Rossi, her small mouth curling into a smile. "A fine match for my Maria."

"But she is engaged to that sweet young boy!"

"Sweet he may be, but rich he is most definitely not." She rolled her eyes. "I would invite you to sit by the fire, but Maria and my husband are not dressed for company."

"That is all right. We are on our way to the market."

"May I call on you later?"

"By all means," answered Zia as she steered me away from the door. As we walked towards the end of the street, the sun came out from the clouds. "I feel quite awful lying, but it's for the best, I assure you."

A group of young men clad in beautiful tunics of lavender, crimson, and emerald walked past us. They were joking and laughing at each other. Each of the four had short swords attached to their embroidered belts.

Women were scarce but the few that glided through the street exposed their marble skin and long hair proudly. Such young women left a trail of whispers behind them. The most stunning ladies wore smooth silks and plush, velvet gowns. Others, myself included, wore warm woolen dresses. The dark blue dress Zia had given me was a little too short, so as I walked down Via dei Benci, everyone could see my purple Converse poking out from beneath.

Zia locked her arm with mine as we made our way through hordes of people. The dusty walls that lined the street were at least thirty feet high, and all the doors opened directly onto the road. The smell of salt-water and fish wafted around the donkeys, chickens, and small altars of the Virgin Mary. The cobblestones were slippery, so I put all my energy into being careful.

When I almost slipped, Zia exclaimed, "Heavens, child, you are clumsy! It must be those peculiar shoes. Be steady, Viola, especially when I am attached to you." She pressed her small hand into my own, and we continued down the street.

The deeper we climbed into the heart of the city, the taller the walls, the wider the streets, and the brighter the light. Makeshift carts made of battered wood and fabric propped themselves up on random corners. Many of the stalls sold wool, used clothing, and vegetables. One stand sold bright flowers. The white petals and crisp green stems of the lilies stood out in spite of the gloomy surroundings.

"Some things don't change." I smiled to myself, thinking back to Angela's Flower Shop on the corner of my apartment building. Flowers have always bloomed, and merchants will always sell them on street corners.

"That is better! I like to see a young girl smile," said Zia, her eyes twinkling, as we continued to tread along the slippery path. "This is called Piazza della Signoria. This is the blessed place where I found you," said Zia as the street opened onto a plaza.

The square was emptier now, but I could still feel the ground vibrate under hundreds of feet, hooves, and wheels. The only evidence of the horror scene that had taken place a few hours ago was the wooden plat-form and the noose. Suddenly, I became more aware of the cold mois-ture in the air and the dryness of my throat.

"It was so horrible," I muttered softly.

"Some call it justice but many call it entertainment. I don't care for it. Somehow that wooden post and bit of rope bring out all that is wretched in humanity. The crowds are unbearable! I try not to come near the piazza for fear of being trampled to death, but this morning it was unavoidable."

Laughter erupted from a rickety stage nearby. Old and young, poor and wealthy, swarmed around the modest stage. The actors played using masks with exaggerated noses, lips, and eyebrows. Even though one of the actors faked their death, there was a steady stream of laughter from the audience. The cheerful sound trailed off with the growing rumble of a clock ticking.

"Do you hear that?" I asked.

"Hear what?

"A ticking sound?"

"I can't hear anything over that racket." She pointed to the stage. Although several towers and storefronts enclosed the plaza, the largest building was by far the most impressive.

"That is where all the important government officials work," she continued, pointing to a sandy brick building that looked like a fortress with its great walls, stepped roof, and looming bell tower.

Through the gaps of the battlement, we could see marching guards clad in polished metal. More than anything, the building looked intimidating and allowed only a few rows of clover-shaped windows for light.

Zia tugged at my arm, and we continued to make our way through the plaza. Before we swerved onto another street, I lingered in the center square. The constant ticking sound had not stopped. Where was it coming from? Was it Idan? Quickly, I counted how many doors there were in the Piazza della Signoria. In total I tallied forty, give or take two. How was I going to try to open forty doors? Maybe I could come every morning and make notes about who goes in and out of each door? The one that no one comes out of should be the door to get back to Mrs. Reed's gallery.

What if I chose the wrong door? They could accuse me of breaking and entering or trying to steal something. They would probably arrest me and drag me up that deadly wooden platform. The anxiety from the early morning pressed against my chest again. Zia noticed my tense body and stoic expression.

"Don't worry so, Viola. Upon my honor, I am an old woman, and I worry less than you. We cannot have that! Let us go down this street instead. I think you will like this next part of the city." Patting my hand, Zia took a sudden right. "All women, the vain and the humble, enjoy this spectacle. My late husband was one of the finest tailors in Florence, and he would often come to this street on business. It is called Via Vac-chereccia," she explained with a proud smile that made her scar vanish.

As we walked down the promising street, the stink dwindled. The cotton canopies of the buildings swirled against the wind's will and the strong rope that grounded them. When we drew closer I could see hundreds of baskets filled with little loose packets of material in a rainbow of colors. Little signs were written on each basket, but I couldn't read them.

"Do you know what is in those baskets, Viola?"

"Material?" I answered. Zia turned and pointed to the store on the opposite side of the street. The shop front was bursting with shelves, upon which neat rows of material shone. "Is that silk?"

"Yes! Those bundles are raw silk, and that is what it looks like after it is woven. Silk is beautiful from start to finish, no?" Zia observed as she approached the store merchant.

He was an older man with a wide nose and a shaggy mustache that concealed his lips. When his blue eyes met Zia's, his hollow cheeks almost reached his eyebrows and in his smile, he revealed a few golden teeth.

When they both spoke in fast Italian, I was reminded of how alien I was. I understood little, but it was evident that the merchant was thrilled to see Zia.

She reached for my hand and passed it to the old man. "This is Viola, my niece from the country. Viola, this is Signore Soldo." The old man cradled my long fingers and gave my hand a scratchy peck.

"Your niece is our blossoming violet among this city of wilting flowers." He grinned at his own wit. In my embarrassment, I veered my eyes towards the silk contained in the shelves. Not letting go of my hand, he led me further into his shop. "Although I cannot boast of having the finest silks in Florence, they are very close." Releasing my hand, he reached to move the footstool. With one last glance at me, he climbed and retrieved two velvets of different colors, sea green and apricot. "Which one do you like best, young lady?" asked Signore Soldo. His question reminded me that it was still my birthday. In answer, I pointed to the sea-green velvet. "Excellent. I thought you would choose that one! The color attempts to match the grace and singular color of your eyes." He wrapped the fabric with thin sheets of cotton.

"Oh, sir, I cannot pay for it!" I said, shaking my head.

"But it is a welcoming gift to Florence … Besides, I only give such exquisite material to the most exquisite ladies." He winked.

"Hush, Francesco! You will scare the girl senseless."

He bowed his head in apology. "God will forgive me as he knows I only speak the truth. Such beauty has obviously been inherited from her aunt."

"Thank you for the gift. I will hem this to the bottom of Viola's dress. She is too tall for it, poor child. We will visit another day."

"Please do visit me again, ladies," he begged.

"Thank you, Signore, for the gift," I said and extended my hand to shake his. Instead, he knelt down on one knee, pulled my hand towards him, and gave it another prickly smooch.

"Another time, Francesco!" said Zia. We weaved our way out of the shop and onto the street of silk. "We are almost there, dear," Zia assured me, turning right onto a street with an inscribed plaque that read "Via Calimala."

I could see that the bright morning light had faded.

Thick smoke drifted into the street from nearby ovens and chimneys. The smell of fresh bread and soil melded with the fumes that burned through my nose. After some minutes of walking, the street opened up into another plaza.

"At last! My feet are tired," admitted Zia.

CHAPTER SIX

Leonardo

Unlike the Piazza della Signoria, the Mercato Vecchio was dense. The walls surrounding it were punctured with hovels that sold baskets of fish, meat on hooks, grains in jars, animals in cages, and milk in canisters. As we strayed deeper into the market, there were several shrines with a cross and a bit of painted fabric draped over its arms. There were also pairs of wooden benches where the devout could reflect. The piazza had a breath of its own, made up of the men, women, children, and animals heaving through it. On one corner of the piazza was a small fountain where children filled their buckets with water.

On the opposite side was a slender column. It had a leaning figure at the top carved from white stone. At the base, several steps wrapped around the column. While some shoppers rested on these steps, most people in the market were bargaining or begging. Several women with simple dresses and hats were seated on barrels and selling their goods on the floor with only scraps of fabric protecting their livelihood. One was only a girl about my age. She was selling chickens, eggs, milk, and cheese. Sleeves rolled up past her elbows revealed forearms that were thick from farm work. Her bored and hungry expression was the same one I had in Mr. Barnett's biology class.

"Zia, didn't you say you needed milk?" I reminded her, gesturing towards the young girl.

"Indeed, I did! But you can usually get better deals farther into the market. Shall we continue on to see if we find a better stock?"

"Why not just buy them here? You also said that your feet were tired, no?"

"That is true," she answered, surveying the plumage of the chickens and the quality of thecheeses.

Zia began to haggle with the girl. Gently squeezing her arm, I pointed to the column steps. "Go on, but remember do not speak to anyone and do not venture off. This market is a maze and a dangerous one for girls," she said. I walked over to the steps and sat down on the side where no one was sitting. It somewhat hurt to sit as the skin of my elbows and knees still felt tight from the fall. Looking around at the market place, I could not help think how bizarre it was that I had not completely lost my mind. Hugging my knees, I peered down at my father's birthday present. The shoes, too, seemed to have added on years from our trip to the past. My poor dad must be worried, waiting with that wretched Mrs. Reed in that terrible house with those awful paintings. Why couldn't we have done something normal for my birthday?

Zia broke my train of thought as she set down a cage with a chicken and a burlap bag with two canisters on astep.

"I thought you were just going to buy milk?" I said, casting a weary look at the chicken. This was the first time I had seen a live chicken up close.

"Well, I am usually less impulsive, but such an unusual day calls for an unusual purchase," she said, wiping her brow with a handkerchief. "Also, I won't have to take this long walk every time I need an egg. The heavenly mother knows I am getting too old for such expeditions. If it pleases you, you can name it."

"Thank you. I'll try to think of a good one," I said, looking at the hen's rusty feathers.

"I am off again to get flour. It will be quicker if I go alone, but I will be back," she assured, counting the coins in her leather pouch. "Oh, I forgot to warn you. Watch out for those palm readers! They are swindlers and will steal you blind. I cannot abide their ridiculousness. Besides, if you want to have your palm read, I know a true seer," she said before vanishing into the bustling market.

While I watched her walk away, I realized that a real attachment and love for Zia was burrowing its way through my heart. What if she really was one of my great grandmothers? Either way, I felt lucky to have fallen by her feet.

I looked back down at the hen. "What would be a good name for you?" I asked. She looked like a George to me, for no particular reason other than being the first name that popped into my head. Nevertheless, she was a girl, so I named her Georgina. After stealing a quick glance around to make sure no one was watching me, I opened my satchel and took out my sketchbook. Once I had flipped to a clean bright page, I began to draw Georgina in all her ruffled glory. Just when I was really getting into it, a voice over my left shoulder interrupted me.

"Not bad!" I turned to see from whom the compliment or insult came from.

He looked about eighteen with dark blond waves and budding facial hair surrounding his wide grin. Although he had a strong, stalky build, when he sat down next to me, I noticed he moved gracefully. His nose's slight bump balanced his sharp bone structure.

"You might think me a brute for saying so, but you will never truly be a great draughtsman or in this case, draughtslady unless you master light and shadow ... May I?" the stranger asked, holding his hand out to receive the bound pages, his smile reaching his hazel eyes.

My hands shook as I passed it to him. He reached into the pocket of his olive tunic and pulled out some charcoal. It was hard to see what he was doing to the drawing of Georgina because his hair blocked my view.

After a few minutes of craning my neck around to get a better look, he parted with the drawing.

"This book of paper is as curious as its owner ... I have never seen a girl interested in drawing before," he said. Scared of being recognized as a foreigner, I held my tongue.

"Viola!" called Zia.

When I looked up, she was practically sprinting with a small sack of flour slung over her shoulder. As she approached the base of the fountain, she looked more relieved.

"I told you not to speak to anyone, sweet girl. You are lucky indeed that it is Leonardo who so imprudently sat down by your side," she huffed.

"Well, Zia Cioni, I must rid your sweet child of guilt. To my own displeasure, she has not opened her mouth once. Fortunately, I have the happy but sloppy manners of sticking my nose in where it is most certainly not welcome. Please forgive me, ladies. When an idea or vision grabs my interest, it rarely lets go," Leonardo concluded with a look that would have melted the heart of Medusa.

"By and by, I am glad you two have met. Tomorrow I am taking her to your master's house to meet and possibly help him around the workshop," admitted Zia.

"*Allora?* But what of Margherita?" asked Leonardo.

"She is far along, and her belly is much too big to be slaving after ungrateful apprentices! No doubt she would welcome some help."

"Zia Cioni, may I point out that you still have not introduced me to your sweet girl?" said Leonardo.

"Viola, this is my nephew's most talented pupil, Leonardo ... You are from Vinci, are you not?"

"*Si,* da Vinci."

"Leonardo, this is my ward, Viola Orofino."

The name Leonardo da Vinci instantly transported me to the tea and cake with Mrs. Reed. She had mentioned the artist as being a "renaissance man" and already accomplished by my age. Although my brain strained to recall all her words, my stomach worked equally hard to keep my breakfast down. This was impossible. Out of all the places I could have gone back in time to, why here and with Leonardo? This was too big of a coincidence. Like it or not, in my gut I knew that he would help me return to the door I had fallen from.

Instead of kissing my hand, he sprung up from the stairs, took off his hat, and gave a low bow. Not being able to stop myself, I beamed at his enthusiastic manners. He slid the sketchbook back onto my lap. After examining the drawing of Georgina, I found myself speechless.

Leonardo had brought her to life on the page with so little effort that I recognized how much I still had to learn. My first reaction was astonishment for Leonardo's talent, but the crisscross lines that made up Georgina's feathers made me feel insecure about my own attempt to capture her.

"Your drawing is incredible," I admitted.

"Aha! Viola speaks ... It is a quick sketch of your excellent hen, but thank you all the same," he said with a curious smile. "Your heavy accent betrays you." He scratched his phantom beard. "Pray, where were you born?"

"Very far from here."

"An orphan?"

"At the moment ... sort of."

"Then we have that in common as I am an orphan as well."

"Leonardo, my dear, that is not entirely true," interjected Zia. "Are you so ungrateful to your father? Was it not Ser Piero di Antonio who recommended you to my nephew, Andrea, and helped you get started in your apprenticeship?"

"Well, my natural father had plenty of chances to legitimize me, but he has decided against it. Please do not think me ungrateful, Zia, as I appreciate the pains he has taken for me," he said, softening the stiff tone the conversation had taken. He offered me his hand and pulled me lightly to my feet. Putting his arm around Zia's shoulders, he said, "But as I see it, all bastards are orphans in a way. If only we all had caring women like Zia Cioni to look after us."

"How can you speak of yourself so, Leonardo?"

"I find it is best to call things and people by the names society or nature gives them," he said with polite conviction.

"As you say, but for my part Florence can keep her names and I my opinions." Zia sighed.

"I must be off, or Master Verrocchio will be cross with me. He sent me to the apothecary to get some ocher and saffron, and I have stopped one too many times on my return. I hope to see you both again tomorrow, Signora Cioni and Signorina Viola."

Mrs. Reed had also mentioned that Leonardo worked in Andrea de Verrocchio's studio. Not wanting to be rude, I shouted back, "It was nice meeting you!" The volume of my voice surprised even me.

Seeing that he was trying not to laugh and not wanting to end the conversation on an embarrassing note, I thanked him for the drawing with a gentler voice. He strode off across the stained stones of the Mercato Vecchio.

"Do you think I was too loud just then?" I asked Zia, feeling a little self-conscious.

"Heavens no, Viola! People do not speak loud enough in my opinion." While I realized my mistake in having asked such a question to an almost elderly woman, Zia had taken out a small notebook where she had begun to scribble some numbers down.

"What are you doing, Zia?"

"Normally, I would wait till I returned home, but with my mind the way it is, it is best to write down the daily expenditures as they happen." I saw the date scrawled on the top of the page.

19 Dicembre 1469

The numbers that made up that combination appeared in Idan's peepholes. At least now I knew that I truly had lost myself exactly 544 years in the past. My dad often said, "knowledge is power," but I did not feel more powerful. With my free arm I lifted the burlap bag and Georgina's cage. After Zia had closed her accounts, she carried the flour, canisters, and the delicate gift of velvet as we walked back to Via dei Benci. After arriving at my new refuge, we placed Georgina in a decrepit coop in the alley behind the house. Zia instructed me to give her a generous bowl of water and several chunks of hardened bread. Meanwhile, Zia prepared her famous goat cannelloni. Before this trip to the past, I was thinking of becoming a vegetarian, but after I saw the head of the goat that was soon to be our dinner, my decision was set. Exhausted, we ate our hot meal in silence while the sun slowly extinguished. Zia lit two candles on the table.

After dinner we said goodnight at the top of the stairs. Zia took one candle into a room on the right, and I took the other to the chamber with the hay bed. Immediately, I took Idan out of the satchel lying on my bed and tried to uncover its secrets. The hand was now between the moon and the rising sun. The combination of numbers had not changed. Now I knew that three of the knobs told the date, but what about the fourth knob? Earlier, I tried to move the knobs, but they did not budge. I didn't try too hard because knowing my luck they might break, leaving me stuck here forever.

It would be a lie not to admit that I had never been so scared in my entire life. The hanged woman's sprite face haunted me. While I felt indebted to serendipity for having dropped me in Zia's path, I dreaded not being able to get back home. Passing by those chanting beggars on the streets reminded me just how terribly things could have worked out. Questions still plagued me as my head rested on the bulky pillow. *Why am I here? How can I figure out which door will get me back home? What role does Idan play in all this?* There were so many mysteries without answers. Yet what I yearned for the most was to wake up to the sound of morning traffic outside my window.

CHAPTER SEVEN

Goat Guts

WITH THE SOUND OF a rooster's crow, any hope that I had of waking up in New York City faded. A fresh water jug and chunk of soap were waiting for me as I stretched my arms in the cool air. I rolled onto my belly to look out the window directly behind the bed. Making a circle in the clouded glass with my fingers, I saw that sunbeams had not yet climbed over the rooftops of Via dei Benci. Falling back on my pillow, I pulled Idan back out of the satchel. It was December 20, 1469 and the mysterious number thirty had turned to twenty-nine. Was Idan counting down to something? It could be counting down days, but 29 days till what? Hopefully until Mrs. Reed found me, but it might not be that at all. I could vanish on the twenty-ninth day.

Thinking it was much too early for all these questions, I put Idan's long chain around my neck and slid it under my nightgown. The cold metal against my navel made my hairs stand up. My lavender sneakers were waiting for me at the edge of the bed, so I pulled them on, grabbed a wool blanket, and descended the stairs to the kitchen. Everything in the kitchen looked gray except for Zia, who was surrounded by a halo of candlelight. She looked even more saintly than the painting of the Virgin Mary hanging in my little room. Her weathered hands moved quickly as she sewed the gift of green velvet to my wool dress. For a little while I stood there basking in the glow of her goodness and watching her at work. As I stifled a yawn, she looked up.

"My dear child, I did not hear your steps! I daresay my hearing is getting worse," she confessed, examining her work. "Stand here, Viola. I want to make sure it is long enough." She pinned the dress against my shoulders and gave me a victorious look. "My hearing might not be what it was, but my tailoring is like a good wine."

"Thank—"

"Stop! Do not finish that word. I know you are thankful, and you can repay me by not worrying so much about it. You are not my guest but part Cioni."

Touched, I knelt down and squeezed her tightly. In our embrace, I could smell the scent of rosewater lingering on her shawl. Her stomach gave a loud grumble, and I could not help laughing.

Pulling away, I asked, "May I make breakfast, Zia?"

"I was hoping Georgina would have laid us a surprise, but she has not yet … I thought you said you did not know how to cook?"

"I said I know a little bit." In the pantry, I found some oats, honey, cinnamon, and walnuts.

Twenty minutes later light crawled its way through the window as Zia and I ate our hot cereal. "How strange this is, Viola. Is this common where you come from?"

"Very!"

"What is it called?"

"Oatmeal."

"O-mil-e?"

"Close enough." I smiled, painfully aware of what I must sound like in Italian.

When our wooden bowls were empty, she urged me to dress. "We are going out soon and cannot be late."

This time around putting on all the layers and newly tailored dress was easier. The sea-green trim of the dress hid my Converse from sight. Although I was appreciative, it felt as if I was covering up Violet Menet for the sake of Viola Orofino. Chrysalises started to hatch in my stomach as the meeting with the workshop owner approached. Somehow, I knew that being close to Leonardo was key to getting back to my life.

"Where are we going, Zia?" I asked as she twisted my hair.

"To church, then to Andrea's workshop. That reminds me, can you carry the goat leftovers while I carry the cannelloni?"

In my head I was thinking "Gross!" But aloud, I said, "*Si, va bene.*"

With last night's supper and a bag of intestines, we left for church. I had not been to any kind of church since I was young. We were all still a family then. If I closed my eyes, I could still see us walking together and feel the pain in my hand from the squeezing contests with Clara.

Thinking about it made me anxious, but I tried to recreate the memory all the same. The heavy swoosh of the bag's contents against my dress drew me back to our walk. It had been about ten minutes when I asked whether we were going to the closest church to home.

"Santa Croce is closer to home, but I know too many people there! When we arrive, you will see how people gossip. If it were not for my piety, I might say that it is the only reason people go to the house of the Lord. To answer your question, no, I would much rather go to San Lorenzo, which is farther away from busy tongues," she said, balancing the leftovers as we walked.

After a couple more minutes, Zia stopped abruptly in a narrow plaza teeming with vendors, gypsies, and churchgoers. In front of us was a jagged building made of pebbles and mortared with sticky mud. There were three wooden doors left, center, and right. Half a dozen elegant horses drank from a narrow stone basin propped against the church. We walked by a shoeless man attending to the steeds while Zia guided me to the door on the left.

"This cannot be the church!" I bellowed. While entering San Lorenzo, I was shocked at the sheer grandeur of the church.

"Hush! Nonsense, child, of course it is. What did you think of us Florentines? We may be quick to make a profit, but we put our money where our mouth is when it comes to the holy family," said Zia with a proud countenance.

Never would I have thought that behind the crumbly exterior was a palace of light suspended by columns, arches, and a golden ceiling. Savoring my amazement, Zia began to give me all the basilica's juicy details.

"San Lorenzo is a very old church, but it was remade into a basilica by a complete madman and genius named Brunelleschi. He has solved many problems that other men have scratched their beards raw over. It took a long time to bring it up to date, but they just finished the interior. Isn't it heavenly?" I gawked in agreement. "Much of the renovation was paid for by the most powerful family in Florence."

"What is their name?" I asked.

"You have already met one of them."

"Leonardo?"

Zia held back a fit of laughter behind her shawl. After a moment she crossed herself and murmured, "No, Viola! Do you not remember the handsome young man, Giuliano Medici, who saved you from the stampede in Piazza della Signoria?"

"Oh!" My eyes began to sift through worshipers, searching for Giuliano's fur cap and brown curls. On either side of the nave were arcades and elaborate altars dedicated to different saints. I noticed the green trim of my dress graze the cobalt and cream diamond tiles. Zia chose to sit at a wooden bench towards the back of the church.

"Why are we sitting here?" I asked, looking at the rows of empty wooden benches ahead.

"Those seats are for people who are part of the grasso class. You and I are somewhere in between the grasso and minuto."

"What does that mean?"

"The grasso are bankers like the Medici family, noble families or wealthy merchants. The minuto, well, they are everybody else," she paused to wipe her nose with a handkerchief. "But in the end, we all make our final journey some down there," she said, tapping her foot on the colorful marble, "and fewer up there." Zia gestured, pointing up towards the ceiling. Following her finger, I looked up at the ceiling and was mesmerized by its geometric beauty. It was covered with white square panels framed in golden lace. In the center of each square was a gold sunflower.

Sorrowful and eerie voices chanted hymns that rang off the walls of the basilica. Zia tugged on my sleeve and nudged her head towards the front of the church. Everyone stood for the procession of priests and altar boys making their way to the altar. They paced through the middle aisle, their draped arms carrying a jewel-encrusted book, a crucifix, and a swinging metal container filled with perfumed smoke.

Standing up, I squinted to see the thick swirly lines of the embroidered fabric protecting the altar and the flowers stacked on its steps. The music, incense, and candlelight caused my eyes to glaze over while my mind wandered through memories.

Once I noticed the singing had stopped, I was the last person standing. Zia tugged at my dress as a sea of heads stared at me. Giuliano was one of those heads ogling me with his swoon-worthy smirk. The glare and serious expression of the man next to Giuliano brought me back to reality. His face looked familiar, but I could not place it. My face felt hot and turned a brilliant shade of red before I sat down.

"Your head is in the clouds, Viola! Do try to pay attention to where you are and why you have come!" Zia whispered.

Although there were many heads and bodies in my line of vision, I saw Giuliano and his austere companion had begun whispering.

Of course, I thought they were talking about how ridiculous I looked standing there after everyone else had sat down. Unable to look elsewhere, I noticed that even though the mysterious man was taller and older, he was not as handsome as Giuliano. On his head was a red turban hat that draped onto his shoulder and grazed his steel blue tunic. Similar to Giuliano, he had a prominent nose, but it was slightly askew as if it had been broken once or twice. The stranger looked very important, as he sat in the first row directly behind the priest. Lavishly dressed ladies and gentlemen surrounded him. The way he carried himself radiated power. My whole body shuddered when I saw the shaved head of the man sitting two seats from Giuliano. It was the man from the hanging. Every fiber of his being gave me a sick feeling. His voice had spoken the words of doom for that young girl who was now no more.

"Who are those two men sitting next to Giuliano?" I breathed.

"The one with the hat is Lorenzo de' Medici. Some call him il Magnifico; he is Giuliano's brother." Once the words left her lips, the divine man seemed to have heard his name whispered and glared at me again.

Immediately, I turned my gaze and decided on the spot that I didn't want to have anything to do with the Medici family. Zia also seemed shaken by the attention, as she did not answer the second half of my question for long minutes.

"The other man is named Pietro Sforza. He is Florence's justice for the year," she said, counting the wooden bead of her rosary.

After the last celestial hymn, Zia and I waited for our turn to leave the opulent sanctuary and gradually made our way through the tall front door. When we finally reached the outside and descended the final step, Zia looked at my hands and asked, "Where is the bag for Andrea?"

CHAPTER EIGHT

Tick-Tock

"Jesus!" I exclaimed.

With that slip of the tongue, I hiked up my dress and ran back into San Lorenzo to get the goat guts. When I reached the aisle where we had been sitting, the stinky sack was nowhere in sight. I had only been in charge of one thing, and I had already lost it.

"Why would her nephew hire me if I can't even keep track of one rotting bag of organs," I lamented as I scanned the aisles.

There were still many stragglers lingering towards the grand altar.

I peeked down at my Converse and modest dress before taking careful strides towards the front of the church. As I approached the altar's floral steps, the shimmer of the women's dresses and the twinkle of the men's jewels caught my eye. Zia's warnings of social class rang in my ears as I crossed over to one of the side aisles to avoid their eyes. It suddenly felt like high school again. I normally take the long way around the school just to avoid being "igknowed"—like that awkward moment when someone who sat next to you in Geometry saw you in the hallway and recognized you but chose to ignore you.

The sound of laughter pulled me from my thoughts. I looked up and saw two men, the one with the red hat that scowled at me and the one with the shaved head. My instinct urged me to run. I searched for somewhere to hide. To my right was a wooden confessional. Without hesitation, I darted inside. Unsure whether they had seen me, I held my breath and listened hard while I waited for their footsteps to pass. For a brief moment, I realized just how ridiculous I was acting.

Why am I hiding? I thought as I peered through the honeycomb hexagons carved in the wooden door.

While I waited for them to pass, a ticking sound began to fill the cramped confessional. I looked for the source of the *tick-tock … tick-tock … tick-tock*. The frequency doubled quickly, and soon I felt a thump against my navel. My eyes bulged when I realized the ticking sound was coming from Idan. The sound and pace continued to increase, and Idan vibrated more violently in an effort to be heard. I slipped its chain from around my neck and tucked it under my bottom to deafen the sound. Even with my whole weight and heavy dress there was a still low tick. Thankfully, the chatter of lingering folk masked the ticking.

"Has Simonetta Vespucci broken Giuliano's heart yet?" asked the man with the shaved head.

The regal gentleman chuckled. "I'm afraid not, Pietro. The good Lord knows it would be good for him but alas she has broken plenty of other hearts." He stopped just short of the confessional. "Speaking of pretty ladies … did you notice that girl that remained standing whilst all others sat during the eulogy?" he asked. A silence followed. My legs turned to mush as I began to shake in my holy alcove. "She wore a blue dress … striking girl but odd nonetheless."

"I confess, your grace, I barely recall her. Why?" asked Pietro.

"Giuliano told me he found her in the most extraordinary circumstances."

"Is that so?"

"Quite! Apparently, she had suffered from some sort of fainting fit during the execution. He said she wore the most peculiar clothes—"

"What kind of clothing?" interjected Pietro. If his companion was surprised at the sudden tension in his friend's voice, he did not show it.

"Tights made of a hard fabric and strange slippers … Are you all right?" he asked as Pietro stiffly turned around. "I merely say this because I think Giuliano fancies her. He seems to believe she was kidnapped," said the gentleman who seemed on the verge of another good laugh.

"Why is that?" asked Pietro.

"He said she spoke Tuscan with a heavy accent." All I could see were both their backs. I tried to calm myself, but my breathing had quickened as the conversation continued.

"Lorenzo," said Pietro, recovering his stiff demeanor. "I think this girl may be … valuable to you."

"I already have a mistress, as you well know."

"That is not what I meant."

"Then how? You just said you barely remember seeing her …" said Lorenzo.

"You must trust me. She possesses an object that is most precious and worth more than all the gold you possess." Lorenzo sneered at this.

"Let us arrest her then," he suggested. The change in the gentleman's playful tone shocked me.

"No," said Pietro, examining the passersby before continuing. "We shouldn't discuss this here." He led the way towards the entrance.

It was several minutes before I let myself breathe easily again, my mind buzzing with doubt. *How did the creepy man know about Idan?* I wondered.

The pocket watch was no longer ticking when I fastened it back around my neck. When an elderly woman passed by my hiding place, I remembered that Zia was waiting for me. I didn't want to leave my hiding place, but I didn't want her to worry either.

My hand shook as I pushed the door open. Instantly, I noticed Giuliano. He was a few rows up and on the verge of untying the bag of goat guts. "I wouldn't open that if I were you," I said, a bit out of breath.

"But you know how curious I am," he implored with a smile that dimpled at the corners of his mouth. "I suppose I will follow your advice, as the bag has a rotten smell toit."

"They are goat bones and organs. We are going to take them to Maestro Verrocchio's workshop," I explained, not wanting him to think I go around carrying stinky sacks of rotten body parts. He held out the bag and as I took it, I noticed he had a large gold ring with five red stones and one blue arranged in a circle.

"I hope you are feeling better, Viola. If I may say so, you look much changed since last we met ... but your eyes are just as brilliant," he said in a charming but sincere voice. Thinking back to yesterday, the last and first time he saw me: mud, blood, and tears caked my face.

"Oh yes ... thank you, Signore Medici."

"Please, call me Giuliano, Viola."

By this point in the conversation I began to fidget with a piece of hair that had fallen from my braided bun. "All the same, I did not get a chance to thank you for carrying me to safety."

"Yes, that... well, it was partially selfish," he admitted. Not knowing what to say, I stood there mute and rooted to the spot.

"My young lord, what a pleasure it is to speak with you twice in only two days," said Zia, who had just entered the basilica. "I must admit I was worried about Viola. She came in such a hurry because she forgot ingredients for my nephew and was taking such a long while. But now I see she has been conversing with the best of company."

"You are kind, Zia Cioni," replied Giuliano with a slight nod of his head. "I did not know your nephew was Master Verrocchio. He is a great maestro indeed! In fact, I am so glad you mentioned his name as I was going to go to his workshop to commission a banner for my brother Lorenzo's tournament. Shall we walk together?"

I gulped hard at the mention of his brother's name.

"We would be most grateful for your company," said Zia.

As we made our way out onto the street, Zia squeezed herself between Giuliano and me. We walked silently in this arrangement until Zia asked Giuliano for his opinion of the sermon. Since we had left the church, I was trying to think of something impressive to say, but everything that occurred to me sounded lame.

"It was a bit long for my taste but ..." began Giuliano, but my attention slowly faded from the conversation as the same clamor of a clock ticking grew—the same tick I heard in the Piazza della Signoria. To make this strange situation weirder, I had the kind of uneasiness that sneaks up your spine when you feel like you are being watched.

Tick-tock, tick-tock, tick-tock, Idan quickened. I turned back to look at Giuliano, but he was still speaking to Zia. What was happening to Idan? Wishing that I could look at it, my fingers moved to dampen Idan's tick.

"Ouch!" I cried out, feeling a sharp pain. I cradled my other arm to comfort my shoulder's sting.

There were deep scratch marks like cat claws. Their talons breached my sleeves and the first layer of skin. Flecks of blood spotted my pink skin and torn fabric. I turned back to see who the culprit was. All I could make out was a blurry profile of a tall man with a shaved head. The upper sleeves of Pietro's tunic had spikes embedded in its leather. A smirk danced on the man's lips while his sharp mustache threatened his cheeks. He stared back at me. Idan's tick slowed as the distance between us widened and the drops of blood filled the void where skin had lived. Just before he turned into the city's labyrinth, he waved.

"What was that?" pressed Giuliano, examining my injured shoulder.

I wanted to point out the man that had hung that girl, the same man that was sitting next to them in church, but he was gone and so was the

Idan's incessant tick. Catching my breath, I realized Giuliano and Zia had stopped walking.

"Who did this?" he asked, looking behind us with my blood on his fingers. Zia's face also looked anxious as she peered up at me.

"Thank you, but I did not mean to worry any of you. Someone just didn't notice where I was walking. Must have been carrying something sharp," I said as Giuliano offered me his handkerchief. "Could happen to anyone." I pressed the muslin against the wound.

The rest of the walk was uneventful. Zia talked about the weather while my mind spiraled around the tick and the stranger. Finally, we stopped outside a narrow three-story building. The bottom level, constructed of dark stones, partially opened onto the street. It had dark wooden fencing and a hard canvas tarp. As we approached the entrance, there was a strong smell of wax and smoke. A melody of hammers and hollers drifted onto the street. Giuliano went in first and the lively noises dulled to a light clatter. Zia and I followed close behind.

The floorboards of the workshop yawned under the many feet of boys and men hurrying around the large room. The studio overflowed with sturdy worktables that supported frames, mixing bowls, brushes, eggs, screws, nails, and glass bottles. Neat rows of familiar and alien tools hung on the walls. Large and small unfinished paintings leaned against surfaces, waiting to be made timeless. Sheets of gold and blocks of marble glittered by the hot oven embedded into one of the east walls. The oven was at chest level and surrounded by neat red brick. A boy around seven years old tended the fire. Other lads were grinding minerals in stone mortars or mixing colors in shallow bowls. The older boys and men were busy drawing, painting, or carving models. Here and there were yards of stiff fabrics draped over furniture.

Zia and I waited at the entrance as Giuliano spoke, hands moving and eyes smiling, with a man in his early forties. He was listening to Giuliano with an attentive expression and his thumbs looped under the belt tightened beneath his round paunch. Suddenly, Giuliano gestured towards the entrance. The man gave us a fleeting smile, nodded, and became serious once more. They both clasped hands before Giuliano walked back over to us.

"I must be off as I have other errands to run for my brother."

"Yes, well you must be incredibly busy. Thank you for accompanying us," said Zia.

"We will see each other quite soon," answered Giuliano as he looked at me. His eyes caught me off guard, so I didn't have time to look elsewhere.

"If it is God's will," Zia replied.

"It is. Please keep the handkerchief." He kissed the back of my hand. When he left the workshop, Zia stared at me with a concerned expression.

"Oh, dear child, I am not sure what to make of that look he gave you, and I can see from the color in your cheeks that you have the same sickness about you. It is not wise for so many reasons! Do not think me a bitter old lady, sweet Viola, I just want to protect you from the harsh world we live in and all its evils. When you meet Margherita, you will know what I mean." She frowned.

The man that had been speaking with Giuliano walked to the entrance with arms spread wide. His dark serious eyes and round face lit up at Zia's face. His chin doubled over onto his white collar and his receding hairline hid under a soft black leather hat. The dust that covered his black tunic almost made it sparkle.

"As usual, Zia, you bring me good luck!" he said as he picked her up in a tight embrace.

"Put me down, Andrea! You will break my bones and then you will have to add me to the long list of people you take care of," she said, clutching his arms.

"You can imagine my surprise at seeing you on the heels of the young Medici. He just commissioned a bust as well as a banner for their family's joust tournament," he said, placing her gently on the floorboards.

"No doubt it will be your top priority!"

"It is just that I have about thirty other top priorities at the moment," he consented, casting a glance around the bustling workshop.

"My dear nephew, you must keep your focus and finish your tasks. You have been that way since you were a child. You could not play with one toy. It was imperative you had insects, lizards, pots, and swords at your disposal!"

"My healthy balance of inquisitiveness and procrastination is my weakness," he admitted. "Leonardo told me that he saw you at the Mercato and to expect you accompanied by a young girl."

"This is Viola, Andrea. She is my new ward." He scanned me, squinting his eyes into slits.

"May I speak with my Zia alone for a moment, Viola?" Verrocchio asked as he guided Zia farther into the workshop.

From a distance, I could see Zia sitting on a chair and Verrocchio bent over her. She pulled out her locket and pointed in my direction. He glared at her as Zia continued to talk. After several agonizing minutes, she gestured for me to join them.

"Zia has explained to me your situation. I beg your apology if in any event, I was rude just now. I had no idea that my Zia had taken on a ward and I did not want her to be played the fool. Could I see your locket for a moment?" asked Verrocchio.

Taking care not to pull out Idan, I unfastened my shawl and took off the locket. He held both lockets in his hand and studied them to the minutest detail.

"They are exactly the same, which is of course impossible," he said to himself.

"Do not bother trying to figure it out. It is clearly an act of God," she said, standing. "I have brought you your favorite cannelloni and to give you the goat's spare bits for glue." She placed both sacks on a nearby worktable. "I also want you to find a job for Viola in your workshop."

Verrocchio stirred from his inspection of the lockets. "Can you not see that this workshop is full of boys and men, Zia? I do not want to be responsible for a pretty, young girl of fifteen. Surely, you can see it is a most precarious situation." At this point of the conversation, not only was I starting to feel like a sack of goat guts that no one wanted, but my eyes caught a painting that almost made me pee in my stockings.

The painting of the angels and the Jesus being baptized, the same painting that had been the door of the tunnel, was resting against the back wall of the workshop. My spirits dampened at the sight of the unfinished painting. How was I going to get back if the painting was missing an angel? Although I had no idea of how to get back, the sight of the painting was also encouraging. It was too big of a coincidence to find myself standing in front of the same painting I had lost myself in more than five hundred years later. Surely, my problem had something to do with the painting.

"I would say the best thing you could do would be to marry her off. But as you say, she has no dowry, and that is out of the question."

"Listen to me, Andrea, she is bright. I trust her completely, and you would do well to take her on as she can help Margherita."

"I see that it has already been decided."

"I can do it, mist-I mean, Master Verrocchio," I blurted. "I want to help in any way I can."

"I can see to it that she makes it safely to Zia's after the day's work," added the familiar voice of Leonardo, who had been eavesdropping at a nearby workbench.

Verrocchio's smile consented to the deal. "Those clothes will not do, Viola. Normally, I give my new boys a uniform. But seeing as you are a girl, I will see to it that you get some clothes fit for work. I can pay you one grosso a week and that is not negotiable." He turned to Leonardo and said, "Since you have played the role of a spy so well, you will be responsible for her care and help me make sure that everyone is on good behavior."

"As you say," he replied with an easy expression and a shrug of his shoulders.

"Margherita!" bellowed Verrocchio.

A young girl of sixteen years or so appeared under a pointed arch. Margherita had a delicate heart-shaped face and red cheeks that were quieted by a few smudges of flour. She wore a dark green cotton dress with sleeves rolled up past her elbows. When she realized that there was a company of people waiting on her, she wiped her dirt-coated hands on an apron tied just above her waistline that fell all around her burgeoning belly.

"Yes, sir?"

"I want you to show Viola around. She will be helping you around the workshop." She pulled back a loose piece of straight blonde hair and tucked it under the pristine white bandana that covered her head.

"I hope you have not been dissatisfied with my work, sir?" She grimaced.

"Not in the least. It is just that I have a soft spot for young ladies in need of work and a worse weakness for my Zia." Still apprehensive, Margherita nodded and offered me her right hand.

"Viola, I will expect you in a couple of hours. Stand up straight and be on your best behavior," Zia said, pinching my cheek before walking towards the canopy.

The phrase reminded me of my father's last words before he left me alone with Mrs. Reed. What I really wanted was to follow Zia out of the workshop, but my determination had grown since seeing the painting. I let myself be guided farther into the workshop.

CHAPTER NINE

Portrait

THE MOMENT WE WERE out of Verrocchio's line of vision, Margherita let go of my hand and warned me to keep up with her pace.

"Since you came dressed for church, there is no point in giving you any real work to do," she said, wiping the beads of sweat from her nose and forehead with her apron. "Not that I can't handle all the work myself, because I can. For now, I will just show you around the shop as the master said."

As she led me up the stone staircase, the scent of flour and citrus rinds followed us. When we reached the landing, there was a dim, narrow hallway that had one high square windowpane at its end. My immediate instinct was to look around for the light switch, an expectation quickly dashed. Margherita pulled out a large key from her apron and walked to the door on our right. When the door opened, the hallway's sandy stone and brick-colored tile were illuminated.

I followed her into a modest rectangular room. The bright light that came from two large rounded windows made us squint. "This is the master's study and where the apprentices come to copy drawings."

The ceiling was made of carved wood; dark wood panels brought birds, flowers, and plants of all sorts to life.

"You are not to touch anything in this room and especially those," she said, pointing towards five shelves bursting with books.

Their colorful spines did look tempting. The apprentices and their master seemed to use the books often as there was no dust on the books themselves.

A plush carpet laden with floral designs stretched across the wooden floor. "Every other day I sweep this room and wash the floors.   You will do that now and you will also be sure not to get the carpet wet and to wipe down the table. Once a month I polish the tables," she said, pointing out the two tables and their sturdy benches. While she continued to explain the many tasks that I would soon have to take on, my eyes lingered on the left corner of the room where there was a divider.

"What is that?" I asked, pointing to the corner of the room. "That is where I sleep." Her cheeks grew a shade more crimson.

"Verrocchio took me on when I had to leave the orphanage ... so this is where I live."

I immediately regretted asking. How was it that I had my own little room with wool blankets to boot and she was pregnant and sleeping behind a wooden panel? Even though she was being short with me, I felt more and more sorry for her.

Margherita steered me out of the room and as she shut the door informed me that door on the other side of the hallway led up to the master's living quarters. "The master's two nieces live in the top apartment and do not like to be disturbed." The reassuring thunk of the lock sounded. Removing the key, she pointed to the door at the end of the hall. "That door leads to the apprentices' quarters. In other words, it is where the boys sleep. You would do well to stay away from there. That is probably the best piece of advice I could give you," she finished with a sad and absent look. Her hand had rested on top of her bulging belly, but she pulled it away when she noticed I was looking.

"When is your baby due?" I asked.

"Should be another three weeks or so ... That is what the master's doctor said, but a gypsy at the market told me it would be sooner."

"You both must be very excited."

"What do you mean you both?" she retorted. Once again, I had put my foot in my mouth. Although uncomfortable, I decided to continue on with the mess I had started.

"Well, you and the father."

She stiffened and let out a sarcastic snort. "The father doesn't care about me or the baby," she confessed and quickly shuffled back downstairs.

I followed her closely, and we continued on our tour of the workshop. As we moved through the center of the principal workroom, I could feel eyes following us. "You must not interfere with the work of the apprentices. The best time to sweep is when they are all meeting in a group with the master." Goosebumps sprawled over my skin, and I began to feel like a fly stuck to sticky paper. "Make sure you do not sweep away something they are working on." She spun around suddenly. Surprised, I took a step back and bumped into someone behind me. "Are you listening to me?" she asked annoyed.

"Sorry!" I said, turning around. The boy who had been putting wood into the oven when I first arrived had been stalking our steps. He was staring up at me with a goofy grin. The young boy had a sweet look but was bone thin. His brown hair fell in a tangle around his shoulders and his face had a chalky layer of soot. Margherita snatched a look over my shoulder to see what the holdup was.

"Renzo!" she said in an annoyed but motherly tone. "Have you been stealing milk from the kitchen?" The creamy evidence of Lorenzo's guilt stuck to the peach fuzz of his upper lip.

"It is already a while past our morning meal, Marga ..." he said, batting his long eyelashes and flashing his white teeth-complete with a missing front tooth.

This seemed to work often as she beckoned him to follow us. Surprisingly, he grabbed my hand and began to strut alongside me looking pleased with himself. Renzo's small hand felt warm against my cold one.

"For the love of our lady, Renzo I don't know how you are so skinny whilst you eat so much! I feel as if I spend half of my time feeding you. You would be so lovely with full rosy cheeks, but the more I feed you the skinnier you get."

We went under the pointed archway where I first saw Margherita and strode into the kitchen. A door ajar to the courtyard sent a chill through the air. A long but shallow stone basin with a water faucet and some brass jars took up the side of the wall lit by the courtyard. The opposite side had shelves built into the wall, and a heavy oven with a curved overhanging structure allowed the smoke to escape. On the work surfaces were some dried herbs picked from the overhanging bundles, sliced lemons, and some pale sausages.

After Margherita served Renzo his second glass of cream, he sat down on a large crate by the door. His long, skinny legs dangled over the crate and drops of milk dribbled down his chin. Margherita pointed to a different cutting board where a pile of figs, garlic, and basil were waiting to be chopped.

When I rolled up my sleeves and began to chop, Renzo's sweet voice sang out, "O though with the milk-white face, the winds are hushed as thou pass by and all the stars caress thee with their beams."

"What is that nonsense you are singing? Where did you hear such ridiculous words?" asked Margherita.

"The old poet in the Piazza del Duomo."

"You would do better by listening more to the master and less to that fool in the piazza."

I tried hard to repress laughter, but it escaped through my nose, and to my horror, I snorted. Little Renzo started laughing and went away bouncing up and down. "It worked! The old poet is a genius!"

Margherita's laugh carried over the crackle-pop of frying sausages. A few minutes later, we carried the midday's meal of bread, cheese, figs, sardines, and liver sausage onto one of the cleared tables. The apprentices were all salivating on the table's benches. We left them to devour their meal in the kitchen, where we both began to clean the pans.

"When you arrive tomorrow, bring something to cover your hair and ears. It dampens the sound of the apprentices, but not so much that if Master Verrocchio calls you, he can't be heard." Her hand pressed her bump in pain. "The baby is kicking hard."

"That means it has lots of energy, right? That can only be a good thing," I said optimistically, but she looked miserable. "I don't mean to be rude as I don't know you, but you don't look excited about having a baby. Where I come from women have rights and you can give your baby to someone who really would love to raise the child. There is no shame in it, and it sounds like you are not happy with the idea of bringing up the baby by yourself. I know I couldn't do it at our age." My words appeared to soften her face a bit.

"It is an unthinkable idea. Why would someone want my baby? I am poor, and my blood is far from noble. Florence knows who I am, and many know I am pregnant. Everyone will think my baby died or that I dropped it off at the orphanage. I could not stand that talk." She resumed scraping the fat off the pan. "I will manage ... Let us clear the table. They are already behind."

To no one's surprise, the food had been demolished, and the floor littered with sardine heads, breadcrumbs, and fig pits.

"Gross ..." I mumbled.

"What does that mean?"

"Disgusting."

"Why do you say that?" she asked.

"Well, they made such a mess of the floor."

"But that is normal. If not, it would be on the table and we would have to clean it up all the same. I do not know how they do it where you come from, but most households in Florence only clean underneath the tables once a week."

As we began to take trips to and from the kitchen, I noticed Leonardo had started working on a sketch. While I was trying to make out the face of his portrait, I felt a hand tug on my skirt so hard that I almost dropped the four dirty plates I was carrying. Turning around, I saw a young man, perhaps seventeen or eighteen years old. His head was covered in perfect ringlets arranged around his high cheekbones and pointed chin. His lips stretched into a conceited smile. Despite his prettiness, the whole of his person gave me the creeps. As I pivoted back around to leave with the plates, he tugged on my dress again.

"Where are you going so fast? We haven't been introduced yet." Frightened, I tried to get Leonardo's attention, but he was engrossed in his drawing. Margherita walked back into the room from the kitchen.

When she saw what was happening, she looked worried.

"My name is Gian Caprotti da Oreno, but everyone calls me Salai," he whispered with his greasy voice.

"What are you doing, Salai? Let go of her dress."

"Margherita ... all she has to do is tell me her name and ask politely." Margherita's strong exterior crumbled at the sound of her name from his pursed lips.

"My name is Viola ... Would you please let go of my dress, Gian?"

"You mean Salai?" he jeered, tugging my dress harder.

"Let go of my lady's dress," interrupted the high chime of little Renzo as he tried to pry off Salai's hands. Salai let out a fit of laughter that stirred Leonardo from his sketch.

"What are you doing, you idiot!" said Leonardo, annoyed that he had been disturbed while drawing. "Take your honey-covered hands off

Viola's dress or I will tell Verrocchio of your insolence. She is under his private care, and you are to treat her as you would one of his nieces."

When he let go of my dress, I could tell that Salai was angry and his pride was hurt. "Go to Landucci's. We need more malachite for The Baptism of Christ." In one smooth motion, he fastened his cloak and made his way towards the entrance, all the while muttering insults under his cloying breath.

As I watched him leave, Verrocchio's words rang in my ears. "*I cannot be responsible for her well-being ...*"

"I see I cannot leave you alone for five moments together," teased Leonardo, cleaning the charcoal from his hands with a rag.

"I tried to catch your attention, but you were drawing."

"Are you a bird without a song? Are you a beggar without a tongue? Speak, Viola! Scream if need be."

"I protected her, Leo!" proclaimed Renzo, pointing at himself. "She is my lady, not yours. It was I who made her laugh in the kitchen with my poetry."

"She is neither yours nor mine. She belongs to herself," said Leonardo and began to further mess up Lorenzo's hair before he continued. "Though it is good she has such an honorable lad to protect her. You are as fierce as you are loud. A match made in the so-called Heaven above. Surely the both of us can be protectors, Lorenzo."

The boy began to stroke his invisible beard and nodded his head in agreement. "Move along then and finish your duties before Master Verrocchio gets back." Lorenzo returned to stirring the oven's embers and splintered wood.

"Do your best to avoid Salai. He will bring you nothing but grief and anxiety. If he comes near you, run the opposite direction, find me, or screw up your face so you don't look quite so pretty. Like this ..."

He finished by making a face to rival the nearest gargoyle. "No need to worry about me, sweet Viola. I am as docile as a dear brother. So that will be the last blush between the two of us, understood?"

"Of course." I pressed on my cheeks with my hands. The corners of my mouth had started to hurt from smiling so much.

"So stop blushing then!"

"Then stop talking about my blush, and it will stop!" I said. Shaking his head, he picked up his abandoned sketch.

Margherita grabbed my hand again, more tenderly than she had this morning, and led me back into the kitchen. Upon entering, we saw a chubby man wearing a long brown tunic nibbling on olives and leftover cheese rinds.

"Stop that, Perugino, or you will get even more well-rounded than you are already," chastised Margherita.

"Margherita, always so lovely. If only everyone called me well-rounded," he said, stuffing the last olive into his mouth. "I think the exact term is fat, but I don't mind. In fact, I think others wish they could be as fat and well-fed as I," he finished, looking at me curiously.

"This is Viola. She will begin tomorrow as another housemaid."

"Everything in this old workshop will smell the sweeter now that we have two young flowers to keep away bad airs." His hungry eyes scavenged the kitchen but did not find anything else to eat. "Alas, I must be off now. By chance do we have any wine to chase my snack?"

"No, but I will chase you out of this kitchen if you do not hurry," she snapped, scraping crumbs into a crate. "Viola, please help me finish these dishes."

Deciding there would be no wine from this kitchen, the apprentice's round face and sense of humor left us to our tasks. I began to wash the dishes. The ice water hurt my hands, and I could not help thinking, *this is what I get for complaining about doing the dishes at home.* After a while my hands turned red and I could not feel the cold as much, but the pain throbbed up to my elbows.

Renzo skipped into the kitchen shortly after I had finished the dishes and announced that the master had returned and needed Viola for the rest of the day. Margherita looked a little disappointed. Her attitude had changed dramatically since this morning.

"Till tomorrow then. Come prepared to work this time," she said.

I smiled and nodded reassuringly as Lorenzo grabbed my hand and pulled me out of the kitchen. "Your hands are freezing!" he said, leading me upstairs two steps at a time.

When I entered the study, the rumble from within hushed. Verrocchio was standing by the window when he signaled me to sit in the chair at the center of the room. "Viola, I would like to create a preliminary sketch of your face," said Verrocchio. Panic was my first reaction to this request. Why did he want to take a portrait of me?

"Therefore, I need you to sit quite still in that seat until we have completed it. If we do not do it now, I am likely to forget about it completely."

Rooted to the spot, my heart worked extra hard to pump blood to the rest of my body. Glancing around the room, I saw Perugino, Leonardo, and one other boy I did not know. They armed themselves with their parchment and charcoal, waiting for me to sit down.

"Please sit, Viola. Boys! I want different angles, so position yourself accordingly.   Do it now," he barked. Verrocchio guided me to the chair, arranged my hair, and tilted my head into his ideal position. "It is best if you look a little towards the floor. It will help you stay still, and you won't be quite so nervous."

Focusing my eyes on the carpet, I could feel beads start to form along my brow. Embarrassed, I wanted to wipe my forehead, but since I could not move there was no stopping it. All I could hear was the fire licking the wood and the soft crunch of charcoal pressing against paper. Was I allowed to talk? Talking was not the same as moving. Typically, I would be too mortified, but I wanted to find out about the painting that was responsible for me being in this predicament in the first place.

"Excuse me, Master Verrocchio?"

"Yes?"

"May I ask something?"

"You already have." The boys chuckled at this, but I pressed on.

"Could you tell me about the painting of the baptism downstairs, why it's not finished?"

"I have my age as an excuse to forget things, but as you are quite young, you should remember what I told Zia this morning. I have a terrible habit of taking on too many commissions."

"Who is it for?"

"What you mean to say is who commissioned it or who is the patron?" He paused as if he was trying to recall a memory. "That painting is for my brother. He is a priest at St. Salvi. It is a priority, but I received a commission from the young Medici. As the elder Medici's tournament is approaching, this is my immediate obligation. Why do you ask?"

"It's..." I hesitated, "...very beautiful ... That is, it struck me more than the other paintings in the workshop."

"It would be if we could finish the missing angel. As to beautiful, I aim to strike a feeling of absolute benevolence."

"What is stopping you from finishing the last angel?"

"You just arrived? Why the hurry?" he asked.

By this time, I had forgotten about the sweat trailing down my neck. His question hung on my consciousness like a bad grade you have to show to your parents. How could I get them to finish the painting? The eerie sense that the painting filled me with made me more certain that it was the ticket to getting back home.

"Arresto!"

The charcoal immediately stopped its course. I saw the pupils examining their work with nervous eyes. Verrocchio was making his way around the intimate room and spent only a couple of seconds on each drawing. Huddled over his students, he had only a handful of words, whether rebuke or praise, for each. When he came to Leonardo, he spent an extra while suspended over his paper.

He put his hands on both of Leonardo's shoulders and squeezed them with a minimalist's approval. "Viola, please collect your belongings ... Your work is done for the day. I am sure Zia has seen to your work clothes, so come back tomorrow with the appropriate dress." Glazing over the eyes of his students he added, "We are done here."

When Verrocchio left the room, one of the apprentices, a fair-haired, boxy boy ground his teeth. Perugino was unaffected and unsurprised at the outcome of the drawing session. Shuffling their feet, they packed up their tools and proceeded downstairs. I soon met Leonardo, who was waiting for me by the entrance. Also on the platform was the recently returned Salai, carrying a full sack of powder and engaged in an enthusiastic conversation with Verrocchio, during which he had enough time to shoot me some sly glances before Leonardo directed me out the door and onto the grungy cobblestones.

CHAPTER TEN

Duomo

ONLY A DIM LIGHT filtered through the clouds and dust onto Via dell'
Agnodo. Across from Verrocchio's workshop was a tannery. The scent of
rawhide, lime, and manure surpassed the confines of its shop. The street
was lonelier than it had been in the morning, and it made for a gloomier
walk as we passed crude shelters sloping against small churches and brick
houses. Outside of these meager wooden enclaves were salvaged bits of
trash and rags, and a persistent ring of flies.

Leonardo and I walked in silence for a ways. His assertive but pensive
stride was offset by my own occasional misstep. Turning my eyes towards
his, I could see they had an absent look.

"Are you all right, Leonardo?"

"*Si* ... Just thinking."

"Can I ask you a question?"

"You don't have to say that every time you have a question."

"Right ... Well, I wanted to know why Verrocchio wanted to take my
portrait."

"I'm not sure," he said with the same vacant stare. There was a long
pause until we reached a corner street called Via della Rosa. Leonardo
stopped, looked around, and said, "You live on Via dei Benci, right?"

"*Si.*"

"Let's go straight then." Above us, damp clothes drooped from several of the balconies that flanked each side of the narrow street. "Most of the time Verrocchio gives us details about why we are doing a specific work. On any other occasion I would say he just wanted to take down your likeness as a drawing exercise for the apprentices' sake, but I don't think that was the case today."

"Why?"

"Because he made a big deal out of it ... When he makes it a competition ..." Leonardo's words trailed off.

"And you were the winner?"

"Of course." He shrugged.

"Well that's good, right?"

He nodded. "In Florence, it's all about coming up on top. The other apprentices take it to heart sometimes, and it bothers me. I just want to create. I do not want to be distracted by petty rivalries. Any time there is a big commission of any value it is opened up as a competition and each workshop or master submits a miniature artwork of sorts. Whomever the panel or grand patron likes best gets the job."

"It seems fair to me, but I understand what you mean. I don't like competing either."

"Sure, it's fair but it's limiting because you have to cater to the patron's tastes while maintaining your own style."

"I wish I had seen the sketch."

"I am sure you will see it somewhere. Whether it makes its way to a painting of the Virgin Mary or crumpled up on one of the workbenches."

Answering him with an ironic laugh, I added, "Oh, I don't think it'll make it that far. I've never seen a painting of a sweaty Virgin Mary. Knowing how well you draw, I'm sure you caught every salty drop."

"I did a decent job, don't you worry."

Despite Leonardo's company, I couldn't help but concentrate on my freezing hands. Trying to warm them up, I started to rub them together until my arms were tired. The backs of my hands and knuckles were already dry and flaky even though the cold was wet. I was thinking how much I missed pockets when we reached Via dei Benci.

"I'm in the mood to go by the Duomo. What do you think?" Leonardo said.

"Um ..." Glancing up, I could see heavy clouds were extinguishing the sun.

"It is a short walk."

"What's the Duomo?" I asked. He halted in the middle of the bustling street. His eyes bulged as carts whistled past us and strangers grumbled at our impromptu stop.

"You obviously have not had the pleasure of feasting your eyes on such a wonder of engineering. It is the heart of the city, mostly because it brings salvation to all us sinners, poor or rich. Andiamo!" he decided. Grabbing my sleeve, we continued onto Via dei Pandolfini. Leonardo picked up the pace, and I followed jogging behind him.

Once we turned onto Via dei Calzaiuoli, the street began to broaden. I could see a geometric building the likes of which I had never seen, not even in New York City. The street opened up into a broad plaza. "Is that the Duomo?"

"No, that's the Baptistery." The building shaped like an octagon was covered in a series of arches, square panels, and columns. Some of the shapes were painted on the surface, while the carved stone engaged others.

"Is the stone painted?" I asked as we walked further into the piazza.

"Of course not, the paint would start to deteriorate right away. Its inlay is green and white marble brought from Prato."

The sound of trumpets caught my ear. Musicians and their instruments spilled out from the bronze doors of the Baptistery. Following close behind was a procession of finely dressed people. A couple hand in hand led the parade and steadily made their way out of the piazza. All of the stragglers left in the piazza had stopped what they were doing and allowed themselves to consume the sight of the veiled woman and her silver train.

"Is that a wedding?"

"And a wealthy one at that ... They are probably on their way to the feast now."

"She's not wearing white."

"Why would she wear white?"

"Well, where I come from a woman wears white on her wedding day. I guess it's a symbol of her purity or something."

"Interesting ... That is kind of obvious, no? Here, that is what the veil is for."

The marble walls of the Baptistery burned orange in the setting sun's light. As we passed, I could feel drops of moisture spray my face. Putting my hands out in front of me, I could see flakes of snow melt against my skin.

"Leonardo, do you think Zia might start to worry?"

Instead of answering my question, he pointed to a set of golden doors and said, "Remember what I told you about competitions? There was a competition put out for the Baptistery's north set of doors. Lorenzo Ghiberti, a master goldsmith, won the contest. Years later he was commissioned to make this east set of doors. He passed away several years ago, but his workshop still overlooks this piazza. I think Verrocchio wants to buy the property." The doors were framed by golden floral and fruit bouquets, as well as several miniature busts. Each square had its own dark frame separating each tale from the other.

Leonardo, seeing my interest, added, "Each panel depicts different scenes from the Old Testament. Do you see Ghiberti's master of high and low relief? And look at his use of perspective ..."

I nodded in agreement. It truly was extraordinary. The section at my eye level portrayed women, men, and children with their arms raised towards the mountain behind them. On top of the mountain was a crouched figure. The rocky surface of the mountaintop and the foliage of the trees felt tangible. The closer the figures were to the center of the panel, the more three-dimensional they were. The flatter the people and landscape were, the farther away they looked.

"What is this panel showing?"

"It shows Moses receiving the tablets of the Law from God. Ghiberti changed the way we cast in bronze." As he was explaining all the building's history with the aid of his hands, I couldn't help smiling in the wake of his infectious excitement. "You will learn more about that in our workshop."

"Does Verrocchio work with bronze too?"

"*Si*, in fact, Verrocchio was a goldsmith's apprentice at first. He himself will tell you he enjoys sculpture more than anything else. He usually only paints when he feels compelled to do so. Usually, he leaves it up to the apprentices to fend for themselves."

"That is the Duomo, right?" Opposite the Baptistery was an immense structure where candlelight burned low within its open doors. People were beginning to file into the church.

"*Si* ... evening mass will start soon. Let's get a look around before it starts." It was cold enough that snowflakes had started to stick to the ground. Leonardo must have sensed my hesitance to enter the Duomo. "Come on, just tell her you went to evening mass, and she will be delighted," he said and slipped through the door.

The church was much bigger than San Lorenzo, but the facade was similar. The bottom part had a few niches with statues, but the rest was the same rough stone that disguised San Lorenzo.

When I entered the church, I could see Leonardo making his way past kaleidoscope designs of green, cream, and rose inlaid upon the marble floor. As I followed his path through the nave, I heard whispered prayers and passed heavy columns sprouting into pointed arches on either side. The air was thick with smoke from the musky incense and hundreds of candles. Leonardo was waiting for me at the altar.

"What do you think?"

"I think it is the biggest church I've ever seen!"

"That is because it's not a church.

"What is it then?"

"A cathedral."

"Oh ..." Surely, I had confusion written on my face because Leonardo continued.

"Meaning, it is the seat of a bishop."

"I understand ... I mean I know that a bishop is a Catholic leader, but what does he do exactly?"

"Viola, take care who you ask such questions to. People will think you are a pagan or even worse ... You are lucky I am not a devout Catholic."

"Why?'

"You are full of questions this evening," he teased. "Firstly, I am interested in more tangible subjects like science and engineering. In my opinion, the spiritual is something people appeal to in days of their old age. Furthermore, it is a healthy assumption that everyone who breathes this wretched air is a zealous Catholic, so no one would ask my opinion anyway." He paused to look up.

Following his suit, I too peered up at the grand dome that hung above us. The brick octagonal dome was indescribably high, and it appeared to be suspended over several dark stained-glass windows. At its center was a circle where a glimpse of the evening's darkening sky was visible.

"What's that circle in the dome called?"

"An oculus," he said without breaking his admiration of the dome's hollow drum. "Sometimes, I come here just to humble myself at the feet of Brunelleschi's genius ... If I have to go along with the assumption that

I am pious, I think I can live with that ... That is to say, I am grateful for what devoutness has done for artists."

"Is Brunelleschi the same architect who designed San Lorenzo?" I asked, remembering that Zia had told me about him at mass.

"The same...There had been many failed attempts to finish the Dome but to no avail. Until Brunelleschi's design, the cathedral had an open ceiling for almost twenty years. He convinced Cosimo Medici that he could complete it and obviously, he did." The sound of a soprano's song echoed off the vaults and disappeared into the drum of the cathedral.

"You still haven't answered my question," I said, rubbing the back of my neck.

"Which one? There have been so many," he asked, smiling.

"About the bishop."

"Ah yes, well above all a bishop is a powerful man. He is in charge of an archdiocese, which means a division of many churches."

As mass was going to begin soon, we decided to resume our march to Via dei Benci. On our way out of the church, Leonardo saw something that caught his eye and stopped.

"Come, I want to show you one last thing," he said, gently tugging my wrist.

He went towards the side aisles where there was a huge painting on the wall. It looked to be about seven by ten feet and at its center was a man dressed in a long red tunic and hat. With one hand he was holding a book out to the viewer so that we could read its contents, and with the other he was gesturing towards a rugged mountainside where a series of naked figures and demons were marching towards the bottom.

On the opposite side was the city of Florence behind its fortified walls. The Duomo was clearly visible. The rosy city walls suggested the sun was setting behind the mount of doom. Behind the man towering over the city spiraled a tiered mountain, at whose top stood the semi-nude figures of Adam and Eve. On each level were several angels and naked souls praying.

"Why did you want to show this to me?"

"The painting was done about four years ago by Domenico di Michelino. The perspective is all off, but it was a good attempt, I think … Anyway, I wanted to show you this man."

"Who is he?"

"His name is Dante Alighieri; he wrote a masterpiece called-"

"The Divine Comedy." Leonardo's sentence was finished by someone standing behind me and with a much deeper voice.

I turned around and to my dread saw Lorenzo the Magnificent. He was dressed alarmingly similar to Dante, all in red. He was quite a bit taller than Giuliano, but his eyes were just as curious. His slight smile was a welcome change from the glares and serious expression he tossed at me in San Lorenzo.

"He was one of the first to write in the common vernacular. His epic poem discusses the afterlife in detail and with unparalleled eloquence. The descriptions of paradise and purgatory are excellent but nothing to the way he talks about inferno." His explanation led way for a profound silence that was only interrupted by the soprano in the depths of the cathedral.

"You must be Leonardo da Vinci," he said, reaching out his hand and Leonardo kissed it. Leonardo's hands shook but his expression remained completely neutral. "And I infer that you must be the famous Viola Orofino." I nodded and gave a terribly clumsy curtsey. He lifted my chin up with his hand. Looking into my eyes he said, "Giuliano is quite right of course. Your eyes are miraculous." My cheeks felt hot as I looked down at the geometric floor.

"It is quite curious you have never heard of him. He is immensely famous even outside of Florence." I looked at Leonardo imploringly, but he had the deer with headlights look on his face. My determination not to say anything to him was becoming increasingly more difficult. "I think Giuliano said you were kidnapped?" he asked, concerned. "But he failed to mention from where or whom."

Long seconds passed by before I worked up the courage to speak. "I was taken from my father in London."

"Yes, you do have a distinct accent," he admitted as his eyes circled around my neck and satchel.

The skin on my arms felt prickly despite the heat everywhere else on my body. Before I could stop him, his hand was on my neck and his fingers had a firm grip on Idan's chain. There was a dim echo of "pardon me," as he unearthed Idan from my dress.

Still as a statue, I stood petrified by his actions. With Idan still attached to my neck, he stared with hungry eyes and felt the delicate engravings of its shell. He was on the verge of opening it when I suddenly found my voice.

"I really must be going, Signore Medici, my Zia is waiting for me." As if drawn out of a trance, he recoiled and recollected himself.

"The gold chain of that interesting object caught my attention … What I was going to ask you was whether or not you had papers."

"Papers?"

"Documents that say who your parents are and if you are legally allowed in this city," explained Lorenzo. My hand moved to my mouth as I looked down at my strange sneakers in silent terror.

"No, signore, I am afraid I don't … What shall I do?"

"Well, you could be sold to a slave trader, sent to the gallows, expelled from the city, or we could simply write up some papers of legitimacy for you," he finished with a wide smile. My body trembled from my lips to my toes. "I will see to it that Giuliano delivers them to you," he finished and then immediately turned and left the cathedral.

Leonardo and I waited a few minutes before stepping out from behind the thick walls of the cathedral that blocked the icy wind waiting for us beyond the entrance. A chill ran down my back as I tried to shake off the threatening conversation. When we stepped in the snow, I could feel the cotton of my shoes start to dampen.

"Let's hurry, Leo, my feet will freeze." It seemed like a good idea to try to forget about what had just happened. Talking about it would probably only make it even worse than the encounter was.

"It's because you are wearing strange shoes. Does it snow where you come from?"

"Yes ... quite a lot actually."

"So that faraway place filled with white brides, snow, and strange shoes is England?" asked Leonardo, wrinkling his brow as we made a left down the deserted Via dei Calzaiuoli. Despite Zia's advice to not trust anyone, I found myself naturally confiding in Leonardo.

"Didn't you hear? I'm from England."

"Where do you come from? You are like a fairy that has leapt out of one of those picture books they give to fair, little ladies. I don't buy the England answer and I don't think il Magnifico did either."

"*Allora?*"

"Yeah, you are at a disadvantage there," he admitted. Snowflakes were falling and melting on his eyelashes. "All Florentines are exceptionally good at telling when people are lying."

"But you are not from Florence!" I protested as cold water sloshed around my feet.

"But I am a fast learner."

"If I told you, you wouldn't believe me. The truth is, I'm not sure myself. The kidnapped part I told Lorenzo was sort of true, but it's kind of my fault too ... It's a long story that I'll have to tell you another time," I explained before we halted outside Zia's front door.

At the sound of our voices, the door immediately creaked open and with it, Zia's expression of relief appeared.

CHAPTER ELEVEN

Fire

"WAKE UP, CHILD!" GIVING Zia my back, I rolled over and mumbled some obstinate words. "I do not know what you are saying, but I do know you will be leaving home without a morsel of food in your belly," she added before slamming the door hard behind her.

For a brief moment I thought she was allowing me to relive what was remaining of a good dream. After only seconds, she strode back in carrying a bundle of clothes. "Come now ... I won't have this idleness." Sitting up, I tried to rub some life into my eyes. "Stand up! I need to help you into this dress as the sleeves are tricky."

"Hurry up, Viola!" hollered Leonardo from downstairs.

"You didn't mention that Leonardo was waiting downstairs," I said, jumping out of bed.

"Wash your face quickly," she urged.

While I busied myself with the water and a lump of herb soap, Zia explained that Leonardo had been waiting for over fifteen minutes and was drinking his second glass of milk.

"You are too early!" I yelled back as I slipped into the secondhand dress Zia had secured for me the day before.

Like my other dress, it was wool, but not as smooth, and instead of blue it was a burnt umber color. The detached sleeves slipped over the underdress and tied together.

"Perhaps, but only because I knew you would be late!" he shouted. "I am not particularly fond of this style as I think it's a little ... too flirtatious. But it is better for working. It gives you more movement," Zia explained while she finished tying up the sleeves.

"I will go and cut up something for you to eat quickly before you head to the workshop," said Zia before rushing downstairs.

When she left, I grabbed Idan's chain from underneath the pillow. The date had changed to December 21 and the mysterious number that had been twenty-nine was now twenty-eight. It was clear that Idan was counting down to something, but I wasn't sure what.

As I headed downstairs, I tucked Idan under my dress and pulled my satchel over my head. Leonardo was working on his third glass of milk while Zia had cut up some slivers of sheep's milk cheese and bread. After I made a sloppy sandwich for the road, I insisted we leave right away.

Leonardo emptied the rest of his cup and Zia protested. "You can't go out with your hair like that!"

Not a minute later I walked out the door with my sandwich wedged between my teeth as I pulled my hair into a side braid.

"Good luck! Try to be home before nightfall," she called after us as we walked into the fishy smog.

I tried to ignore the smell as I ate, wrapping my head around how I was going to get home. What could I do now? Did I have to wait twenty-eight days? It seemed like an eternity.

"Leo, how long would it take to finish the Baptism painting?" I asked, brushing crumbs that had stuck to wisps of the wool dress.

"Not long; tempera paint dries very quickly. If all goes to plan and Verrocchio allows me to paint the missing angel, I would work with a new kind of painting technique. It involves using oil to bind the pigment instead of tempera's vinegar, water, and egg."

"But oil takes so much longer!" I protested.

"You've used it?" he asked, completely stunned.

"Yes, it's common in ... London," I lied.

"Shocking! Well, anyhow, it is highly uncommon here. To finish the painting, it is more a matter of finding the time to sit down and do it. Or rather, it's about Verrocchio feeling the pressure of a deadline."

"Well, we need to speed it up."

"Why?"

"I can't tell you just yet."

"So many secrets, Viola ... Will I be in danger if you tell me?" He grinned.

I shook my head and put a finger to my lips to silence him on the subject. "How can we hurry it up?" I pressed.

"As I already hinted, I am trying to convince Master Verrocchio to let me paint the missing angel. Two days ago, I sketched a young boy at the market who would be perfect for the angel. His face is still very clear in my mind."

Idan's sporadic and low tick had started up again. My eyes skimmed the dark frosted street for the bald stranger with the sharp mustache or some other weird happenstance. It was still quite early and few people, apart from shop owners and farmers, had stepped out their front doors.

"Could I go to the church that commissioned the painting and ask them to inquire after its progress? Would that help?" I looked at Leonardo to see if he noticed the low *tick-tock ... tick-tock*.

"Maybe. We'll have to see. I think I have him almost convinced." The tick grew louder and so did my frustration. There was no one around.

"What's that sound?" he asked.

"You hear it too?

"Wait," he hushed. "It just got fainter?"

"Yeah," I agreed. "Hold on." When I retraced our steps, Idan's ticking quickened. There was an archway on the right, and I took it. Leonardo followed me and the growing clamor into the Piazza della Signoria. Maybe the stranger was here?

"Viola, I think the ticking is coming from you," insisted Leonardo.

Drawing Idan out of its hiding place, I placed it in my palm, feeling it pulse. I looked around but the only thing that was nearby was an empty wall with a faint outline of a door. People in the piazza were scarce and the fog added to our secluded situation.

Leonardo's nostrils flared and his pupils doubled as he gawked at Idan. "What is that?"

"It's a watch of sorts," I heaved.

"A watch?"

"A small clock."

"That is nonsense. Clocks cannot be so miniature," he said, narrowing his eyes at Idan's engraving.

"Well ... it's very dear to me for that reason." I shifted awkwardly.

"I think your small clock is broken. I might be able to fix it for you in exchange for a secret or two. I am skilled with that sort of thing, you know. That is, tinkering and trust ..."

His voice trailed off as hope started to consume me. Was this where the door was? My heart started to skip beats at the thought that home might lie beyond the wall.

"What are you doing?" asked Leonardo as I slowly approached the door.

The morning's sandwich was stuck somewhere between my throat and stomach. Once I got closer, I clearly noticed the outline of where the door used to be. Someone had gone to great lengths to make the sure barrier could not be breached. Entirely crushed, I turned away from the wall, but Leonardo moved closer to it. After a few moments, he said, "Look here! There is a note wedged underneath the stone."

Spinning back towards the door, I saw he was right and reached my hand down to pull the note out. My fingertips could feel the sandy surface of paper.

My body quaked with frustration. Why did I get my hopes up so high? This whole time I'd been cursing my circumstances and trying to find my way back at every turn. It occurred to me then, in that moment of distress, how ungrateful I was. Since I stumbled into this city of wilting flowers, my path had been so easy. One might say too easy. I could have been starving, begging, or worse. Instead, my very great- grandmother serendipitously found me. A coincidence I still had trouble explaining. Ever since my birthday, she has clothed, sheltered, fed, loved, and worried for my well-being.

"Viola, are you feeling all right?" Leonardo asked, pulling me to my feet.

He stood by my side almost forgotten. To assure him I was fine, I nodded and gave him my best attempt at a smile. Although grateful for Zia, I was almost equally thankful for meeting the genius that would be Leonardo. Despite my confusion, I had found a friend in the most unexpected place. Concern shone through his frown when he passed me his pristine handkerchief.

"Why are you handing me this?"

"Because you are crying."

Feeling the dampness, I said, "I didn't notice ... *grazie*," I brought the linen to my face, patting it dry. The fog was lifting as carts, donkeys, and breadwinners filed into the piazza.

"I don't mean to be ... insensitive, Viola, but we should head to the workshop now or we will be really late."

"Right," I agreed, realizing that my left hand still clutched Idan and the mysterious letter.

All this time wasted! I should have just read it immediately. Leonardo had already begun to stride towards one of the entrances of the piazza. Slipping Idan and the envelope into my satchel, I ran across the damp stone to catch up with him.

Our journey was silent, but my imagination kept me busy. Idan must have started ticking for a reason. Today it had led me to the door I had come through and all the impossibility of it. Yesterday it ticked when the stranger had cut me. Idan must have sensed something different about him. Maybe the letter belonged to him and that was why Idan led me to the door? It could also be totally unrelated. Two lovers might be using the crevice in the peculiar door to write to each other in secret.

The familiar scent of rawhide and burning fat hinted we were close to the workshop. Leonardo ducked in, and I followed almost out of breath. When I entered, Leonardo had taken to the stairs, and Margherita was sweeping away curls of wood that littered the platform. She stopped and wiped her face with her apron.

"Good morning, you are right on time ... almost too close for comfort. I woke up Leonardo extra early to make sure you would be here on time." She was barely audible because of the racket going on in the workshop.

"Thank you, Margherita ... I promise to arrive earlier tomorrow."

"Go up to my space in the study. There is something waiting for you. It is probably a good idea to put your satchel up there while you are at it."

Following her advice, I climbed the steps to the study. The room was almost blinding with light. As instructed, I went to Margherita's space behind the decorative dividers. There was a narrow feather bed with clean sheets accompanied by a modest dresser. A painted wooden set of the holy family embellished the dresser. On the bed lay a cotton apron and on its neck strap was my name stitched with purple thread. *Margherita must have done this yesterday*, I thought.

Truly touched by the gift, I took off my satchel with the intention of tying the apron around me, but I stopped when I saw the corner of the cream envelope poking out. The temptation was too great. Guiltily, I moved my fingers over the paper. It had a scarlet seal embedded with the head of a horse. Using my fingernails, I broke it and began to read the sheet of fine paper.

20th of December

Viola,

With a little help from Idan, I hope you find this letter before it is too late. It is most imperative that Idan does not leave your person. Without it, you will be unable to make it back to your proper time, ever.

The creak of the door disturbed my reading. Reluctantly, I stuffed the letter back into the satchel and rushed to put on the apron. Between the cracks of the divider, I saw Salai softly closing the door behind him. Salai looked about the room before approaching the bookcase. He then took out four books from the top shelf and placed them aside. Metal scraped as he fidgeted with a box. After opening it, he began to stuff the contents of the box into a small pouch tied around his belt. The sound of coins jangling against each other rang heavily against my conscience. Hoping against all odds that Salai was not stealing, I squeezed myself farther into the small corner I found myself.

"Viola! What is taking you so long in the study? You are needed in the kitchen!"

Fear immobilized me. Sure that even the next-door neighbors heard her, I decided to run for the door. Remembering the warning, I took Idan from my satchel and hid it underneath my brown dress. After, I quickly tossed my satchel underneath the mattress and ran to the door but Salai had already blocked the door with his body. He looked down at me with a smile that oozed malice. He silently caressed the loose locks of hair that had fallen out of my braid. My bravery extinguished. His voice and touch made my skin crawl.

"What you think might have happened ... well, it did not." His perfumed fingers started getting closer and closer to my face. "Is that not so?"

"Please stop, Salai. I need to go downstairs." Suddenly his hands grabbed my face and my legs went numb with panic as I tried to pry them off.

"Maybe you didn't hear me clearly, sweet flower," he whispered. "You didn't see anything ... right?" His face was too close to mine.

"Right," I consented.

"If I see so much as see a glance that I don't like from you ... Well, it would be a shame to see poor Zia's house on fire." Horrified, I stood there wishing someone would save me. "I'll wait till she has left for the market or church of course. I am not a monster," he added and then pressed his terrible lips against mine. After I struggled violently, he finally let go of my face and moved aside.

Heaving the door open, I flew downstairs. My heart felt as if it would leap out of my chest and make it to the kitchen before I did. Margherita's chastising words were lost on me as I stood there petrified and useless.

She pointed to a dead chicken waiting to be plucked. Probably noticing the frightened state I was in, she kindly added, "Clean and chop those mushrooms instead." I took the knife from the cupboard without a word. "Are you all right, Viola?"

"Yes, of course," I managed, wiping off the mushrooms. The water was icier than the day before, but the feel of its cold stream against my hot palms quieted my distress.

"Did you not like the apron?"

"Yes, it was so thoughtful ... I meant to say as much when I first came into the kitchen, but I forgot." Margherita's hands moved effortlessly as she plucked the chicken's buttery feathers.

"I'm glad." She smiled. "Master Verrocchio bought the apron, but I had some free time in the evening."

"Thank you, Margherita, I really like it."

While I continued to clean and chop, my mind kept drifting back to Salai's warning. Why had courage failed me? I could have screamed, kicked, or confessed what happened the moment I reached the stair platform. It was an aspiration of mine to be fearless, but somewhere during my growing pains, bravery had marooned me. Not wanting to risk Zia's safety or her beloved house, I kept what happened in the studio to myself but with great difficulty. Having secrets always made me feel trapped, so I seldom kept any. Now I had enough secrets to make up for all fifteen years of my life.

Once the mushrooms were chopped and the chicken plucked naked, Margherita began to prepare the day's first meal. "It's your turn to sweep the workshop," she said while she picked some dried oregano from an overhanging bushel. Dreading any encounter with Salai, I walked quickly into the workshop, trying to avoid anyone's eyes.

Little Renzo made my lame attempt impossible when he reached for my hand. He soon let go to finish his chores by the oven. The workshop was not too loud, as they all seemed to be involved in quieter tasks like painting or drawing. The apprentices courteously moved their feet and models out of the broom's path as I made my way around the large room. The burning oven made a warm haze that rose and traveled to the rest of the studio. A few boys were making a constant crunching noise as they ground plants with their mortar and pestle. The redheaded boy next to Leonardo was mixing egg, vinegar, and a rainbow of powders to create singular hues of paint.

When I reached Perugino's table, he had a heavy piece of navy velvet fabric stretched across his table. "I thought I smelled lovely flower." He chuckled. "How are you doing on this fine day?"

"Well, thank you, and yourself?" I replied, sweeping underneath his workbench.

"Hungry but splendid, the usual," he added cheerfully. "What are you working on?"

"A young lord's banner for the upcoming tournament ... It will be a portrait of his young love." Perugino was using chalk to trace the contours of the girl's face. "Don't judge me just yet. I have only just started," he said playfully after he realized my interest. "We always get several commissions like this from young men when tournaments are approaching. They have their coat of arms and beautiful ladies painted on their banner. This way, the crowds can marvel at their nobility and a lovely lady as they ride in on their excellent steed."

"You paint a spectacular sight," I said encouragingly.

"I do my best, but you will see it for yourself, surely. If I am not mistaken ... it is three days hence." He lowered his voice to a whisper. "You don't by any chance know where Margherita hid the wine today?" His question made me smile, and I assured him she had not shared its hiding place with me. He looked slightly disappointed. "It is probably for the best."

"I will leave you to your work."

"Also, probably for the best ... We wouldn't want to upset our young noble with an unfinished banner, correct?"

"Correct," I agreed, finishing my chore.

The hours of scrubbing and polishing went by quickly with the aid of Margherita or Renzo's conversation. Later in the afternoon Verrocchio came into the kitchen to check up on me and see how I was getting along. For a brief moment, I thought this was my chance to confess what I saw earlier that morning, but the opportunity came and went. Before long Leonardo tapped me on the shoulder, and it was time to walk home.

While we navigated past the black slush, Leonardo told me about a commission the workshop had received to crown the Duomo. He was talking breathlessly about the copper orb that Verrocchio was planning. If possible, Leonardo was even more excited about the mechanism he was designing to raise the orb to the top of the dome. As we approached Zia's neighborhood, a steady and thick cloud began to hover above the street. The smell was intoxicating.

"That is all very good news, Leo, but don't forget about the Baptism painting."

"I haven't," he said unconvincingly. "Where is all that smoke coming from?"

"Not sure, it could be anything. Let's go check it out." We started to move rapidly towards the direction of the black eruption of smoke. It was slow progress as many people and animals moved in the opposite direction. When we arrived at the source, my cold hands sought solace cupped around my warm breath. A mass of people crowded around a burning house. The crackling sound of fire licking at the wooden remains greeted us. Several people were coughing, crying, and supporting loved ones for their loss. Spectators carried buckets of dirt and water just in case the fire decided to attack their own homes. Grabbing Leonardo's hand, I urged him to leave the miserable scene.

For minutes later all I could smell was burning wood. Salai's threat from this morning bounced off the walls of my skull.

"What was that?"

"Someone must have died in the house from the Moria, or it could be the health inspectors were tipped off about the house containing bad airs. Or it could be an accident."

"So they burned it down, just because someone told them it had bad airs coming from it?"

"It's likely."

"You're telling me that anyone could go to the health inspectors and say, 'I think my neighbor's house smells like death' and then they will just burn it down?" I asked. Leonardo looked equally disturbed by the scenario.

"Well, they are supposed to inspect it but ... no one wants to get the Moria. So to them, it's the safest course."

The thought of Zia standing outside of the only thing she had as it burned down in front of her brought me close to tears. Eager to be alone, I waved a curt goodbye to Leonardo. Zia was sitting down at needlework when I entered the house. Once I pulled up a chair close to her, Zia asked how my day had gone and what kind of spices Margherita uses to cook. While she talked of her encounter with a fish merchant, I stared lovingly at our surroundings. With the wood furniture and ceiling, Zia's home would be cinders in seconds.

"Viola, I would be grateful to you if you check in on how Georgina is doing with her eggs." Exhausted, I dragged my feet down the steps of the pantry and outside to the little alley where the chicken was resting.

She had two eggs waiting for me on a makeshift shelf. Finding myself quite alone, I sat on the step and took out the letter.

By now, you must have reasoned that Idan is counting the days until the door and time loop will reopen. You MUST go through the door with Idan at dawn on the last day. There is only a small window of opportunity when the passage will lead you forward so be sure to be punctual. If you manage to get back, it will lead you to the gallery, exactly ten minutes after you went behind the painting.

A warning, Idan is sensitive and possesses a mind of its own. The time may change drastically from one moment to the next. Therefore, be sure to keep a close eye on your precarious companion.

Although there was no signature, I had a good idea who it was from. I slowly tore up the heavy paper and scattered its fragments through the open gaps in Georgina's coop. With the two eggs, I walked back inside the house with a heart filled with anxiety.

CHAPTER TWELVE

Mice

MY EYES OPENED BEFORE the sun could call on Via dei Benci. The restless night had been cold in spite of the woolen blankets piled on top of me. For hours I lay on my belly staring out at the modest view the window offered. The half-moon's face illuminated the patchwork of empty rooftops clumped across the skyline. Every now and then a gang of boys would pass by the deserted street, singing slurred songs of love. Usually, when I couldn't sleep, I would sneak onto the roof of my New York apartment building. Sleeping bag in tow, I would stare at the thousands of twinkles arising from the city and count their constellations until I fell asleep.

Once I pulled on my green sweater and an extra pair of socks, I tiptoed through the darkness down to the kitchen. With a flint, I lit a few candles and started to boil some water for me and some milk for Leonardo. From the cupboard, I grabbed some dried fruit and honey. While I waited for my tea to cool, I opened Idan's gold covering. After reading the mysterious letter, I decided to wear Idan around my neck always. It was too great a risk not to. The number 27 told me that Idan was sticking to its day-by-day countdown. So many days... it seemed an eternity.

The curt letter's red seal and my own instinct told me the letter came from Mrs. Reed. It was good to know she hadn't totally abandoned me and that my dad wouldn't be worried sick. The scuffle of footsteps approaching prompted me to get up and look out the window. Leonardo's broad back was leaning against the door as he gnawed on an apple core. When I opened the door, he looked pleasantly surprised.

"Thank you, Viola! Florence froze overnight," he said, stepping into the house.

"Why are you up so early again?"

"Well, truth be told, I do not sleep a whole lot. In fact, sometimes I feel like I am always awake while the rest of the world is asleep. Not only physically but metaphorically," he admitted, scratching the shadow of his growing beard. "That and I thought you would get behind if I were any later ... Is that milk?"

"Yes, it is." I shot him a skeptical look.

"Excellent," he said, pouring the cream into a ceramic cup.

"There is more if you like. Zia was worried she would not be able to keep up with your thirst, so she bought a cow. It's waiting in the back alley and armed to fill all your thirsty needs," I joked, and his eyes crinkled.

"So she has a sense of humor after all." Leo took a sip and white foam hung to his upper lip. "I hope this means that you are coming out of your shell. If that's the case, be sure to slip a secret or two my way while you're at it."

"I will when the time is right. Scout's honor."

"What are *scouz?*"

"Never mind ... and I do too have a sense of humor. I'm just shy is all."

"Shy? No, you are too curious to be shy. I think it is something else."

"What do you mean it's something else?"

"What you call your shyness."

"What is it then?" I asked, trying hard not to sound defensive. Taking a sip of my cold tea, I braced myself for the blow.

"You're scared." He shrugged.

"Yesterday ... I might have seemed—"

"No," he interrupted. "Since the day I sat next to you, I saw it. Your frightened blue eye and your brave brown eye are having a fierce competition. I'm curious to see which one will win."

Leonardo had surprisingly put his finger on the real interior battle that warred within me. It was as if I was having a conversation with my subconscious.

"What is it I'm frightened of?" I asked, taking another sip of my tea. Light crept through the windowpanes and under the muslin curtains.

"Life," he said plainly.

"That's going a bit far."

"It's not going far enough." He stood up to serve himself another glass of milk. "You are scared to walk out that front door and even more worried about what time you will walk back through it. Not to mention that you are petrified of Salai... In that there might be some sense," he paused to see the effect his speech was having on me. I was nervously biting my fingernails. "Before you say anything, you hesitate because you are scared that you will hurt someone's feelings or that you may say something wrong."

"Sounds like you have me all figured out," I snapped. Unfortunately, he was right, and I felt like a coward. The last sip of my sweet brew left a bitter aftertaste in my mouth. I stood to put my cup in the basin, but Leo followed me and put his arm around me.

"Don't take it badly—but you should take it to heart," he said while engaging his most charming smile.

"I know you are right, and I know I needed to hear it, but it's hard to listen to all the same."

"Come on and get dressed! We have a stop to make before the workshop."

"I don't really—"

He shot me a stern look and pointed to the stairs. Not wanting to seem any lamer than I already did, I dragged my feet up the stairs. Zia was at the top of the platform.

"Why are you up so early?" she asked, squinting through the early morning dust. "Is that young Leonardo I heard downstairs?"

"Yes, he is waiting to take me to the workshop so I need to hurry and get dressed."

"That's a good girl," she said to herself as she stifled a yawn.

It took me a little longer because of the laces on the sleeves, but we left the house with plenty of time to spare. The morning was bright despite the overcast sky that hung over us. We hurried past two young men tinkering with a tall ladder. They were setting up a garland of pink and lavender flowers that hung across the street. The blond boy got distracted and lost his step.

"Keep your eyes on your ladder and your mind on your bride, my friend," Leonardo called over his shoulder to the fallen boy. The man's companion bent over in laughter. "Can't take you anywhere, Viola," he teased cheerfully.

"Hope he's okay," I said embarrassed. "How do you know he has a bride?"

"That is what the garland is for ... She must live on Via dei Benci." We continued our walk past the Piazza Signoria until we reached a church called San Pierto Scheraggi.

It was hard to believe the scene unfolding in front of the church's small plaza. "Ciao Jacopo!" called Leonardo giving the burly giant of a man a hug.

"How is your father?" asked Jacopo.

"Tolerably well, still no brothers or sisters, but all good things come in time. How is your lady?"

"She is sassy today," he said, pointing to the great lioness in the cage.

She was sitting upright in all her glory. Amber eyes hid beneath her lulling eyelashes. Although she appeared tranquil, her rounded ears were alert. Her sandy fur moved up and down with each heavy breath.

The cage that imprisoned the lioness was the exact reason I never liked going to the zoo. Even though trapped, she radiated power and majesty. Bold children were playing with a tiny cage near the lioness. Through its wooden bars, I could make out several fuzzy field mice. Both boys of four or five years old were giggling and probing the helpless mice with sticks. "Those are treats for when she behaves." Jacopo sighed, sitting back on his oversized chair. With his teeth, he ripped a chunk of salami and placed it back on the small table's still life of mugs, cards, and a coiled whip.

"Where is her other half?" asked Leonardo.

"Not here, and it's a good thing too. The lion usually upsets her," grumbled Jacopo as he took a swig from his waterskin. Scarlet drops dripped down his double chin and onto his long brown tunic.

"The lion is the symbol of Florence. When she has cubs, it is considered a sign of good luck for the city," said Leonardo, staring at the tranquil lioness. "Personally, I hate this."

"What do you mean?"

"I can't stand or justify the idea of causing unnecessary suffering of animals. People can judge me all they wish, but I won't partake in the beastly ritual of eating animals ... It's just wrong to me."

"Why did you bring me here, then?"

"It's a metaphor, Viola," he replied as if it was obvious. "Assuming you had to be one of the two, the mouse or the lioness, which would you choose?"

"The lioness, of course," I said, understanding what he was getting at.

"If that's the case ... be her." He turned to walk in the direction of the workshop.

Following behind, I mulled over his words. Honestly, I wanted to be the lioness, but at the moment I was most definitely one of the many field mice. Salai, Mrs. Reed, and Idan were the sticks poking at my sides and causing me to scurry around in anxiety.

"Are you happy with your work in the workshop?" His questions broke my train of thought.

"Everyone is very nice, and Margherita is sweet."

"That she is. Did you know that you would make a magnificent politician?"

"Why do you say that?"

"Because you have an uncanny way of not answering my questions," he jeered. "Let me put it another way. Would you be content with cleaning and cooking for the rest of your days?" There was a brief pause. It was difficult to have a serious conversation as we weaved through food carts. "You are hesitating."

"No, I'm not!" I protested.

"Just say it."

"No, I wouldn't be happy."

"There it is," he said with a gratified grin.

"No, the truth is I don't want to be doing this job at all. I want to be an apprentice."

"Why don't you tell Verrocchio, then?"

"There are no other girls working as apprentices."

"Even better. You would be carving the path ... I think you would be surprised to find how open-minded he can be."

"I don't really think this is fair."

"What?" he asked.

"You could take a lesson from the lioness as well," I said, meeting his sideways glance. "Why haven't you asked Verrocchio about finishing the angel in the Baptism of Christ painting? You told me you wanted to paint the angel in oil."

Leonardo opened his mouth to say something, but no words came out. We turned the corner on the industrious street of the workshop, but Leonardo stopped in front of the canopy.

"He has yet to allow me to paint figures," he admitted with crossed arms.

"But he chose your drawing of me in the library only a few days ago."

"Exactly! Drawing." He strode under the workshop's canopy.

"You would be surprised how open-minded he is," I mimicked before we separated at the foot of the stairs.

Once I left my satchel under Margherita's mattress, I rushed downstairs to meet her in the kitchen. The steam that rose from the boiling cannellini beans converted the stone room into a warm sanctuary. While I peeled a tower of ripe tomatoes, the sound of Margherita's heavy breathing thickened the air.

"Are you all right, Margherita?" I asked.

When I turned around her eyes were squinting in pain. One of her small hands slowly turned the stew with a wooden spoon while the other rubbed the underside of her belly.

"Yes ... I have just been getting these pains. I think—" She was interrupted by the quick skip of little Renzo.

"Viola, there is someone waiting for you in the courtyard," he said in a quiet voice.

Margherita and I both turned around to see who it was. Although the windows were foggy, we could both make out the tall but lean figure of a finely dressed man. His hands twisted behind him as he impatiently paced the humble courtyard.

"Is that...?"

"Yes, it is," I said, suddenly hyper-aware of my coarse brown dress and the red pulp under my fingernails.

I tried to rub off the smell of the tomatoes and garlic with some of the lavender soap in the basin. After untying the handkerchief from around my head, I attempted to tuck the loose pieces back into the braid.

"But why would he want to see you?" she asked.

"I'm not sure."

My cheeks felt hot. In an attempt to cool their color, I splashed some of the chilly water on my face. Margherita helped me undo the knot in my apron that my fumbling fingers failed to do.

"There you are," said Giuliano as I walked through the courtyard. The deep purple of his velvet tunic and the dark fur lining of his cape gave him a regal appearance.

"What a nice surprise," I admitted.

"Why are you surprised?"

"I wasn't expecting you," I explained.

"Don't you remember what I told you when we parted?"

Even though I did, I shook my head. His hands reached for my own, but they were wrapped in fists in an attempt to keep me from fidgeting. When he unclenched them, he held my hands tightly against his warm palms.

"I said we would see each other quite soon."

"Yes, that's right."

I looked up at him. His almond eyes had hazel flecks. The faint lines that surrounded them spoke of laughter. Although I was nervous, I could meet his gaze, which was something I had been unable to do.

"Here we are." I broke the silence.

"Well ... I ... just wanted to see you and hear your strange accent."

"I thought it was getting better."

"It is but don't work on it too much. I like it just the way it is ... I also came to give you this," he said as he withdrew a bulky envelope.

"What is it?"

"Something from my brother," he said.

"Thank you."

It was strange how different they were. Giuliano was so charming and easy to talk to, whereas Lorenzo was intimidating at best. Although I knew these papers meant to help me, I felt uncomfortably indebted.

"You can thank me by coming to the tournament on Sunday."

"Some of the apprentices have been telling me about it. From all they've said, I would like to see it."

"I can arrange it for you ... if you'd like. I do know where you live, after all." He grinned.

"No, that's all right. I'm sure I can manage it," I replied.

"Brilliant," he said, moving closer. Little Renzo ran into the courtyard with a package for Giuliano. Embarrassed, I slipped my hands away from his.

In a soft voice, he said, "Thank you, little one." Renzo did not appear to like the nickname "little one," even if it was coming from the unofficial prince of Florence.

"Well then, I will see you at the tournament?"

"You will," I agreed.

"Until Sunday then," he said with a slight bow and turned on the heels of his tall boots.

As I walked back into the kitchen, I slipped the envelope into the apron pocket. When I stepped through the doorframe, the whole workshop had been crowded around the foggy window.

"Hey! Whatever happened to a thing called privacy?"

"Never heard of such a thing!" exclaimed Perugino. "We tried to stop Renzo, but he couldn't take it anymore and burst out onto the courtyard." All the boys erupted in laughter. One by one they left the room with mocking jokes and reenactments.

Margherita offered me a faint smile. "Viola, please set the table." Once the plates and silverware were stacked and my arms loaded, Margherita stopped me. "Be careful there."

"I have only broken one thing in two days!" I protested.

"No, I mean with the young Medici."

"Oh yes ... well, I'm not sure why he keeps talking to me. I think he's just curious."

"Well, I didn't know why either, but now I do. Giuliano Medici and you are not in the same class," she explained as she sliced the rye bread. "Where you come from that might not mean anything, but here it means the world. I don't want you to end up like me." My arms were sinking from the weight of the dishes, but my feelings for Giuliano were struggling against Margherita's wisdom.

"I know you are concerned, Margherita, but you needn't be ... honestly."

"Your blush says otherwise," she pointed out. "Keep your distance. Powerful men are always used to getting what they want."

She placed the basket of bread on the pillar of plates. Once the table was set, I began cutting thin slices of mortadella while Margherita served the stew into shallow bowls. She mentioned something about cleaning chamber pots, and I instantly lost my appetite.

"Viola." I turned at the sound of my name. Master Verrocchio stood in the kitchen; his hands clasped behind the drapes of his black tunic.

The expression in his voice and face was grim. "I need to speak with you." My heart sank in my chest. Fear led me to suspect it had something to do with Salai's theft. Trying not to appear as guilty as I felt, I wiped the cold cuts' oily fat from my fingers. "Now would be a good time, if you please."

"Sir, we are about to eat. It will get cold," implored Margherita.

"This cannot wait," he insisted.

Margherita and I exchanged worried glances before I left the kitchen. Arming myself as I ascended the steps, I whispered, *"Be the lioness."*

CHAPTER THIRTEEN

Massimo

A TRAIL OF MUDDY footprints led to a door of varnished wood. A fire within beckoned me to enter the cozy living area. Verrocchio sat at an ample chestnut desk in the corner of the room. This was the only space that had any sign a man lived there. The untidy desk and its contents stood out drastically against its delicate surroundings. Eclectic floral carpets concealed the floor's brown tile. Two stiff sofas topped by mustard cushions were arranged around paneled windows. Faint light sifted through the salmon curtains. Discreet ceramic bowls of dried flowers gave the apartment an intense rose aroma.

"My nieces spend their time decorating. No doubt, it keeps them entertained." Verrocchio pointed to a chair facing his desk.

Before I sat down on the pale blue cushion, I moved the abandoned needlework from the chair. Exotic figurines of jade and ivory weighted down piles of parchment on the desk. Broken bits of charcoal and scraps of wax littered the surface. At the center of the chaos was a heavy book lying on its spine with hundreds of numbers scrawled in minute print.

On the back of Verrocchio's chair, I saw the familiar leather strap of my satchel. "Oh no!" Verrocchio took the satchel from its hiding place. "Sir—"

"Is this your property?" he interrupted, laying my satchel on the book's open face.

"It is," I admitted. He grumbled something under his breath I couldn't understand. "I had been keeping it in Margherita's ... space," I added, unsure where the conversation was going and shocked at the workshop's lack of privacy.

"It saddens me to say that yesterday someone took a generous sum of money from me." Unmoved, he let the information hang in the fragrant air.

"Sir, I know who took the money." Verrocchio's serious eyes tried to penetrate my armor, but his silence told me to continue. "I didn't say anything before because the person I saw take the money threatened to hurt someone I care about." Still, he said nothing. His eyes now fixed absently on my satchel. "I am sorry for not saying anything earlier ... but I was scared." Nervous, I started compulsively rubbing my hands and arms.

"It's interesting," he said, withdrawing a bottle of ruby liquid from underneath the flawlessly carved desk. Pouring the liquor into a shallow blue glass, he continued. "Someone in the exact same chair told me an almost identical tale." The liquid smelled strongly of licorice. A numb sensation that had started in my legs began to spread to my other limbs. "I'm sorry I had to search your belongings, but such was the nature of the accusation. Trust me when I say this class of ... happenings are my least favorite fire to put out." He took a sip from the glass.

"There might have been something I was unclear about regarding our relationship. In fact, now that I sit here, I do not recall having that conversation with you at all. Most likely because I have little time to spare for words." With his fingertips, he briefly soothed his temples. "When I welcome someone into my work, I am also inviting them into my home and consequently my life. This is a leap of faith. Although not stated directly, it is implied that I expect this trust to be reciprocated."

Verrocchio took off his black cap. For a man in his thirties, his face looked tired. His receding hairline added years to his appearance.

"Viola, can you assure me that you have been completely honest with me?"

"No, sir," I answered, feeling wretched. His guilt trip was worse than the one of my mom's. From my satchel, Verrocchio withdrew a heavy pouch that made a definite clinking sound when it hit the desk's cluttered surface. The anger that surged through me brought my extremities back to their full power. Before I knew it, I was standing. Everything that I had witnessed behind the cracks of the divider poured out of me. My Italian had never been so good.

"Viola," he interjected as he pointed back to the chair, "Do you have anything else you would like to share with me?" He maintained his calm but serious composure. My mind was so clouded by rage I could not think clearly.

"What about this curious item?" he asked, holding up my sketchbook. Immediately, it reminded me of a conversation I had shared with Zia, during which she advised me not to share my sketchbook with anyone including Verrocchio.

"Well, is it yours?" he pressed.

"Yes, it is."

"Are you responsible for the contents in this book?"

"Sketchbook," I corrected.

"We will get to that." Taking up his glass, he drained the few drops of remaining liquor. Still I said nothing.

It took all my energy to regain control over my feelings. That monster Salai had framed me and my privacy had never been so violated. He had no right to look through my stuff—or did he? The off-white bows on my sleeves reminded me where I was. Lost in a place where women were commodities meant to fulfill the needs of men. Misplaced in a time when women had to marry against their will and literate girls were dangerous or an oddity at best. There would not be rights for women for hundreds of years to come. Maybe at this time, I did not have the right to privacy? A liberty that I had taken for granted in the twenty-first century.

Verrocchio, who had been sitting patiently, cleared his throat. He was still waiting for me to claim the sketchbook.

"Yes … it belongs to me," I confessed. He began to sift through its pages.

"Are you telling me, that you, Viola Orofino, are responsible for the entire contents within this book?"

"Yes, sir. Oh! Except for a drawing of Zia's hen. Leonardo helped me with that."

"Leonardo knows about this?" He held the book up as if I could not see it clearly. "I can't believe he didn't tell me about this," he muttered more to himself than to me. Verrocchio's poker face disintegrated bit by bit. His eyebrows knitted together, creating deep creases around his eyelids and forehead.

"Who else knows about this?"

"Zia," I answered. A gurgling growl from Verrocchio's stomach interrupted our confession. Ignoring its yelp, he continued. "So you can read and write?"

"Yes," I admitted. All the while I wondered where these questions were leading. *Was I still being accused of stealing?* Although my stomach was not making noises, my emotional anguish had worked up an appetite. At this point in the inquiry, Verrocchio looked down at me as if I was a hallucination conjured by his licorice treat.

"Do you come from England?" Assuming he was talking about my writings, I answered,

"Sort of, I mean… English is my first language." The fire that had allured me into the cozy examination room was quickly fading.

"Why do you speak Tuscan?"

"My mother is Ital— I mean Tuscan."

"And your father?"

"His family is French."

"So what is your other surname? Orofino must be your mother's last name?" The blue cushion felt increasingly uncomfortable underneath me. Why was he so curious about me, and why was I telling him so much? Not accustomed to keeping secrets, I was a terrible liar. Truth slipped from my lips before I had a chance to stop it.

"I'd rather not say, Maestro," I said. A knock at the door disturbed Verrocchio's interrogation.

"Who is it?"

"Margherita, sir." She came in bearing gifts. Cold cuts, focaccia, olives, sharp cheese, and crimson wine weighed down the tray.

"Thank you, Marga," Verrocchio said as he made a clearing on his desk for the meal. She turned to me before she left the room, but I could not reveal enough information in just a glance. When the door closed behind her, I reached for a slice of cheese.

Moving the tray slightly out of my reach, Verrocchio protested, "As you heard, I am hungry as well, but I think it would be best if we finished our conversation first."

I retracted my hand. In an attempt to allow more light in, he peeled back the curtains of the closest window. When he sat back down his expression and posture had softened.

"I will not pretend that Salai is an honorable young man. I knew he was lying to me this morning, and I knew that pouch belonged to him. But I confess, I wanted to see how honest your testimony would be. When I found you in possession of this ... sketchbook, it was so hard to believe it belonged to you. May I ask one more question?"

Although relieved I was no longer being accused of stealing, my hunger had mounted to the point where I was almost incoherent. "Then can we eat?"

"Most gladly ... How did you come here and why?

"I'm still trying to figure that out.   All I know is that I was running through a dark hall of stone. The next thing I remember was the execution and being trampled on by hundreds of people in the Piazza della Signoria."

"That is when Zia and the young Medici found you," he added. There was a brief pause. My mouth filled with saliva. "Well, what would you have me do, Viola?"

"Excuse me?"

"You are hardly fit to be a housemaid," Verrocchio explained, cutting the bread.

"Are you letting me go, sir?" I panicked.

"Go where? Home?" He turned to look out the window he had just cleared. "There is still work to be done. We have not even savored our food yet." Passing me a generous serving, he clarified, "What I meant to say is it seems a terrible waste to have you sweep floors when I have so much work on my hands."

Not believing my luck, I seized the opportunity. "Master Verrocchio ... I am a most willing student. I would love to be an apprentice."

"It would be most singular to have a female apprentice," he pondered aloud. Shoving two black olives into his mouth, he mulled over the possibility. "It would be unprecedented and not entirely legal." The thought of doing something for the first time emboldened me.

"I don't think it is fair that I too want to learn but can't just because I'm a girl." The master looked at me sympathetically.

"You have been quite a handful, I must say, but I do not think there is a better place for you than here. Your talents are most unusual for a girl, and they are absolutely impossible given your class standing."

"You mean because I'm minuto?" I took a bite of bread.

"Something like that ... To get to the point, we cannot make use of your talents as a girl, so you will have to continue your work with

Margherita in the kitchens and cleaning." The gloom of the winter day mirrored my reaction to his jail sentence.

My thoughts readied for a rebuttal when he said with a smile, "At least in the morning. After briefly considering your situation and all the work I need to get done, I have decided to give you a choice. Apart from your early morning tasks, you may also be my apprentice in the afternoon."

"Yes!"

"Wait, I am not finished. If you agree, I will give you some money and Leonardo will accompany you to pick out some boys' clothes that suit you."

"So I have to work in the workshop dressed as a boy?"

"Unfortunately, those are the times we live in. I want to make clear that this is quite a risk, for the both of us. I am not sure what the Signoria would do if they found out I had a young girl as an apprentice dressed up as a boy ... but I am certain they would not be pleased. There could be penalties."

"What kind of penalties?"

"Prison, fines, maybe even a trial if we are particularly unlucky."

The scarred scene of the crying woman, knotted rope, and people cheering stirred from my memory. Never had I been so close to death. Even though it hadn't been my own life in the balance, an overwhelming sensation of dread had consumed me. Despite the risks, becoming an apprentice felt like it was the only way to move forward, to become a better artist, and make my time here worth something.

Verrocchio had polished off the rest of the food while I reflected on the dangers of my decision. "You must understand why it is so important to be secretive. It would be best not to tell Zia, as the less she knows the better her nerves will be." He poked the fire back to life.

The idea of lying to Zia was bothersome, but I didn't want her to worry either. To conquer Florence, I needed to become part of the city. Being the mouse was no longer an option. I needed to be the lioness.

"Master Verrocchio, I still want to do it."

"You agree then? Understanding the circumstances and perils?"

I nodded. Verrocchio stretched out his hand, and I squeezed back to seal the pact. "You realize our pitfall might be your eyes. It makes this charade most difficult. They are so singular you are almost impossible to disguise. Save those who have not met you already," he said with the grin of a mischievous boy. "We will do our best. We must trust our family down there creating away," he concluded as he stared at the blue-green vignettes painted on the opposite wall.

"What about Salai?" I asked. Verrocchio took a deep sigh and put his feet up on the desk. The tender black leather of his boots hung over the corner of the desk.

"Salai is bound to me ... he came to me fatherless, and I cannot bring myself to throw him out. He is also what some may call the black sheep of my boys, and I do have a soft spot for those." Meeting my eyes, he continued seriously, "Be cautious, Viola. If I were a girl, I would not look him in the eye. Margherita had to learn that lesson the hard way." He stood up and walked around the desk. "As I said at the beginning of our conversation, it is a leap of faith. I believe I can manage him, mostly because he has nowhere else to go."

"I will not let you down." I stood up. With a fatherly motion, he placed his palms on my shoulders.

"You are strong beneath all that fear. It would do my nieces good to be more like you. Instead, all they do every day is keep to their rooms, sleep, and demand potions to make their hair smoother and skin fairer."

He walked to the door. "Leonardo!" he boomed. While we waited for Leonardo to appear, Verrocchio told me we needed to figure out another name for me.

"How about Massimo?" He suggested.

Before I was able to protest, Leonardo entered the room. The sleeves of his gray undershirt were rolled up past his elbows. His short navy tunic was spotless, and his lion-like hair was pulled back into a loose ponytail emphasizing the stubble protruding from his jaw.

"You called?"

"What do you think of the name Massimo?"

"For who or what?"

"For Viola," said Verrocchio. Leonardo looked confused at first, but understood his meaning when he saw my open sketchbook on the desk. "Massimo ... sounds perfect."

"You are joking," I blurted. Both men laughed. "That is the worst name you could have chosen for me."

"Massimo it is! Leonardo, you will take her to get clothes for Massimo, no?"

"That will be interesting."

"Excellent. While you two are gone, I will explain to the workshop our new situation."

"Master Verrocchio?"

"Yes, Viola?"

"I think that Leonardo wanted to ask you something." Verrocchio and I both turned towards Leonardo. His eyes focused on his boots as he shifted his weight from side to side.

"Out with it, Leo. It is unlike you to keep your opinions to yourself. You are making me terribly nervous." Still Leonardo stalled. "Honestly, I am busy and if you don't speak up, you will most definitely sour my excellent mood."

"I want to paint the angel."

"What angel?" asked Verrocchio.

"The missing one from the Baptism of Christ."

"Oh yes, for a moment I forgot about it entirely," Verrocchio confessed, scratching his head. He looked Leonardo over for a moment. "You have a model in mind?"

"For several days now ... It's a boy I drew by Mercato Vecchio."

"If you feel you are ready."

"I do," assured Leonardo.

"Wasn't there something else?" I added, feeling bold.

"Yes..." Leonardo cleared his throat "...I wanted to paint it in oil."

"I don't care how you do it as long as it's glorious."

"It will be," said Leonardo, beaming ear to ear.

As Verrocchio handed me my satchel, he placed three coins in my palm. "Be quick about it. The day is almost over." Not being able to contain my gratitude, I gave him a tight squeeze.

"*Grazie!*"

"*Prego*, Viola," he returned.

CHAPTER FOURTEEN

Ponte Vecchio

WE HAD ONLY MADE it halfway out the door when Leonardo gave me a shoulder nudge that said, "I told you so." A cloud of feathers surrounded us as plundering pigeons flew from our path.

"Why do you look so pleased with yourself?" I asked.

"I thought my smile said it all."

"Your smile is lacking some information."

"That's not its fault." He shrugged. "The guilt lies with my secretive companion."

"Ugh, you always have to have the last word," I protested.

It was difficult for me to trust anyone, especially after Salai had threatened me. After my confession to Verrocchio, I felt better than I had since I arrived in Florence. It felt like gravity had loosened its strangling grip on me.

"You're right. Maybe I have been a bit too ..."

"Elusive? Mysterious? Distrustful?" he mocked.

"Any of those would work."

"I know."

"Do you also know that sometimes you can be... bossy?" I said.

"That's a nice way of putting it, and yes, I know that too ... I will lay off a bit," he consented, offering his arm out for me. "Almost forgot to say thanks for pushing me to ask Master Verrocchio."

"More like forcing you, but you're welcome all the same."

The sun was about to make its descent behind the heavy layer of clouds. Frost was settling in between the cracks of the cobblestones. The road's travelers scattered to finish their day's business.

I did not see any other women on the road we were on. After pausing for thought, I realized that I seldom saw any women walking on the street. Rarer still were girls my age. Perhaps I noticed it then because I was thinking about how lousy it was that I had to pretend to be a guy just to be an apprentice.

"Why are there no women around?"

Leonardo laughed. "There are many. You just can't see them because they are barricaded in their homes and only come out for church. As a rule, women do not walk around Florence. I might even go as far as to say it is highly discouraged. So most of the women that must walk on the street are old, impoverished, or accompanied by men."

"Why?"

"Many think a woman's proper place is at home. Anything outside of it, especially the street, is considered a man's domain."

"You don't believe that, right?" I asked incredulously.

"Of course not," he said, turning onto Via Della Porcellana. It was sad to think of all those girls cooped up behind their balconies. Suddenly, the foul but free air smelled sweeter.

As we passed a pit where workers quarried porous stone, we heard a voice call out, "Leonardo!" We turned around to see a man in his early twenties with wavy auburn hair.

"Ciao, Sandro!" returned Leonardo. The young man approached us with a wide smile. Similar to Leonardo, he wore an indigo tunic that fell just above his knees. The taupe cloak draped about his person gave him an ancient Roman appearance.

"It has been a while," said Sandro, grabbing Leonardo's free hand.

"You have been lost. Last week was the first time I have seen you miss a guild meeting."

"You are not even in the guild yet and you take attendance," laughed Sandro.

"That is a mere formality."

"Yes, I know ... Well, my father has bought the property just there ..." He motioned to a quaint two-story house four doors down. "I have converted the bottom floor into my own workshop." Sandro's smile was handsome but not brilliant. He had a strong face in that instead of his features mixing harmoniously, each feature was so pronounced that it stood out separately. His bottom lip weighed down his curvy upper lip.

Green eyes bulged from his manicured brow and accentuated his straight nose. His chin was prominent, but he had a jawline that most models on the advertisements in Times Square would envy.

"Come in and see," he pleaded. Not waiting for an answer, he pulled Leonardo into the workshop, and I followed.

The workshop was bare. Three worktables and benches arranged in an L-shape huddled around the fireplace. The pools of wax on their weathered surfaces suggested late nights at work. One table had a cracked human skull at its center with fruits and flowers arranged around it. A few tools hung on the wall opposite the fireplace. Piles of wood were scattered about the workshop. On three easels were paintings of the Virgin Mary in different poses. The silhouettes were striking; each figure was elongated and curved around the painting's panel.

Leonardo and Sandro were talking about the wonders and woes of running your own workshop when I noticed a boy who looked to be only a year or two younger than me. He was silently preparing a wooden panel for painting. Sawdust from leveling the gesso clung to the buttons of his rust-colored tunic.

"I was sorry to hear about Master Lippi," said Leonardo.

"Yes." He grimaced. "Very untimely if you ask me. Actually, he was the picture of health the last time I saw him, which was only two weeks before his death. I mean a little round about the edges but ..." His eyes were alert and his tone disbelieving.

"What are you trying to say, Sandro?" asked Leonardo.

In the midst of their conversation, I noticed an open sketchbook on the worktable. It was too tempting to resist. I tiptoed closer so it would be easier to steal a few casual glances.

"What you're hearing my friend, think—" He stopped and glanced over at the corner where the boy was working. Sandro shook his head, pointed at the skull. "Memento mori."

Drawn in dark pencil on the open sketchbook page was the head of a gorgeous girl. She had long curls that jumped off the page and red chalk for lips. The mysterious lady's nose was delicate and petite, and her eyes were inlaid perfectly underneath her slightly arched eyebrows.

"True, one of the only truths we really know ... All will die," agreed Leonardo.

The morbid conversation led way for an awkward silence. On the opposite page were more portraits of the same lovely girl. My eyes grew a little wider when I saw that one of the portraits included a full nude drawing. I had seen nude women in paintings or statues. However, it seemed weird to look at the stark body in the middle of a workshop full of modest Virgin Marys and even stranger amid conversations of death.

"Well, we must be going. We have to get to Ponte Vecchio before the shops close," announced Leonardo.

"But you have not introduced me to your fair friend," Sandro pointed out.

"Yes, sorry about that. This is Viola. She is a new housemaid at Verrocchio's workshop ... Viola, this is Sandro Botticelli."

"Nice to meet you," I said, tilting my head. "Likewise."

"It's too bad Verrocchio swept you up. As you can see, I am in need of a housemaid. You don't by any chance have a sister with your extraordinary eyes?"

"No, I do not," I answered uncomfortably.

"But she does have a twin brother with those same eyes," interjected Leonardo.

"*Allora*? I am fascinated by twins."

"As am I." Leonardo winked at my surprise. It was amazing how naturally he spun such coherent lies. "Who is that diligent boy in the corner?"

"I, too, have neglected the duties of introduction," he consented. "Fillipio, come please."

The boy walked over to the entrance of the workshop, his eyes barely leaving the stone floor. The dark hair that framed his face and ears was covered with a round blue hat.

"This is Fillipio Lippi, son of my late master. Fillipio, this is Leonardo da Vinci and Viola ..."

"Orofino," I finished. Fillipio politely nodded his head after each introduction.

"Well, it was nice meeting you, but we must be off."

"Would you mind if we accompanied you? I have a mind to eat meat this evening but have none in my pantry. It would do us good to walk, would it not, Fillipio?"

"We will be almost running to make it on time, but you are more than welcome to come along," warned Leonardo.

Botticelli grabbed a red hat off a hook near the staircase. "Mama! I am going out! Come watch the shop," he yelled.

After we heard the creak of the floorboards above, we headed out to continue our journey to Ponte Vecchio. Leonardo and Sandro led the way while Fillipio and I fought to keep up with their swift steps. It felt good to be at the rear and have someone else block the wind. The smell of rotten fish met my nose before I could glimpse the river. My insides winced at the stench. To soften the scent, I started breathing heavily through my mouth.

"It stinks, right?" said Fillipio.

"Yes! No one ever talks about it, so I just assumed I'd get used to it ... eventually."

"I am new here as well." He had lovely tear-shaped eyes that drooped a little at the corners of his face.

"Sorry to hear about your father," I said.

"Oh ... thanks," he said, scratching at the cleft in his chin. "Are you training to be an artist as well?"

"Yeah, I was training to be one under my father, but he died, so my mother asked Botticelli if I could continue my apprenticeship with him," he explained with a slight lisp.

"Did you move here?"

"Yes, about a week ago, but so far I don't like the city much."

"Why?"

"It's small."

"*Allora?*"

"I was living in Spoleto, so I am used to lots of green and wide-open fields. Here you are constantly surrounded, and like I said, the smell is awful," he added.

"Viola, this is a cursed and unlucky ditch," called Leonardo.

"What is?"

"The Arno," he answered, slowing down his pace to walk beside me. "A year after I arrived in Florence, the river flooded the lower parts of the city. It got so bad that benches from Santa Croce floated around here. When the flood subsided, it left a sewer of waste behind."

"How lovely," I said, looking at the river.

"Maybe you will have the same luck," teased Sandro.

As we teetered a little closer to the bank of the river, I looked down to see makeshift piers made of tattered wood scraps. Women and men were pouring buckets of dyes and obscure compounds into the river. Garbage littered the surface and moved with the current of the river. Florence's waste lapped against the sides of the banks.

"That is so sad," I said.

"Look at that, a much more pleasant sight for the eyes to rest upon," proclaimed Sandro.

He was pointing to a stone bridge. The bridge's broad arch connected both sides of the riverbank. Its long passageway was lined with shops and thick defensive walls were punctured by tiny windows. As the sky darkened, lamps flickered across the skyline. We hurried across the bridge. The walls that surrounded the bridge provided shelter from the rain but little else.

Every shop owner had a sturdy wooden table upon which he displayed his goods. It was clear we were late by the sloppy second pickings left over. Several men haggled high prices for mediocre or poor meat. The bridge's shops mostly sold meat except for the occasional second-hand clothes dealer. Leonardo found the vendor he was looking for.

While he browsed and negotiated prices with the vendor, a scarecrow of a man with a huge nose, the street began to quiet. Four men clothed in chest armor and stripes of blue and red marched across the bridge. As they approached voices hushed and breaths were held. The helmets that shielded their heads shone silver and plumage exploded from their tops. All four approached, an elderly man's stand on the opposite side of the bridge. When Leonardo realized something was happening, he beckoned me to get underneath the shelter. Sandro took Leonardo's cue and used his body to block me from view.

"But I want to see what's going on!" I protested.

"Hush!" said Leonardo.

"You are being—"

"Bossy, I know ... now get down and tighten the shawl over your head."

Bending down, I looked through the gaps their legs allotted. The shop owner was a kind-looking man who had an uncanny resemblance to my only grandpa. His tidy white mustache matched the finely cut hair that circled his bald spot. He had a face both round and sweet. His bottom lip was trembling with his hands clasped together. Cries of help followed as the guards unsheathed their long swords. The old man's eyes widened as he grabbed for the few baskets of fish he had left on the table. The men began to mercilessly pound on the table. The shop owner fell back and the fish in his baskets flew in every direction.

My heart flooded with pity. The merchants and market stragglers didn't spare a glance. I was shocked to see their hollow expressions— the same apathy I had seen the day of the execution. In an attempt to stop the flow of tears, I shut my eyes and covered my ears. The thrashing stopped.

When I stood up, the guards were walking back in the direction they came from and the older man remained where he had fallen. His hands supported the weight of his head. He looked so alone. No one had to tell me this would not be fixed by buying a new table. Something serious had happened. The guards had broken more than his table.

"Viola! Don't!" urged Leonardo as I rushed past him and over to the weeping man. The baskets of fish he had tried to save were overturned. Kneeling down next to him, I could feel his helplessness.

"Signore ..."

"Leave me," he gasped. It would have been impossible for me to leave him. Instead, I gently touched his shoulder.

He looked up at me, both surprised and distraught. Anger crossed his face briefly but shame followed.

"You have a face of an angel," he whimpered.

"I can tell you have the soul of one," I said. He tenderly grabbed the hands I offered him. His eyes were sapphires. "Can I help you, sir?"

"I am afraid not," he said picking up a shard of the broken table. "I'm so ashamed I don't think I can even stand up."

Years of toiling under the Tuscan sun had darkened and thickened the flesh of his hands and face. He had the look of a man who had lost too much weight in too little time. As I held his hands, I could hear him quietly recounting his troubles to himself.

"How will I pay back the loan if I cannot sell my goods? What if I go to jail? Who will take care of my grandsons?" I tried hard to keep it together but with each plea my heart gave way to a new wave of sympathy. Leonardo, Sandro, and Fillipio walked over and began replacing the fish in the reed baskets.

"How much for the fish, sir?" asked Sandro. The man looked at Sandro as if he had just said a bad joke. "I mean it in earnest."

"They are ruined."

"Hardly ... a bit of hot water will set them right." Sandro left a chunk of coins beside the man. "There is extra there for the basket," he said, picking up the basket.

"Sir, you have given me too much!" protested the old man.

"Nonsense, this is an excellent basket!"

"Sir, I would like to buy the other basket," I insisted.

From my satchel, I grabbed the money Verrocchio had given me for the clothes. Leonardo bent beside me and handed me a few coins of his own. I took the old man's hand and placed the coins in his palm. Sandro and Leonardo helped the elderly man to his feet.

"What is your name, dear child?"

"Viola."

"You are a gift," he said, kissing my hand. "My name is Alfredo Moroni. For the few years left in me, I am at your service." I shook my head at this gratitude and bid him farewell.

We left the Ponte Vecchio with all of Signore Moroni's fish in our arms. We parted ways with Sandro and Fillipio at the end of the bridge. Leonardo and I continued on to Zia's house. The streets were slippery, and I had to hold on tight to Leonardo's arm. So many questions were buzzing around my head. I didn't even know where to begin.

"Why did those armed men break Signore Moroni's table?"

"He is bankrupt and has debt that is overdue ... It's a common practice," he admitted as we turned left onto Via dei Benci.

"A debt with whom? Who would do such a thing? It's like Moroni said. How will he pay the debt if both his table and his pride are broken?" I raged.

"No need to tell me. You're better off talking to your admirer about that."

"What admirer?"

"Giuliano."

"Why?"

"Well, I would bet money that our new friend's debt is with the Medici bank. Has Zia not told you that they are the major bank of the city? You might even say the world. Even the Pope goes to the Medici for money."

The dozens of burning wicks shining from Signora Rossi's house illuminated the wedding wreath's pastel blossoms. A duet of strings and whistles escaped from the cracks of the jubilant household.

"Will you be early again tomorrow?"

"Even earlier, so make sure to prepare extra breakfast," he said, disappearing into the shadows.

CHAPTER FIFTEEN

Marriage

A FIRE FLICKERED BENEATH the stovetop. A few tallow candles burned low. In an attempt to mask their beefy odor, Zia boiled cinnamon sticks in one of the pots that steamed above the flames. She came out of the pantry carrying mushrooms and flour. After placing the basket of fish on the top of the table, I removed the shawl from my head and moved closer to the fire. The corners of my mouth burned from the cold, but it felt good to let the warm air wash over me.

"Dear child!" lamented Zia. "You get home later and later each day. I am going to have a talk with Leonardo ... Look at the state you are in!" Once she had safely placed the ingredients on the counter, she felt my forehead. The back of her hand felt hot against my skin. "Your hair is damp ... a sure sign you will catch a cold." Zia began to search through the brass canisters that lined the shelves surrounding the oven.

"Tonight, before the fire goes out, you will slip these stones into the fire. When they are nice and hot, carefully put them under your sheets," she instructed. "Go put on that warm green thing you have."

My feet felt heavy as I scaled the steps. Once I removed the first two layers of clothing, I slipped on my warm wool sweater. When I squeezed my braid, I could feel the dampness hiding within. Unweaving the braid, I let my hair frizz around my shoulders.

"What in Mary's name are all these *triglie* doing here?" Zia cried from the kitchen.

"Sorry?" I called, descending the stairs.

"Fish!"

"Oh yeah! I was so tired that I forgot to tell you," I admitted. After sitting down, I told her what had happened at the market except for the bit about why we were there in the first place. I explained how between the four of us we bought all of Signore Maroni's fish. "Since Leonardo is a vegetarian, that means more fish for us." I smiled. While I was telling her the story, she seemed upset, but by the time I got to the end, her expression had softened.

Without saying a word, she picked out four of the *triglie* she liked best and placed them on a nearby plate. Then she unlocked the door, took up the basket, and left. From the open door, I could see her waiting on the footsteps of the Signora Rossi's house. When the door opened, music burst onto the street. The master of the house, a squat, chubby man, was all smiles at seeing Zia and her offering.

It was not until she was mixing the flour and eggs that she said, "Well, now there is no need to get them a wedding present." For a brief moment, I thought I was safe from being lectured. "You're a sweet soul, Viola, and I am happy that you were able to help someone else, but you worked hard for that money, and make no mistake we could put that money to good use," she said kneading the dough.

I was annoyed. Although I saw sense in her words, I hated that I was being chastised for doing something kind. She had not been there to see his despair. While I recounted the long list of reasons to hold my tongue, I took a step back and realized that the person I was really mad at was Giuliano.

It was impossible to think of anything else. Olive oil and mushrooms sizzled, and their savory scent drifted through the kitchen. Zia rolled out the dough to push out the air until it was paper-thin. Next, she cut long but wide vertical rectangles and slid the fresh pasta into the boiling cinnamon pot. Soon after, we sat down to eat our supper of pappardelle, mushrooms, and fish. Zia held my hand and said a long prayer. Only after taking a generous bite of the pasta did I break the peace.

"Leonardo thinks that it was the Medici who broke Signore Maroni's table," I blurted.

She raised her eyebrows at the mention of the Medici. Every part of me wanted the slander to be contradicted and Giuliano's guilt to magically disappear.

"Young Leonardo is most probably right," she said, slurping on the fish head. "He is most probably indebted to the Medici."

How could I allow myself to like someone who would do such a thing? Then again, it was really his family that was responsible. It would not be right to hold that against him. That would be like Juliet hating Romeo because he was a Montague. His family's deeds were not necessarily his fault, right?

"The fault lies with Signore Maroni," she added. "He bit off more than he could chew. That said, what that poor man has suffered is cruel and humiliating." She looked at me with sympathy. "I wasn't going to say anything unless the subject was brought up. Mostly because I, better than anyone, know the disaster that can come of meddling with the affection two people have for each other. I was hoping it would cool but that is obviously not the case." She finished the few bites left on her plate before adding, "I say this because Verrocchio came by the house today." Resolved not to fall for the silent trap again, I stuffed another mouthful of the wide noodles into my mouth. "He told me you had a visitor at the workshop today."

Crossing my arms, I bit hard on my oily lips. "He came to pick up something he had ordered from the workshop," I justified. The white scar on her cheek disappeared in the folds of her grimace.

"Surely, you saw the garland down the street?"

"*Si.*"

"Well, that is a tradition in Florence. The day of the wedding the groom hangs a garland of flowers across the street of his bride," she explained. "Although that is a lovely custom, here the tradition of marriage is far from the rosebuds that hang on its ribbon." She stood up to grab a knife and two overripe apples. "We do it to bear children and to fulfill the holy sacrament. But it is also a contract," she said, peeling the fruit's wrinkly skin. "As you know, my late husband was a tailor. We lived well in that we never lacked for anything. Coming from humble origins, neither of us had valuable connections. Fortunately, we were able to start a dowry fund for our two girls."

She poured herself a shallow glass of white wine. "One night, the Devil came and stole my oldest, Giovanna, while she was in my arms. Ginerva, only five years old at the time, accumulated a generous dowry upon her sister's death ... You see, she was our only child who made it past her ninth birthday. It was most important for us that she be well taken care of and above all secure." She took a sip of wine and waited for the wave of emotion to pass.

"The boy's name was Antonio. He and his family moved from Pisa to a house a few doors down. What a fair boy he was," she added as the wrinkles on her forehead searched for ways to describe him. "He was more handsome than our young Giuliano and with a heart that was ... true. I cannot remember where I last put my smelling salts but I remember the day Ginerva and Antonio first met. She was thirteen years old and he only three years her senior. We were walking to mass at Santa Croce when we ran into our new neighbors. I felt the fervor that closed the space between the two young hearts. Antonio saw Ginerva through the starry eyes that the young Medici looks through when he sees you."

She took another sip of wine before scraping all the fish bones onto one plate. I held my breath fearing how the story would end. "Two years passed. They exchanged notes that spoke of love and dreams of country life. I turned a blind eye to this because I couldn't take away her happiness," Zia reflected sadly. "That is how I like to remember her now, every day ... It was not much longer before her father noticed. My husband liked and felt for Antonio, but that did not curb his ambition. He was a good man but stubborn and determined that Ginerva would marry a young man from a wealthy Florentine family." She took off the embroidered handkerchief that covered her gray hair, the strands wispy and fragile. "My husband revealed to Antonio his plan for Ginerva's marriage to the Agolanti family."

"Did Ginerva know?" I asked, hanging on Zia's every syllable.

"No, Antonio told her."

"What did she do?"

"Nothing." Zia sighed, passing her fingers over the embroidery of her handkerchief.

"Nothing?"

"Needless to say, I was very conflicted about my husband's decision, so I delivered the notes that Antonio would slip into my basket before he headed to his woodshop. I watched her read the letter from Antonio about her father's intentions. As she read, his words stole all the joy and zeal that once radiated from her. It was terrible to watch her disintegrate in front of me." Zia's chin shook. I wanted to tell her that she did not need to finish the story, but my anticipation would not let me.

"On the day we walked under her garland and up to the ceremony at San Giovanni, she looked like one of my nephew's beautiful statues. Lovely to behold but cold as marble. It tore me apart. I pleaded with my husband, but he would not go back on his decision. Poor Antonio insisted on walking the whole procession despite my entreaties to go home and save himself the pain. I will never forget what he said to me that day. "The only soul I am meant to walk this life with is my fair Ginerva. But if it is not God's will, it is my will to walk alone."

Her chest heaved. "His words pierced straight through my flesh, bone, and heart. The marriage did not end well. It was an act of God." It was when I got up to get her a glass of water that I realized the low light of the candles had hidden her tears. She took a long drink of water. "My dear, I don't think I can finish telling you this story, at least not today," she apologized. My curiosity would have to rely on imagination to piece the rest of the tale together. "Why was I telling you about Ginerva and Antonio?" she asked.

"I think you were trying to make a point about marriage."

"Yes ..." She took another gulp of water. "Ginerva will not speak to me, so I am alone ... except for you, sweet Viola," she said, weaving her fingers through mine. "Marriages are for advantageous reasons only, money or connections."

"Zia, but I'm only fifteen! I'm too young to get married," I protested. The conversation seemed so ridiculous. The pasta twisted in my gut at the thought of being married at such a young age.

"That is beside the point. Giuliano Medici will marry a wealthy noble like his brother Lorenzo, who is engaged to Clarice Orsini." She stood up and began to clean the plates and pots.

Good for him, I thought with a sneer as I stood up to throw the smooth stones into the low fire. *Who says I want to marry Giuliano... or anyone, for that matter?* The idea of marriage felt light years away from me. All I wanted was to spend time with him. Maybe stare at him and dance with him. It would be dreamy to kiss him for a few seconds, minutes, or hours. After piling the stones back into the metal canister, I walked towards the stairs.

"Before you sleep, I want you to think long and hard. Then ask yourself whether Giuliano's intentions with you are honorable." Her words must have not had the effect she was hoping for because before I could disappear up the last steps she added, "Think about poor Margherita too." She had said it, the one phrase that would turn my dreams of romance into nightmares.

CHAPTER SIXTEEN

Surprise

FLORENCE WAS REBORN WHEN the clouds darkened, and rain poured onto its stone. The city's filth drifted away, leaving a new beginning. The air smelled crisper but the cold bit harder. By my feet I could feel the polished surface of rocks. Fumbling under the stiff sheets for Idan, I found it by my waist. Its hard shell was warm from my body heat. The tips of my fingers grazed the bumpy imprint Idan's cover had left on my skin. Still groggy, I pried open my companion. I held Idan close to my face in the darkness.

The arrow pointed to the rising sun but the numbers surrounding its opal center told me that today was December 22, 1479 and that I had eighteen days left. My spine straightened, and I rubbed the grogginess out of my eyes before I looked and the numbers again. The words of the anonymous letter hung in my conscious. *"Idan has a mind of its own."* Startled, I looked at its diamond case as if it were the first time I had seen it. Three days ago, the remaining time had been thirty days and now there were only eighteen. Excitement that I had barely let myself feel bubbled up inside me. I would be home sooner than I thought.

The day before, Zia had found some old boots that belonged to her husband. Embarrassingly enough, they fit my gargantuan feet. After I slipped on the black boots, I walked downstairs, past the pantry, and through the door to the back alley. The makeshift wooden roof of Georgina's roost protected her rusty feathers from stray raindrops.

It turned out that chickens were a smelly business, but on this early morning, the air was fresh. It felt good to take in the gray break of day. The slope of the roof above created an opaque curtain of raindrops. Water splashed onto the boots' pebbled leather. Outside, it was still and quiet. My eyes closed as I tried to imagine Ginerva and Antonio exchanging notes of longing in the alley.

"Lovely morning for a swim." The sound of the unexpected voice almost made me jump out of my skin. "Just now, your face was priceless," laughed Leonardo.

"What do you expect, creeping out of the shadows of a dark alley in the rain?"

"I wanted to see if you were really keeping a cow back here." He smiled. "Speaking of rain, let's go inside, I'm frozen."

Once inside, Leonardo hovered by the stove until a flame sparked while I rummaged through the pantry. We were silent while we prepared breakfast together.

"I have something for you," he said as I stirred the milk.

"What is it?" I turned my head. He had taken off his hooded cloak, and I could see a rough leather-bound notebook wedged between his arm and brown tunic.

"My sketchbook."

"Wow! Things are getting personal. Next thing you know you'll be hanging a garland of flowers on my street," I teased.

"Ha, ha," he mocked. "Very clever. How long have you been waiting to say that?"

MARIA C. TRUJILLO

"Centuries."

"Let's get back to business," he said, preparing his toast with more honey. "Yesterday, before we ran into Sandro, you said perhaps you have too many secrets ... So here I am, bright and early, to lighten your load. I even brought a peace offering." He held up the book and then let its weight fall onto the table. After finishing my improvised tea of orange rinds and lemon juice, I sat down at the table and reached for the sketchbook. Leonardo blocked my hand before I could open it.

"I'll show you mine if you show me yours," he said.

I thought about his proposal for a moment. Leonardo scratched at his chin. His beard was growing quickly. Here and there, red hairs clashed with the blonde and brown stubble.

"That is hardly fair. You have already seen mine," I pointed out.

"Correction, I drew in your sketchbook. Which is not even close to what I am offering," he defended, moving his sketchbook closer to his body. Looking into someone's sketchbook was just as personal as looking into someone's diary. Leonardo was offering me a glimpse into his soul.

"Fine." I returned in moments with my sketchbook.

We both exchanged our most private possessions at the same time. After taking a sip of my citrus brew, I turned to a random page. The hot liquid that filled my mouth almost came rushing back out.

"Leo! What is this?"

"I was just about to ask you the same thing." The page I had turned to had a series of different hand gestures. Everywhere in between was narrow but curvy scrawl. Bringing the notebook closer to my face, I tried to decipher the script, but it was beyond my ability. The words flowed from right to left like Hebrew.

"Is this Latin?"

"Of course not! Latin is severely overrated and all those stuck up people who aim to make themselves seem better by speaking and writing it can't help themselves," he said without looking up from the page he had flipped to. "If Tuscan was good enough for Dante, it is good enough for me." His protective tone told me I had found a soft spot.

"Well, I can't understand a single sentence."

"That makes the two of us." The page Leonardo had turned to was a drawing of my boy-next-door crush, Louis Martin.

This looks so stalker, I thought. It was one of several drawings I had done of him in AP English class. Any time he was in a one-mile radius of me, my bones would go jelly-like and I became seriously stupid.

"Did you admire him?"

"What? Uh ... no ... I mean, why?"

"Well, you took great care with this sketch and with all the other drawings of his face." It was a good thing he could not read English. All around the sketches, I had professed my undying love for his caramel skin and black curly hair.

"So what language is this?"

"It's English."

"So you're from where exactly?" His face screwed up in confusion.

"You wouldn't believe me if I told you," I answered. Leonardo drummed his fingers impatiently on the table.

"You have said that before," he groaned. "Try me."

"I have no way of knowing for sure, but I don't think I'm allowed to tell you or anybody. It's not about trust, I promise you."

"Fine, what did you want to talk about, then?"

With no further delay, I told him about everything that had happened to me once I had fallen into the crowd in Piazza della Signoria. I told him how I had witnessed the execution and woken up in Giuliano's arms. The story of what had happened in the study with Salai unraveled before I had a chance to stop myself. After I finished telling him about Idan being my key to getting back home, I sealed the explanation by sharing with him my feelings for Giuliano. Leonardo stared back at me blankly.

"Speechless. This must be a first for you."

"I like that you're smiling. I love those who can smile when they're in trouble," he said softly. "First thing I mean to do when we get to the workshop is punch Salai in his pretty face."

"Oh, so what you are really saying is that you want to turn Zia's house into a pile of firewood?" I asked sarcastically.

"He's all talk."

"All the same, I can't take those kinds of chances," I insisted, gulping the last of my cold tea. "These are all secrets by the way. Just to make sure we are on the same page."

"*Scouz ono.*"

"What's that mean?"

"It was what you said when you promised to trust me one day."

"Oh! You mean scout's honor?" I smiled, repressing a giggle.

"Yes ... that. Are people always so obvious where you come from?" Rolling my eyes, I picked up the dirty dishes and placed them in the basin. "Now, about your sketchbook ..." Leonardo cleared his throat.

Bracing myself for the worst, I sat back down. "Have you tried drawing people or animals in motion?"

After thinking about it, I realized I usually drew things that were steady. "If I have, I can't remember right now. Why?"

"In order to truly master drawing, painting, or sculpting, you need to be aware of all the muscles and bones of the human body and animals alike. Only through the study of how they work together to create motion will you perfect your skills. To this, you must further associate yourself with how the muscles and skin clothe bones on bodies, young or old." He leaned over the table and turned to a page in his notebook.

"Look here." The page he showed me was covered with micro- studies of dogs fighting, walking, or running. On the opposite page was an anatomical drawing of a dog's hind leg. "You are talented, but you lack in naturalism." He paused to see how I was taking his criticism, but I was too interested in what he was saying to care. "By rule, I like to work in solitude, but we could try some movement exercises together. It's difficult but that is probably why it's my favorite." He moved to get a refill of milk. White drops hung from his budding mustache as he continued his lecture. "It is my belief that every great artist should carry a notebook around so as to draw what is happening around him."

"Or her," I corrected.

"Yes. For example, what do you think I was doing at the execution?"

"Hopefully not because you like that sort of thing," I said.

"No, I was sketching."

"You were what?"

"I was drawing her fear, her body, the tension of the rope around her neck, the life escaping from her. Do not look at me like that! Honestly, the way I remember her is much more wholesome than many old women crushing her in between rosary beads."

"I guess," I consented, recalling Signora Rossi's harsh words of judgment.

"Well you could hardly carry that beast with you all day," I said, gesturing toward his thick sketchbook.

"That is what this is for," he said as he withdrew a thin notebook the same size of his hand. "Sometimes when I am walking, I see an interesting face and before I know it, I have a pencil in my hand, and I've spent the whole day following that face."

"That sounds kind of creepy," I teased.

"Said the girl with pages covered with drawings of the same boy?"

"Well played," I surrendered.

Suddenly, there was a light knock at the door. From the window I could see a flurry of red hair. Opening the door, I could see Giulia's flustered face with two babies in her arms. One was Luca and the other must have been her little girl.

"*Buongiorno*, Viola, is Zia up yet?"

"Not yet, should I wake her?"

"If you don't mind watching Luca for an hour there is no need to wake her. I need to go to the market early, and I need at least one free arm. My husband forgot to tell me he had found a good day's work in the quarries." Not waiting for me to answer she moved close to my chest, and I made a nest with my arms. Little Luca was sleeping soundly. "I just fed him, so he should be no trouble. I will be back soon!"

"Who was that?" asked Leonardo as I sat down at the table. It felt so nice to hold Luca close to my body. He smelled like soap and his little hand was so soft.

"A neighbor … Leonardo, you still haven't explained your writing," I added, giving him a pointed glance.

"Well, I write in my own kind of shorthand because I have ideas and inventions in there that I would rather keep to myself." The soft tap of Zia's footsteps descended the staircase. "Also, since I am left-handed, it is less messy to write from right to left," he explained, taking the last bite of his toast.

"Leonardo?" Zia squinted at the bottom of the stairs. "You are here before the sun! If you continue to walk Viola home at such a late hour, which I don't approve of, I will start making up a bed for—"

A knock on the door interrupted Zia's speech. It was still rather early, and Zia's expression told me she was just as surprised as I was at the unexpected sound.

"Who in the world?" Peering out the window, I tried to make out who it was, but they were standing too close to the door. "What are you doing with Luca?" asked Zia amidst the confusion.

"Giulia had to run to the market. She will be back soon," I assured her as I carefully passed her the baby.

"Don't, Viola! You are not dressed!" she urged, but my hand was already on the door handle.

When it flew open, I suddenly became aware of the old boots, tangled hair oversized green sweater and semi-transparent gown I was wearing. There stood Giuliano in all his glory—his black cape lined with soft brown fur. The red tunic underneath blazed against the shadows of his cloak. I must have looked wild as we both stood speechless in the doorframe.

"Who is it, dear?" Zia's voice cracked from within.

"*Buongiorno*," I said, finding my voice.

"*Buongiorno*, Lady Viola." He nodded.

"Again, you surprise me," I said, signaling towards my dress.

"You look lovely," he said before Zia tiptoed behind me to catch a glimpse of our visitor.

"Signorino Medici! Please, please, come in!"

"Pardon my intrusion, Zia Cioni. I hope I did not wake you."

"Not at all, young sir." She signaled to him with her full arms to come into the house.

"I came in the hopes of escorting Viola to your nephew's workshop," he explained, stepping across the threshold with his chest held high.

"What a wonderful notion. It's just that my nephew's pupil Leonardo arrived earlier with that exact same design," said Zia.

Giuliano had just noticed Leonardo, who respectfully stood up. "I have been beaten to it. I don't believe we have met before," he said, extending his hand to Leonardo.

"We have not. Leonardo da Vinci."

"Of course, I have heard of your exceptional talent."

"Thank you," said Leonardo, squeezing his hand.

"Shall we all walk together?" I suggested.

Neither looked excited about being a third wheel. Taking their silence as a yes, I flew upstairs and squeezed myself into a stiff gray dress and swapped the boots for my sneakers.

They were both waiting outside. Zia raised her eyebrows at my loose hair. Before we left, she passed me her embroidered shawl as a polite reminder. At first, our walk was quiet. Even pigeons were scarce. Ice lodged itself under my nails and in the cracks of my lips. The air was sharp. Rearranging the stole around my neck, I tried to take short breaths.

"Are your hands cold?" asked Giuliano.

"Very," I admitted.

"Here," he offered, prying the fine leather gloves off his hands.

"I couldn't! Really, then your hands would be cold, and I would feel bad."

"I have other pairs ... I insist."

"I do too," I persisted.

He seemed a little disappointed. For one reason or another, I did not want to take anything from him. The seed of doubt that my friends had planted was growing. Angst pulsed against my ribcage.

"What's that you have hanging around your neck?" asked Giuliano, pointing to Idan.

I had forgotten to tuck Idan underneath my dress in my rush to leave the house. I tried to look casually at Leonardo, but he was completely lost in his own reflections. Just like his older brother, Giuliano made a grab for it, but I beat him to it.

"Oh, this? It's a family heirloom. The only thing left I have from my parents," I softened my voice to make it sound more convincing.

"But what ... is it?" he stressed.

"It's a compass."

"Interesting family heirloom."

Usually, I considered myself pretty good at reading people. On the subway ride to school, I would glance at the familiar or strange faces of commuters and try to make out their lives through the clues they wore or what dangled from their bodies. The tightness in his beautiful smile seemed forced.

"My grandfather was a pirate ... It's sort of broken, so I rarely open it, otherwise I would love to show it to you," I said.

My terrible lying skills always managed to come through. A pirate? What was I thinking? Trying to change the subject, I asked him if he was excited about the joust. His eyes sparked as he glanced at Leonardo.

"Yes! It is going to be spectacular. You're coming, of course?"

"I think so," I replied.

"My brother is eager to renew his acquaintance with you. We both would like to invite you to the dinner and festivities after the joust."

Although distrust crept into my heart, it did not make me like him less. I was beginning to understand that stereotype about how nice girls fall for bad boys. The thought of dancing in a palace wrapped in the arms of Giuliano was incredibly tempting. It took me a while to answer.

"I am honored, but I don't think that would be wise. Please tell your brother I appreciate the invitation."

"Leonardo?"

"Si?" he said suddenly as if abruptly pulled from the depths of his conscious.

"Could we have a few moments alone? We will be right behind you," asked Giuliano. Leonardo looked at me and I nodded.

"I will walk behind. I am in no rush," he said before stopping.

"Why will you not come to the palazzo?"

"I don't think Zia will approve."

"And?"

"And I don't have anything ... appropriate to wear."

"Both obstacles can be easily rectified. We will not take no for an answer," he insisted. His body moved in closer to mine and beneath his cloak, I could feel him searching for my fingers, but I crossed my arms.

We were getting close to the workshop, but with every step the tension thickened.

"Have I done something to upset you, Viola?"

"No," I replied too quickly.

"Forgive me for persisting, but it seems like you have something on your mind," he said.

I had a lot of things on my mind. It was difficult to pinpoint what was bothering me more: Zia's warning or Signore Maroni's shame.

"Yesterday I went to Ponte Vecchio." I let the words hang in the heavy fog surrounding us. "While I was there guards came and broke the table of a sweet elderly man named Signore Maroni." Giuliano's head hung and his eyes fixed on the wet floor. "He is a poor fisherman who is the sole caretaker of his grandsons and has no way to take care of them if he has no table. He can't—"

"So you are upset because you think I'm to blame?" he interrupted. His warm brown eyes narrowed.

"No, that's not what I meant to say."

"So you think it's my family's fault?" he snapped. Choosing not to make the situation worse, I tried to avoid the question. We stopped in front of the workshop. "In fairness, we provide a service and your dear Signore Maroni should not ask for a loan if he does not have a plan to pay it back with interest." In truth, I knew he was right, but it made me mad all the same to hear him speak to me condescendingly.

"But a million and one things could have happened since then."

"If we treated everyone on a charity basis, we would be the ones with our tables broken on Ponte Vecchio," he said before he gave me a curt nod and strode away. Somehow, I had turned a pleasant walk into a disaster.

CHAPTER SEVENTEEN

Masaccio

"Is it just me or was that as awkward as it looked?" said Leonardo.

"Not helpful, Leo," I said, bristling my shoulders, but he just shrugged it off.

"He will be back ... unfortunately." He coughed. Trying not to laugh, I elbowed his side as we walked under the canopy of the workshop. When I entered the kitchen, Margherita accosted me. She had positioned herself on a stool by the doorframe.

"Are you crazy?" she shouted. "You do know that what you and Verrocchio are about to do is borderline sacrilege?"

It was an intimidating sight. Her belly seemed to have gotten bigger, and her face was scarlet from the heat of the stove.

"I know it's strange but—"

"What if you get caught?"

"I don't know ..."

"I do! You will be put into jail or worse." Even though we were almost the same age, she seemed so much older than me.

"I want this."

"Why?

"I want to be a great artist … and I don't think it's right that men get to do it and we can't. We deserve to be treated equally and not handed about like property or slaves."

Margherita just shook her head from side to side. "You have such strange ideas."

"They may be strange, but they're true."

"And impossible," resigned Margherita as she reached for the broom propped against the pointed arch. "I hope for your sake they don't get you into trouble."

"Me too," I breathed.

The morning was turning out to be wretched. Margherita rattled off a long list of chores that started with scrubbing the workbenches. The day's hours passed by quickly, except for the part I spent sweeping the frozen courtyard. Verrocchio came into the kitchen while Margherita and I were finishing our meal of pasta and beans.

"Is Massimo ready to start his apprenticeship?" he asked. I scarfed down the last of my lunch and stood up.

"Margherita, fetch Renzo and go upstairs with Viola to help her dress."

"But, sir, we didn't buy any clothes—"

"Leonardo told me about the old man … He was also so gracious as to give you some of the clothes he outgrew. Despite the way it appears, I am not running a charity. So before you give all my money away, think on it twice," he said before walking into the workshop.

Margherita and I followed him into the smoky studio. The apprentices were finishing their lunch as well. Little Renzo was at the head of the table playing with his cutlery. She whispered in his ear and his eyes widened.

"*Grazie*, Renzo and Margherita for helping me," I said as the door of the study closed behind us.

"I think it is a great idea!" piped Renzo.

"I think it's a terrible idea," said Margherita.

"How about you two go behind there, and I will throw the clothes over?" he suggested, motioning to the partition.

"It's freezing so we should do this quickly, Viola," said Margherita, staring at the empty fireplace.

"You mean Massimo," corrected Renzo with his finger pointed in the air. As it was too early for his face to be covered in soot, the bright pink of his cheeks made him even cuter.

"Not yet, she isn't."

Between Renzo's instructions and Margherita's knot-tying abilities I managed to put on a pair of thick, black tights and a short, wrinkled tunic with long sleeves that fell at my wrists. This was the first time I congratulated myself on still needing to shop in the girls' bra section of most stores. Otherwise, this plan might not have worked out so great. The olive tunic had laces at the top and was far too big for me around the waist and hips.

"Let's use that belt of yours," suggested Margherita, taking the neon orange belt from my dress. She fastened it around my waist and the heavy fold of the tunic hid it from view. "You forgot about the shoes." She pointed down at my purple sneakers. At hearing this, Renzo raced out of the room and returned with a foul pair of soft leather shoes.

"Oh no!" I protested.

"But they're the only pair!" retorted Renzo.

"Are you sure you want to do this?" asked Margherita, holding up the pair of tattered shoes by a handkerchief as if they would attack her.

"I've come this far," I said, putting on the shoes the way people rip off a Band-Aid.

"It is good your hair is not long, otherwise we might have to cut it," she said.

There was a hard knock at the door before Verrocchio stepped into the room. "Are we ready?"

"*Sì*, signore," we chimed.

I stepped out from behind the partition. Even though I did not have a mirror, I felt convincing. Verrocchio had his hand in a fist blocking his mouth. It was hard to tell if he was thinking seriously or laughing.

"Your eyes will get us in trouble," he said, clearly amused by the situation. "Maybe we can get a hat for you. ... Yes, that might be best. Let's head down. There is a lot of work to do." We all filed out of the study and followed the workshop master downstairs. The nervous feeling from this morning that had started in between my ribs had infected every cell in my body. A sharp whistle caught the attention of the apprentices painting, chipping, and chattering away.

"As discussed yesterday, we have a new and ordinary apprentice named Massimo," Verrocchio announced, making sure to stress the word "ordinary." He motioned for me to come out from behind him.

Once I stepped forward, one of the boys burst out laughing and the others quickly followed until the room shook with every type of laughter. There was the kind that left a stitch in your side, the loud and obnoxious, and last but not least, the gasping for air type. As usual I started to sweat with embarrassment. In retrospect, it must have been funny to watch me, but in the moment I didn't think it was even a little bit funny.

Leonardo had started clapping and shouting the cheer, "Long live Massimo." Other boys followed and the laughing slowly turned into applause. Verrocchio held up his hands for the room to quiet.

"That's quite enough! I hope you all got it out of your systems. Let me stress, again, the importance of normalcy and secrecy," he said, looking into the eyes of each pupil but lingering on Salai's sour expression in the corner of the room. "Back to your duties," he boomed. Gradually, the clamor reached its usual level.

Verrocchio put his hand behind his back and looked at me hard. "Have you ever heard of Cennini, Viola?" I shook my head. "Well, he was a workshop master too, and he would say something very wise that went something like this ..." he paused, "If you with a lofty spirit are fired with this ambition, and are about to enter the profession, begin by decking yourselves with this attire: enthusiasm, reverence, obedience, and constancy. Are you ready?"

"*Sì!*"

"Good!" He clapped his hands together. Today, you will be our new *creato*. Meaning you will perform the most basic tasks."

"Like what?"

"Color grinding, preparing gesso, sanding, and making charcoal pens." He must have realized my less than enthusiastic spirit because he leaned a little closer and added, "It's important because this is the only way you will be able to value the work of others. Not only that, but it will give you an understanding of colors and their different properties. Renzo will walk you through the different tasks."

The young boy had been standing next to me the whole time, thrilled with his new assignment. Distracted by Perugino's painting of a land-scape, Verrocchio moved closer to investigate.

Renzo took the opportunity to grab my hand and led me to the opposite side of the workshop. As we walked, I could see Leonardo, who was staring beyond the painting in front of him. It was his first day painting the missing angel and he looked slightly unnerved. The wooden palette rested at his side laden with pale and dark hues of red and blue. Although his sleeves were rolled up, his posture straight, and his hand armed with a paintbrush, he was completely still.

"Go on! It's getting tiring just waiting for you to start!" I said as we walked by him. Not stopping to see his reaction, I continued following Renzo.

He stopped in front of a cluster of shelves with an array of bright colors encased in glass jars "These are all the powder colors we have; their names are written on the lids." He took down one of the jars filled with a white powder and read, "Lead white."

"Oh!" I said a little startled, as I was pretty sure that lead paint was toxic. "I think that is actually really bad for you," I said.

"I don't really know if that matters or not," he said with a shrug and took another jar from the shelf. "Malachite." It was a beautiful turquoise color.

"What about that one?" I asked pointing to a tiny jar.

"We are not allowed to grind or touch that one," he warned. "It is called ultramarine." I remembered using a paint tube with that name in art classes.

"Why not?" I asked.

"It's made from a stone called lapis lazuli, and it's really expensive. If a patron wants it for a painting, he will ask for it specifically or get it himself. This little bit is just leftovers that we carefully swept off tabletops."

Renzo and I spent the rest of the time grinding red ocher and making gesso. He told me they used the goat scraps I had brought on my first day to make the gesso along with some plaster. My fingers bled orange, and my arms hurt from grinding. It was boring work but better than scrubbing the floor.

The moment Renzo left to attend to the fire, Salai slithered towards me. "What a dangerous position you have put yourself in," he said, pushing the ringlets from his eyes. "You are asking quite a lot of us to keep your secret."

"You should probably share that with Verrocchio because it's his dirty secret too," I snapped, but he pretended not to hear me.

"Does the sweet Viola feel tougher now that she is in boys' clothes?" His eyes darted about my face. "How would your Zia react if she found out you were lying to her?"

"Stop blackmailing me, Salai … I know you have nowhere else to go."

"Is that what the master told you?" He looked cross. "I have talents I can take elsewhere … There is no place to grow here anyway when you have fools like Leonardo taking up all the attention with his 'genius' scribbles. I know Latin!"

"Good for you, but you are a fool to think Leonardo is one," I said braver than I felt.

"Now that's not necessarily true. I can definitely be foolish," said Leonardo. I turned around to see Leonardo's smile, but it was taut and rigid with anger.

"Go ahead and change, Massimo, we need to walk back." The glint in his eyes made me question whether he was forgetting our pact from this morning.

"Scout's honor," I reminded him and quit the workroom. Changing out of the boys' clothes was much easier than putting them on. While I waited for Leonardo beneath the canopy, a plump rat ran so close to my feet I screamed. He came rushing out of the workshop asking me what happened.

"I saw a huge rat!"

"That's all?"

"What do you mean 'that's all?'" I said, glaring at him.

"If everyone screamed every time they saw a rat in Florence, there would be no peace because all you would hear is one constant shrill from sunrise to sunset," he said and walked onto the street.

During the day, carts, feet, and hooves had kicked up the mud from this morning's rain, creating landmines of filthy puddles. Fresh dirt coated the stone walls on either side of us.

"Are you tired?" asked Leonardo.

"Not completely. Did you begin the angel or did you just sit there?" I asked.

"Where was that attitude two minutes ago?" he asked. "Yes, I did, but it will take longer to finish because it's oil."

"That's true. I forgot about that."

"Let's go visit Masaccio."

"Who's he?" I asked. Leonardo shuddered as if I had sworn something awful.

"Every artist needs to meet Masaccio, but it's even more important to appreciate him. If not, you will end up like Perugino and repeat the same ten figures in every painting. His is an incredibly dull business."

"That's not nice."

"It is not like he doesn't know it. Perugino uses the same poses and faces because they are popular and lucrative, but that is not the point. The key is Masaccio," he said as we turned into the crowded Piazza del Duomo. We crisscrossed onto a series of short streets until we arrived at a smaller plaza. "That's the Basilica di Santa Maria Novella."

He didn't need to point it out as it took up most of the plaza. The façade of the basilica had two levels. The top portion's triangular pediment towered directly above the basilica's base; at its center hung a rose window. A band of white marble decorated with dark green square outlines separated the two levels. Pointed arches divided by pilasters were decorated with the same zebra stripes that were visible throughout the beautiful basilica. All the elements seemed rounder than the Duomo and made it feel more welcoming.

"What is that next to the basilica?" I asked, pointing to an arcade attached to the church.

"That is a cloister; it is where the Dominican monks live and work."

On the opposite side of the piazza was another arcade but the arches were rounder and it had two stories. In between the arches were sky-blue medallions with little angels.

"What about that building?"

"Let's leave that for another day," he said.

"Sure, but what is it?"

"It's an orphanage."

"Oh," I said, staring at the steps that led to the round arches.

"It was designed by the same architect who finished the Duomo."

"Brunelleschi?"

"Good girl." He smiled.

"I am going to say, 'good boy' every time you do something I approve of and see how you like it," I said.

"Then you won't be saying it often." He grinned and walked towards the double doors of the basilica.

Similar to San Lorenzo, it had a nave with a side aisle on either side separated by an arcade. The same black and white stripes covered the ribs of the ceiling. The hundreds of candles that marked the passageways burned with a mystical glow. Leonardo walked towards the left aisle.

Supporting the basilica were several pillars that made up the colonnades. An elevated horizontal band of stone attached itself to one of the pillars. An elaborate staircase leading to the suspended porch wrapped around the pillar. A round disk that looked as if it had cut into the stone lay suspended above the round capsule.

"What's that?"

"It's an ambo," he replied, lowering his voice. "It was designed by our friend Brunelleschi, but I think his adopted son ended up finishing the job." Elaborate floral motifs were carved into the ambo. Its borders framed scenes from the Bible. "An ambo is where they read from the scripture," he explained, grabbing my hand.

Midway down the left aisle, we stopped in front of a wall that had a painting of Christ crucified. Leonardo and I stood in respectful silence for the masterpiece. The painting was rather morbid and dark. Only the muted light struggling through the stained glass could touch the painting. The color palette ranged from burgundy to taupe and dark blue. It looked to be about twenty feet tall.

We both had to look up at the gloomy figures that occupied the painting's space. Close to the bottom lay a stone sarcophagus supporting a bone skeleton. A string of words appeared as if carved into the stony crypt.

Above the crypt, two heavily draped figures flanked each side of the painting. The one on the left was an older man clothed in a dull red cloak with his hands clasped in prayer, staring up at the cross. His companion on the right was in the same pose but dressed like a nun in black from head to toe. Further into the painting stood two figures; I assumed one of them was the Virgin Mary because of her halo. She had her arm up in a gesture that suggested she was presenting her son. The standing figure opposite her also had a halo. In between them was Christ crucified.

What really stunned me about the painting was the figure behind Christ. The figure was a robust older man with a white beard and another halo suspended over his head. He was lifting up the cross that held Jesus.

"Is that supposed to be God?"

"*Sí!* Gutsy, huh?"

"I suppose. I don't remember seeing another painting of God. I've only seen paintings of Jesus," I said.

"That's your biggest question?" he asked, astounded. "What about his use of perspective? It is almost flawless! Do you not see how realistic he made the arch or barrel vault that sets the scene? How he painted the coffers in the ceiling that shelters the father and his son?"

"Keep your pants on! That was just my first question," I said, crossing my arms over my chest. "What does it say there by the skeleton?"

"In Latin it says, 'As I am now, so you shall be. As you are now, so once was I.'"

"To remind us that we are all going to die?" I asked.

"Exactly ... memento mori, a reminder of death."

"Who is the figure standing next to Mary?"

"That is John the Baptist, the patron saint of Florence. The two kneeling on the floor are the patrons that commissioned the painting."

"What about the white bird right above Christ's head?"

"That is a dove that completes the Holy Trinity meaning ... the Father, the Son, and the Holy Ghost."

"How did he paint it on the wall?"

"It is true fresco, which is done by painting directly onto wet plaster. It's usually done in parts."

"That's really incredible but it sounds kind of stressful."

"It can be. That is probably why Master Verrocchio never does frescoes. Essentially, this is a painting of a chapel instead of an actual one."

"He seems to really understand the human body," I said, noticing the stretched muscles of Christ's body being pulled down by gravity.

"It was and still is revolutionary. Everything in the painting leads to one point ... right below Christ's feet." His face was full of awe.

"I appreciate it, Leo."

"Good girl," he teased. "Let's head back to Zia's. I don't want to test her patience again."

"Look who's scared now?" I said as we passed devout whispers of devotion.

"It is not about being scared. It is about being considerate," he joked.

The long walk home reminded me of what my dad used to say when it was particularly cold outside. *"Doesn't this chill make you feel more alive, Violet?"* he would ask. I had never been away from him this long before. A bittersweet feeling stirred every time I thought of him. Missing Dad made time pass by so much slower. All these reminders of death might be meant to spook everyone, but they just made me appreciate what I had even more.

CHAPTER EIGHTEEN

The Banner

"Dear girl!" squeaked Zia as the door swung open. "You almost scared the soul out of me ... I wasn't expecting you home so early."

"Leonardo wanted to surprise you." I locked the door behind me.

"That is a good lad," she said, loosening her fingers from the heavy fabric that fell across her lap. "Did you have a good day?"

"I did."

"Why are your fingers so orange?" she asked, staring at my hands. "I looked down at my fingers to see that the creases in between my nails and skin had turned a rusty orange.

"One of the apprentices spilled ocher powder, and I had to clean it up," I said truthfully.

What I failed to mention was that I was the apprentice who knocked over the jar. Overall, I was proud that I had not set anything on fire. As Zia had started to embroider again, I made my way to the stairs.

Before I could reach the platform, she said, "A boy came to deliver a package for you."

Turning around, I saw a bundle wrapped in sandy linen waiting on the table. From the corner of my eye, I could tell that Zia was searching for a reaction. I could feel her searching every line and quiver of my expression. Once I approached the table, I saw there was also a note with my name carefully written. Pressed into the seal's red wax was a coat of arms with six circles and two crossed keys. Recalling this morning's walk, I held my breath while I broke the wax and unfolded the letter. Unlike the illegible scrawl of Leonardo, the hand that had wielded the blue ink was elegant.

Viola,

When I arrived at your door this morning, I had imagined our walk would turn out differently. It would have begun by slowly walking alone together, side by side. I would invite you to the banquet tomorrow, and you would say yes. I would warm your hand with my own. In my attempt to charm you, I would stumble, you would laugh, and if I was exceptionally lucky, I might steal a kiss. Alas, my imagination got the best of me. The constant kindness in your expression was absent this morning. I regret your distress over Signore Maroni's situation and my defensive behavior. I hope you accept this apology along with the gifts I have sent.

Until tomorrow then.

Yours,

Giuliano de' 'Medici

Slowly, my lungs let out the air they had been holding tight. "What does it say?" asked Zia innocently.

My cheeks grew warm at her question. I was annoyed but not surprised by her curiosity. I definitely couldn't tell her everything the letter said; that would be way too embarrassing.

As I stared at the letter trying to come up with a good edit, Zia said, "I am not very good at reading, and with these weary eyes it is almost an impossible thing," she confessed.

The irritation I tried to conquer melted into guilt. I read the letter aloud, censoring the parts about any kind of bodily contact. After I had folded the letter, I looked to see her reaction but it was stoic. As I opened the package, a small paper fell onto the tiled floor.

"Oh my God," I said, peering down at the parchment.

"My child, do not use the Lord's name in vain. It is a capital sin."

"Zia, Giuliano acquitted Signore Maroni's debt," I said, showing her the note. She just held it up close to her eyes then far away in an effort to understand the minute lettering. "Look there, it says, 'Signore Maroni, this receipt confirms that your debt has been paid in full.'"

"Heavens! That is gracious of him," she said, her eyes widening. The way Zia's mouth and eyebrows contracted spoke volumes of the inner struggle inside her.

When I unraveled the last layer of linen, I felt the smooth pebbled surface of leather. The tailored gloves were a rich coffee color and lined with smoky fur. I could not help but smile at how perfectly they fit. My bitten nails and dry skin looked undeserving of the lovely gift.

Zia took the other glove and carefully examined the stitching and material. "An exquisite gift," she admitted.

Placing the glove gently on the table, she walked over to the garlicky stew that was simmering on the stove. While she stirred our supper, I tried to think of ways to bring up the tournament tomorrow. I thought it would be easier if I did not meet her eye directly.

"Where is the tournament tomorrow?"

"In the Piazza de Santa Croce."

"Oh! So it's very close," I said, my eyes wide with excitement. For a moment I waited to see if she would say anything, but the only sound came from the simmering pot. "I imagine there will be a lot of people

… should we leave early to get a good spot?" I said, trying to insinuate it was a given.

Only on rare occasions did I have to ask for my parents' permission. My dad encouraged me to be independent and to explore the city. If I asked him if I could go to a party, he would practically push me out of the house. I guess he was always concerned I was not social enough.

"I haven't decided whether we are going at all," said Zia. Right away, I knew her response had everything to do with her misgivings about Giuliano.

"You don't want to go?" I asked.

"Of course I do … Such festivities are few and far between," she paused, covering the pot. "However, sometimes what we want to do and what we should do are at odds with each other."

"You don't have to worry about me," I assured her. She broke off some rosemary from an overhanging bundle and slipped it under the pot's lid. "I would love to see the tournament. I have never seen one before."

Zia passed me plates and spoons to set on the table. "What did you say when he invited you to the banquet?" She grimaced.

"I thanked him for the invitation, but said I couldn't go."

"I don't believe we will go to the tournament either," said Zia, staring down at the tiled floor.

My heart skipped a beat. "Why?"

"Well, first of all, you don't have papers. What if something happens and a guard asks you for them?"

"I do have papers," I said, suddenly aware I had never told Zia about my strange encounter with Lorenzo de' Medici.

"You what?" she asked, stepping closer to me.

"Lorenzo de' Medici gave me identification papers."

"Why haven't you spoken of this?"

"I am sorry ... it slipped my mind."

"Why do you think he did that?" she asked with her hands on her hips. "Men like the Medici always have a reason." Honestly, I had never stopped to think about it.

"The papers state that my name is Viola Orofino and that I am visiting Florence for a time at the request and courtesy of the Medici family."

"What a mess this is!" She huffed. "I know this decision will upset you, and it is not my intention."

I clenched my fists and could feel frustration boiling up from inside me. I needed to be alone. As I scaled the stairs Zia said, "It is for the best, Ginerva."

"My name is Viola," I corrected her, my voice corroded with anger.

I took off my many layers of clothing in a rush to slip under the blankets. It felt safer there. Beneath the woolen blankets I felt comforted, and it was okay to cry myself to sleep on an empty stomach.

Daybreak and unusual sounds from below woke me. Just by tilting my head back, I could tell it was going to be a beautiful day. I had not slept in so late since I arrived in Florence. The soft blue sky was spotless, but it was a sunny day I wanted nothing to do with. From outside my window I could hear excited voices and feet rushing past. I pulled the heavy covers over my face to block out the light and fervor of all those allowed to go to the tournament.

"Why did the tournament have to be so close to my window?" I lamented, my stomach grumbling almost as loud as my mouth. A knock at the door interrupted my brooding thoughts.

"Viola ... are you awake?" asked Zia. It was hard work to be mad at her. The door groaned open. "My dear, come down and eat," she implored, sitting at the foot of my bed.

When I stole a peek from my shelter, I could see how conflicted Zia was. The grooves of her wrinkles ran deeper, and her skin looked even paler than usual.

"I'll be down soon," I assured her.

"This morning I went to get some fresh bread and—"

"Caterina Cioni!" called a man's voice.

We both crammed the narrow window to see who it was. Signore Soldo, the silk trader I had met on my first day, was on the doorstep with a golden grin, holding a basket. Before she rushed out of the room, I caught a glimpse of the blush that had bloomed on her white cheeks.

Painfully aware of my hunger, and that this encounter might be the single most exciting event of the day, I hurried out of bed. After splashing water on my face and pulling a shawl around my shoulders, I tiptoed towards the top of the stairs. I paused and listened to the conversation unfolding below.

"What do you mean you aren't going?" asked Signore Soldo.

"I trust old age hasn't gotten the better of you yet ... What you heard the first time. Viola and I are not going to the tournament."

"Why ever not? Is she ill?"

"Heavens no!"

"Then what?" asked Signore Soldo. The smell of sizzling ham wafted up to my hiding place.

"I'm doing it to protect Viola!" she retorted.

"From who?" he asked, completely clueless of her frustration.

"The Medici," she whispered loudly. A reverent pause followed the name.

"But how could that sweet girl ..."

"She didn't offend them, if that is what you're thinking," she said defensively.

"I think I see it now," he said with boyish delight. "Which one is trying to court her then?"

"The prince," she said, setting plates and cutlery on the table.

"Giuliano? The boy? What are you worried about then?" he said, waving her trepidation aside.

"They are such a powerful family, Francesco ... and I mean to keep her safe from harm, even if it means not going to a silly tournament."

"A silly tournament indeed! What is silly is this conversation. The harm that haunts you will never come. He enjoys her beauty and no doubt her other unique qualities, as do all those around her. He will soon tire of this chase or decide one day he fancies red hair instead. Those are the ways of boys who want for nothing." Sitting in my hiding place, I knew Signore Soldo's words were probably true, but they stung all the same.

"That's what Andrea says," Zia confessed with a sigh of relief.

"Your nephew and I are men ... Leave these sorts of matters to us."

"That might be, but the last time I left such matters to men, my only daughter shunned me."

"You and Ginerva still aren't speaking?"

"No, she lives in Vinci and cannot forgive me for turning her away," said Zia miserably.

"Come now! I want no more of this sad talk. I will be your escort to the tournament and will have no more nonsense about two of Florence's most beautiful women not going! You will surely spoil my appetite if you continue to defy me," he said cheerfully.

"There she is," he said after I crept out of my hiding place.

"*Buongiorno*, Signore Soldo." I smiled.

"How old that makes me sound. Please call me Francesco, I insist!" he said, placing a scratchy smooch on the back of my hand. "I thought I heard someone's stomach grumbling." He winked. The usually modest table was loaded with fresh bread, soft cheese, and honey ham.

"Shall we eat?" he asked.

"*Si*," I said, quickly finding my place. With no delay, I served myself a juicy slab of ham and a thick slice of walnut bread. I took a generous mouthful of the sweetmeat before I dressed my bread with butter.

"So, Viola ... from what your aunt has shared with me, I hear congratulations are in order," he said as he rolled up the burgundy sleeves of his tunic. "You're the lucky girl who beguiled the handsome Giuliano de' Medici ... Surely you are the envy of every young heart in the city."

"Thank you, but I don't think he likes me that much. He is probably just bored with nothing else to do or think about," I said tactfully in between mouthfuls. Zia looked surprised at these words.

"See that, Zia! And you were worried about Viola. We should be fussing over poor Giuliano, who will be the one left with his heart broken," he teased.

"He is anything but poor," pointed out Zia.

"Well, enjoy his attentions while they last, then," encouraged Francesco.

"I am so glad you came," I said.

"As am I."

He stared at Zia. Since I finished breakfast first, Zia sent me upstairs to put on my dress with the sea-green trim. Zia had sewn up the torn sleeve and washed out the bloodstains from Pietro Sforza's spike tunic. After I had slipped on my Converse, Zia came holding something in her hand.

"Zia, I wanted to say sorry for being so ungrateful last night," I said. "I know you were just trying to protect me."

"This belonged to Ginerva," she said, showing me a web of woven string and purple iridescent shells. I thought maybe she did not hear me but then I realized this was her way of forgiving my foolishness. "Would you like to wear it?" she asked

"I would! How does it go?"

She began to comb my hair back with her fingers. Shortly after she had gathered and secured all my hair in the net, we met Signore Soldo by the entrance. Before the door shut behind us, he pronounced himself the luckiest man in the world.

The sunlight that toppled over the houses warmed me from the outside in. Via dei Benci was swarming with carts peddling fried food and beverages in questionable ceramic cups. The smell of manure, wet hay, and cooking meat were hosting a competition of their own. Apart from the vendors were parents dragging lines of children stringed together by little hands. The usual scarcity of women reversed overnight. It seemed that for every man, there were at least two women and an elderly person bringing up the rear. What we all shared in common, other than dressing in our finest clothes, was our excitement as we marched towards Piazza de Santa Croce.

Among the mass of moving citizens were knights clad in a confetti of different metals. Each had an escort of young boys carrying their tools of chivalry or guiding their horses. The brave men brandished a collection of colorful banners as they weaved through the *popolo*. A few of the knights spoke in alien tongues or sported thick accents from foreign lands.

As we drew closer to the piazza, clumps of bright tents sprouted from the ground. "Those are for the knights participating in the tournament. Some sign up on their own accord while others are invited," explained Signore Soldo, clearly enjoying my amazement.

The Medici had erected a vast circular fence for the occasion. Statuesque guards manned posts along the wooden divider. Elevated balconies were built against the stone buildings surrounding the piazza, each decorated with draped fabric and intricate patterns. Inside the luxurious alcoves were clusters of wealthy families crowding to find the best seat. Ladies with hair ornaments almost as extravagant as their fur-trimmed gowns pointed at the strutting men and their horses inside the circle.

The grandest building in the piazza was the church that loomed over the festivities. On the steps of Santa Croce was the largest balcony. The crest of the Medici house waved proudly in the strong breeze.

Shielding my eyes from the sun, I searched for a sign of Giuliano, but much like the other balconies, it was full of ladies, distinguished elders, and prim children.

Meanwhile, the rest of Florence fended for a good spot. Luckily I was tall for my age and could see the men practicing at their swordplay behind the barrier. Soon after we started to push forward into the crowd, I felt hands tugging on my dress.

"Just what do you think you boys are doing?" demanded Francesco.

Two little faces full of freckles peered up at me. Both boys looked close to five or so.

"Nonno said to look for a girl with one blue eye and one brown, tall, with chestnut hair," one recited.

"We are supposed to bring her to where Nonno is," said the other.

"Where is your grandfather?" asked Zia, kneeling closer to them.

Without further delay to their mission, they pulled me through the crowd. There were many rough comments and lots of "mi scusi" on my part. We finally reached a clearing right by the fence that Signore Maroni had been fighting to keep. When he saw his grandsons leading me, the corners of his white bristle-like mustache crinkled into a smile. He went to one knee. My face burned with embarrassment when his grandsons mimicked his example.

"Thank you, my lady, for lifting my burden," he said earnestly from behind his spectacles.

"What?" Zia and Francesco had finally arrived at the clearing.

"Without your intervention, I know I would be in debtors' prison. I would be unable to provide for my grandsons, let alone take them to this tournament." His piercing blue eyes brimmed with emotion.

"Please! There is no need," I protested, glancing around nervously. To my horror, almost the whole of Verrocchio's workshop, including the master himself, had surrounded us. They were all staring, amused by the scene before them. *For sure I will be teased for this tomorrow*, I concluded, catching a mischievous smirk from Perugino.

"Signore Maroni has been saving your seat all morning," said Sandro Botticelli, who was standing next to Verrocchio.

"That is most kind," thanked Zia.

"It is nothing," he assured us.

The trumpets sounded and the crowd pushed forward, forcing us to cozy up to one another. Zia was wedged in between her nephew and Signore Soldo. Perugino, who was lifting little Renzo on his shoulders, was on my left and Leonardo was on my other side. From the corner of my eye, I could see Sandro looking up nervously at the Medici box.

"It's starting!" shouted Renzo. All the competitors were lining up on their steeds with their banner boys and pages following close behind.

As they filed in the arena, the master of ceremonies stated the rules. "Let us all take a moment to thank the most illustrious family in Florence and congratulate Lorenzo the Magnificent on his future nuptials!" boomed the announcer.

The crowd roared. Leonardo was shouting something at Perugino, but I could not hear it over the cheers. Perugino grabbed my hand and pointed it at one of the banners.

"Does that look familiar?" he yelled in my ear.

"Oh my God," I mouthed, squinting my eyes. "Is that me?" I screamed back. Leonardo and Perugino nodded.

CHAPTER NINETEEN

Joust

"I TOLD YOU THAT someday you would see the portrait I drew of you," said Leonardo when the sound died down.

"Did you know about this?"

"No ... and honestly I am a little annoyed. It is my sketch. I should have painted the banner," he said.

"Well, it would have been nice if someone could have asked me before they put my face on a banner," I said, but Leonardo's face screwed up in confusion.

The shock of seeing my face framed by blue velvet still had not lifted. My eyes followed the pole that bore the flag to Giuliano astride his black horse. The moment I saw him I understood what Signore Soldo meant this morning when he said I was the envy of every young heart in the city. Giuliano gleamed in silver arms slashed with golden bands. His plumed helmet was propped on his saddle while he waved at the crowd ahead of him.

Why would he like me? I wondered, as I fought the temptation to pinch myself.

Next to him was his elder brother, Lorenzo. It was surprising to see him smiling atop his ivory horse, his hands clasped together in a grateful gesture. Instead of a lady, Lorenzo's banner displayed lilies made of gold thread accentuated with precious stones.

"Despite the way this looks, the Medici are not the only powerful family in Florence," explained Perugino. "Next to Lorenzo are the Pazzis … They're an even older and more noble family." Pointing to Giuliano, he continued. "On the other side are members of the Salviati and Pitti." The line dispersed and so began the games.

First there was a series of sword fights, one of which included Giuliano against a member of the Pazzi. The clash of metal on metal bounced around my skull. Perugino must have felt my nervous jerks.

"In the good old days, they would fight to the death. Now they just get points." He stifled a yawn as Giuliano unarmed the Pazzi.

The next game was the mace. "*Boys,*" I sighed as I watched them beat each other up with a spikey ball. People were crowded so close together that I was actually hot, despite the clouds of breath that evaporated into the fervent air. Leonardo passed me a flask of warm honey wine. I drank a few sips even though what my itchy throat longed for was a cold bottle of water. A short break followed the mace while they set up for the joust. The ache in my legs told me that it had already been several hours. Poor Sandro had not been able to stand still the whole tournament.

"Are you okay, Sandro?"

"Yeah! Why? Do I not look all right?" he asked, pulling his auburn hair over his ears.

"He is in love," piped his apprentice Fillipio. It was unclear whether Sandro had turned scarlet from anger or mortification. The whole tournament he had been staring at the Medici balcony and now I knew why.

"No need to explode, Sandro. There is not a man in this city who is not at least half in love with Simonetta Vespucci," said Perugino.

"Shut up!" demanded Sandro.

"Who is that?" I asked.

"The fairest lady in Tuscany," a lust-filled Salai declared from the knot of people.

"She is the one with the long blonde hair in the front row," directed Verrocchio.

It was difficult to see her from so far away, but she certainly looked beautiful. Sandro's arms were crossed, and he was trying hard to look everywhere except the Medici balcony. Music announced the beginning of the joust competition. The wooden lances were much longer than I had imagined from movies. Although each opponent was clad in armor from head to toe, it looked violent all the same. At the cue of the trumpets, horses and their poised riders launched at each other from opposite sides of the long rope barrier. The fabric cloaking the horses danced against the breeze as strong muscles geared up for motion.

Right before they collided, I chickened out and hid behind Perugino's shoulder. Leonardo smiled at my cowardliness. The sound of splintering wood and the groan of the crowd followed. I saw one triumphant man about to do a victory lap and the other bent over his saddle, limp as a rag doll. Two other duels went on following a similar pattern before it was Lorenzo's turn.

"He is going against the Salviati," said Perugino.

Although Lorenzo cut an opposing figure in his blue armor with veins of black, his opponent was equally splendid. Salviati looked taller and stronger than Lorenzo. His horse was covered with an indigo and shell print that looked like train tracks.

"Shields are overused nowadays," reflected Leonardo.

"Oh, you think you can do better?" Verrocchio challenged.

"Certainly. They are always the same. They have a girl, some saint, or worse ... their coat of arms. Just in case we forget who they are."

"You sound arrogant, son, even for Piero da Vinci," said an unfamiliar voice.

"Good day, Father," greeted Leonardo.

"I will have to take you up on your boast and commission you to make me a shield."

As I stared at the both of them, I realized Leonardo was almost the spitting image of his father. Piero was the same height and looked as fit as his son, except he was balding. A closely manicured beard framed a pleasant grin radiating through crooked teeth. "I hope you do not mind if I watch the end of the tournament with you and your friends," he said looking me up and down.

"The people behind us surely will mind, but I don't," replied Leonardo.

"So," he said, shifting his weight, "tell me what you would put on my shield, if not a saint?"

"Something that would frighten any man off his horse."

"Even Giovanni Salviati?"

"That's a lot of man to throw off," doubted Sandro.

Once again, the trumpet sounded, and the mob of people held their breath. For seconds only the beat of pounding hooves and tolling metal of armor met our ears. The horses sprinted as the men locked their elbows to steady their lances. Lorenzo's lance hit the corner of Salviati's shield, causing his shoulder to turn at an unnatural angle. Lorenzo's opponent had overshot his target, forcing him to drop the lance. Wood chips scattered and fell onto the hay that littered the stone floor of the piazza. As the distance between the men grew, so did the blare of the masses. An eruption of hoots and applause followed.

"What now?" I asked.

"Now they give out the prizes," answered Verrocchio.

The ceremony was short. Each knight received a wreath of laurel from the fair hands of Simonetta Vespucci. The Gondi family won the mace competition, the Pazzi triumphed in the swords, and the Medici conquered the joust.

"There is only one grand prize and it is going to go to Lorenzo, of course," said Leonardo.

"Who wants to place a bet on what it will be?" suggested Perugino.

"It is going to be a helmet," said Verrocchio.

"A sword!" shouted Renzo. "A lute?" offered Fillipio.

"Anything but a shield," hoped Leonardo.

To all our great amusement, it was a helmet. After the prizes were awarded, the master of ceremonies declared the tournament officially over. The crowd stalled awhile, enjoying the last few minutes of entertainment before they began to shift and stretch their limbs. Peddlers took final requests for wine and cream pastries.

"I expect to see you for dinner tonight," pronounced Leonardo's father.

"Agreed."

"Feel free to bring your lovely friend. The house could use some cheering up," he said before disappearing into the swarm of people surrounding us. We had all made a silent pact to wait for the horde of spectators to thin out.

"Viola?"

I knew Giuliano's voice right away. Before I spun around, I tried to brace myself for his armor and dimples, but it was no use. It was as if he had been copied and pasted out of a fairy tale. Even the sweat that gathered around his cheeks looked godly. I meant to say something but forgot what it was. Instead, I stood there gaping like a fish out of water. Everyone in a mile radius stared at me like I had an infectious disease. I could tell what they were thinking: "Why is a Medici talking to that girl?"

"Did you enjoy the tournament?"

"Yes!" I stuttered. "Congratulations on your victory."

"Thank you, my lady," Giuliano said with a low bow.

"You are wonderful ... I meant were! But that doesn't mean that you aren't also ..." I stammered, hoping that someone would stop me.

"As are you, Viola," he said, fighting back his laughter. "I see you are in excellent company." He looked around at my entourage of men and Zia.

"Yes, I'm very lucky," I agreed, my eyes widening as Lorenzo approached. He was only clad in half armor revealing the black tunic and gold threading below his breastplate.

"Hello, Signorina Orofino," offered Lorenzo.

"*Buonasera*, Signore Medici," I said, respectfully lowering my head.

"Greetings to you all," he added politely to the hundreds of eyes upon us. After whispering something in Giuliano's ear he turned to Zia. "I understand that you are Viola's aunt." Zia's pupils doubled in size. "I wanted to personally invite Signorina Orofino to the banquet this evening at our Palazzo." Zia looked to me and then to Signore Soldo who nodded.

"We are honored by your invitation," she consented.

"Excellent! She may bring along a chaperone of your choosing. Shall I send a carriage?"

"No ... thank you, sir. We will manage without."

"Good evening to you all," he said before walking off towards the large party that awaited him. Once Lorenzo had left, Giuliano resumed his easy air.

"A page boy should be waiting at your house with your mask."

"Mask?" I asked.

"Yes, it's a masked banquet," he explained before grazing his lips against the back of my hand. "And now I must follow my brother's example ... till this evening then." While I tried to pull myself together, a chorus of workshop boys blew kisses and whistles.

"Stop that!" I shouted, but the noises just got louder. I looked around the crowd for Zia and saw that she was having a conversation with Sandro Botticelli, who was on his knees. "What's going on?"

"This young man was just swearing his life to protect you," said Zia, amused.

"With all due respect, Zia, I think you should let him," advised Leonardo. "He's a gentleman and he will make sure she gets home earlier than I do." It never occurred to me that I might have another chaperone other than Leonardo.

The sun hung low in the sky by the time we had finished the chaperone arrangements and said our goodbyes. Zia, Francesco, and I did our best to avoid the manure traps and mud holes along the path home. As promised, a dark-haired boy was sitting on our doorstep with a large wooden box.

"That's a big mask," chuckled Signore Soldo.

"I hope you weren't waiting long," said Zia.

The boy, about the same age as Renzo, shook his head, crunching almonds in his mouth. "Are you Viola Orofino?" he murmured through a mouthful of sweet slivers.

"Yes."

"This is from the Medici family. I am meant to tell you that your presence is required at sunset," he recited.

"*Grazie.*"

"Would you like something to drink before you go?" asked Zia, but he gave her a polite "No, thank you," before dashing off.

While Zia opened the door, I picked up the box. It really was too cumbersome and heavy to be just a mask. Zia and Signore Soldo gathered around the table as I opened the box. On top of folded fabric lay a copper mask. Delicate chiseled lines framed the pointy eyes and ears of a fox. While I tried to tie the side strings around my head, I could feel its scalloped edges rest along the bridge of my nose and cheekbones.

"Viola!" exclaimed Zia.

"*Si?*" I asked, twisting the strings into a bow.

"This is much too fine!"

"The mask is real—"

"No! The dress he has had made for you," said Zia.

"Not a dress," corrected Francesco. "A masterpiece."

He unfolded the dark cherry fabric. My fox eyes saw that throughout the dark red velvet were strips of silk with painted violets. Trails of tiny pearls framed the bodice and sleeves. The dainty lace and open crevices foreshadowed just how difficult it would be to put on.

"What's that for?" I asked, pointing at a long-sleeved dress made of a stiff, almost transparent material.

"That goes under the dress," explained Zia.

"Zia, I think you're right. This dress is too generous of a gift," I said, running my fingertips over the tiny pearls and lush fabric. There was no doubt that it was the most expensive thing anyone had given me. "I can't accept it... right?" Zia did not answer, her eyes transfixed by the gown.

"You don't have a choice," said Signore Soldo. "Besides the fact that it would be unthinkably rude, it was made for you. They had it tailored with you in mind. Gowns like these are not ordered on Silk Road. They are commissioned like works of art. They thought of your skin and eyes when they chose the material," he explained seriously. Signore Soldo carefully pulled the regal gift out of its box and let it breathe in his arms. "I could go on, but you have little time to get ready before a certain lad comes knocking." He passed me the gown as he would an infant.

"Go wash up, Viola. Sandro will be here shortly," instructed Zia.

With arms bursting with velvet, I ascended the stairs. Once I laid the dress on the bed, I slipped Idan under the pillow. While I scrubbed myself red with the lump of soap, I fantasized about the hot shower waiting for me at home. Despite the cold water, nervous excitement boiled inside me. Zia came in and ordered me to put on my regular first layer as she dumped the basin's water onto the street. She then gathered the shimmering organza layer over my head. The sleeves fell past my wrists and its collar peeked around my neck. It took the two of us to get on the exquisite but heavy dress.

"This gown must weigh as much as Giuliano's suit of armor." Zia laughed a bit and overall her spirits seemed to have improved.

Her hands tightened the laces until I could hardly breathe. "We will keep your hair just the way it is," she said, tying the sleeves' crimson ribbons. "This reminds me of when my husband and I had finished Ginerva's first grownup dress. When she tried it on, her beauty blossomed before our eyes and all the tender life within her filled the room," she reflected.

"Thank you, Zia," I said, holding her tightly in my lanky arms.

"What did I tell you about saying thank you?" She shook her head. "If you ever feel uncomfortable tonight, I want you to tell Sandro and come home directly, you understand?" I nodded earnestly. "I think Sandro is already here. Don't be long," Zia said before leaving the room. It wasn't until I heard her footsteps reach the stairs that I reached for Idan beneath the pillow. A folded parchment tumbled from the same hiding place and onto the floor.

The red horse that fused the letter's secrets together stared up at me. My hands shook as I opened it. After rereading the first sentence over and over again without understanding it, I folded the paper and tried to steady my heartbeat. After a deep breath, I opened it again.

23rd of December

Viola,

You have thrown yourself into the path of dangerous people. If you hope to make it to the door, avoid the man of justice named Pietro and the Medici family despite temptations. An unquenchable lust for control lies behind every powerful man. It would not do for a young girl full of secrets to dine with such characters. With a bit of luck and wit you will not be hearing from me again.

The playful excitement I had allowed to build fizzled. *What a disaster*, I thought to myself. It was as if the fairy godmother had turned the pumpkin into a coach and then decided Cinderella could not go to the ball at all. My mind tried to find a happy medium between going and heeding the letter's warning. Either way I looked at the situation, there was no way to do both. I was sick to my stomach of always doing the right thing.

"I never do anything I'm not supposed to," I snapped at the letter. "There is no way I'm going to let anyone spoil my evening," I said, hiding Idan's chain beneath all my layers. But deep down I knew the letter already had. My mother's locket hung outside the dress, just in case Lorenzo got handsy again. Picking up the train of the dress, I left the room and the letter before sense got the better of me.

While I maneuvered down the steps, Sandro was fidgeting with his own costume. He was dressed in olive and wearing a round mask with a wide nose. Sandro almost looked surprised to see me.

"You look nice," he stammered.

"Nice? A grown man like you should be able to make a woman fall madly in love with you in five syllables. Viola will give that famous Simonetta a run for her jewels." Zia hushed Signore Soldo with her eyes as she helped fasten the fox mask.

"You'd better be the proper gentleman, Sandro ... and don't you dare let her out of your sight," cautioned Zia, guiding us to the door.

"Of course, signora," said Sandro with a nod before we stepped out into the brisk air.

The sky above us was streaked indigo and orange. My bare neck and ears were cold but everywhere else was toasty. *It's still so dirty*, I thought, lifting up the dress' thick fabric. The foul smell followed us as we turned onto Via dei Neri. "So what are you supposed to be?" I asked.

"A frog."

"Oh," I said, trying not to laugh.

"It's all I had."

"But it looks good on you."

"*Grazie.*" He reddened as we passed the Signoria.

"So why did you want to be my chaperone?" He was quiet for a long moment before he answered.

"Since I just opened my workshop, I don't have many patrons. My prosperity would be certain if the Medici supported me."

"So this is for your business?"

"Yes."

"So this has nothing to do with Simonetta?"

"I would be lying if I said no," he admitted.

Sensing he did not want to talk about her, I dropped the subject. We reached a corner where a line of people wrapped around a tall, narrow building. Their hungry eyes lingered on the pearls of my dress.

"What is this?" I asked, pointing to the ornate windows and niches that cut into the sandy stone.

"It is many things ... but mostly a church and the granary for the city. The people in front are most likely waiting for charity."

"I see," I said, feeling increasingly uncomfortable in my clothes. "It is called Orsanmichele. Those..." he pointed at the niches that harbored de-tailed statues "...are depictions of saints and the Virgin Mary. Different guilds commission them. In fact, it is my understanding that Verrocchio is working on one for the Merchants' Guild of Christ and St. Thomas."

"If you keep explaining it like that you are sure to kill her of bore-dom," said Leonardo. Sandro and I turned around. There he was, dressed in a flattering pink tunic with his mane pulled back.

"What are you doing here?" I asked, thrilled to see him.

"I am coming with you … You are walking into the lion's den," he said, tapping his lion mask. "You will need more than one chaperone."

"I am perfectly capable of—" protested Sandro.

"Of staring into Simonetta's eyes all night," finished Leonardo.

"How will you sneak in?"

"I won't have to, I'm wearing pink."

"How will that help you?" I asked.

"No one will protest against a man who wears pink," smiled Leonardo. "Cosimo Medici himself used to say that two bales of pink cloth made a gentleman," he said before leading the way to the Palazzo Medici.

CHAPTER TWENTY

The Garden

FLAMES WAVERED ON THE wicks that illuminated the grand walls of
Palazzo de' Medici. Unlike the houses on Via dei Benci, the square mansion wrapped around an entire block. Its first floor was built with heavily carved stones. In between the arches that framed the tall windows
were iron stakes that held the sweating candles. As we passed their
glow, I looked up at the two rows of arched windows. At the corner, we
could see a set of guards looming over the entrance. I looked at Leonardo but he seemed calm.

"Signora Vespucci?" he called.

A young woman ten feet ahead of us turned around at the sound of
her name. While Leonardo had quickened his stride, Sandro slowed to
an awkward tiptoe. The lovely lady wore a gown of teal with flecks of
gold that shimmered. Thick blonde waves unraveled artfully down her
back. She looked curiously at the handsome Leonardo from behind her
peacock mask.

"How stunning you are," Leonardo said with such easy charm that I
blushed, even though the compliment was not meant for me. The girl's
pink lips curled before she could stop them.

"I am sure every gentleman behind those walls will tell you the exact same thing for it is truth itself. But, I am so happy that I was the lucky one who told you first."

"And who are you, sir?" she hesitated.

"Hopefully your escort into the palace and by doing so the envy of every breathing man in Tuscany?" My mouth fell open almost as wide as Sandro's. He looked inconsolable as Simonetta Vespucci took Leonardo's arm and glided past the guards who barely spared a glance at his pink tunic.

"Well, I guess you will just have to settle for me," I said, pulling Sandro along towards the tall paneled doors.

The guards bid us goodnight as we stepped through the doorway into a sparkling courtyard. Lorenzo and Giuliano were greeting guests that lined up by one of the staircases. We took the open space right behind Leonardo and Simonetta.

"Hello again," said Leonardo. "My lady, allow me to introduce my friends. This is Viola Orofino, and this is the famous artist Sandro Botticelli."

"Yes ... of course," she said, holding her hand out for Sandro. Whether she really knew who he was or not, it was clear that the famous artist did not care as he rushed to kiss the hand of his golden opportunity. "How fortunate we are in meeting each other!" she exclaimed. "I have been meaning to get my portrait painted." Her sugary words could not have reached a more grateful ear. We switched partners and all was as it should be.

"You are so lucky," I said, glancing at the triumphant smile below the lion's whiskers.

"Luck has nothing to do with it."

"So you just had that mask lying around the workshop?"

"Handsome, no? It is one I made for my father ... I suppose Signore Soldo just threw a few scraps together when you got home," said Leonardo, tugging at one of my sleeves.

"Very funny. You know it was a gift, and you have already figured out from whom."

"Now that we can both agree we look dashing, let's talk about your sweetheart's palace."

"He's not my sweetheart."

"What do you think then?"

"Of what?" I asked. Leonardo rolled his eyes and put his arms up.

"Of the palace!"

"Oh, well it smells wonderful," I observed, breathing in the perfumed air.

"That is it?"

"Of course not," I replied, peering into the courtyard's arcade.

"It's very nice ... I mean elegant. Maybe it's more discreet than I had expected."

"That is true. It is classical," he agreed, staring at the empty pedestal in the middle of the courtyard. "What a shame."

"What's a shame?"

"I think that is where Donatello's David usually is," he explained. "It is actually one of the reasons I came."

"Oh, thanks."

"That was poorly phrased." He grinned. "What I meant to say was that I have heard so much about its beauty that I was eager to see it with my own eyes."

"Maybe I can ask Giuliano about it?" I offered just before our hosts greeted us.

"*Buonasera*, Viola," said Giuliano, tilting his handsome head.

"*Buonasera*," I managed with an awkward bow. "Your home is beautiful."

"I am so glad it is to your liking." He beamed. "You look ..."

"Out of place?" I suggested.

"Wonderful," he said, passing my hand to his brother. The tingly feeling fluttering around my heart instantly vanished.

"How purple is thy bloom, fresh Viola," interjected Lorenzo. "And oh how white the hand that gathered thee." He pecked my hand. When he looked back up, I noticed his face was rosier than usual and his eyes less alert. "Did you like that?"

"Excuse me?"

"My couplet?"

"Oh, yes it was ... original."

"Poetry is one of my many passions," confessed Lorenzo. The corners of his mouth were welcoming despite the notes of wine in his breath. "With your permission, I would like to introduce you to someone during the course of the evening." Bewitched by the incandescent atmosphere, I nodded. "Excellent. We will be up shortly. Straight up the staircase."

After climbing the stone steps, we followed the trail of candles and laughter down a long hallway. The path was outlined by rich carpet and pedestals crowned with proud busts. As Leonardo and I walked past the shut doors that flanked the passage, I wondered what marvels they might hold. I broke off from the procession when I spied one door that was slightly ajar. It was hard to see much since the room was not lit. The round elegant lines of the architecture were outlined by the moonlight that entered through the windows.

"Viola! Andiamo," implored Leonardo. "Supper hasn't started, and you are already sneaking around!"

"Hush!" I placed a finger to my lips while I waited for my eyes to adjust to the faint light. Magnificently carved furniture held countless books. The scrolls' spiral parchment budded from the many shelves that bordered the room. Dark padded chairs spread across the marble floor. As I approached the large table at the center of the room, I could make out loose parchments, silverpoint pens, and two empty wine glasses that burdened it. Smoke from a smoldering fire added to the haze that consumed the study.

"It's amazing how you can be so scared of some things but—"

"I can't believe it."

"What?"

"That is mine!" I pointed to a meticulous drawing of Idan that lay on the top of the paper. "How could he—"

"After he saw your small clock at the Duomo, he must have drawn it."

"What does that say?" I asked, staring at the script that surrounded the drawing. Leonardo squinted in the dark.

"My Latin isn't very good," he admitted.

"Excuse my intrusion," signaled a boy's voice from behind us. We both spun around, guilty as thieves. It was the same page boy that had delivered my dress. "Were you looking for the chamber pot room?" There was an awkward pause until Leonardo spoke up.

"I tried to tell her that it wasn't here. But she was in such a hurry. You know, when nature calls ..."

"Yes, well, it is actually just past the dining room," the page boy said, gesturing back towards the door.

"Thanks for throwing me under the bus," I whispered, thoroughly embarrassed.

"What is a bus?"

"Nothing. What it means is that you blamed it all on me."

"Well ... if you recall, I was against going in there," said Leonardo as we entered the blazing dining room.

"But if we hadn't, I wouldn't have seen the drawing," I retorted.

The detailed drawing of Idan brought the letter's warnings back to my mind and with it a bouquet of emotions. Each one threatened to wake me from the dreamy fairy tale I was living. A symphony of string instruments tried to lull me back into the delightful banquet.

Flames danced off the painted ceiling and its golden frame. Above our heads, tiny angels glided between fountains while birds flew against the rose sky of the overhanging beams. Many guests had already sat down and begun drinking the red wine that the servants were pouring into the glasses. The tables were arranged in a horseshoe shape with silverware settings on only one side.

"That way no one has their backs turned towards one another," explained Leonardo as I gazed with wonder at the scene before me.

"Is that so everyone can be seen?"

"That's part of it. This way they can see the jewels that dangle from their necks and judge each other's table manners."

"Everyone does seem to have put in a lot of effort into how they look."

"Not a lot," corrected Leonardo. "All their money, time, and care. In Florence, there are sumptuary laws. People cannot show off their wealth. The laws are especially strict about women's dress."

"You mean the few times they are allowed to step out their front door?" I snapped.

"Yes."

"Like what kind of dress is illegal?"

"They are not really allowed to wear trains," he said, pulling on the back of my dress.

"Oh!"

"What about where you come from?"

"Well ..." I stalled thinking about the busy streets of New York City. "In the city that I am from you can wear anything you want." Leonardo's eyes bulged at this and he was on the brink of flooding me with questions when the music died down.

"Thank you for waiting," pronounced Lorenzo. The gray mask he wore looked like a dog and matched the silvery thread of his periwinkle tunic. "We are glad you are all here and will not be content until you enjoy the amusements and your neighbors' company. Therefore, let us be the merriest of parties." He raised his glass. While his guests followed his instructions, the instruments came back to life.

"Where do we sit?" I asked Leonardo.

"Anywhere," he answered, grabbing the closest chair. I had barely sat down at the seat next to him before someone touched my shoulder. Giuliano smiled down at me from behind his brown bird mask.

"I had to make sure no one else took my seat," he said, taking off his mask and setting it on the place setting next to me. "I actually have to sit by my brother for a while, but I'll be back soon."

He strode back towards the main table. Leonardo let out a low whistle, and I jabbed him in the rib with my elbow. Austere-looking men sat at the table where Giuliano was required to sit. Among them was the man with the shaved head.

"What are you doing?" asked Leonardo.

"Nothing," I murmured, bending my ear towards my tummy. "I'm checking to see if Idan is ticking."

"You mean your little clock? I wish you would let me tinker with it ... I bet I could fix it for you."

For a moment I thought I could make out a faint beat, but the music was too loud. "It doesn't need fixing," I insisted, sitting up. The servants flowed in and out of the dining room carrying large jugs and platters laden with exotic foods. "I don't think you will be eating much here," I said, staring at the platter of roast beef wedged between us.

Leonardo quickly exchanged it for a plate of sharp cheese, green grapes, and sliced apples. As I served myself, I could feel the gaze of many around me. "Where did Sandro go?" I said, seeing Simonetta across the way. She was cutting tiny pieces but eating nothing. The gorgeous lady was surrounded by young women dressed in equal splendor.

"I'm right here," he said through a mouthful of a dark pudding. He was seated on Leonardo's other side.

"Honestly, if I would've known that the only dish without meat was going to be cheese and fruit and that all you would be doing was flirting the night away, I would have stayed with my father," complained Leonardo.

"More food for us then," added Sandro, cutting a thick slice of mutton covered in hot butter. "What were you expecting?"

"I thought there would be more ... drama. At the very least, I hoped for better food."

"Sorry you are disappointed," said Giuliano coolly. Leonardo tried to hide his embarrassment in a gracious smile.

"Viola, would you like a tour of the house?" asked Giuliano, leaning close towards my ear. One of his stray curls rested against my cheek.

"I would!" I said, getting to my feet. He grasped my hand and led the way out of the dining room. Giuliano was almost running down the hallway. "Why are you in a hurry?" I asked.

"I want to spend as much time with you as I can before we are missed."

Grinning, we rushed down the hallway and leaped down the stone steps two at a time. Once we were in the courtyard and I saw the empty pedestal again, I remembered what I wanted to ask Giuliano.

"Giuliano?"

"*Si?*"

"I heard that you have a wonderful Donatello sculpture here."

"Had."

"What do you mean?"

"It was stolen."

"Oh ... I'm sorry to hear that."

"Don't be. We will get it back soon. Then you will have to come back and see it," he said, guiding me under a portico of trees.

"How can you be so sure you will get it back?"

"Because Lorenzo cannot bear any other secrets other than his own," admitted Giuliano. "This is all quite serious talk! I wanted to show you the garden and take you away from all that." He waved at the flickers of light that came from the windows overlooking the courtyard.

Beneath the cover of leaves, I took a deep breath. How crisp it smelled beneath the courtyard's damp green canopy. It had been so long since I had seen trees.

"What I wanted to show you is farther along," said Giuliano, squeezing my hand and leading me into Eden. He stopped at a clearing where there was a stone bench.

Giuliano let go of my hand and crouched down by the bench. The bottle-green fabric of his tunic stretched across his athletic form as he reached for something behind the bench. When he turned around, he held a potted plant with one purple flower blooming beneath a glass case.

"It is probably the only one in the city, at least at this time of year."

Even in twilight, the violet's petals were vibrant. The plant's round leaves touched the sides of its crystal prison. It struck me then that I felt like that flower. Mrs. Reed had plucked me from my home and planted me in a time I did not belong. "The glass is what keeps it from wilting," said Giuliano placing the flower back behind the bench.

"It's beautiful."

"But it is not as rare or as warm as my Viola," he said, drawing me closer to the bench. "Do you know why this is called the city of flowers?" I shook my head. As Giuliano leaned closer to my face, I could feel his breath brush against my face and smell his minty cologne. My whole body felt like it was on fire. "It is said that during the Roman Empire, Florence was nestled in between hills and covered with flowers." His warm fingers wrapped around the nape of my neck.

My heart was beating louder than Idan's tick, and I had lost feeling in my legs. He looked at my face for a moment. First, he stared into my eyes, but then his gaze roamed over every freckle and bead of sweat. With his other hand, he pressed the small of my back. As Giuliano locked his soft lips between my own, time sat still on that garden bench. His right hand moved up from my neck and into my hair and I could feel his arms pulling me closer to me.

"Giuliano!" called Lorenzo from beyond the garden path. I pulled away, but Giuliano rested his forehead against mine.

"I'm sorry, Viola," he whispered.

"For what?"

"No matter what happens ... I truly—" Lorenzo's footsteps drew closer.

"Truly what?" I asked. Giuliano got quickly to his feet. His brother came into the gap of trees.

"Giuliano ... Viola," he said, his eyes catching my disheveled hair net.

"I was just showing her the violet," said Giuliano.

"I hope that is all you were showing her." Lorenzo frowned.

"It's clever. That is, the glass case you have the violet in," I said, blushing.

"Yes, it is," replied Lorenzo, resuming his formal manner.

An eerie feeling began to weed itself through the empty space that Giuliano's kiss had left. How could it have all been over so quickly?

"Would you be so kind as to grant me your promise?" asked Lorenzo.

"Promise?"

"To meet my acquaintance," he said, offering me his arm. Before I took his arm, I glanced back in time to catch Giuliano's miserable expression. "I trust you are enjoying your time?"

"My time?" I asked as we walked back into the courtyard.

"Yes, your time here in Florence."

"Oh, yes of course," I said. While we climbed back up the steps, I wanted nothing more than to run out of the palace as fast as my poor running abilities would allow. "I sometimes forget that I am not really from here."

"I have not," said Lorenzo. Dread strangled me as I loosened my grip on his arm. "That is ... forgotten that you are from a different land." With every step we took down the hallway, I shrunk smaller and smaller. The candles that had once seemed so magical were now leading the way to my funeral. It was strange to think that only minutes before, I had blissfully raced down the hallway. The music grew louder as we approached the dining room.

Upon entering, my eyes darted frantically around the room for my chaperones. Sandro had worked up enough guts to talk to Simonetta again. He was kneeling attentively by her side while she picked at her custard. Leonardo was not in sight. As we moved further into the room, I could feel Idan's steady tick quickening.

"Pietro," called Lorenzo. The man with the shaved head turned around. Idan violently beat against my skin. "Allow me to introduce, Viola Orofino," said Lorenzo, gracefully moving my hand to the stranger's. Unlike Lorenzo's hand, Pietro's hand had enough calluses to rival Verrocchio himself.

"*Please don't let the music stop,*" I whispered under my breath.

"Enchanted," he said, kissing my hand. "I am Pietro Sforza."

"Pietro is a visitor as well," explained Lorenzo. "We invite a foreign judge from outside Florence as to not upset the scales of justice with our own city's private rivalries."

"Yes, I am actually from Milan, but I am enjoying Florence immensely," smiled Pietro as his eyes considered my every blink.

"I find Pietro quite indispensable. We seem to share all the same academic pursuits ... Alas, he is leaving us soon and there is still so much more I hoped to learn from him." Pietro's smile broadened at Lorenzo's words.

Tick-tock, tick-tock, pulsed Idan.

"Surely, you give me more credit than I deserve."

"I always say exactly what I mean ... Viola, Pietro has led me to so many brilliant discoveries, scrolls by philosophers long forgotten, artifacts that even Verrocchio would find hard to replicate. Unfortunately, time has ravaged many of the scrolls."

"But no matter how long I stay, time will pass. Many a brilliant creation will decay, and we will be none the wiser."

Tick-tock-tick-tock!

"The very thought hardens my soul. To lose humanity's revelations, its progress!" lamented Lorenzo.

"Yes, but what you seek is an impossible thing."

"What do I seek?"

"To control time," answered Pietro without removing his eyes from me.

"I would give up all you see before you for such a gift," admitted Lorenzo.

Rubbing my salty hands against my dress, I tried to plot my escape. Suddenly the music stopped. Poor Idan, who had been screaming to be heard, finally rang out.

"What's that sound?" asked Lorenzo.

A flash of understanding crossed Pietro's face. The creepy smile that curled up the sides of his face clashed with his sharp features and pointy mustache. From the corner of my eye, I caught Leonardo's pink costume. He was urging me towards the entrance, but I was cornered.

"Excuse me, Signore Medici and Signore Sforza, but I really must be going. My Zia has long been expecting me."

"Not so fast, Viola ... before you leave, I wanted you to show Pietro that curious trinket you have strung around your neck."

"If you insist."

"I do." I grasped for my locket, but before I even had it in my palm Lorenzo protested. "No! That wasn't it at all."

Tick-tock-tick-tock!

Pietro seemed to be waiting for something to happen.

"I think you told Giuliano it was an heirloom. Something about your grandfather being a pirate," added Lorenzo. The lie sounded even dumber the second time around.

"If I may be so bold, might it be on the other chain hanging around your neck?" insisted Pietro.

I looked down and saw Idan's gold chain peeking through the translucent material of the under dress.

"Damn this organza," I cursed under my breath. The whole elaborate plan dawned on me. Giuliano's betrayal put me on the verge of tears.

"What was that?" asked Lorenzo, who was poised to pounce on my neck.

"Would you excuse me, please ... I am suddenly in need of the chamber pot room," I said and strode off before they could protest.

Leonardo raised his eyebrows as I approached the door. Once we turned the corner, we bolted down the hallway. Voices shouted our names from behind us, but we did not stop. We could not stop.

CHAPTER TWENTY-ONE

Wings

LEONARDO WAS CLEARLY ENJOYING our escape. He howled like a wolf as we ran through dark passageways. We skipped every pothole and veered past piles of manure. Rude complaints rang down on us from awoken sleepers. We darted past the cage of the lioness and flew down the Duomo steps ignoring drunken men stumbling home.

"I am so out of shape," I gasped. My throat felt like I had swallowed sand.

"You really are," agreed Leonardo, drenched in sweat.

"Well let's switch clothes and do the course over again."

"That might be fun," considered Leonardo with a distinct twinkle in his eye. "So come now, tell me what happened."

"Nothing," I said, trying to steady my legs with my hands. "Other than the Medicis conned me." I balled my hands into fists, unable to quiet the anger fermenting inside me.

"Did they hurt you?"

"Not physically ... It was all an elaborate trick. The banner, the dress, the kiss ... it was all part of a plan," I tried to swallow the lump of emotion that swelled in my throat.

"Wait, wait! He kissed you?"

"All they wanted was Idan!" I said, pushing aside his question.

"Why not just sell it to them? I am sure they would pay you well."

"I can't!"

"Why not?"

"It's my only way to get back home," I confessed.

"How can a tiny clock aid such a quest?"

"It's not a clock!" I cried out in frustration. It was exhausting trying to keep everything bottled up inside of me.

"Then what is it?"

"It controls time, but I haven't figured out how yet. What I do know is that I need it to get back."

It was dark on the street save for the dim light coming from Zia's fireplace and the half-moon's radiance. Still heaving, I leaned against the porous walls of my safe haven waiting for Leonardo to interrupt the silence.

"Are you saying you come from a different time?" I looked up and down the street, terrified at my own outburst. "Viola, I think you need some rest. Perhaps you need to sit down? I know you are upset but—"

"I am upset!" I rubbed my eyes on the embroidered sleeves. "But I am not crazy."

"I made no such—"

"You didn't have to. Your look said it all."

"But you are speaking of time travel!"

"I've only done it once." Gathering the train of my dress, I sat down on the step. "Do you have any more of that honey drink left? My throat is killing me." Leonardo pulled out the flask from his cloak and passed it to me. I drank the last mouthful. The honey felt wonderful as it traveled down my raw throat. "You don't believe me," I said, passing him back his flask. I had been so hot from running that the cold's breath was just beginning to shake me.

"It is not that I don't believe you ... it is more that I choose not to believe anything I cannot see, touch, hear, or taste. In short, I trust nothing that I cannot dissect or deduce."

A cough ripped us from our private conversation.

"Did you hear that?"

"Probably just a fisherman." He peered in the direction of the sound. "I like the idea of something as ambitious as time travel," he whispered. "I mean time traveling itself does not interest me. I am fine where I am. The concept of a device that moves the whole world interests me ... but it is impossible."

"I liked your first word better. Ambitious."

"Sometimes I have ambitious ideas but, then I just never explore them because I think they are doomed to fail."

"Like what?"

"You will laugh," he said, staring at his feet.

"I just told you I time traveled."

"True." He smiled. "Well, for example, flying or being able to swim underwater without surfacing."

"I think you need to get out of your own way," I said.

"What do you mean?"

"I mean ... I might be scared by a lot of things, but I'm never frightened by my own ideas."

"Wise words, dear sister," said Leonardo, helping me to my feet. "So what happened with Idan?"

"They wanted to see it."

"Did they?"

"Of course not! Although, I guess it doesn't really matter. Lorenzo already had a pretty good drawing of it."

"How did you get out of it?"

"I told them I had to go to the chamber pot room." I smiled.

Leonardo burst out laughing. He had a wonderful laugh. Its low and hearty rumble was infectious. Zia and Signore Soldo opened the door to two teenagers bent over and barely able to breathe from laughter.

"What do you two think you are doing? You will wake up the whole neighborhood with all this noise," chastised Zia. She bid Leonardo a goodnight and ushered me inside. Too exhausted to talk anymore, I ascended the stairs dragging my feet one by one.

"Well! How was it?" asked Francesco as Zia helped him with his cloak.

I thought about it for a second and then settled for the standard. "It was fine."

"Fine?"

"Yeah." I yawned.

"How can a Medici banquet be just fine?"

"I'm sorry to disappoint you."

"The food must have been exceptional." Signore Soldo's eyes widened as he imagined the spread.

"Zia's is much better," I said.

"That is truth itself, Caterina. You have set the bar unreasonably high." She smiled at his praise.

"*Buonanotte*, Signore Soldo, thank you for everything," I said before disappearing upstairs.

I let my body slump onto the thin mattress. Without changing, I curled my knees towards my body. The giddy feeling the laughter had brought helped me fall asleep. As usual, I awoke with a start. All the anxiety that Leonardo had overwhelmed me.

"I just ran away from the most powerful family in Florence," I told the darkness.

I looked out the window half expecting a battalion of guards waiting to take me away. But there was not a soul on the sleepy street. Knowing well that I would not be able to sleep anymore, I traded the elaborate dress for my simple wool one. Today I wanted to be me, not Massimo or a fine lady. I thought about cinching the brown fabric at my waist with the neon belt. Swinging my green sweater over my dress, I snuck past Zia's door, down the steps, and out the door. My eyes took a while to adjust to the light of the empty street. I trod carefully down the cobblestones with my arms wrapped tightly around me.

Despite my bad mood, it was refreshing to walk through the streets alone. Quickly, I chanced a glance at Idan. I had concluded that if Idan were a person, it would be a guy. Only a boy could cause so much mischief and be even more indecisive than me. One hand was pointing to the rising sun and the countdown's number was sixteen.

The digits hung heavily on my conscience. I closed his cover and through a flock of pigeons that were picking at discarded trash from the joust. While they flew away, one was kind enough to leave me a white wet gift that dribbled down my shoulder.

"The cherry on top of my cake," I complained to the houses that flickered to life.

As I turned the corner of the workshop, I almost knocked Leonardo over. He did not seem surprised to see me.

"Is that pigeon feces?" he pointed at my shoulder.

"Good morning to you, too," I said, "and yes, it is."

"Well, that was almost good luck." He shivered as we approached the workshop.

"Almost?"

"Yeah, if one defecates on your head it's supposed to be good luck."
"The shoulder doesn't count?"

"I'm afraid not." He shrugged, walking under the frozen canopy.

The workshop was still waiting for the apprentices to wake up. Leonardo went back upstairs to his dormitory. All was quiet. Not even the constant crackle-pop of the fire could be heard. The kitchen was also still. I lit a fire and tried my best to clean the pigeon poop off my shoulder. After I thoroughly washed my hands, I began to knead the dough that was rising on the countertop the way Margherita had taught me. After forming the dough into loaves, I dressed them with egg wash. Using the long wooden spatula, I set the bread to bake. Slowly, the smell of bread filled the snug kitchen.

Margherita came into the kitchen as I was boiling water for tea. She placed her cloak on one of the hooks by the archway. Each one of her moves was slow and forced.

"Thank you for making the bread, Viola ... I was not expecting you so early," she said, wiping her face with a handkerchief. The black circles around her eyes told me she had not slept for days.

"Why did you think that?" I asked, breaking off rosemary and lavender from overhanging bundles.

"With your banquet and all, I figured you would sleep in a bit."

"Oh, you heard about that." I poured the boiling water into a ceramic cup.

"The boys told me everything when they got back," she said, sitting down on the castle of crates at the back of the kitchen. "Did you have-"

"Margherita, are you feeling all right? Where did you go out at such an early hour?" I interjected.

"I went to call on the midwife," she said, resting her free hand on her enormous belly. "I was feeling awful, and I have been getting these terrible pains all over."

"What did she say?"

"That the baby will come soon."

"What is soon?"

"Tonight or tomorrow."

"Wow, on Christmas! That's a good sign, isn't it?" I said trying to cast a positive light on the situation.

"I don't know ... it seems more like a nuisance to drag people from their feasts and mass to have a baby I cannot afford to keep." She wiped her eyes with a moist handkerchief.

"What will you do?"

"The idea of giving the baby away to a complete stranger or worse, watching her grow up unloved in the orphanage as I did ... it makes my heart ache."

"Don't worry about that right now. We'll figure out something. I'll ask Zia what she thinks." Poor Margherita looked like she was hurting in every which way. "What can I do to help you?"

"For a start, take out the bread." She smiled weakly. I did as she said, but it was a few minutes too late. The top was blackened. "That is fine. They will eat it. Besides that, there is nothing you can do. Unless you know someone who wants to keep my baby," she scoffed.

Moving the hot bread into a basket warmed my icy hands. After choosing the least burnt bun from the dozen, I offered the soft knot to Margherita, but she shook her head miserably from side to side. With all my heart, I wished that I knew more than six people in the whole Florence Renaissance. I longed to know a happy couple that would jump at the opportunity to care for Margherita's baby. Not one of my acquaintances would be able to take on such a responsibility. *Perhaps Zia?* I thought as I slathered the piping bun of dough with butter. It was one thing to take on a girl of fifteen but another thing entirely to take on a day-old baby. The salty cream melted in my mouth when my teeth sunk past the crust. Suddenly, an idea struck me.

"What about..." I said aloud through a mouthful of flakes.

"What about what?" asked Margherita.

It was clear I did not know a soul who could take care of her baby, but I had heard of a couple that might. Not wanting to get Margherita's hopes up just yet, I kept my discovery to myself.

Shaking my head, I said, "What about lunch?" She tried hard to mask her disappointment, but it hid itself in the deep creases of her mouth.

"I knew something was off. So while everyone was out yesterday evening, I cooked this evening's Christmas Eve feast."

"I should have been here helping you," I said, feeling lousy.

"Nonsense." She waved my apology aside. "If I was not so giant, I would have been out there cheering with the rest of them."

"You should go rest. I'll set up the table for breakfast."

"I think I will," she said. I held out my hand to help her stand. "We are fasting because it is Christmas Eve. So there is no lunch to prepare," informed Margherita before she left the kitchen.

Leonardo and Renzo were the only ones working when I followed Margherita into the workroom. Renzo helped me set the table, and soon after the boys filed in. They barely resembled humans until they had at least two thick slices of bread in their guts. When I realized that I had not eaten either, I squeezed between Salai and Perugino. Salai did not seem as threatening anymore now that I was on the Medicis' bad side. After Salai made a few rude comments about the singed bread, I told him to shut up and eat it or he could cook all his meals. My boldness amused Perugino and granted me a few thumbs up at the table.

"That's not very ladylike ... I'm not sure your boyfriend would approve of that," retorted Salai.

"I'm not sure he would appreciate anything that comes out of your mouth. Especially what you say to me," I snapped, my patience depleted. Salai's olive skin turned pasty white but he continued to eat the bread.

Wanting to be alone, I shoved half the buttery toast in my mouth and collected some dirty plates for washing. While I warmed some of the ice-cold water for washing, there was a soft knock at the archway.

"Sandro!"

"*Buongiorno*, Viola," he replied, looking away.

"Are you all right?"

"That is what I came to ask you," he said, his eyes relieved to see me in one piece. "I also came to apologize for last night."

"What for?"

"For being the worst chaperone in history." I smiled at the sincerity of his apology. "I realized you were in trouble when you and Leonardo bolted down the hallway."

"What happened when we left?"

"Lorenzo looked furious and shouted something at Giuliano. Then the young prince got up and ran after you with two other young men," said Sandro, fidgeting with his round cap. "It took a while before Signore Sforza was able to pacify Lorenzo's temper. I don't think anyone has ever turned their back on him before."

"When did Giuliano get back?"

"He didn't catch up with you?" asked Sandro. I shook my head. "I don't know then. I left shortly after you ran off."

Sandro's concern made my heart drop a few inches. I put my hands behind my back to hide their trembling.

"Don't feel bad! It was nothing you could have prevented. Did you enjoy yourself?" I asked, trying to mask my anxiety.

"I got a commission to paint a portrait of Simonetta."

"Congratulations!" I hugged my clammy arms around his square shoulders. Sandro's auburn hair felt soft against my ear. When I pulled away from him, I could tell he was still feeling guilty. "Seriously, I don't want you to feel bad about anything. It wouldn't have mattered if I had had a hundred chaperones. The evening's escapade would have been the same."

"If you say so."

"I do."

"Viola!" called Verrocchio. "Yes?"

He stepped into the kitchen abruptly. His dusty tunic was messier than usual, and his hands were caked with clay. "Fetch Massimo! There is too much work to be done. Did you hear all that?" Verrocchio shouted to the apprentices. "There will be no feast until I see you have all put your backbones into it."

"Who is Massimo?" asked Sandro.

"Are you busy or would you like to help out a bit?" asked Verrocchio, who was looking at Sandro like he was a mirage. "I am quite overwhelmed."

"I suppose I have a bit of time to spare."

"That's a good man!" exclaimed Verrocchio. "Viola, I still need Massimo."

"Well, you will have to make do with Viola today. Margherita is sleeping, and I don't want to disturb her."

"You mean you are going to work in the shop?" asked Sandro, his eyebrows disappearing behind the fringe of his hair.

"Exactly," I said, hiking up my sleeves and walking into the shop before either of them could stop me.

Verrocchio soon directed me on preparing a wooden panel with gesso. While I waited for the layers to dry, Renzo asked me to help him make more brushes.

After Renzo's nimble fingers formed neat clumps of white hog hairs, he instructed me to wind the coarse hair into bundles with waxed thread. He lodged a tapered stick of maple in the middle of the bunch and told me to keep wrapping it until the thread concealed the ends of the hair.

We repeated this until we had twenty new brushes. Apprentices were waiting by our table grabbing them as we finished securing the wrapping.

"We have to do the same thing but with miniver hair," said Renzo smudging the soot all over his face.

"What does it come from?" I asked, feeling the soft brown hair.

"They are much higher quality and are made from squirrel hair. They are used to paint the finer details," explained Renzo, trimming the supple hair with tiny scissors.

"Viola, I need you to work on tracing this drawing," ordered Verrocchio.

I left Renzo and walked over to the table where Verrocchio hovered. A large square of fabric about five feet wide had an elaborate angel conversing with a man sketched on it.

"You are to trace the lines by making pinpricks along them like so." He demonstrated. "I know you may find this tedious, but it is extremely helpful to me," he said before hurrying off to check Salai's gilding technique.

Once left alone with the intricate drawing, I decided to start on the angel's feathered wings. I was only halfway done with the top portion when I felt someone peering over my shoulder.

"Do you like it?" asked Leonardo.

"I do."

"Good, I helped out with that one."

"How is what I am doing helpful?"

"Well, it helps us lay down the sketch on the panel. We spread cinnabar or another kind of pigment over the drawing leaving a soft outline that we can then model and hatch in. It is especially useful with proportions."

"That's smart."

"We try." Leonardo shrugged. "Leave this and grab a board and some parchment. Then meet me in the courtyard."

I cast a wary glance at Verrocchio, who was fully absorbed in a plaster mold. I found both items quickly before walking out of the shop, through the kitchen, and into the drafty courtyard. When I stepped outside, Leonardo was cradling a snowy dove between his hands.

"How did you...?"

"Her wings are clipped," he said, frowning. "Once they grow back out, she will fly freely out of the courtyard," he explained more to the dove than to me. Leonardo let her down in the center of the courtyard and then tiptoed towards me. The dove examined him. "Remember what I said about drawing things in motion?"

"Yes."

"Well, this is the best exercise I could come up with that did not involve anything illegal." He smiled and handed me a piece of charcoal. "I'll move around the bird while you sketch. Ready?"

After settling on the floor, I nodded and off she flew. The charcoal, my eyes, and the dove's wings were one. Waves of frustration came and went as I tried to capture the dove's struggling flight. While Leonardo shuffled the dove about, I tried a combination of thick contour lines balanced by quick hatching, but it felt like an impossible task. My mentor walked towards me to see how I was getting along with the assignment.

"It's really difficult," I said.

"More difficult than time traveling?"

"Somewhere in between flying or swimming underwater without coming up for air," I teased.

"All in all, it is a pretty good try. Let us get back inside before Verrocchio notices we have gone."

Upon entering the workshop, I was surprised to see so many apprentices crowded in one corner. It was the same nook Leonardo had been working at all day.

"What's going on?" I asked.

"Not sure."

"Is that the baptism painting?"

"Yes."

"They all look starstruck," I said, noticing their open mouths and glassy eyes. Verrocchio was at the center of the huddle and clearly moved.

"Alas, my painting days have come to an end," declared Verrocchio.

CHAPTER TWENTY-TWO

David

DURING THE AFTERMATH OF Verrocchio's outburst and quick retreat, I went to see if it was the angel I saw for the first time in Mrs. Reed's gallery. The boys' mixture of jealousy and awe rendered them easy opponents as I elbowed my way to the front of the pack. The angel was not the same as I had remembered. This angel's face was far more radiant than my memory. For now, I knew better the genius that wielded the brush. The softness of Leonardo's ethereal angel was inspiring. The wisps of hair that fell around the head and the eyes that stared up at Jesus really set it apart from its angel counterpart. There was nothing awkward or wanting from the blue textile that draped naturally against the kneeling figure. Leonardo was standing next to me, his body stiff with apprehension.

"Should we get going?" I asked.

"Yeah." He crossed his arms.

"What's wrong?"

"Nothing," he grumbled. "Just thought you would have something to say is all."

"I expected nothing less of—"

"Brilliance?" he offered.

"Exactly." I smiled. "The angel's natural gentleness is misplaced in the workshop. It makes all the other flat figures stuck behind their panels sick with envy."

"All right! That is enough." He reddened. "Let us get going, then."

"I'm going to check on Margherita first. I will only be a minute," I said, making my way towards the stairs. I knocked lightly before I entered the library, but no sound came from within. "Margherita?" I whispered.

When I peeked behind the divider, I saw a crumpled blanket at the foot of the bed and her body shifted to one side. As I moved closer to check on her, a sporadic snore rose from her delicate mouth. The pillow was damp, but I could not decide whether it was from drool or sweat.

I grabbed a dry linen from the hallway cupboard and carefully lifted Margherita's head. After turning the pillow, I laid the fresh linen on top of the damp one. While I covered her with the blanket that had been thrown off, I noticed she was shivering. It was with a heavy heart that I met Leonardo by the stairs.

"I do not feel right about leaving Margherita with no one to take care of her," I admitted to Leonardo as we crossed the street.

"Then why are we on our way to Via dei Benci?"

"Because I need to talk to Zia alone first. I also don't want Zia to be alone on Christmas Eve."

"The feast at the shop is usually not fancy," said Leonardo. "Verrocchio sometimes joins his nieces, who almost always go to a banquet at one of their cousins' houses."

"All the same, I think it right I should be near Margherita."

"I think last year she made roast chicken."

"So hungry! Everything sounds glorious right now."

Tick-tock, tick-tock, tick-tock, beat Idan. I stopped and looked desperately around me waiting for something or someone.

"What is the matter?" asked Leonardo.

Pietro Sforza came rushing out of the house opposite us with such speed that he did not even notice us or the pair of young boys he almost ran over. Once he had disappeared onto a side street, I spun around to get a better look at the house he had fled. It was pieced together with an array of bricks of different sizes and colors. The building looked older than most. It had let go of its original square shape and curved outwards towards the alley that abutted it. The passage seemed to be part of the property. That or the owner of the dwelling had annexed it. Long strips of canopy hoarded its contents from wandering eyes. The odd alley also had a metal gate that had been poorly shut by its owner.

"This used to be just an empty dead end," observed Leonardo. "I mean empty, if you do not count the poor folk trying to find shelter."

"I think this is his house," said Leonardo as I approached the gate and stole a glance around at the few strangers on the street. "I saw him unloading a bunch of bundles and crates here not too long ago when I was on my way to Mercato Vecchio. It was the same day I met you." Leonardo scratched his head.

"He looked like he was anxious to go unnoticed." I held Idan up to my ear, but he was still. My hands widened the gap of the metal gate. Once again, my curiosity had taken over my reason.

"Viola!" cautioned Leonardo with a sharp whisper. "What are you doing?"

"I want to see what he's hiding," I said. Leonardo flashed me a look that showed me how crazy my scheme was. He moved closer to the gate but lingered on the precipice. I was already on the other side of the metal bars.

"So you are too scared to watch a joust, but you are fine with breaking into a judge's home."

"Well, when you put it like that ... I'm just curious."

"What if you get caught?"

"We won't!"

"We?"

"Yes! Idan ticks like crazy when Pietro is close by, and I want to find out why. We will have plenty of time to run back out."

"You are forgetting that I do not believe in your magical Idan," he said with a raised eyebrow.

"Come on, we are losing time," I said, walking further into the alley.

"Viola," moaned Leonardo from the gate.

"Don't be such a mouse." The gate creaked open, and Leonardo followed me inside. "I wish it were lighter outside."

Crates covered with wax and clay scrapings were propped against the house's curved wall. A makeshift oven had been built at the end of the alley. As we drew closer, we saw a red glow coming from the wreckage of discarded objects.

"Oh my God."

"What is it?"

"He is trying to cast something," he said, pointing to the empty glowing cylinder. "He must have just finished."

"How do you know?"

"That is a crucible..." he motioned to the cylinder suspended between iron bars "...it's used to melt metal. Those handles are for pouring the bronze." We both looked closer at the litter that covered the floor. "This," he said, picking up a metal rod, "this is what keeps the wax mold in place."

"Why would a judge be casting a sculpture?" I wondered aloud.

"What is even more worrisome is that he is doing this alone," added Leonardo. "This task should never be done by oneself. It can go terribly wrong."

"He must not want anyone else to know," I suggested, noticing a side entrance into the lopsided house. Idan was still quiet. When I opened the door, the little light that filtered through the alley brightened the cluttered chaos within. "This place is a mess!" I said, treading carefully through the wreckage. Old plates of food and papers were scattered everywhere. The room reeked of fat, wax, and smoke.

"He must have left in a hurry," said Leonardo, looking at the smothered embers in the fireplace. There were only two pieces of furniture in the broad room, a chair and a massive table, upon which stood a sculpture.

"Viola! That is the David!"

"The David?"

"Donatello's David sculpture! The one that is usually in the Medici courtyard."

"Oh no," I said, suddenly aware of the danger we were in.

"What?"

"Giuliano said it had been stolen."

"How could you not tell me that?" exclaimed Leonardo.

"Hush! Don't yell at me. I just forgot." The statue looked to be of a young boy and was about five feet tall. David was wearing a soft hat with a floral bouquet crowning it. Fair hair caressed his shoulders and neck. Other than the hat, he wore knee-high laced boots. "Why is he naked?" I asked.

"He is not naked, he is nude," corrected Leonardo.

"But he's wearing a hat and boots ... If he was nude, he wouldn't be wearing anything. The few items of clothing make him look more naked than if he wasn't wearing anything." My mom and I had had a similar discussion before about some sculptures in the Metropolitan Museum.

Leonardo considered my words for a few moments as he admired Donatello's work. "Well maybe he is naked to emphasize how he refused to take the armor offered to him before he faced Goliath."

"Who is Goliath?" Leonardo laughed at my question.

"Just tell me! No need to make me feel stupid." He put a hand on my shoulder and pointed at the giant mass David was standing on.

"That is Goliath." After I moved closer to get a better look, I realized the mass was actually a giant severed head. "The story is from the bible. It takes place when the Israelites and the Philistines are at war. Goliath, the Philistines' best warrior, proposes man-on-man combat to end the whole battle. Not one of the Israelite warriors was brave enough to accept the challenge. David, who was too young to be a soldier, accepted the proposal. The leader of the Israelites offered David armor and weapons, but he refused, opting to use his trusty slingshot. That is why he is holding a rock in one hand," explained Leonardo.

"But what about the sword in his other hand?"

"Well, David knocks the giant down with his slingshot but then severs Goliath's head using the giant's own sword."

"He looks like he couldn't even lift the sword, let alone use it," I said.

"It is believed that God gave him the incredible strength he needed to defeat Goliath." Leonardo drew closer to the sculpture. "I'm not sure you are properly impressed."

"What do you mean?"

"This is a completely unsupported, freestanding bronze sculpture. It is an incredible challenge."

"He looks kind of … dainty?" I said. "It almost looks like a woman's body from certain angles."

"Perhaps that is intentional."

"It feels—"

"Sensual?" offered Leonardo.

"Bordering on the scandalous," I added, my eyes lingering on the plumage going up David's leg. "I haven't seen anything like this in Florence."

"Well, it is in a private home for a reason. I suppose it is revolutionary. Hopefully a sign of the times to come," said Leonardo.

I took a step back but my heel slipped, and I fell on my butt. The culprit was a huge block of plaster.

"Congratulations on finding the cast," breathed Leonardo through fits of laughter.

I rubbed the small of my back tenderly as I sat up. Taking advantage of being down there, I grabbed one of the many papers tossed on the floor. It was one of many detailed studies of David's face and subtle smile.

"I think that's a copy of Donatello's hero," I said, tapping the plaster block with my foot.

"I agree," seconded Leonardo, who was sifting through the loose-leaf papers by Goliath's head. "That's strange."

"What is?"

"All of the writing on these pages looks like yours."

Tick-tock, tick-tock, tick-tock rang Idan. I jumped to my feet and snatched the sheet in Leonardo's hands.

"We need to go, Viola!" pressed Leonardo. My eyes scanned the scrawl of the paper. To my amazement, it was in English.

"How could it—"

Leonardo stole the paper away from me, grabbed my arm, and forced me through the side door.

Tick-tock-tick-tock-tick-tock! Idan quickened.

"We won't make it to the street in time," I warned. "He's almost here! Let's just hide behind the junk piles."

"We'll make it," he said, practically carrying me through the gate.

Pietro turned the corner just as the gate closed behind us. He looked up from his polished boots and locked eyes with me.

"Did you come to call on me?" said Pietro as we stood foolishly outside his house. "I had to step out a moment." He smiled.

"Uh ... no, we were just walking home," I mumbled, placing my palm over Idan.

"You were sorely missed after your chamber pot departure," said Pietro, rubbing his shaved head. "Which reminds me ... I never did get a look at that family heirloom of yours."

"Oh yes. Perhaps another day."

"Someday in the near future, I imagine," threatened Pietro over my shoulder. Once we were out of earshot, I told Leonardo about Sandro's visit and what he had said about Giuliano running after us.

"Do you think the cough we heard on the street may have been him?" I asked anxiously.

"We will never know ... I didn't see him or hear his footsteps behind us."

A shiver slithered up my spine at the thought of what Giuliano might have overheard. "Sandro said Lorenzo was incredibly angry."

"But you already suspected that?"

"Yes, but it's different when your worst fears are confirmed," I said.

"So you are worried?"

"That's an understatement," I replied as we swerved onto Via dei Benci. The sparks beyond glass windows smiled down at the strangers passing through the shadowy street.

"Do not start worrying until after Christmas."

"That is your comforting advice?"

"It is a good concession," he said. "The family will probably be too busy to even think about you between their services and parties. But after Christmas it will be business as usual," said Leonardo, scraping the muck off his shoes on a protruding stone.

"Meaning?"

"Then you can start worrying."

"Thanks," I muttered, grasping the door handle.

"Viola, I am not going to lie to make you feel better." He shrugged. "We'll figure something out between now and then. In the meantime, I'll send Renzo over in a bit to fetch you."

"All right," I said, resigned, moving to open Zia's door, but it would not budge. I knocked but no one answered.

"Viola!" called Zia from across the street.

She was chatting with Giulia in the doorway. The young woman rocked a baby in her arms while Zia pinched Luca's chubby cheeks. The scene of Zia with the happy baby reminded me of my promise to Margherita. Before Giulia vanished into her house, she waved at me.

"I'm sorry, my dear. Giulia had such a nice fire going that I really could not resist her offer. I completely lost track of time," she said, unlocking the rickety door. My body shook against the chilly air. I could feel all sorts of sand, wax, and clay glued to the rubber soles of my sneakers as I bent to start the fire.

"How is baby Luca?" I asked, arranging the wood in the pit.

"Heavenly! He is getting so fat." She beamed.

While my fingers struggled to kindle a spark, I wondered how to move forward with my plan for Margherita's baby. I knew that Zia alone would not be a good match, but perhaps with the help of a long-lost daughter, Margherita's baby might have a chance at a happy life.

"Zia?"

"Yes?"

"What would you do if someone gave you a baby?" I asked, blowing life into the flame that had caught on the twigs.

"What a question indeed!"

"I'm serious." Zia reached for the broom propped in the corner of the room.

"There is not much I could do," she said, her tiredness gathered in sacks around her eyes. "I'm almost seventy and have not the energy to raise a child."

"But you like babies!" I protested.

"I do," she agreed. I debated for several minutes trying to decide whether the time was right.

"Do you have any grandchildren?" The scraping of the broom's hard bristles on the tile made me cringe.

"No, I doubt very much whether Ginerva will ever be able to have a baby."

"Why?" I asked, excitement swelling inside me.

Zia leaned on the broom's pole for support, as if deciding whether she wanted to open that wound. "The marriage my husband had arranged for her was an unhappy one, and then she became so violently ill that we all thought she was dead. The doctor and the priest both pronounced her to be dead, but it turns out she wasn't."

"What?" I blurted out.

"She woke up in her husband's crypt." My teeth clenched tighter with every sweep of the broom. "She managed to return to her husband's house, but he thought her a spirit, so he sent her away. Then she came to her real home, this house," she continued, the wrinkles around her chin trembling. "It pains me to say that her father acted the same as her husband. He too thought she was a ghost that had come to haunt him."

"Were you awake when she came?"

"I woke up when my husband came back to bed, but he was struck with such a fear that he could not speak until the next morning."

"So what happened to her?"

"Ginerva went just down the street to Antonio's house. He opened the door for my poor sick child." Zia's voice cracked; her eyes glassy from the water that longed to leave them. "He waited on her and healed her back to health ... but most of all he nursed back the happiness that I had taken from her."

"So you saw her again?"

"Yes, at the hearing with the bishop. Ginerva wanted to annul her marriage so that she could marry Antonio."

"What was the verdict?"

"The bishop agreed to annul the marriage since her previous husband had pronounced her dead when in fact she was not." Zia stopped sweeping the already clean floor.

CHAPTER TWENTY-THREE

Christmas Eve

ZIA ABANDONED HER BROOM by a nearby chair. The oven's embers fought off the dark night. Zia set a pot to boil on the stove before heading into the pantry.

"Many need children to bring them their happiness ... My Ginerva is happy with her Antonio," she said, emerging with jars stuffed with chestnuts.

"But don't you think that the happiest child would come from parents so in love?" I asked.

"No doubt children could only add to their happiness," admitted Zia, throwing the chestnuts into the boiling water. "I can see these questions are leading somewhere. Do you mind telling me where?" Of course, she was right, but I did not want to reveal my intentions yet.

"Just curious." A soft knock interrupted Zia before she could probe further. The door opened.

"It is so cold out there," shivered little Renzo, rushing to the oven.

"To what do we owe this pleasant surprise?" asked Zia.

"Are those chestnuts?"

"They are."

"Oh, how I love chestnuts!" squeaked Renzo.

"Well, how lucky we are that you have come to call on us." Zia beamed. "But there will be no chestnuts for you until you wash your face."

"Can you bring the chestnuts to the workshop?" asked Renzo.

"Are you not having a feast of your own?"

"That is why I have come," he cleared his throat and pushed the reef of brown curls that fell across his eyebrows. "Master Verrocchio wanted me to invite and escort you and Viola to our Christmas Eve feast," he announced with an air of importance. Zia smiled with amusement at the gallant invitation, forgetting for a moment the woe she had just suffered.

"It is a little late," she said, glancing at the black window. "Tell me, Renzo, are we invited to enjoy the feast or to prepare and clean it up?"

Renzo's smile faltered but he found refuge in staring at the neat black boots that fastened around his ankles. "Both?"

"So I take it Margherita has started her labor," Zia said. Renzo's eyes bulged with quiet affirmation. "Viola, would you be so good as to grab two logs of salami and a jar of honey from the cupboard? Could you snuff out the fire Renzo? Mind you, do not ruin your lovely tunic."

He nodded dutifully before carrying out his task. Once the chestnuts cooled, she put them in a wicker basket. After all was in order, we set out onto the wintry path back to the workshop.

The fires that burned from within the neighboring windows cast an orange glow onto the smooth cobblestones. Stragglers hurried past us to get home for their feasts, and merry families moved quickly to their gatherings. Lonely lights from the Piazza della Signoria reminded us that guards were still on duty.

"Come, Viola," urged Zia, hurrying me past frosted roofs and balconies barricaded by icicles.

They reminded me of the ones my dad would snap off our own balcony. Every Christmas Eve, my family would eat turkey but with an array of immigrant twists. My dad would make cauliflower gratin, and my mom would make her risotto while Clara and I played games against the murmur of old Christmas movies. It panged me to remember it as I knew that those precious years of celebrating Christmas together had come and gone without me realizing how truly special they were.

"Has the midwife arrived?" asked Zia. The concern in her voice shook me from my melancholy daze. Verrocchio and Leonardo bent over what looked to be a chess game. The other workshop boys were grumbling from hunger or hovering over the shoulders of the two players.

"Yes, they are upstairs in the library," said Verrocchio, looking up from the match. Zia turned to the staircase and ordered me to begin preparing dinner.

"No, I want to see Margherita first," I protested.

After a short stop in the kitchen to drop off the food, I followed her up the steps. The scent and flicker of tallow candles seeped into the hallway from the cracked door. Upon entering the room, I was surprised to see how many women were quickly bustling about. The midwife, a hefty woman in her forties, shouted directions at her two daughters, who were either arranging neat piles of pristine sheets or pouring clean water into a basin.

A polished chair stood in the middle of the room. A wide round hole had been carved out of the seat's center. The dividers had been pushed back to conceal the stacks of books, converting the library into a hospital room. Zia chatted with the midwife while the daughters waited for further instructions.

Feverish groans gushed from Margherita's dry lips. She had her back propped up by feather pillows, and her skin was pasty white. Fear filled her wide blue eyes. Streams of sweat slid from her scalp and down her neck. I tried my best not to look alarmed at her frail condition.

Once she realized I was in the room, she called me forward. "Viola," she heaved, "did you find a good family for my baby?"

"Yes, of course. I told you I would," I said, peeling strands of hair from her hot cheeks. "I found a couple who can't have children but are happy and much in love."

"How nice that sounds," she said, closing her eyes.

"Can I get you anything?"

"Is Salai here?"

"I'm not sure." My jaw tightened in an attempt to hold back the emotion rising inside of me.

"I wish he was, even though I know I shouldn't ... Isn't that terrible?"

"Don't worry, he still might turn up!" I lied, trying to pacify the wave of anxiety swallowing her.

Her face contorted in pain while her fingers clenched together. I stroked her hair and hummed happy thoughts. She looked so young lying there. Her maturity and hard years usually masked her youth. It seemed so cruel that a girl of sixteen had to suffer so much pain.

"Viola, please follow me," Zia said, walking towards the entrance.

She shut the door behind me and proceeded to the kitchen. "We need to start supper." Although she listened patiently to my protests, she shook her head. "That room is far too small to hold so many people scampering about. Margherita needs space." The kitchen was warmer than usual because some hungry person thought they would get ahead of things and warm the stove.

"Did you make all this?" asked Zia, uncovering the large pots that sat on the burners.

"I wish," I said, cutting the cured salami meat. "Margherita prepared it yesterday."

"Bless her," she prayed, wiping her face with her handkerchief. "Well let us hurry and heat this up. If we finish in time, we can make mass at the Duomo."

"Can't I stay behind?"

"No ... she will be well taken care of and an extra body in the room would be a nuisance. You could help her much more through prayer."

My temper had reached its breaking point, and I was officially sick of people telling me what to do. Searching for an outlet, I ran into the courtyard. An icy gust tried to cool my temper while I stood ignoring Zia's words. I was shivering but didn't care. It was nothing compared to the pain that Margherita suffered. My ears perked up at the approaching footsteps.

"Now is not a good time, I promise."

"What is the matter?" asked Leonardo.

"I don't want to go to mass! I want to be in the library with Margherita."

"That makes the two of us."

"Are you serious?"

"Dead."

"Why?"

"What is happening up there is a miracle of science. I wish I could be there to record how it all happens ... and to support our dear Margherita, of course," he added after noticing my disgust.

"She is not a science experiment, Leo! What if something bad happens? There is no doctor here to help her. No hospital for an emergency."

"You do not have to tell me," retorted Leonardo, squaring his shoulders. "That is the way of it here. Midwives are very skilled in their profession. She is in good hands. By your skeptical tone, I imagine they do it differently where you come from."

"I think it is safer, at least in many parts."

"Why is that?"

"Because medicine is more advanced—"

"And how did it become so?" he snapped. "Through observation and study." He folded his arms. I parted my lips searching for a clever comeback, but nothing came. With only my bad mood for company, I left Leonardo in the courtyard.

When I came into the kitchen, Zia was serving the polenta and salty trout to the hungry boys. As everyone ate, I brooded in my corner. Although I was starving, I barely touched the food she served me.

Somehow, it did not seem right to eat the meal prepared by Margherita while she was suffering upstairs. There were only eight of us at the tables. The girls and the midwife took turns coming down to eat. Each one told of how well Margherita was doing.

"Such a young, strong girl should not have any trouble at all," they said, piling food into their mouths.

Once the last daughter had vanished upstairs, I interrupted the loud chewing and lip smacking. "Where is Salai?" The boys and Verrocchio himself shook their heads uncomfortably. "What a coward," I hissed, loud enough to make sure they heard me. Never in my life could I recall ever disliking someone so much.

"Andrea, you will clean the plates while Viola and I go to mass," announced Zia, fastening her cloak.

"Which mass?"

"At the Duomo. If anything should happen, send Renzo."

We rushed out of the workshop amidst lads arguing as to who would be the lucky one to clean the stack of dishes. Our feet soon joined the flock of devotees that rounded the corner of the Piazza del Duomo.

By the time we finally spilled into the cathedral, the nave and side aisles were bursting. We had to stand close together near the entrance of the Duomo. The bishop leading the mass was a speck in the distance. Thousands of candles glittered across the sea of people that chanted the prayers. The smoke of the musky incense swirled up towards the ceilings, adding itself to the layers of soot covering its painted surfaces.

I didn't really want to be there. I wasn't even sure what praying truly was. Shutting my eyes tight, I prayed so hard for Margherita and her baby that the moments under the domed cathedral felt like an instant. The occasional bump of the shoulder by a late arrival snapped me out of my meditative state.

"*Scusi! Scusi!*" repeated Leonardo as he pushed and hurled his way through the crowd. When he met my eyes, he did not stop but plunged forward into the mob with more determination.

"Zia..." I bent to whisper in her ear "...Leonardo is making his way to the front of the church." She stopped rubbing her rosary beads between her fingertips.

"Are you sure?"

"*Si*, he didn't stop to talk to me."

"Then we should wait for him outside ... we will need to hurry."

"Why? What's wrong?" I asked, treading carefully past our pious neighbors. Once we were out the golden doors, I knew something had gone terribly wrong. "Zia! Please tell me what's happening."

"I will not need to, sweet Viola," she said, staring at her rosary beads. Just then, Leonardo came out from behind the giant entrance.

"Leonardo! Tell me—" I cried. A young priest soon stepped from behind the door waiting for Leonardo's instructions.

"No time to explain, we have to run," pressed Leonardo as he and the priest took off at a sprint. Zia and I followed their wake at the quickest pace she could muster.

"I'm sorry, my dear, that I cannot move faster," she lamented. But her apology just made me sadder. In less than ten minutes, we were rushing over the workshop's threshold. A baby's cry echoed through the abandoned workshop. When we entered the room, one of the midwife's daughters rocked the baby. Verrocchio, Leonardo, and the priest loomed over Margherita.

"No!" I gasped. Suddenly, I realized what was happening.

The neat white piles of sheets had transformed to heaps of fabric soaked in scarlet. A jumble of instruments lay on a tray in a shallow murky puddle. The babe's cry had reached a high pitched scream. Zia and the midwife were trying to talk over its wail, and the priest was doing his best to compete with the tragic cacophony that filled the room. It took me a while before I was able to work up the courage to look at her. Margherita was losing so much blood that the sight of it made my knees buckle and my head dizzy.

When I reached the foot of the bed, Leonardo's hands were covering his mouth, but his eyes did not stray from Margherita's beautiful face.

While her neck stretched across the pillow, her lids rested over her frightened eyes. Blonde hair lay in a matted nest about her. I shivered as I witnessed her ivory skin turn gray. Death was slowly sucking the once precious life from her splintered lips. She mouthed something but no one heard her quiet plea. Verrocchio drew his ear close to hear her wishes.

"Viola, come quickly!" He moved aside, allowing me to squeeze to the side of her bed. I kissed her clammy hand and held her limp fingers in my own trembling ones.

"I want to see you hold her before I go," she breathed.

"Pass me the baby," I hollered over the noise. The baby girl was a beacon of life in a room shrouded in sorrow. Her scream calmed to a whimper in my arms.

"What shall we call her?" she asked

"How about Margherita?"

"A new beginning," she heaved. "With a happy couple in love." The tears that dripped down my face lost themselves in the baby's blanket.

"I'll always..." I looked up from little Margherita's pink skin, but her mother was gone.

CHAPTER TWENTY-FOUR

Milk

MY HEART BROKE. *WHAT a loving mother she would have been if only the world had been less cruel*, I thought as one of the midwife's daughters took the baby from my arms.

The midwife swaddled the baby with the only clean linen left while the others cleaned up the debris of childbirth. The acrid smell of blood hung in the room, and the taste of metal lingered in my mouth. It was impossible for me to stay, but I knew that once I left it would all be real. The hope I had clung to the entire wretched night would be dashed. Worse than that, one of the few friends I had would turn into another painful memory.

Once I finally moved, I was the only one left in the room. I wanted to kiss her goodbye but the fear of death that infects so many suddenly forced me from the room. Zia and Verrocchio blocked the hallway as they discussed the miserable situation.

Little Margherita had fallen asleep and was being rocked by Zia. "So the father wants nothing to do with the babe?"

"He has yet to admit he fathered the child." Verrocchio grimaced. "And you have such a scoundrel in your employment, Andrea?" retorted Zia.

"He was himself abandoned as a lad ... perhaps he knows no better."

"So what are we to do with the babe? Does Margherita have any family?"

"No, she was left at the Ospedale delgi Innocenti," explained Verrocchio. "I am sad to say she has no one."

"It appears she will have to share the same beginning as her mother."

"No!" I protested. They both exchanged wary looks as I entered their conversation. "She will have a different beginning. That's what her mother wanted."

"Viola, I'm not sure you understand. Yes, it is an orphanage, but there she is sure to never lack for food or warmth. They have an army of wet nurses and nuns that will take good care of her. For a little girl who does not have a family, she will be protected and educated," said Verrocchio.

"You mean taught how to sew, clean, and cook?" I interjected bitterly, but he ignored my outburst.

"When the babe grows up, she can decide either to become a nun or get married. If she decides to marry, they even help secure a dowry for her."

"So those will be her options, a nun or a wife?"

"She could also set out to find work on her own," said Verrocchio, trying just as hard to convince himself.

"Like Margherita?" I asked biting my lip.

"What would you have me do, Viola?" he spat. "It is not that I am indifferent. I feel partially responsible for this catastrophe. Not to mention I cared for Margherita a great deal," he confessed, rubbing his eyes on his dusty sleeves.

"I would have you give me little Margherita for a few days while I try to find her a family that will take good care of her."

"You will have a tough time of it," warned Verrocchio.

"That might be true, but I have to try ... I promised her mother I would give her a new beginning, not the same one, and especially not the same ending."

"Sweet Viola, I admire you for wanting to fulfill your promise but—"

"But what?" I interrupted Zia.

"Well, correct me if I am wrong, but you do not know the first thing about caring for a baby."

"That is true ... but you do."

"When this baby wakes up, she will be very hungry and we have no means of feeding her." I thought for a moment on this and paused to admire the wonders of modern-day baby formula.

"What about Giulia?" I asked triumphantly.

"I don't think she will take her. She already has a contract for Luca, and she has her own baby girl."

"Why are you both so determined for this to fail?" I yelled, no longer able to cap my feelings. Although the hallway was dark, I could see the pity in their eyes.

"Margherita entrusted a small savings to me. You are welcome to take it, but I'm afraid it will be just enough for some clothes after you pay Giulia for a few days of work," he said before disappearing upstairs to his living quarters.

"I'm sorry, my dear, I know you are upset. We all want what we think is best. Would you hold her?" she asked, carefully laying the baby in my arms. "I'm afraid that I am attached already."

When Verrocchio returned, he handed Zia a small drawstring bag and a blanket. "I will take care of the funeral arrangements. Renzo will call on you shortly to tell you where the ceremony will be held."

Zia nodded and led the way downstairs. Before we braved the frosty night, she meticulously wrapped the baby with the woolen blanket. It was not until we turned the street corner that I realized we were walking under the early morning's twilight. The stones were slippery with drops of the impending dawn. The sky was clear but grew pale as we walked towards Via dei Benci. It was a slow pace, but Zia was happy to oblige.

"I have never seen anyone die before," I said.

"Bless you, child," she said in between puffs of breath. "It is one of life's reminders of how swift it all can be."

"Life?"

"Time," she said, turning onto our street.

"I hope she is awake," I said as we approached Giulia's house. The windows were still dark when we knocked on her door.

Margherita was still sleeping but I could feel her squirming restlessly beneath the layers of fabric. It took a few moments before any signs of life came from the house. Above we could see Giulia's long red hair peek out of the window. Soon the locks twisted open, and we were ushered into the house.

"Are you both all right?" asked Giulia, surveying us.

It was clear we had woken her. The stamp of sheet folds still clung to her right cheek. Her eyes watered as they struggled to widen. Giulia's house was warm even in the absence of a fire. Like Zia's, the house was neat, but her furnishings were finer. The polish of the wooden table and empty crib gleamed even in the low light. A tidy pile of clean kitchen towels waited on a nearby table. I instantly recalled the pristine towels piled in Margherita's room before they dripped with blood.

"Yes. We are fine and so sorry to wake you," said Zia. Giulia tightened the shawl around her shoulders and stifled a yawn.

"So tell me, what brings you and your niece—" Her words faltered when she noticed my bundle.

"My friend, she ..." I tried. The lump in my throat swelled as I fought to find the words to explain what had happened only a few hours ago. How could I express the terrible evening and all the anguish it had brought? Zia saved me from relating the desperate circumstances that brought us to her doorstep.

"And so we were hoping that you would take this babe on for three days or so," said Zia cautiously. "Just until we find the little girl a family."

Giulia glanced at Margherita with a sad smile. She stepped back pulling nervously at her thick red hair. "I really cannot. I have a contract with a good family and my own little girl," said Giulia. "If they found out …" Margherita's movements became more restless. Her eyes blinked lazily as her mouth gaped at the sweet and sour milky scent that perfumed the room.

"Please, Giulia! We can pay you and it would only be for two days, not even three," I begged. My arms felt tingly and sore under the weight of Margherita.

The cry started as a whimper then transcended into a high wail. I tried to rock her in my aching arms, but the cry worsened. The baby's pink face was desperate. Giulia was looking around her cozy home, clearly conflicted. Without further hesitation, she unbuttoned her nightgown and took Margherita from my arms. Zia left the bag of modest savings on the table and guided me towards the entrance. The bawling had stopped. Before the door closed behind us, I whispered my gratitude to her back while she fed Margherita. Zia fumbled with the key to open the front door.

"Why did you tell her two days when you really have no idea how long it will actually take?" asked Zia.

"Because I am taking her tomorrow or the day after to her new family," I said, stepping through the front door.

"So what makes you think that this family you have in mind will take the baby?"

"Because of what I have been told about them … and I know they can't have children of their own, so I'm sure one baby would be more welcome than none."

Zia's wrinkled frown and forehead told me she understood my plan. "And when were you going to share your plan with me?"

"After the baby was born?" I said, not even sure what the real answer was. The plan had sort of unraveled on its own.

"How do you expect to get to Vinci?" It was hard to say whether she was excited or anxious about my brilliant plan.

"I was going to ask Leonardo to take me since he is from there," I said, making up my mind as the conversation progressed. Zia did not respond to this. Instead, she stood with her hands on her hips, staring absently into the empty hearth.

"And what if they cannot afford a baby? I have no idea of how they are living in Vinci," said Zia, keeping her eyes fixed on the ashes. Long silent minutes stretched by before the solution came to me.

"I'll sell my dress."

"The Medici gift?"

"Didn't you say it was exceptionally fine?"

"I did." She raised her eyebrows. "Get some sleep before Renzo comes. You will need it if you expect to travel." Zia relinquished her resolute pose to resume her needlework. Halfway up the stairs, it occurred to me that Zia had not really mentioned anything about my plan.

"Do you think she will take Margherita?" I asked.

"I couldn't say," she said, pulling the ebony thread through the taut linen. "I don't really know who she is anymore."

CHAPTER TWENTY-FIVE

White

SOON AFTER RESTING MY head on the pillow, sleep came to visit me. It held my hand for a while and whispered comforting clichés. It told me how everything would turn out all right and how good time is at healing all wounds. As quickly as it had come, it left. Slumber abandoned me before I could argue, and I awoke with a start. The terrible adrenaline that had kept me functional had now dulled to the pain. If I closed my eyes and tried to identify the feeling, it would slip away. Something else was lurking behind the ache. Was it fear?

"I think it is," I said to the sweet portrait of the Virgin Mary and child that hung at the foot of my bed.

Perhaps the feeling was more tangible now that I knew that on top of my grief I was scared, too. *But of what exactly?* I wondered, pulling the darkest dress I had over my head. Once I had filled the basin with icy water, I grabbed the soap and worked it into a lather around my face and neck. The rooster crowed while I splashed water on my skin and watched bubbles form a film on the basin's surface. *Probably death,* I thought, patting away the dampness with a dry cloth. It was an inevitable end that I always avoided thinking about.

When I was five, I had a rollerblading accident. My older sister dared me to roll down a steep hill near my grandfather's house. I didn't want to do it, but I also didn't want to lose my nerve in front of her crew of friends, so I did it. The six wheels spun me down the hill at a frightening speed. Not really knowing how to use the rubber brake, I shut my eyelids tight and hoped for the best. The curb hurled my body across a summer green lawn. I walked away with only a few scratches on my knees and face. It was not until I was in the bathroom washing off the dry blood that I experienced the fear for the first time. I remember staring in the mirror and counting the years I might have left to live. For the first time, that naked, terrified five-year-old was coming to terms with her own mortality. By the time I got to the impressive number of ninety-three, I shrugged my shoulders and decided to worry about it later. Well, ten years had passed, and it was "later."

With time on my mind, I checked Idan's countdown. "Four days," I breathed. That was how many days I had left in Florence, and how few I had to find Margherita a family. Earlier, when I had closed the door of Giulia's house behind me, I made a pact with myself. I would be strong until the baby was happy in the arms of her new mother. Then I could fall to pieces, but not before.

Not wanting to be alone anymore, I hid Idan under my dress and went downstairs to the kitchen. Zia had fallen asleep at the table. A fresh pang of sympathy struck me. Zia stirred at the squeak of my sneakers on the tile floor.

"Renzo will be here soon," she said in a muffled voice.

"Why didn't you go to your room to sleep?" I asked.

Zia ignored my question by posing one of her own. "Are you hungry?"

"Hungry?" The sound of the word triggered a groan from my insides. Zia moved to get up but I told her to stay seated.

Four of Georgina's eggs were frying in a pool of olive oil when Renzo knocked at the door. He slumped into the house shielding his puffy eyes with his hat. He sat on the cool tile with his palms raised towards the oven's fire.

"Would you like some too?" I asked the sad boy crumpled by the hot embers.

The sight of his wet face softened my resolve to be tough. Quickly looking away, I cracked two more eggs into the iron pan. We ate to satisfy our stomachs with only the snivels of Renzo's runny nose for conversation. Once the breadcrumbs and dried yolk were cleaned up, we took up our march to the church where Margherita's funeral would be held.

The sun warmed my back and my spirit despite my determination to be gloomy. It was only a few minutes before our path diverged from Via dei Benci. Our feet carried us across Santa Croce's stone plaza. The echo of the giddy excitement I felt just days ago recoiled off the phantom balconies surrounding the piazza. Families with cheerful smiles walked past us carrying trays laden with creamy pastries and sausage links hung over their shoulders. The basilica's jagged stone facade covered us in shadow as we climbed the low steps. Since the rough exterior was so similar to San Lorenzo's, I almost expected the grandeur that waited for me within. The ceiling's nest of painted beams momentarily relieved my misery. An ethereal light and air radiated from the lofty stained-glass windows as we walked down the broad nave. The massive piers that flanked us supported the pointed arches that housed the side aisle's chapels. While we made our way to the east end, my curiosity devoured the ornately painted niches.

"Oh my God!" I said, breaking the hazy fumes of incense.

"Shhh, Viola! How many times must I tell you not to take His name in vain?" warned Zia.

"It's Christmas," I said, staring at the nativity scene we were approaching.

"Of course ... Yesterday was Christmas Eve, don't you remember?" She stopped to feel my forehead.

"I forgot," I said, gently removing her hand. It was true that I could be forgetful, but I had never forgotten Christmas. Finely carved statues played against a landscape of painted fabrics.

"It is a pretty scene," she said, following my gaze. "Saint Francis of Assisi started this wonderful tradition. I suppose it is fitting that you see it in a Franciscan church," she observed.

Before we could reach the figurines of Mary, Joseph, and the barn animals, Renzo veered towards the right. We followed him down the transept of the church until we reached the foot of a chapel.

Workshop boys flanked the few steps that fell from the jewel-like sanctuary. Their heads hung limp and their backs leaned against its painted walls. Feet huddled around the cold remains of the warm Margherita. She lay on a wooden slab with thick handles at each corner. Her long blonde hair brushed to her waist. It looked golden against the stark white dress that dropped off the sides of the stiff bed. I forced myself to look on her, and in turn, on death. I had not known Margherita for long, but my affection for her ran deep. My sadness sprung from knowing that such a sweet soul had been ripped so violently from this world.

Although I did not know every boy's name that stood around me, I recognized their faces and the sound of their voices. It only took me a quick glance around at the brilliant walls to see that everyone was there, except Salai. Rage rose from the surface of my thoughts while the same young priest from the night before preached words of forgiveness. No longer being able to look on Margherita's ashen skin, I searched the painted walls that surrounded us.

The narrow, colored glass behind the priest had been precisely pieced together to form portraits of holy figures. The blue backdrop of the saintly strangers dimmed the sunshine that lit the chapel. Every surface and crevice of its walls were richly painted. The ribbed ceiling that stretched above us shone with constellations of lead white stars against a lapis lazuli sky. Vines of flowers sprawled from the center of the ceiling and down the vault's skeleton. The painted walls told stories through their frescoes.

Normally, I would have asked Leonardo about the murals, but he was standing next to Verrocchio near the priest. *What brought all these portraits, paintings, and stained glass together under one altar?* I wondered.

When I looked at a painting where the Virgin Mary was presenting Jesus to the shepherds, it dawned on me that all the images appeared to relate to Mary's life. I was admiring the softness of the figures' bodies and drapery when the sound of a beautiful instrument brought me back to the funeral. Leonardo was playing something that looked like a violin but was wider at the top where his fingers pressed at the seven strings. A soprano's voice sang from within the crowded chapel. Renzo's song cracked among the beautiful words that rang out from his lips.

> To the low light and the ring of shade I have come, and to the snow-
>   ing hills.
> There is where we see the colorless meadow. Nevertheless, my long-
>   ing remains green as It has taken root in the heart of stone.
> Wholly frozen is this blossoming lady, Even as the white that lies
>   within the dark. For she is no more alive than is the stone By the
> sweet spring which warms the hills And paints them anew from
> white to jade
> Casing their sides once more with flowers and grass.
> When on her mane she sets a crown of leaves The mind has no spare
> thoughts for another lady, Because she weaves the sunshine
> with the grass.
> How does that lady love lie down there in the dark–
> Love has imprisoned me within those low hills.

She is brighter than the most precious gem And the wounds she left
    behind may not be healed. I therefore have fled far from prairies
    and mounds.
But from her brightness nothing may hide– Not behind any peak,
    nor barrier, nor spring-green.

When the song finished, I peered around at the new crowd that had
gathered on the outskirts of the chapel. From their looks, I could tell
that the choice of song was peculiar, but for those that remembered her,
it was perfect. Boys began to shove each other for the honor of lifting
Margherita out of Santa Croce. They carried her with great pride while
they navigated the mass of people trying to see if they knew the girl
whose hair and dress flowed gracefully out into the air. I fell to the back
of the procession that moved up one of the side aisles, wiping my face
with my long sleeves.

Before I was able to step out into the afternoon, a hand grasped my
shoulder and pulled me into the shadow. Startled, I tried to scream but
a hand anticipated it and hushed me. The ringed fingers that waved in
front of me belonged to Lorenzo de' Medici. Terror coursed through me.

"No need to be frightened, Viola," said Lorenzo with such sincerity
that my limbs stopped shaking. He straightened his red hat before he
politely said, "I am sorry for your loss. She must have been quite a lovely
girl to deserve a funeral like that."

"She was," I replied.

"I do not mean to interfere with your mourning, but I am going
away today for a few days and this was my only chance to ... talk to you."
It was then that I noticed his unusually humble traveling cloak. "I came
to extend an invitation to you," he said kindly.

"I'm sorry, Signore Medici, but I don't think—" I started. The rubbing sound of leather that came from his clenching fists signaled the
dramatic change in his demeanor.

"How do I put this?" he said, taking a step back to collect his composure. "Let us be honest with each other ... you know what I want," his gaze clung to the chain around my neck. "I am a persistent man, and I am aware of the fact that you are attached to your heirloom. But I assure you I intend to use it for purely academic purposes."

"Excuse me, sir, but I need it to—"

"Go back home?" He snickered.

I struggled to hide my shock. The curl of his mouth confessed he knew my secret. The letters' warnings echoed in my mind.

"How about we try again?" He paused to scratch his crooked nose. "I would be most pleased if you could grace me with your presence at the Signoria at sunset three days hence." The sarcasm that played in his invitation made it clear this was an order and not an invitation. "I will expect you in the entrance hall," he said, moving out of the shadows. "I forgot to mention, in the unlikely event that you do not show up or have another chamber pot emergency ... Well, let us just say it would be best for everyone if that were not to happen," he said before stepping beyond Santa Croce's threshold.

CHAPTER TWENTY-SIX

Charm

MINUTES PASSED AS I stood at the basilica's entrance feeling the frosty breeze numb my ears. *What was I going to do?* I panicked against the murmured psalms.

"Viola?"

"Yes?" I broke my concentration.

"Are you all right?" asked Leonardo.

"No." I looked down at my dirty sneakers, wishing I could click them together and miraculously fly home.

"I just saw Lorenzo leave, and I thought something happened." After I reenacted the entire conversation, Leonardo shook his head. "He must have heard our conversation and believed the part when you rambled something about time travel."

"If only he thought I was as crazy as you do."

"Not crazy ... just lost. We will come up with something. In the meantime, do not trouble yourself until we cross that bridge."

"Aren't we already standing in front of it? It's not an ordinary bridge. But the hanging kind that ropes together two mountaintops with a deadly drop in between," I said, trying to get a grip on my hysteria.

"You forgot to tell me about your plan to go to Vinci." Leonardo crossed his arms. In my desperate search for a plan, I had forgotten to tell the only person who could help me with it. "Zia just told me, and I pretended as if you and I had plotted it together."

"Thank you." I sighed. "I was going to tell you, but with Margherita … the baby … I'm not sure if I would even call it a plan. I've just been making it up as I go along."

"Zia has left to sell something to a secondhand clothes dealer. I'm not sure how lucky she will get, it being Christmas and all."

"She left without me?"

"Yes."

"Did she say anything?" I asked.

"No, because I told her you would be coming with me to dine with my father."

"I am?"

"Certainly. You will charm him until he is ripe for the picking. Then I will ask him to lend us his horse to travel to Vinci."

"I am not sure how charming I can be," I said, slumping my shoulders.

"With talk like that we will be walking to Vinci," he said, leading me out of the Santa Croce. The air around the piazza was crisper than it had been the day of the joust.

"What about Margherita?" I asked, looking around the piazza.

"They are arranging for her burial now." Leonardo frowned. Maybe it was because it was Christmas or that underneath our superficial layer, we were miserable, but everyone who walked past us seemed too happy.

"By the way, you never told me you knew how to play an instrument!" I said, trying to lighten the mood. Leonardo blushed. "What is that instrument called?" I pointed to the case strapped over his shoulder.

"It is called a Lyra de Baccio."

"I didn't know you liked music," I said as we moved around herds of families on their way to mass. "Do you play anything else?" I asked when we reunited.

"A bit."

"That means a lot, right?"

"I have some ideas for different instruments," he said as we walked into Piazza della Signoria.

"To create new ones or alter ones that already exist?"

"Both," he said, turning onto Via della Prestanze. Leonardo stopped short of a door situated under a round arch. The wall that butted it belonged to the Palazzo della Signoria. Leonardo grabbed the metal rings attached to the entrance and knocked. One of the doors groaned.

"*Buonasera*, Leonardo," said a housemaid.

"*Buonasera*, Maria."

"I don't know if your father is expecting you," said the girl. She was young in figure alone; her face looked more worn than Zia's.

"That sounds about right," said Leonardo, widening the gap in the door. "Could you set two more places for supper?" He handed her our cloaks. "Is my stepmother at home?"

"*Sì*."

"And my father?"

"In the hall."

"This way, Viola," signaled Leonardo, taking the steps in giant leaps.

The ceiling rose high above us as he led me into the den. Tapestries of feasts and flowers hung against the stone walls. Ser Piero sat on an elegant cherry wooden chair engrossed in a book. A fire crackled near his upholstered footstool. On the opposite side of the room was a long dining table set with silver candelabras. Ser Piero looked up from his book at the sound of our approaching footsteps.

"What a surprise!" He beamed, welcoming Leonardo with arms spread wide.

"What are you reading?" asked Leonardo, examining the book in his father's hands.

"It is about astronomy," answered Piero. His son shook his head disapprovingly.

"And it is in Latin?" said Leonardo as if it couldn't have gotten any worse.

"Have you said hello to your stepmother?" asked Ser Piero, while I admired the ceramics sitting on the mantelpiece.

"Not yet," said Leonardo.

"Go check on her, then." Leonardo dutifully left to greet his stepmother.

"Do you like those?" asked Ser Piero. I mulled over how I was supposed to charm someone who was already so enchanting.

"They are beautiful."

"They were made by my mother. They are quite good, are they not?"

"Very, signore." He looked me over trying, to politely unravel my situation.

"Would you like to see something?" I nodded. He walked over to a finely carved chest and from it withdrew a leather folder. As he moved closer to me, he untied the folder's knotted straps. "These are the drawings I showed Verrocchio before Leonardo became an apprentice," he explained, turning the pages tenderly. It was startling how naturalistic the drawings were.

"How old was he when he drew these?" I asked.

"I think there is a mixture here, but somewhere between twelve to fifteen years of age," he said, pausing on a drawing of a kite.

"They are amazing."

"I thought so too." He grinned proudly. "But to make sure, I wanted to show them to Verrocchio. Once I did, he wouldn't let me leave until I promised to let him take on Leonardo as an apprentice." Most of the drawings were studies of insects, animals, or flowers. "After my

first wife and father died, Leonardo and I moved to Florence. In the beginning, it was difficult for him. He was extremely fond of them both.
Growing up in the country didn't help."

The sound of approaching footsteps from beyond the den reached
us. Piero quickly went to place the drawings back in their hiding place.
Maria strode under the doorframe carrying two more place settings.

"That must have been hard for you and him."

"I had already been doing work in Pisa as a notary. So moving to
Florence was not much different. Nevertheless, it was a great loss to our
family. Slowly our situation has improved," he said, clasping his hands
behind his back. "Now for instance! You are the first friend he has ever
introduced me to."

"*Allora?*"

"Indeed," he stressed.

The silence stretched as I recalled how often my dad had complained
about something similar. At least once a month he would remind me
that we were both not allergic to people and that if I invited a friend
over, he would promise not to embarrass me.

"You have a lovely home, signore."

"Thank you," he said with a slight bow of his head. "I told Leonardo
he is welcome to come and go as he pleases, but it seems he is more
comfortable in the workshop." He motioned for me to sit down in the
chair opposite his. It was easy to see who Leonardo got his easy manners from, as I took in his warm smile.

"Well, I wouldn't take it personally, sir. It's probably because all the
other boys stay at the workshop."

"Perhaps." He stared at me, and I looked away from his eyes, busy-
ing myself with the spines of books that were stacked on a nearby table.
"What appears to be certain is that you have a kind heart, Viola."

"Thank you," I said, trying to maintain a normal skin shade.

"Sometimes, I worry whether Leonardo will ever forgive me," he said.

The sudden confessional tone of our conversation caught me off guard. Leonardo had said to be charming, so I tried to think of one of my mom's witty anecdotes that she would say to dinner guests. Yet none seemed helpful. The arrival of a young woman escorted by Leonardo interrupted Ser Piero's confession. She was sickly thin and about a head shorter than me with lips stuck in a constant pucker.

"This must be Viola," she said, barely moving her mouth. As she approached me, she waved her beige gown back and forth emphasizing the gold thread that made the fabric shimmer. "Leonardo was just telling me all sorts of wonderful things about you." Her eyes darted between me and Ser Piero.

"Good things, I hope," I replied. She looked to be about my older sister Clara's age, and at least half the age of Ser Piero.

"My love, our family has just arrived, shall I tell them to enter?"

"Please do."

"I am sorry for our unexpected visit," I said, realizing they had guests.

"Nonsense," replied Ser Piero.

The guests soon spilled in, and their voices filled the broad room. The whole family was a jolly party. Each one took my hand and introduced themselves in Italian so fast I could barely keep up. When we sat down to the Christmas feast of roasted fowl and sautéed mushrooms, Leonardo sat on my left side and one of the relatives on my right. The supper that covered the table sat on creamy linen and red velvet. Sage steamed from the hot platters. Before we ate, Ser Piero led us in a long prayer that left more than one person licking their lips in hungry anticipation.

"Amen," he concluded, and so the gentle race for the best bits began. Leonardo looked quite content to have his plate of fried eggs piled with mushrooms.

"Is he ripe yet?" asked Leonardo. A few pieces of egg white hung from his mustache.

"I think you should clean your face first."

"No!" he protested, licking the corners of his mouth. "That is for seconds," he smiled before wiping his face on the purple napkin. "You have to look like you're listening to us, agreed?"

"Agreed." While Leonardo turned to his father, I perked my head forward.

"Papa?" interrupted Leonardo. His father's shake of the head hinted he already knew what we were about.

"Son? What is it you want?"

"I just wanted to tell you that I miss Grandma and Uncle Francesco." His father raised his eyebrows at this. "When are you going to Vinci next?"

Ser Piero took a sip of red wine. "Not for another month or so."

"That is too long ... I have been telling Viola all about the farm and she is eager to see it."

"When did you want to go?"

"Tomorrow?" Ser Piero was in danger of spitting out his wine. "Viola and I get a few free days from the workshop ... so I wanted to take advantage."

"Viola!" interrupted Ser Piero. "Have you tried the pigeon?"

"Umm ..." I winced at the thought of eating something that in New York City were regarded as rats with wings.

"You really must. It is Maria's specialty."

"Please, Papa, don't avoid the question."

"I knew it," said Ser Piero, tearing off a piece of ciabatta.

"Knew what?"

"You only come to visit me when you need something."

"That is not true," protested Leonardo. "I know you are busy, and I do not want to get in your or Francesca's way.

"You mean your mother's way," corrected Ser Piero.

"Sure." A silence soon ensued, which lasted until dessert was served.

Meanwhile, I was debating what I should say between mouthfuls of tangy custard.

"Leonardo, be a good lad and play us something," Ser Piero broke in.

"You know I don't like playing for strangers," muttered Leonardo.

"And I don't like taking my horse out of the stables on such short notice. In any case, they are not strangers but family."

Leonardo grumbled all the way to what looked like a guitar but with an oval drum propped against the wall. The guests quieted as Leonardo tuned the strings to his liking. He took a deep breath and stroked the instrument's chords.

Oh lovely Rosa
My sweet spirit
Do not abandon me to parish
In princely love
Nay abandon me
To torment, I who am
Forced to wait and be faithful
Save me now
From my heartache Rose of my heart
Do not leave me in pain

Leonardo led the party through another chorus before he put down the instrument. My mouth was dry despite the oily custard that rolled around my mouth.

"Have you heard that song before?" asked Ser Piero. I shook my head. "It's called 'O Rosa Bella.' It is one of Johannes Ciconia's most famous works."

Leonardo took his place again amidst the dying applause. "Why are you looking at me like that?"

"Like what?"

"Like I still have egg white hanging from my incredibly masculine facial hair?"

"You're just full of surprises."

"I could have told you that." He winked. It was not long before it was impossible to control my yawn. "Shall we?" said Leonardo, pivoting his head towards the door. We both stood and rounded the table with lots of "grazies" and "Merry Christmas." Once we arrived at Francesca and Ser Piero, we stopped.

"The horse will be ready and saddled at daybreak." He kissed his son on both cheeks.

"*Grazie*, Papa."

"Thank you ..." I added, unable to voice how grateful I truly was.

"Say goodbye to your mother, too."

"I will," said Leonardo.

Our mood on the way home could not have been more different. This one bright triumph shone a light on what had been a dark day. With the piazza and streets abandoned, we practically danced towards Via dei Benci, and I only tripped a few times on the slick stones.

"I will pick you up in front of the house, so be ready," he ordered before heading back to the workshop.

"Yes, sir!" I called after him.

I deliberated in the damp night whether I should visit Giulia and Margherita. The glow from within the cozy house concealed itself behind thick curtains. My hand was already on the metal knocker when Zia whistled. I turned around to see her short frame outlined by the fire's brightness. She waved her arm in a hurried motion, beckoning me to cross the street.

For the first time, it was hot in the house. Usually, I could see my breath evaporate in front of me, but that night we enjoyed a blaze kings could only boast. Zia bustled about preparing a bag and a large basket. Though she was not smiling, I could feel her excitement.

"I got a small fortune for your dress, Viola. There will be plenty for a wet nurse and clothes.   I used some to buy some extra firewood in case Ginerva decides to visit." My heart melted at the notes of hope in her voice.

"What a good idea."

"This bag has apples and calzones for your trip," she said, pointing to a burlap sack.

"What's that?" I pointed to a woolen blanket tied in an elaborate knot.

"That is for Margherita," she added cheerfully. "You weren't expecting to hold her the whole way. Your arms would fall off."

"How long is the trip?"

"It depends on the horse and how fast you go ... but since you have two people and a baby you will need to travel at a slower pace."

"So how long?"

"If you leave at dawn you should get there by midday."

"Oh!" I said surprised by the long journey.

"I talked to Giulia. She promised to feed Margherita until she was good and full. So hopefully she will sleep the whole journey," she said. "If she wakes up, she will be hungry, and your long journey will seem an eternity."

CHAPTER TWENTY-SEVEN

Rosa

THE BLANKET OF PALE yellow that covered navy skyline signaled dawn's arrival. It was a chilly morning but the heat from last night's fire lingered through the small house. Zia was cooking a medley of cream, honey, and leftover chestnuts. The nutty fragrance that wafted from the pot gradually lifted the spirits of the small kitchen. A jumble of different sized sacks waited to be packed onto the horse. I fidgeted with Idan as I stood by the window waiting for a sign of Leonardo. Zia's sudden change in attitude towards my Vinci scheme invigorated my confidence in it. My heart lightened at the prospect of being relieved of Margherita's heavy charge.

"Shall I go get Margherita?" I asked.

"I dare say you will have her long enough. Let her rest," said Zia. I was nervous about meeting Ginerva and the Medici rendezvous.

My nerves were as raw as they had been when my parents separated. Everything someone said or did around me would mingle with the turmoil fermenting inside me. That was how I felt, vulnerable. Zia moved quickly around the kitchen, finishing breakfast. In the past week, Zia had shed decades off her age. When I first arrived in Florence and peered up at her from the kitchen table, she looked as though she would not see next year. Now, as she hummed a tune that sounded a lot like the one that Leonardo had sung the night before, she looked rejuvenated. Even the scar that engraved her cheek was lighter in the early morning sun.

"Is that, *Oh Lovely Rosa?*" I asked.

"Yes ... how do you know it?"

"Leonardo sang it to his father's guests last night." The sound of horseshoes pacing against the cobblestones interrupted us.

I went to open the door for Leonardo. He was leaning forward on top of the copper horse and whispering sweet nothings in its pointed ears.

"You're late."

"I was just being considerate. Didn't want to make you feel bad for being behind," he teased, sliding down from the horse.

"You look like a regular cowboy." I laughed as he tied up the horse's reins to a metal ring embedded in the house's wall.

"A what?"

"It's a guy who is really good with animals or works with them on a farm," I explained, but Leonardo did not look convinced. "They are very ..."

"Resourceful?"

"Yes!"

"You forgot to add incredibly handsome to that description."

"Oh, you mean the horse?" I replied.

"That is precisely what I meant," he said, stroking the horse's long muscular neck.

"She is handsome and tall."

"Almost sixteen hands ... a long way to fall," he added, catching my hesitation.

"What kind of horse is it?"

"A mutt, but mostly a Maremmano."

"What's her name?"

"Rosa." The horse's hair was paler around her muzzle.

"After the song?" I asked. Leonardo nodded, taking out a handful of chopped carrots from his cloak. "That's why you chose to sing that song last night?"

"Oh lovely Rosa ... my sweet spirit," serenaded Leonardo. Rosa's black mane shook and her long tail swished.

"What are you up to out here?" called Zia. "Your breakfast is getting cold." While we ate the chestnut porridge, Zia placed an envelope on the table. "I want you to give this to Ginerva."

"Who wrote it for you?" I asked.

"Yesterday, while you were out, I called on Signore Soldo, and he helped me piece it together," she said. "I was anxious about the whole thing, but I felt better after the letter was done."

"What does it say?"

"To trust you and it talks about the baby's mother and well..." her bottom lip quivered, "...it tries to explain as best words can ... how sorry I am and how much I miss her."

The letter doubled the pressure that I already felt on my shoulders. Not only did I need to find Margherita a home, but I was also attempting to reunite a family that had been feuding for years.

"I will, Zia," I said, tucking the letter into my satchel.

Leonardo sniffled as he busied himself with loading Rosa. Once I stood up, Zia slipped the woolen sling over my head and shoulder.

"Be careful on the road and keep those eyes of yours sharp. There can be nasty people about the road," she warned.

The wind pressed against me as we crossed the street to Giulia's house. The door opened before we reached it. Margherita was snoozing in Giulia's arms. In only a few days, her face had changed. The red apples of her cheeks popped against her stark white skin and her crown of hair stood up on its ends.

"She will have lovely ringlets," said Giulia, tenderly touching the soft hair. "Never have I held such a gentle babe." Her eyes were puffy and the network of vessels that surround her blue pupils burned.

"I'm sorry you were dragged into this, Giulia," I said.

"I was hesitant to take her on because I get so attached to them." Tears trailed down her freckles.

"You have loved and cared for Margherita when the baby girl needed it most," added Zia, wiping Giulia's face with fingers. "May God always smile on you."

Giulia carefully placed Margherita into the sling's nook. "She just fell asleep. Mind you she has eaten enough for three. She shouldn't need another feeding for several hours. If she wakes, just rock her best you can."

"Thank you Giu—" I said as she escaped behind the door.

Zia placed her hand on my shoulder. "Don't worry, she'll be fine in a day or two."

"We must get going before it gets too late," said Leonardo, placing a kitchen chair by Rosa.

"Be careful, child!" cautioned Zia. Holding onto the warm babe at my chest, I stepped up on the chair.

"What are you waiting for?" asked Leonardo.

"I've never been on a horse before."

"How strange you are!" he laughed stepping on the chair. "Turn around slowly." Leonardo's sweet breath warmed my nose. He put his hands around my waist. "I'm going to lift you on three. Hold on to Margherita ... Three!" He heaved me onto the leather saddle. Once I regained my balance, I kicked my left leg over the other side.

"Viola! What are you doing?" exclaimed Zia. Leonardo grinned as he pulled himself onto the horse.

"What did I do?"

"You can't ride like that! It is highly indecent for a woman."

"It was hard enough to get on here. I'm not changing my position ... It's not fair that men get to ride this way and women can't."

"Go on then, hurry up before people wake up and see you," she said.

I could feel Rosa's heartbeat quicken beneath me as we lurched forward. Before we left, I wanted to wave to Zia, but one arm was supporting the baby and the other was holding onto Leonardo. We trotted along the Arno until we reached the city's fortified walls.

"Ciao," said Leonardo to the guard posted at the city's threshold.

"Ciao, Leonardo ... Where are you sneaking off to so early?"

"No sneaking involved, just going to visit my family in Vinci."

"Who's your pretty friend?"

"She is my cousin."

"As you say," he said, clicking his tongue against the roof of his mouth. "Papers, please."

"Come off it! You have never asked me for papers before."

"Well that was before il Magnifico told me to keep my eyes out for a young pretty girl named Viola Orofino," he said, scratching his rough jaw.

"Right, as I said this is not any such person. This is my cousin, she has her baby with her, and it will be such a mess if we go looking for the papers." The word baby drew his attention from my face to the baby sling around my shoulder. "Take this as a parting present and let us be on our way," said Leonardo, passing him the wineskin slung around the saddle. Marco looked around before accepting the bribe.

"Well, Medici didn't say anything about a baby," concluded Marco while two other guards parted the heavy doors.

"Good man, Marco," said Leonardo before we trotted past the thick walls and out into the country air.

We traveled in silence for a span, each of us enjoying the fresh air. Margherita squirmed against the confines of the fabric swaddled around her. She was tiny; the rhythm of her breath was soothing. We soon came upon the river again. Along the city's lifeline were modest mills and pull boats tangled in nets. Fields of withering crops and vacant hills frosted with dead flowers haunted both sides of our path.

"It is a shame you could not see this in the summer," said Leonardo.

"Why?"

"It is covered with grapevines, and there are infinite fields of sunflowers."

"Are you a poet as well?"

"I dabble ... There is not much of a breeze at that time of year. But the sun is so strong that it blends a perfume of turned soil. If there is a Heaven, that is how it looks and smells."

"You must miss living out here."

"I do," he admitted while I stared at the dark brush that spotted the rippling landscape. "I love progress, but I hate the city ... I suppose you cannot have both."

"I've always lived in a big city, but sometimes I daydreamed about what it would be like to live out here."

"Once you know what it is like, you will never see city life the same. It is still hard for me, and I have lived there three years."

"Why did you move?" I asked.

"My father was concerned about my education, and he was anxious for me to follow some sort of career plan. But it wasn't until after my stepmother and grandfather died that he ever took action."

"I'm sorry to hear that," I said feeling his shoulder tighten.

"In honesty, it was hard. I was extremely fond of them both. My father was working as a notary in Pisa and Florence while I was growing up. My grandparents cared for me and gave me the freedom to be myself, to explore," reflected Leonardo as the sun hid behind the sparse clouds. "I was separated from my birth mother, so the only one I have ever known was my father's first wife, and she died the same way Margherita did," said Leonardo. I squeezed his arm, unsure of what to say. "I cannot complain though. By bastard standards, I grew up in a loving family where I was free to roam around and study what I wanted."

"What sort of things would you study?"

"Plants, bugs, birds ... horses."

"Did you always know you wanted to be an artist?" I asked.

"I was always good at it. I love nature and enjoy studying anatomy. My father would say I had a natural ability for drawing."

"You did."

"How do you know?"

"Your father showed me. He keeps your drawings in a chest. It's an incredible gift ... I think your father loves you very much," I added.

"But not enough to claim me by law," he retorted. "It is fortunate I am able and enjoy being an artist because if I did not, I would be in a precarious situation."

"What do you mean?"

"There are not many opportunities for children born out of wedlock."

Our conversation quieted but was kindled back to life by passing travelers. Poor Rosa's sweat soon soaked through my dress and stockings. My thighs were sore from rubbing against the wool dress and saddle.

We stopped short of Vinci to give Rosa a rest and to pacify Margherita's growing whimpers. It was a small village with one tiny inn. Leonardo inquired after a wet nurse. The innkeeper's wife offered to take care of Margherita as she herself had a brood of young children. We paid her handsomely for her generosity.

"Not much longer now," said Leonardo as we munched on the calzones Zia had packed for us.

It was only an hour before we were back on the road. Despite my eagerness to make a statement, I decided to sit sidesaddle the rest of the trip. We veered off the road following the posts that directed us to Vinci and then to Anchiano. The wide paved road narrowed to a dirt trail. We rode along a rising hill that overlooked olive groves. In the far distance, clouds threw the villages below into shadow. After we rounded the corner, we broke from the path and traveled through dormant gray trees."

A rectangular stone cottage came into view. Leonardo quickened our pace. Tall cypress trees framed the pleasant home. Square windows looked out across the flat courtyard and down into the valley below.

Leonardo reared Rosa into a sudden halt. Margherita stirred when Leonardo jumped down to help me off the horse. As he banged on the door, I carefully scooped Margherita out of the sling, letting her breathe the fresh fragrance of the potted herbs by the entrance. A stout bearded man opened the door.

"Leonardo!" he said in a deep voice that resonated through the house.

He pulled Leonardo into a man hug but froze when he saw me. His attractive face flashed from delight to alarm. Hurried steps from the house drew closer until a striking elderly woman appeared. She had long wavy hair that flowed around her.

"What a lovely surprise!" she said with a voice so loving that it made my heart ache.

"Leonardo, who is this?" asked the bearded man in a tone that was barely civil.

"This is Viola."

"Oh, my dear boy, what have you done?" asked the grandmother, pulling her arms from her grandson.

"Does your father know?" said the man, suddenly severe.

"Of course, that is his horse after all."

"How could you?" she gasped. "After what you went through as a child."

"Excuse me?" I interrupted. "I think there is a misunderstanding," I cleared my throat. "This isn't my baby and it's not Leonardo's either." Relief flushed their faces, and their smiles returned.

"I don't know why you had to ruin the joke so soon, Viola! It was going so well." Leonardo smirked.

CHAPTER TWENTY-EIGHT

The Carpenter

"Francesco," said the bearded man before kissing my hand. "I am Leonardo's zio. This is my mother, Caterina." He presented the elderly woman with the youthful spirit.

"I am Leo's *nonna*."

"Very nice to meet you both." I nodded.

"Well, let us not stand about around here! Come inside and sit," said Nonna.

Margherita was making smacking noises with her lips. Ducking under the low doorframe, we entered the house. Inside it was wonderfully open and bright. Windows pocketed the painted walls. There were no partitions breaking up the space, so every part of the room fused together.

"Please sit and make yourself at home," Nonna said, motioning towards a comfortable corner toppling with books and mismatched chairs.

I chose one with a worn green cushion. While the others arranged themselves, I let Margherita's weight fall in my lap. My neck was sore from the sling. Margherita looked up at me with eyes that shifted in color.

"Ana, please prepare some hot cider for our guests," said Nonna to the woman who was working on mincing a large pile of turnips and garlic.

Ana had a petite frame; her tan face was plain, not remarkable or unpleasant. Nonna strolled back to the corner where we sat. I noticed that she wasn't wearing a dress but a long tunic with tights.

"You must excuse my dress," she said noticing my gaze. "I was not expecting company."

"I think it's wonderful."

"I agree," seconded Leonardo.

"I do not," laughed Zio, "but I have learned that subject to be a lost battle."

"Indeed, it is," she said. "You speak from lack of experience. When you try on one of my gowns and work the field in it, then we can discuss the matter."

"Work in the fields? Last time I checked, Uncle never left this corner except to relieve himself," said Leonardo.

"Take care, nephew ... such wit will scare off our guest." Ana served the cider on a low wooden table covered with what were probably Leonardo's doodles. The mugs were of all different designs. I cupped one glazed with orange and green.

"These cups are really nice," I said.

"Thank you, dear, it is something I enjoy doing." The fumes from the cider revealed cloves and cinnamon.

"I hope you do not find me nosy, but could you tell us whose baby that is if it is not your own?" asked the uncle, who had settled himself in an odd chair that leaned back.

"Well that is what we are here to find out," answered Leonardo.

"Pardon?"

"Her mother used to work in Verrocchio's workshop with us."

"And where is she now?" asked Nonna.

"Dead."

"She died from childbirth," I said.

"The same way ..." said Leonardo, his words failing.

"I promised her mother I would find a home for her," I said.

"Don't they have an excellent orphanage in Florence?" asked Francesco.

"Yes, that is what they say," I said, peering down at Margherita.

"Why not let them take this burden from you?"

"The same reason you did not take me to an orphanage," said Leonardo bluntly. "We want her to be loved, not just cared for."

"It is a noble cause," said Nonna. "How can we help?" she asked, taking a long sip from her cup.

"We were told a married couple lived in Vinci ... their names are Antonio and Ginerva," I said.

"The carpenter?" asked Zio.

"I think so," I said, trying to recall if Zia had said anything about his profession.

"They live closer to town, but he runs a shop in Vinci. A good man; he made me this chair. The best one I have ever sat in, and as Leonardo told you, I rarely leave this nook."

"Right, well, we will need to go right away," said Leonardo.

"What will you do if they refuse?" asked Nonna.

"I haven't even thought about the possibility," I admitted. "I have money to pay for a wet nurse but I—"

"*Scusi*, Signora Caterina?" said Ana, the housemaid.

"*Si?*"

"Might I offer to take care of the babe for now? You know my little Teresa is weaning. I could use the extra money."

"Thank you, Ana. That is a most generous offer ... Well, you will stay the night of course?"

"Ask the maestro," said Leonardo, pointing to me.

"That would be kind," I said, thinking more of my chafed thighs than anything else.

"Of course, but supper will not be served for some time."

"That's all right, we should go now anyway."

"Ana, would you mind washing our little guest for her outing?" asked Nonna.

"Not at all, signora," she said, rushing over to our corner. I handed over Margherita, who immediately began to cry. It took a few moments, but Ana's experienced arms lulled her back to bliss.

"You may use the lavender water."

"Very well, ma'am."

Once Ana had left with Margherita, there was a long pause. Those still moments were a needed pause from the responsibility that had been temporarily given to me.

"How is your Ser Piero?" asked Nonna.

"He is fine," said Leonardo.

"And your stepmother?"

"She is still my father's wife."

"Leonardo, you must accept and forgive. Spite does not suit you."

"He could have waited ... my real stepmother was barely cold in her grave before he remarried."

"He is just anxious to have children," said Nonna.

"Because I am not enough," snapped Leonardo.

"It is a peculiar situation, and I do see your point," she said, imploring Francesco to participate with her eyes.

"Do not look at me that way. I quite agree with Leonardo. I do not really understand Piero's ambitious motives," he said.

"Yes. Well, would you please excuse me? I have to finish something by the kiln," said Nonna before walking outside. Leonardo and I did not stand up until we heard Ana walking towards us with Margherita.

"I am going into town with the cart if you three want to ride in the back. I'll drop you off in the piazza," offered Zio.

"That would be great," I said, wrapping the sling over the fresh shoulder.

Once Zio parked the cart at the front of the house, Leonardo and I stepped up on the back and settled ourselves between clumps of hay. As we rolled down the hillside, I closed my eyes. Even with my lids shut, I could feel the brightness and see the dark shadows of the branches. I had dozed off underneath the sun's snug blanket. The cart jerked me awake. We had stopped in front of an old church with a pointed bell tower.

"Antonio's shop is right over there," said Zio, pointing to an open door opposite the church.

"Thank you, Signore Francesco!"

"*Prego* … Take your time. I came to get away, so I am not in a rush." He kicked up his feet onto the cart railing. Leonardo helped Margherita and I get down from the cart.

"I will wait for you here," said Leonardo.

"You're not coming?" I asked nervously.

"I think it would be better if you went in alone … It is such a sensitive situation that I think the fewer people involved the better it will turn out."

"Maybe."

"Do not look so nervous! You will do great."

I sighed before walking towards the carpenter's shop.

"You must be on your best behavior," I whispered to Margherita as we approached the shop. "They will fall in love with you. I am sure of it."

No noise came from within the tiny studio. Tools hung on the walls in neat rows. A hint of sawdust flew about in spite of the owner's meticulously clean workshop. At the entrance, there were a few furniture samples for the eyes to rest on.

"Buonasera?" I called out to the empty room.

"*Scusi!*" A man of thirty years came rushing in from across the street. "I'm so sorry to have kept you waiting, signora."

"It's *miss*," I corrected. He glanced at the baby.

"Forgive me," he said politely. I could see why Ginerva had fallen for him as he combed the cluster of gray hair back into his black ponytail.

"How may I help you?"

"Well, I'm here on a more personal matter." I gently rocked Margherita. He looked surprised but waited for me to continue. "I hope you don't think me rude, but I need to know if your wife's name is Ginerva."

"It is." He crossed his arms.

"Is she well?"

"Who would like to know?" It was clear from the crow's-feet that spread from his pale jade eyes that he had a kind personality, but his defensive demeanor made me wary.

"Her mother, Signora Cioni."

"She is well," he said curtly, rolling up his white sleeve. He walked past me and further into the workshop at a loss of what to say. "Was there anything else I can help you with?" he asked, pulling on his gnarled work gloves.

"Yes, I have something for you." I paused as an idea struck me. "Would you help me to get it out?" He stood up from his workbench. "Could you hold her a moment while I grab something in my satchel?" I asked, already leaning her up against his chest.

Shocked by the brevity of the whole transaction, he had no time to object. For a few minutes, I pretended I didn't know where the letter was. While I searched, I stole a look at the two. He smiled when Margherita's eyes widened at him. She took a deep breath and leaned her round cheek against his arm. "Here it is! Sorry about that," I said, placing the letter on the work table. "I can take her now."

"She is lovely," he said, gently holding her out to me.

"And as sweet as her mama was," I said, sweeping her back into my arms.

"Was?"

"Yes, her mother died a few days ago, right after the baby was born."

"I am sorry for your loss." He frowned. "You must be her aunt?"

"No, I'm just a friend. The letter on the table should explain the whole situation." He looked confused. "I'll be waiting for your answer at Signore Francesco's house right outside of town. I believe he bought one of your chairs ... Please come as soon as you can, I am leaving in the morning for Florence."

"I have no knowledge of the letter's contents, but if it is from Signora Cioni, I can tell you that my wife has not spoken to her mother for five years. I would not like you to wait for a reply that may very likely never come."

The prospect that the plan might fail angered me beyond reason.

"You mean she wouldn't read it?"

"It is possible ... she has not read any of her past letters."

"That's so cruel!"

"Excuse me?" said Antonio, raising his eyebrows. "My wife has been through a lot."

"I know ... Zia told me."

"You mean she gave you her version."

"I can promise you that she didn't paint a pretty picture of herself," I snapped. "She helped you deliver your notes to Ginerva ... Have you forgotten that?" I probed angrily.

"I haven't, but I also remember that she did not stop that wedding. Instead, she told me to hide like a coward."

"What could she do when in this place women have no rights, no social standing? When they are given away like objects for sale? She was trying to spare your feelings and her own! It broke her heart to see your suffering." He said nothing but just blinked at me as if I were a hallucination—a vision of a strange teenage girl with an even stranger accent yelling at him about women's rights and digging out the skeletons in his closet. "I brought Margherita to you because I wanted her to grow up with a happy family that wouldn't hold her back."

"Who is Margherita?"

"She was a kind soul who was tricked by a little devil, a girl who died wanting only a new beginning for her baby." Still he said nothing. "You have the day to talk it over with Ginerva. You know where I am staying," I said before turning out of the studio. As I crossed the street towards the cart, I breathed a little easier.

"How did it go?" asked Leonardo, tossing back a handful of pickled olives.

"I'm not sure."

"How can you not know?"

"Well, I think at one point I was yelling at him," I said.

Zio chuckled. "That is a good sign," he said, stroking his beard. "All men like to be yelled at by a woman now and again, even if they do not know it. It makes them realize how human they are."

"I do not like to be yelled at by anyone. Least of all by women," said Leonardo.

"Like I said..." Zio spits out pits onto the packed dirt floor. "...even if they don't know it. Does he know where to find you?"

"*Sì.*"

"Then let us get going." Once we resumed our ascent, Margherita began to whimper again.

"Unreal!" I said. The clouds above us rolled past. "What happened?"

"I think Margherita can sense when I'm worried."

"Give her to me then," said Leonardo sitting up. "I'm never worried." I passed her to Leonardo. Immediately, she quieted.

"See! She knows."

"She might," he agreed.

It felt good to stretch my aching arms out over my legs that dangled off the cart. The chilly wind picked up. It pushed around the cart's edges and breathed against our few patches of bare skin.

"What will I do if they don't come?" I asked, rubbing my sore shoulders.

"You have done your best."

"Have I?"

"I think so, and I am a tough judge," said Leonardo. "Her mother would have wanted you to look after yourself now."

"What do you mean?"

"Come tomorrow, you will not have time to worry about Margherita because of the Medici."

"Si, you're right ... I'm totally screwed." I leaned back on the pillow of hay. "Maybe that's why I am so focused on this. There is a big elephant in the room, and it looks like Lorenzo Medici."

"Elephant?"

"Doesn't matter."

"Have you thought of a plan yet?"

"No," I said, fidgeting with Idan's chain. I opened its case and brought it up to face. My heart sank into my empty belly. "Oh no!"

"What is it?"

"I have less than two days left!"

"For what?"

"To get back to the home."

"How do you know?" he asked.

I sat up to show him Idan's face. "That number there..." I pointed to the window where the countdown appeared "... it keeps changing. I should have checked on it sooner."

"Are you sure it is not just broken?"

"Stop it with that." I elbowed him. "Just because you don't believe in it does not mean it's broken, and it's also not a free pass to dissect it."

"For the record, I hope you are just delusional."

"Oh, that's sweet of you, Leonardo."

"No, I mean it."

"Why?"

"Because on the off chance there is a grain of truth to what you say, it means you will leave me."

"I could kiss you right now."

"That and it would also mean I was wrong about Idan ... and I hate to be wrong." He smiled.

"You're lucky you are holding the baby, otherwise I would throw you off this cart."

"Guess I am a lucky guy," he said, withdrawing his hand from Margherita to pick out the straw stuck to my hair.

"Have you thought of a plan?" I asked as the cart pulled into the courtyard.

"I have, but I hope it does not come to that. It is kind of a worst-case scenario scheme."

"Hope you are all hungry!" sung Nonna from the doorway. "Supper is ready."

"I'm starving," said Leonardo, passing Margherita to Ana.

Supper lay on a chunky wooden board placed at the center of the room. Stray droopy wallflowers decorated the table for the occasion. We spoke of Leonardo's work on the *Baptism of Christ* and the tournament. I watched while they laughed at Leonardo's comical rendering of the joust. We washed down the roasted chicken and vegetables with spring water or the table wine from the family's vineyard. Leonardo agreed to a card game with his uncle while Nonna and I cleared the table.

"What beautiful hands," she remarked as I passed her the dirty dishes. She placed them in the sink and took my hands in her own. I was wondering whether she was serious or not when she rubbed at my callouses and stared at my tinted cuticles. "You have artist's hands."

"People usually say piano hands."

"What is a piano?"

"Oh ... sorry, never mind."

"Well, they are creative ones. May I show you something? Leave those plates there and grab that candlestick," she said rushing out of the house. We turned the corner of the cottage and kept up our hurried pace heading for a square hut with a large chimney. "This is where I work."

It was a modest space and the polar opposite of Antonio's studio. Clumps of clay caked and splattered onto the walls. Wooden tools, worn rags, and broken scraps of ceramic covered the only table in the hut. The tiny space felt liberating.

"It's a sanctuary," I said, scanning the shelves of shallow bowls and miniature animals.

"I like to think so," she said.

"It will be so hard to return to the city after being out here in the country. It feels so ..."

"Free?" she suggested.

"Si!"

"Are you sure there is not another reason you do not want to return other than the horrid stench and strict rules?"

"Is it that obvious?" I asked. She nodded, her long gray waves flying wildly about her face.

"Although the reasons you gave are enough, there is something else." I followed her out of the hut and under the star- stenciled sky.

"I am running away from someone."

"I realize I might be nothing to you but a silly old lady ..." She turned to face me, and her smile left. The aura of youth radiating from her disappeared. "May I be so presumptuous as to give you some advice?" I nodded. "It is natural to be scared, healthy even. It helps us survive. But as most things, too much is dangerous. My words of wisdom are to accept your fear. It will never go away, but you can harness it ... Most importantly, do not let it hold you back here or anywhere," she said before leaving me to the critters hiding from the moon's light.

CHAPTER TWENTY-NINE

Late

"WAKE UP!" SOMEONE HIDDEN behind matted sandy hair shook me awake. The dreamy fog I had enjoyed all night slowly lifted. "Come on!" urged Leonardo, flailing his arms towards the door.

It took me a second to orient myself. I had spent the night in Nonna's room. In the past, I might have felt strange about sleeping next to a stranger, but instead, I felt safe. Nonna Caterina did not seem like someone I had only met the day before. I was comforted in the dark of night hearing someone breathing next to me. Her presence reminded me of the lullabies my grandmother would sing to me.

Leonardo was having a fit in the hallway, waving a bundle of clothes at me. I slid off the bed, snatched my shoes, and creaked across the wooden floor. "You took forever," grumbled Leonardo as soon as the door closed behind me.

"What's the problem? Is Ginerva here?"

"No."

"Then why did you wake me up so early?" I scratched the sleep out of my eyes. "It's still dark outside."

"If we do not leave now, we will not have time."

"For what?" I asked, but he ignored my question by handing me clothes. "Whose are these?"

"They used to be mine, but I have outgrown them."

"Why do you want me to wear them?"

"Can I answer your questions later? Just put them on." I shot him a suspicious look. "Please?"

"Turn around then." I changed quickly hoping no one would come into the hallway. "I'm done." Leonardo spun around.

"You look like you could be my brother." He grinned.

"You really know how to make a girl feel good about herself," I said, hiking up the green tights and straightening the black tunic.

I followed Leonardo down the stairs to the bottom floor, abandoning my underdress on one of the chairs. Leonardo had already ventured out into the brisk morning. Rosa sniffed at the meager grass that spotted the path down the hill and onto the road.

"Hurry up, you are so slow!" he said, straddling the horse.

"I just woke up!" I protested. He leaned forward to offer his arm. "It's too high."

"I have you," he said, grabbing me by the forearm while I pushed off my feet. What ensued was an awkward version of trying to get out of a swimming pool without taking the stairs, but it looked twice as stupid. Rosa was already walking down the lane by the time I regained my balance.

"I'm so sore."

"You are such a wimp," teased Leonardo, keeping his eyes on the uneven slope.

"Then you are a bully," I snapped back. "Waking me up—"

My words were lost when Rosa sprang into a gallop. I threw my arms around Leonardo's waist so as not to fall off the horse. We cut a trail through the thick air and damp mist. Using Leonardo's back, I protected my face against the cold wind that whistled by. Once the

Anchiano hamlet lay behind us, the gray twilight transcended into a new day. Up ahead was the foot of a valley. Jagged rocks and coarse thorny bushes collided around one of the low mountain's base. Leonardo rode Rosa around the hill's slope until we reached a small clearing. Once he had tied Rosa's reins to one of the scrawny trees, he helped me down.

"Where are we?"

"A place I would often explore when I lived here," he said, walking through the thicket. "Are you glad you did not wear a dress?"

"Yes!" I said, scaling the rocky route.

"It is just around the turn." He sprinted ahead. Once I rounded the corner, I saw Leonardo standing in front of a gash in the hillside. The cave's mouth was wide but its ceiling low. "I would walk here growing up. Often, I would just stand here and stare for hours, terrified."

"You? I thought you were only scared of breaking into houses."

"Seriously, I was struck by fear, but I also had an overwhelming desire to go in. I imagined all sorts of terrible monsters lived within ... Why are you looking at me with that face again?"

"Because that contradicts everything you ever told me."

"How?"

"Have you ever seen, touched, or heard a monster?"

"You failed to understand my meaning. The keyword I used was imagine." He fussed with a branch, rock, and a knife. "I have an active imagination." Sparks caught to the scrap of fabric he had pulled from his cloak. Soon the branch burned a modest light. "Shall we?"

"After you," I insisted.

He crouched down and through the opening. I followed close behind him and almost immediately the cave's low rock ceiling transformed into a cavity of darkness. I stood up to chase Leonardo's bright beacon.

"What do you think?" he echoed.

"It's a great hiding place."

"You could hide here until the Medici tire of you."

"No ... I don't like bats," I said, staring at the towers of guano.

"I would love to paint this one day," he admitted, casting a glow over the sediment's stepped surfaces.

"How would you do it?"

"Study it and use it in a landscape."

"A landscape of what?"

"The only thing I am really allowed to paint ... portraits or scenes from the Bible."

"Why can't you paint anything else?"

"I can paint whatever I want. But if I want to eat, I will need to stick to commissions." Several rocks boasted curves where mossy plants fought to conquer them. "Does it happen to you that certain memories are so sharp that the rest are pale by comparison?"

"I have a few, and you?"

"This cave is one of the few vivid memories I have from my childhood."

I tried to recall my earliest memory in the flickering darkness, but my conscious clung to the sound of our voices ricocheting off the rocks that rose in towers around us.

"I'm glad you shared it with me, then," I said.

"Well, if you are not going to hide out here, we should head back."

"Hopefully Ginerva will be there by now," I said.

Rosa was stretching her neck impatiently when we found her at the clearing. The ride back was quiet. All of the freedom that the open country had given us gradually disappeared as we scaled the hill. Once we arrived at the house, all the pressure that we had left behind in Florence had resettled on our shoulders.

"Is breakfast ready?" asked Leonardo, walking through the door.

"Almost ... Oh good, there you are, Viola. We thought you had vanished into thin air," said Nonna, holding up my white underdress.

"Mamma, look what you have done!" said Zio, seated at his usual spot. "The girl has not even been here a full day and she is dressing like a boy." Nonna gave me an approving look.

"That was my doing. It was more practical for what we were doing," said Leonardo. "Ana, could I have four fried eggs?" She nodded.

"Did anyone come this morning?" I asked the busy room.

"Not a soul," said Ana. "But Margherita only woke up four times."

"That's good?"

"For a newborn babe? Very! She is a peaceful babe."

"Oh, well, I'm glad it wasn't too much trouble for you then," I said, attempting not to look as disappointed as I felt. "I'm going to go change just in case they come." When I returned all three had gathered around the table waiting to slop their brown bread into the golden yolks.

"I am sorry you two could not stay longer." Zio frowned.

"Me too." I smiled.

"We will have to leave right after breakfast," said Leonardo before folding the entire runny egg into his mouth.

"They're not coming," I said.

"I'm afraid that is true," said Nonna. "If they were coming, they would have been here at the crack of dawn to make sure they did not miss you." I looked out at the sunny window, resigning myself to the failed mission.

"We can't wait even a little longer?"

"If you want to be locked out of the city," he said, refusing the cut of bacon his uncle waved in his face. "Anyway, do you not have an appointment at the Signoria?" Fluids and morsels gushed around my stomach as I tried to keep my food down.

"I am sorry, my dear. I wish we could take her on, she is such a lovely babe, but we just cannot," said Nonna.

I politely finished the goat cheese left on my plate even though my appetite had left. I tried to delay our departure, but Leonardo had the horse packed and ready to ride within the hour. Before we walked outside, I paid Ana for all her help.

"I would say until we meet again, but I know that we will not," said Nonna while she embraced me. "You have a good spirit ... Let it shine bravely."

"You best be careful at the Signoria," warned Zio, lifting Margherita and I up onto Rosa. "I heard they will stick anyone in that tower of theirs." My heart skipped a beat. "Just joking." He laughed.

"Well now that you have thoroughly spooked Viola, we will be off," said Leonardo.

"Come back soon, my boy."

"Nonna! I am hardly a boy anymore," he said, nudging Rosa into gear.

"Arrivederci!" he yelled before we cantered out of sight.

The closer we came to Florence the more I would turn back to see if anyone was following us. Menacing clouds loomed above us as the number of outer city hovels and villages increased. Margherita's milky breath warmed my skin. "You have a lovely family," I said, breaking the stillness.

"They liked you too."

"Really?"

"What a thing to say! Of course, they did. What is not to like?"

"You are just being sweet because you know there is a troop of guards waiting outside Zia's house."

"No, I really think that. But it pains me to say that you are right about one thing."

"Just one?"

"*Si*, you're not going to make it to the Signoria by sunset. Which means—"

"I'll be late," I finished. As we ascended the road to the colossal doors of Porta Romana the wind bashed us and the overcast thickened. "I'm sorry, little lady," I whispered to the woolen nook. "I failed you."

"That is false," said Leonardo in an unusually soft voice. "Her mother would understand." The door was about to close when we rounded the last curve. "Oy! Marco, wait!" The doors stopped.

"Cutting it too close, Leonardo," whistled the guard. Despite his taunting, he looked relieved to see us. "Why did you lie to me?" he asked staring me straight in the eyes.

"About what?"

"Don't peg me for a fool, Leo, you know exactly what." He pointed to me.

"I am sorry, friend, it was an emergency ... and we are back now, so no harm done, right?"

"Wrong," he said, his nostrils flaring. "I had to lie to the most powerful man in Tuscany to cover your tracks. Almost pissed myself."

"You were covering your tracks, too," barked Leonardo. Marco's mouth gaped as if he were about to say something awful.

"I'm so sorry, Marco," I said. "It was for the baby that I left. I hope you aren't in too much trouble." His mouth closed and the furrow on his high forehead resided.

"And I hope you find your way out of trouble, young lady."

"Me too."

"Off with you then," said the guard with a shooing motion.

Leonardo jolted tired Rosa back in motion.

"Where are we off to?" asked Leonardo as we turned off the main street. "The Signoria or the orphanage?"

"Neither. Let's go to Zia's."

"You are sure?"

"Yeah, they'll come and get me anyway. It doesn't mean I have to make it easy for them."

"As you say," said Leonardo. It was not long before Rosa's tired hooves resonated off the cobblestones of Via dei Benci. A lively fire gleamed through the curtains of Zia's house. "I will go in with you."

"You don't have to," I said.

"How else will you get down?"

"True."

"You should not have to face Zia alone."

"Thanks, Leo," I said as he helped me down. "Here it goes." I knocked on the door. The scurry of footsteps from within gave me time to prepare myself to watch Zia's hopeful face fade to disappointment.

"*Buonasera,*" said an unfamiliar voice. I looked up from my special cargo. A woman in her late twenties was standing authoritatively in Zia's doorway.

"Where is Zia?"

"She is here," said the woman, kindly glancing at my sling. She stepped away from the doorway to give us enough room to enter the steamy room.

"Oh my God." I breathed when I noticed Antonio sitting at my chair by the kitchen table.

"*Buonasera,* Viola," he stood up. Zia came out of the cupboard carrying a dusty bottle.

"Oh, my sweet child! I was so worried that the gate would be closed before you returned. It kept me up all night as I remembered after you left that I forgot to tell you about the curfew." Even though she was sharing her worries, I could see that inside she was all lit up. She was not smiling, but she radiated goodness.

"I'm sorry I worried you, Zia."

"How is Margherita?"

"Sleeping," I said, placing a protective hand over the sling. The wool cloth had rubbed away at my skin to the point that blood had started to ooze from my pores. My eyes lingered on the young woman with the raven hair. She stood away in the corner at a safe distance from me.

"Viola and Leonardo, this is my son-in-law, Antonio, and my daughter, Ginerva."

"Why didn't you come to meet me in Vinci?" I asked Antonio, ignoring Zia's civil introduction.

"We didn't know who you were," said Antonio. "We came to talk to Zia and make sure this was not a trick."

"It was not our intention to worry you," added Ginerva. I was livid, but I could not pinpoint why. She took a step closer to me. "I realize I have handled the situation poorly. No words can turn back time, but we have spoken, and we will both try to fill the void that has grown between us for so long."

"Just like that?" I said, locking eyes with the mysterious woman. Her black straight hair fell to her hips and matched the dark circles around her eyes.

"No, it will take time ... I can understand your anger. You must think me an abominable person."

"I wouldn't put it in those exact words, but I'd rather see Margherita grow up in an orphanage than be with a family torn apart by grudges."

"I agree. That is why we are moving back to Via dei Benci."

"You are?"

"Yes."

"You have brought us together again," interjected Zia, grabbing hold of my hand.

"Ginerva didn't make it easy for me," I said, looking at the envelope on the table.

"That is for you," said Zia, following my gaze.

"Who brought it?"

"A woman, but since she was veiled, I could not tell who it was." She shrugged.

I picked up the envelope. The crimson horse seal dripped sloppily down the envelope.

"Open up!" sounded the metal fist against wood. "Official Medici business!" The boom grew louder.

"Viola, what is this? What is wrong, my child?" a panicked Zia asked.

I broke the wax and unfolded the parchment. There was only one word on the page.

Run!

CHAPTER THIRTY

Window

RUN? WHERE AM I going to run to? You forgot to leave the address of your hideout, Mrs. Reed, I thought bitterly, crumpling the note in my hand.

"Open the door!" repeated the man behind the door. Antonio walked to the door.

"What does it say?" asked Leonardo but the question was lost in the chaos that ensued when Antonio opened the door. An official guard clad in half armor crossed the humble threshold. A cold breeze broke through the room's comfort.

"I'm here to escort Viola Orofino to the Palazzo della Signoria," he said.

Zia approached him, armed with her renewed vigor, looking as though she could take him down in one blow. Antonio stood between them, unsure of what to do. For a brief moment, I debated running out through the pantry door, past Georgina's raggedy coop, and down the alley. The guard was tall. I could tell by his wide calves that tapered from his tunic that it would not be long before I would feel his hand yanking my sweater collar. The guard's eyebrows reared in shock at Zia's harsh protective threats. It was unclear whether he moved towards me to escape Zia or to seize me.

"Wait!" I yelled over the confusion. "I will go ... Lorenzo and I have an appointment after all," I admitted to the surprise of all. "I apologize for being late. Signore Medici must have been worried and sent you, right?" The guard looked uneasily around the room and cleared his throat.

"*Si*," he said.

I crossed the distance that separated Ginerva and me. Margherita's eyes winced as I moved her from out of the woolen womb. I bent my head to kiss her fuzzy forehead. It was heartbreaking to nuzzle my nose against her smooth skin. Hints of our adventure remained in the lavender notes that stuck to her dark hair. As I gently offered her up to Ginerva, I was saying a prolonged goodbye to her mother.

"I hope you give her a beautiful beginning," I said, peeling the sling from the dry blood that had gathered beneath the wool.

It was good to see the motherly spark in Ginerva's face before I followed the guard towards the entrance. Zia grabbed my sleeve before I made it to the door. I did not mean to be such a coward. Although I knew it would be hard to say farewell to Margherita, the idea of leaving Zia forever was unthinkable. Deep down, I thought it would leave a gash so profound that nothing would stitch it together. She had welcomed, clothed, and loved me with all the sensitivity that only a selfless mother could offer. Tears ran through the wrinkles of her face. I gathered all my bravery to spare her any grief.

"Why are you crying, Zia?" I asked steadying my trembling mouth. "I'll be back soon."

"You say that, but I don't believe you, my sweet Viola."

"How can you be so sad? Look what a happy family I leave you with."

"But you are also my family," she said. Her knuckles whitened as she gripped my wrist. I squeezed her tightly against me and kissed her gray scalp.

"I love you, Zia," I whispered as drops streamed down my nose. I looked up at Leonardo for comfort, but his sulk left me wanting. The guard clutched my arm and pulled me out the door. I looked behind my shoulder to the despondent huddle that stared after us. "There is no need for you to hold on to me," I said.

"Pardon?"

"I'm a terrible runner," I said, drying my face with my free hand. He did not let go but his grip loosened when we turned onto the Piazza della Signoria. The clouds' drizzle only added to the low fog that fumed about the square. As we drew near a set of guards opened its doors. The entrance opened onto a large courtyard supported by massive columns, thick with elaborate carvings of winged figures flying among splendid gardens. I walked into the courtyard, but the guard directed me to a staircase that broke off from the entrance. He guided me through a room with gold coffered ceilings that harbored dozens of glittering rosettes and gilded lilies. It was not until we walked through the next room that the guard let go of me. Lorenzo sat at a long table that stretched the length of the narrow room.

"So good of you to come," he said without lifting his eyes from the paper.

"It didn't seem like I had much of a choice," I said.

Lorenzo raised his eyes but the hand armed with the quill finished its thought. Crossing his arms, he leaned back against the chair's stiff bolted leather.

"Do you like choices?" he asked. I let the trick question pass away unanswered. "I promise to give you a choice in a few moments." He stood up abruptly. "No need to worry … I always keep my promises. Unlike a certain little flower I know."

"I never bro—"

"You broke an engagement," he said harshly. "Pray do not interrupt me. I cannot abide it." As he strode across the room, the sound of his boots' heels dampened against the tapestries that hung along the walls. "I'm a busy man, Viola. So when I tell you to meet me at sunset that means …"

I stared at my shoes, unwilling to play his game. He forced my head up with his right hand. I could see the veins around his temples burn and his mouth twitch with irritation.

"Bind her hands and then you may leave us, Alessandro." The guard clasped my hands behind my back and wrapped them tightly with rope before leaving the room. Lorenzo let go of my face and held his hand out expectantly. "I do not mean to be impertinent, but I am sure you will understand," he said, slithering his dry fingers around my neck.

I cringed as they grasped Idan's chain and pulled it. "I am upset, Viola." He smiled at Idan's intricate cover. "Do you know why?" I said nothing. "Because I don't enjoy acting the role of a tyrant," he continued. "You see, I never asked for this …" He gestured towards his surroundings. "In order for my family to survive, it is my duty to maintain and foster the power that has been given to me most unwillingly." He moved towards the fireplace. "You see, I am just a scholar with little . . . time. I need it to pursue what I love." He walked closer to the fire. "It is not a selfish mission. All humanity will benefit from every discovery I make and every artist I employ to realize my vision. Now, enough about me, tell me about yourself and Idan, of course."

He opened Idan's case. As he peered down at its face, his shoulders tightened and his back arched. Long minutes of eerie silence slipped past. Even the flames burned without a sound. I looked up at the woven angels for help, but none came. His jaw had loosened from his scowl, and his eyes gaped at the pocket watch.

"I did not bring you here to listen to myself. You shall speak. If you choose not to, you will regret that choice, my dear," he said, pulling out a knife from his belt.

"My name is Viola Orofino," I broke.

"Is it really?" he asked, putting Idan's chain around his neck.

"Yes."

"And you come from where?"

"I don't remember."

"How convenient," he said, piercing an orange from the table's fruit bowl with his knife. "I did not want to remind you, but you leave me no choice." He peeled away its skin. "Do you remember those papers Giuliano gave you at the workshop? Well, as they clearly state, you are my guest. As a result, I am the only one vouching for your legitimacy.

Unfortunately for you, your status has changed." He held a piece of parchment to my face.

"I am a prisoner?" I read aloud.

"It is a shame."

"On what grounds?"

"I have yet to decide." He popped an orange crescent in his mouth.

"You can't hold me if I haven't done anything wrong," I said.

"How interesting it must be where you come from." He laughed. "I do not need to remind you where you are because threats will only anger me. I hate dealing them out, so be a good girl and your punishment will be less severe." He sighed. "Now I trust you will be more forthcoming with your answers." Juice dripped down his chin. "Explain to me how Idan works? What do all these numbers mean?"

"They have to do with the time we are in right now. Three of the numbers show the date it is today. The other tells you the days I have left till the door opens."

"What door?"

"I'm not sure but it faces the Piazza della Signoria. I don't think the door will appear until the countdown stops." I shook my head.

"The door will open at dawn the day after tomorrow." I cringed watching him handle Idan. "It's my only chance to get back home."

"You have yet to tell me how to control it," he wiped the juice off his chin with his red sleeve.

"No one can ... at least, I don't know how."

"Do not lie to me, girl." He dropped the orange rinds on the floor.

"I'm not, I swear," I pleaded.

"It is hard to believe you when everything that has come out of your mouth has been a lie. Where would this door take me?"

"If it did, it would take you to the future."

"How far?"

"About six hundred years." Lorenzo looked hungrily at Idan.

"How would I get back here?" he asked.

"Again, I don't know."

"Why did you come?"

"I was tricked," I said.

"It is quite sad that you have never had control over your own cir-cumstances ... sort of like now," he said, chewing on the last orange slice. "I think this conversation is at its end ... at least for now."

"What about my choice?"

"Oh yes, thank you for reminding me," he said, cleaning the sharp knife on the tablecloth. "So you get to decide where you stay. I can of-fer you a cell in Le Stiche, which has a wide variety of vermin, a potent stench, and is overcrowded with prisoners of all sorts. Or, you could stay in the tower here at the Signoria. I should warn you it is awfully high and cold wind blows through there. What shall it be?"

"The tower."

"Excellent, that is most convenient for me as well." He smiled. "Ales-sandro! Come in." The door flew open. "You can take her to the tower," he ordered.

"Under what charges?" I yelled as Alessandro led me by the neck.

"I am not sure, but I am leaning towards stealing."

"*What!*" I protested. "I have never stolen a thing in my life."

"It was that or imprisoning you for breaking our dress and gender laws with all that Massimo nonsense. The fact stands, Viola, that you have no record of your identity. Therefore, I am the one writing your past, and let us be honest, your future."

"But why stealing?"

"What a coincidence it is that the day you arrive in Florence, my family's Donatello statue of David goes missing."

"You have no proof!"

"I do not need it. You may take her now," he repeated to Alessandro. "What's the punishment?" I asked, dragging my rubber heels against the tile floor.

"Death."

I scrambled to escape Alessandro, but it was too late for that. My legs and arms flailed, but the guard merely pulled me over his shoulder and carried me out of the room and through the gold-ceilinged room. His breathing struggled with each step he took up the stairs. Judging by his balding head and the broken veins around his handsome nose, I guessed he was middle-aged. His shoulders shook from supporting my body weight.

"You can put me down now," I said, but he continued to fight. After ten more minutes of slow progress, he caved.

"Go on ahead then," he heaved as he let me down.

We climbed up two flickering flights of stairs dripping with candle wax. The steps ended at the crenelated battlement that bulked out of the building below. Sand covered the floor that soldiers paced back and forth. Between the battlement's steps, I looked down at the few lights that burned in the city below.

"No point now that you have nowhere to escape," said Alessandro cutting the rope that bound my hands. "That way." He pointed towards the tower. There was a small platform before entering the tower's spiraling staircase. Before we reached the top, Alessandro stopped short of a low door that broke away from the steps. He fumbled with a heavy set of keys until the door opened. "In you go," said Alessandro. I ducked into the cell, but someone was already there.

"Alessandro," said Giuliano, "I would like a few moments alone with Viola. Would you keep a watch outside to make sure we are undisturbed?" Alessandro looked uncomfortable with this situation.

He cleared his throat and pulled at the tight armor around his neck. "I was given orders that she was to have no visitors."

"I too rule here, and my word is equal to my brother's," retorted Giuliano. Alessandro's shrug told me that it clearly was not the case.

"Come, Viola," said Giuliano.

"I don't want to even be in the same room as you. Let alone listen to you," I said.

"Please ... You'll want to hear what I have to say."

"I doubt it." Alessandro closed the cell door. I moved to the farthest corner from Giuliano in that small stone chamber. Pale beams traveled through the only tall window casting a faint outline on the dusty floor.

"I came to apologize for how things turned out," said Giuliano, twisting the leather brim of his hat.

"Oh, that's nice to know because I am too. I'm really sorry that I fell for your act ... let alone allowed you to kiss me."

"I meant what I said in the garden. I really do care about you."

"If that's true, what am I doing stuck up in a tower?"

"I think my brother is just trying to frighten you. He would not go through with a hanging."

"You think?" I hated his beautiful face so much that I could not think straight. "How did you know I was here?"

"I was listening from behind the door while you spoke with my brother."

"Why didn't you stick up for me?" I asked. He ran a hand through his curls. "I thought I was a coward until I met you. You give a new definition to the word." I slumped against the corner until I felt my knees hit my chest.

"I wanted to! But my brother rarely listens to me."

"Oh! He only listens to you after you spy on me and manipulate me with fake compliments and gifts."

"Any word about your person that has left my lips has been genuine!" exclaimed Giuliano. The wind howled during the quiet recess. "I brought you something," he placed a wool blanket on the only piece of furniture in the cell, a rigid bench. "My grandfather Cosimo was imprisoned here at one point. Every time I asked him about it he would always tell me how cold it was and that was in the month of September, so I brought this blanket, and I'll leave my cloak too," he said, unclasping the dark purple fabric that draped over his body.

We sat together in silence for at least an hour, my hands and face buried into my sweaty dress. I shivered, too proud to grab the blanket.

"I will work on persuading my brother...Do not worry," he said, slipping through the door.

CHAPTER THIRTY-ONE

Visitors

IT WAS NOT UNTIL the locks turned behind him that my panic turned into loneliness. "What will I do? Surely, Mrs. Reed will figure out a way for me to get out. She couldn't go back without me, could she?" I told the moonlight that stole through the window. "But how did I know it was really Mrs. Reed? There were hints and the notes ... but they could have been written by someone else, maybe Pietro?"

My mind ventured into a gloomy hopeless place. I tried to rock myself to sleep so I could suspend the pain that had crept up on me. The chill that frosted the stone surfaces made it impossible. That was when my pride surrendered. I strode to the opposite side of the cell and covered myself with the thick purple woolen cloak. Sometime in between the sobs, I fell asleep underneath the warm huddle perfumed by Giuliano's minty cologne.

I woke to the sun caressing my back. My subconscious scrambled after the dream that was slipping away. It had been a bad dream, but it was better than the nightmare I had awoken to. There in my cloth cocoon, I was safe. It had cost me my pride and possibly my own fatal judgment. With each inhale I allowed myself to think on Giuliano's dimples, but with every exhale I cursed my weakness. My body was in survival mode searching for fat to feast on. My limbs moaned, and my scabby skin felt taut. Dry flakes of blood from the sling stuck to my fingers.

There was a faint knock at the door before it opened. Alessandro came and placed a tray on the floor. Without saying another word, he left. I rolled out of the narrow bench. Novels had prepared me for ashen muck with a side dish of anonymous hairs. To my great surprise, there was fresh bread, soft cheese, an apple, and some juice. With the tray in tow, I retreated to my bench and savored the breakfast with little bites.

As I chewed the morsels, I tried to prolong the inevitable—my future. Giuliano had promised that Lorenzo would not hang me. At least he was being positive. How much was his promise really worth? I couldn't really tell the truth apart from the lies. Hanging or no hanging, it was clear I would never see my parents or my sister again. There was no way out. Tomorrow at dawn the door would open to a tunnel that would carry me home to my family. Stranded three hundred feet in the air, I would miss that open door and my only opportunity.

"How awful," I groaned, realizing I could see the gap where the door would appear from my window. I would not be able to go home but I could watch my captors go through the tunnel's threshold.

Up until that moment the ramifications of what might happen if the door did open for the Medici had not occurred to me. Worse than not being able to go home, I might be single-handedly responsible for imploding history. Those were the thoughts that kept me company when the locks turned again.

"*Buongiorno*, Signorina Orofino." A shaved head and its sharp features snuck past the door. Pietro's lips puckered as they repressed a smile.

"*Buongiorno.*"

"What unfortunate circumstances we find ourselves in," he said, rubbing his scalp. "No doubt you are scared about your punishment." He let this reminder hang in the cold air before he continued. "But I have come to tell you there is no need to trouble yourself." In any other scenario I would have jumped for joy, but my time in Florence had taught me to be skeptical if not defensive.

"Why is that?"

"Because I am willing to strike a deal with you ... and forgive and forget what has occurred between us," said Pietro.

"I'm sorry? Forgive what?" I asked. He pressed his fingers against the pressure points between his eyes. Before lifting his head, he counted softly.

"What do you say you and I drop this charade?" he said in sounds that were distantly familiar. It was so strange to hear English again and even more so to speak it. "You tell me where the statue is, and I will make sure you don't die. What do you say? I don't think you could refuse such a deal." My tongue wagged a bit trying to find my bearings. "You are taking too long ... which means you are trying to come up with some story."

"What statue?"

"The one you saw at my house only a few days ago?" he said, impatiently tapping his left foot.

"I haven't seen it since." He stared at me a long while before speaking again.

"Do you have any idea how long and hard I have been working on that replica?"

"Are you talking about the David you stole from the Medici Palazzo?"

Pietro's eyes darted towards the walls, half-expecting them to come to life. In one swift movement, he jolted forward, grabbing my neck between his rough hands. "I'm not to be played with, Viola ... Again, what have you done with my sculpture?"

"I don't know where it is," I gasped, feeling his grip tighten.

He looked straight into my eyes searching for deceit, but when he did not find it, he let go. I coughed trying to move the lump in my throat.

"She must have taken it," he murmured to himself. Pillows rested underneath his sunken eyes and wrinkles creased his dark tunic. He turned back to face me after regaining his composure. "It is unfortunate we were unable to help each other," he said, starting for the cell's entrance. He banged on the door and the keys scraped. "I'd keep Donatello's David a secret just between us if I were in your shoes," he said, smirking at my grungy converse. "Oh yes! And just in case you were wondering, she won't come for you. Trust me, I know her well." He walked through the door.

"Who? Do you mean Mrs. Reed?" I shouted before the door slammed behind him.

In a short conversation, my hopes of a rescue had vanished. I screamed something shrill that rang through the tower before I collapsed back on the bench. Hours of brooding crawled by as I mulled over the events of the past two days. Didn't Leonardo have a plan? Or was he bluffing? Maybe I should have stayed in the cave. If only Zio knew how right he had been about the tower. Alessandro came back to switch the food trays, but the new meal lay forgotten on the terracotta floor. *I could tell Lorenzo about the David ... but who would he believe? I thought desperately.*

An argument was brewing behind the door. I stood up and moved towards the raised voices. Even though my ear was pressed against the wood, I only caught a few words, "father," "problem," "trouble," before I heard the locks shift again. I ran back to my bench and waited for my second guest.

"Signore Maroni!" I rushed towards his kind face and plump belly. "How did you—" I stopped when I felt a hard shell where his soft stomach should have been. "What?" I asked but he hushed me by placing a finger to his lips. His brilliant blue eyes winced with urgency.

"I have come to check on you, sweet girl," he said in a loud voice, lifting up his tunic shirt. Beneath his tan undershirt, someone had coiled strong rope around his chest and past his paunch. He motioned for me to help him while he continued to spout fatherly concerns.

"Why have you not eaten your lunch? Is that a calzone? How lucky you are!"

I tried to move as quickly as my heartbeat. I kissed the top of his head gratefully after I unraveled each layer. He blushed behind his square spectacles. He pointed towards the blankets.

"Do not worry, Viola, I'm sure the Medici will be merciful on you," he said while I hid the pile of rope under the cloak. "Don't be sad, you will see how much better you feel after nightfall." He passed me a parchment that had been folded over several times. "Be sure to eat your food." He winked, knocking on the door. "Starving yourself is not the answer," he advised before tipping his hat at Alessandro.

The guard glanced at the discarded plate and grumbled something that sounded like "girls" before the door closed again. I waited several minutes before I loosened my fist around the note. Once I had unwrapped it, I immediately recognized the cryptic scrawl.

Viola,

Since I could not wrap enough rope to cover the distance between your window and the piazza, you will have to swing it. There is a metal clasp knotted to one end of

the rope. Press on the circle to release what I like to call "the claw." It should secure the rope to the window ledge. Swing to your left, as you are facing the tower, and then jump onto the rooftop right behind the Signoria. I'll be waiting for you there. Do not descend until the fun begins, just after nightfall. You will know when the time is right. Whatever happens, be the lioness.

Leonardo

My body trembled as I took a second look at the long fall between my window and the piazza. I stuck my head out and looked towards the right. The edge was barely visible from my limited vantage point. Tomato sauce speckled the paper while I reread the escape plan a hundred times over. I did not shred the paper until I had memorized its contents. Sore muscles twitched at each creak, squawk, and yelp. A bad case of the jitters infected me as I waited in nervous anticipation. I tried to rest and conserve my strength, but my eyelids kept blinking open trying to gauge the changing colors of the clear sky. Gradually, my pupils expanded with the dimming light.

The freezing wind blew through my only hope of escape. As instructed, I pressed on the protruding circle of the metal knot attached to the rope. The lever released sharp edges forming a spiky hook.

"How clever," I said as I used its thorny talons to rip through both layers of my dress.

Using both hands, I tore the fabric until it fell in a jagged line around my calves. I wrapped the salvaged strips around my palms. Night came soon after, and I waited, listening hard. It started as a low rumble and then grew into a symphony of shouts, hurried footsteps, and horn blows. Something had obviously gone wrong. Cries carried up to my tower from the piazza below. This must have been the sign Leonardo was talking about, but it seemed rather ominous. I hooked the spiked clasp into one of the window's corners until it had sunk into the sediment.

Lifting one knee at a time, I hunched into the small arch. I looked down at the sheer cliff that fell beyond the windowsill. Before I could retreat, the scraping of metal locks rushed me. One leg, then two, dangled above the face of the Signoria. The cell door creaked. Alessandro's blue-green eyes looked back at me just before I gripped the rope around my bandaged hands and disappeared behind the window. There was no time to think about how I could splatter all over the cobblestones far below. Suddenly, I was hyperaware of my body's jumble of bones, muscles, and skin. My arms locked, and I wrapped my left leg around the rope and crossed my right foot over my left leg. In my delirium I could not help but be grateful for Coach Phillips forcing me to do rope climbs in gym class. Alessandro's balding head poked out from the top of the window.

Little by little, I slipped down the rope until I hung near the stepped battlement. My arms were already tired. I kicked off the surface, all the while anxiously eyeing the edge of the window. My hands were sweating and causing my grip to slip.

"One last jump," I groaned, pushing off with all the energy I had left.

The rope curved around the edge and I let go.

CHAPTER THIRTY-TWO

Refuge

I LANDED HARD ON my knees, sliding forward onto the sandy pavement.

My stockings ripped and so did the scabbed gash on my knees. Scarlet beads dripped onto the white sand as I ran. I looked over the rooftop but in my breathless state, I saw no one.

"Over here!" called Leonardo, his frame hooded in darkness. There was a four-foot drop to get to the next roof. "Hurry up!"

I leaped and tumbled over slightly. My legs shook as I started to slide. Leonardo caught my hand and pulled me back onto the flat edge. "We're late," he said, tugging me along the ridge. We stopped at the edge. While Leonardo examined the tiles, I tried to catch my breath. "There it is," he said tugging at a rope with an identical metal claw. "Right, so grab the rope like this and you are just going to slide a little ways 'til you reach the balcony. Wait for me there."

I looked over the precipice. "That's not a balcony. That's a shelf!"
"Which leads to a balcony ... Come on! This is easy compared to what you just did."

I sat on the roof's edge and held on to the rope with my splintered fingers. With my back to the fall, I started sliding down. My fingers surged with pain as the sharp straw pressed against my skin. Once the balls of my feet reached the narrow ledge, I leaned forward and grabbed the open window frame. Doubling over, I pulled my torso into the portico. After my legs were safely inside the balcony, I tugged at the rope. Within seconds, Leonardo swung into the balcony with one smooth nimble motion.

"You're such a show-off."

"How about ... 'thank you, Leonardo, for getting me out of prison.'" He paused. "Then you could follow up with something like, 'not only are you a genius but you are also my hero,'" he said, opening the door beyond the roofed balcony, which led down a dark corridor.

"That goes without saying," I whispered.

"Why are you whispering? This is my house," he said, pointing towards the room we had dined in on Christmas.

"Oh! That is right, it was right behind the Signoria." We hurried down the stairs and stopped at the main entrance. Leonardo pressed his ear against its wooden surface. "What are you listening for?"

"Lions."

"Excuse me?" I asked.

"Remember my friend Jacopo, the giant who takes care of the lions?"

"Yes."

"Well, the Signoria keeps several of them in a hall on the first floor. A few hours ago, he fed them a few extra deer. When they were good and full, he opened the gate ... by accident." He winked.

"They could have hurt someone!"

"No, they could not. They are too lazy. Even if they did, serves them right for cooping them up where they do not belong. At least they got to stretch their legs a bit," he said, handing me his cloak and then opening the door.

"Where are we going?" I asked, fastening the cloak around my neck.

"Shhh! You'll see."

The cool night deepened, and the strong wind that had been my cellmate had calmed to a breeze. Its presence soothed the burn of my scrapes and cooled my sweat. Leonardo led me in a half-circle through a series of back streets. The familiar fumes of campfire floated past us as we turned onto Via Vacchereccia. The decadent displays of silk bundles and luscious textiles were absent from the hanging canopies. Leonardo walked up to Signore Soldo's shop, but before he could knock, I seized his hand.

"Wait!"

"Why?"

"I don't want to get him in trouble."

"I promise he will not be in any kind of danger. Anyway, it is too late for that. Let us be honest, without serious help you would not have been able to do it alone," said Leonardo.

"I know." I frowned.

"For your information, I did not force anyone, no more than you forced me. They were all eager to help."

"What do you mean *they all*?" I asked. Leonardo turned towards me, placing his hands on my shoulders.

"What, did you believe that all prison guards are as gentle as Alessandro, and prisoners get to eat sausage calzones? Or that they all let in sweet-looking grandfathers to visit prisoners?" Leonardo knocked twice at Signore Soldo's shop door.

"So you're saying Alessandro was involved too?"

"Luckily for us, Alessandro is Signore Maroni's son," said Leonardo.

"That is why he helped us?"

"If it was not for you, his sons' only caretaker and beloved Nonno would be locked up in debtors' prison."

"Who's there?" called Signore Soldo.

"Brunelleschi," answered Leonardo. The door cracked open.

"Heavens above, Viola, look at you! What did they do to you?" asked Signore Soldo as he bolted the door behind us. His eyes lingered at the jagged hem, bleeding knees, and bandaged hands.

"No one ... I did this to myself."

"I think she looks great!" added Leonardo. "Like a proper warrior."

"A proper mess more like it! Go back to the pantry. There is a bucket of water that should still be hot," said Soldo pointing past the shelves of silk. "I brought your things from Caterina's house. They are back there too." I walked towards the back of the shop.

The pantry was much like Zia's. Jars teeming with pickled food and spools of thread lined the cabinets that covered the walls. In the center of the pantry, a metal bucket steamed. A lump of pink soap bubbled at the bottom of the warm water. One by one, I peeled off the grungy layers that had protected my body. Their crusty surface made a hard sound when they hit the tile floor. I lathered the dirt and blood until the red color changed to white. My knees took the longest. Each soapy stroke was torturous. The brown water was lukewarm when I finished. Naked, I looked around for my dress, but instead, I found my ripped jeans, purple scarf, and black undershirt. It felt strange pulling on clothes that seemed to belong to a stranger. As I wrapped the scarf around my neck, I could smell the musky books and the flowery perfume that rested on my dresser in New York City. The chime of Renzo's voice reached me before I left the pantry.

"What are you doing here, Renzo? You could get in an awful lot of trouble," I said, walking towards the shop front.

"But more importantly, did you tell anyone you were coming?" asked Leonardo.

"I wouldn't risk my maiden's life!" exclaimed Renzo defensively.

"Well, you better hope you were not followed. I do not know how long it will be before they realize Viola is gone."

Signore Soldo stirred the pot of lentil soup before ladling it into four shallow bowls. We pulled out the table pushed to the side during shop hours and sat at its benches.

"I'm afraid it's not Zia's cooking, but at least it's piping hot," he apologized. "I have had to learn to fend for myself, you know. I just assume adding a healthy dose of garlic makes anything taste better." He placed a basket of brown bread on the table. "I am also convinced it keeps me young."

"Cooking or the garlic?" laughed Leonardo.

"The garlic! Sit here by the fire, Viola."

"Thank you, Signore Soldo ... for everything," I said.

"It is my absolute pleasure," he said, taking a seat at the bench across from me. "What you have done for Zia..." he choked "...there are no words."

"He thinks you are an angel, Viola," said Leonardo.

"So what if I do? It makes a lot more sense than the rubbish you have all come up with. To be frank, I care for my version much more."

It was hard not to harbor that fuzzy feeling inside as the fire warmed my back, and I looked around at my brilliant rescue party. After only a few ravenous spoonfuls of silence, there was a rap at the door.

"Who is it?" called Signore Soldo.

"It is Andrea del Verrocchio," answered the voice.

Leonardo got up to check the tiny peephole. Soon after, Verrocchio's large figure stepped into the shop. He sighed with relief when he saw me.

"How did you know we were here?" asked Leonardo.

"I followed Renzo." The poor boy looked around and scratched at the phantom lice nibbling around his ears.

"Well, I was being extra careful! I did not hear anyone behind me."

"To his credit he was," added Verrocchio. "Once I saw him knock at this door, I decided to come by on my way back from the hospital."

"Why did you go to the hospital? Are you unwell?" we asked.

"Nothing like that," he said, removing his hat and taking a seat at the bench. "I've been looking for Salai since Christmas Eve and have only just found him. The nurse told me they spotted him crumpled in a ball by the Ospedale degli Innocenti. What had started out as a bad case of drunkenness almost turned into pneumonia."

"I don't feel the slightest bit sorry for him," I interjected, not meeting Verrocchio's eye.

"Well, I do," he said. "It was a pitiful sight, seeing him there. He's not as heartless as you suppose him to be."

"I'm not convinced."

"Then it is a good thing I did not come to convince you of anything," he said, accepting the glass of wine from Signore Soldo. "I came to apologize."

"To me?"

"Yes, I realize I did not really teach you anything."

"You were busy," I said, wiping stray lentils from my mouth. "And I did learn a lot, especially from Renzo and Leonardo." He took a long drag from the wine glass. The lines on his forehead spoke of regret. "There really was not enough time. How long do apprentices usually stay with you?"

"It depends on the apprentice, but usually about a decade." Another thump at the door interrupted the many side conversations happening at once.

"Who's there?" repeated Signore Soldo for the fourth time. "Medici," said the deep voice beyond the door. I was halfway to the pantry and into a panic attack when I heard Sandro's stifled laughter.

"Just kidding! It is Botticelli." We all let out a sigh of relief when the door opened, and Sandro brushed passed Leonardo.

"You scared me to death!" I said.

"But now you are so glad to see me! I just wanted a bit of fun is all."

"How did you know I was here?"

"Well, I felt a little responsible for what happened to you."

"It had noth—"

"If I would have been a proper guardian, this might never have happened."

"That's not the case, but it seems I won't be able to convince you otherwise."

"You're right."

"You still haven't answered my question," I said.

"Well, I went to Verrocchio's workshop after I heard the news to see if I could help in any way."

"He helped me to test out the claw," said Leonardo, who stood up to join the conversation.

Verrocchio reached up to pat Sandro on the back, congratulating him on his new patron. The interruption allowed me a brief moment to look around the shop.

"What is wrong?" asked Leonardo. I shook my head. "Why is it with all women you must ask what is bothering them three or four times before they actually tell you?"

"It's just, I know that when I go back, I'll never see any of you again. I'll be leaving behind the few friends I have."

"You have no friends where you come from?"

"Does my father count?"

"Definitely not." He grinned.

"Then no, I don't."

"As people that care about you, we want you to be safe. That is no longer possible for you in Florence. I say this with all the love of a brother ... you do not belong here. I do not think you will lack for friends ever again."

"How can you be sure of that?"

"I cannot be too sure of anything so abstract, but the Viola I met at Mercato Vecchio would not have dangled off the side of the Signora."

"You might be right," I said, chewing my lip.

"By the way, do you have any genius ideas for getting back?"

"We need a way to be in the piazza watching for the perfect moment to take back Idan," I said.

"How are you planning on that?" asked Leonardo.

"All we need is half of a good plan, but mostly great timing."

"You can be performers!" said Renzo, squeezing himself into the middle of the huddle.

"There is that theatre troop that performs in Piazza della Signoria," Leonardo agreed.

"How would we manage that?" I asked.

"Sandro and I can make the masks," explained Leonardo, his voice escalating with excitement. "We just need volunteers ... Two is a suspicious number."

"How many times do I have to say that I don't want anyone else getting in trouble!"

"One person in a costume is scary at best," pointed out Leonardo. "As I was saying, you also need to put on a cloak and a hat that covers most of your head ... Come to think of it, my father has a couple of those. I guess he's a little self-conscious about his balding. I will grab those."

"I want to be a performer," implored Renzo.

"I have always had a flair for drama," offered Signore Soldo.

"And I," said Sandro, tossing back the remaining red wine.

"But what if you all get caught?" I asked.

"Stop worrying so much," said Leonardo. "The minute you make a slow run for it, we will take off at a much quicker pace."

"Very funny."

"It is a natural gift," teased Leonardo. "Unlike your running skills."

"Are you done?"

"Yes." He stood up, and Sandro followed his lead. "We will be here in a couple of hours." A cold gust squeezed through the crack in the door as they opened it.

Once it closed behind them, the fire dampened. Verrocchio beckoned me to sit next to him. I could tell by the batting of his eyelashes that the glass he held in his hand was one of several.

"I also wanted to give you this." He pulled out my spotted apron from the workshop. "I thought you would want to keep it as a memento," he said as I traced Margherita's embroidery with his thumb.

"Thank you ... I'm sure you must miss her," I said, accepting the folded apron.

"More than words can express." He clenched his jaw. "I will also miss you, Viola."

"You mean Massimo?"

"No, I mean Viola." He pulled me into a hug and without another word finished his wine and left.

CHAPTER THIRTY-THREE

Dawn

THE RESCUE PARTY WAS down to Renzo and Signore Soldo. While they both set up a makeshift bed of fabric and patterned cushions, I moved to put the apron in my satchel and clean the dishes. Signore Soldo's eyelids drooped farther and farther over his eyes until he excused himself. While I watched Renzo roll around on the shop's mattress of silk, I took out my sketchbook. At first, I doodled whatever my imagination unloaded onto the paper: hybrid animals a sphinx would be jealous of and composite monsters that sported similar knee wounds took form from the ink. I'm not sure when my pen dropped nor when my cheek leaned against the fresh doodles. I woke at the knock of the door. Half-dazed, I opened the door. Leonardo and Sandro filed in with their arms full of props.

"You did not even ask who it was!" complained Leonardo, who looked fresher than ever.

"I'm sorry," I said, stifling a yawn. "I'm surprised I fell asleep."

"It is a good thing you are going to wear a mask."

"What's that supposed to mean?" I asked defensively.

"Because you have ink stains all over your face."

"Pretty typical I guess," I replied, trying to rub them off with some saliva and the cuff of my sweater. "Renzo is sleeping."

"Wake him up! We need to get going. Dawn is almost here," said Sandro. Nerves quickly replaced my sleepy haze, the kind you get before you go on stage at a school play or just before you get on a plane.

"I'll wake up Francesco," said Leonardo, walking towards the stairs at the back of the shop.

"Renzo, wake up." I rubbed his back.

"I don't want to," he grumbled.

"That's fine if you don't want to," I whispered reassuringly. "You can stay here in bed."

"I'm not scared!" He stared up at me.

"Then why don't you want to get up?"

"Because that means you will be leaving me, just like Margherita," he said with all the sweetness and innocence that showed the virtue of his age. At a loss for words, I kissed him on his forehead, and he squeezed my hand.

"This one is yours, Viola," interrupted Sandro, holding out an orange mask.

"It's hideous!" I protested.

"Leonardo's orders." I accepted the orange mask with the chubby cheeks and long, pointed nose. "Here is the hat." He tossed a bulky brown turban into my lap. "This one is for you, Renzo." Sandro handed him a fawn-like mask.

Once Leonardo and Signore Soldo came downstairs, they too were dressed in full costume, complete with less ugly versions of my mask. Signore Soldo helped me bundle all my hair into the turban while the others waited outside.

"Almost forgot," said Leonardo, passing me a cane. "What's this for?"

"It's to make your costume look more convincing. Also, if you're hunched over no one will be able to see your weird shoes."

"But my cloak is covering them."

"Barely," he said, eyeing the hem of the cloak. "It is also a good weapon."

"We have to hurry!" urged Sandro.

Early birds eyed us with amusement as our troop of bizarre actors walked past them. Signore Soldo's shop was just around the corner of Piazza della Signoria. Although it was a small distance, the walk felt even shorter as I remembered the first time I had walked down Via Vacchereccia arm in arm with Zia. Straight ahead lay the tower and the window I had looked out from my prison cell. Never did I allow myself to hope that I would be standing where I was. Lone grocers and their goods carted off across the piazza. While we walked towards the stage that had been abandoned in the plaza, I chanced a glance at the door frame, but there was no one near it.

"Do not be nervous," encouraged Leonardo. "You are not really that bad at running ... you know I just like to tease you."

"I know that," I said, trying to swallow the lump that was growing in my throat.

Our troop climbed the stage and each one took turns doing what they thought actors did. Some rehearsed sonnets they knew. Others fussed with the torn canopy or tumbled across the floorboards. Still, there was no sign. The sky seeped violet and ginger as the sun approached.

"They are coming," whispered Leonardo.

I scrambled to look busy, but I could not think of anything to do as four figures turned onto the piazza. The tallest and leader was Pietro, who was quickly cutting a path through the faint fog. Following close behind him were the Medici brothers and a guard. While I turned to face Leonardo, I knew my time had run out.

"Leonardo ... I—"

"Do not say it," interrupted Leonardo. "I cannot stand goodbyes."

"Stop being so bossy!" I said, watching the pack of four pass the stage. "I wanted to say ... that I will miss you more than I have ever missed anyone." Trying to grasp the words, I looked down at the wooden boards. "What you have done for me, well, it's been—"

"I think I know what you are trying to say."

"I love you dearly," I said. "I've never had a friend like you, and I know I never will."

"You took the words right out of my mouth," he said, giving me one last smile. "I don't have a sister, but if I ever do ... I hope she grows up like you."

"I'd kiss you goodbye, but I think you gave me this big-nosed mask so I couldn't."

"How clever you are," he said before he kissed my cheek. "You had better keep an eye out for your perfect moment."

I picked up my cane and was about to face the rest of my rescue party until I realized what a good time they were having with their new actor roles. It seemed a shame to ruin it with salty goodbyes. I wanted to remember them just like that, Renzo and Sandro having a handstand contest and Signore Soldo their judge. Slipping quietly off the stage,

I crept towards the door's shadow. Giuliano was closest to the passageway's faint outline, but Lorenzo held Idan. His eyes flashed from the door to Idan. With each step, I could hear Idan's high-pitched tick escalate. Pietro's gaze was fixed on the concrete wall. I blinked once and an oak door was there where the stones used to be. The stunned guard dropped his guard, shifting all his weight towards the hip that boasted his sword. My gut told me the moment had come. I spared one look back at Leonardo, but he was no longer there. They had all run away, just as they promised.

It was my turn to do the same. I took a deep breath and bolted. As my legs pushed hard off the ground, my healing knee caps screamed.

Hurdling towards the door, I shed the cloak and mask. I was upon them. Giuliano's eyes doubled in size with surprise. A shrill scream pinched the quiet morning. Lorenzo turned to its source but instead, he got a shove in the belly and the pocket watch he worked so hard to get was snatched from his hands.

"Giuliano!" shouted Lorenzo.

Only two leaps remained between the tunnel and me. My hand was on the knob when Giuliano caught me by the waist. I struggled as hard as I could but to no avail.

"Do not let go of her!" threatened Lorenzo as he grabbed his side.

"Why could you not stay put?" whispered Giuliano in my ear.

"Because I don't belong here," I pleaded. "You know that! Please let me go!"

"I care for you, but I cannot—"

"Prove it then!" His grip loosened and I wiggled free.

"Giuliano! No!" was the last thing I heard when the door closed behind me.

I rushed into the tunnel, Idan's chain safely tangled around my neck. As the tunnel narrowed, I crouched so I wouldn't crawl on my gashed knees. It took me a moment to realize that it was not just my heavy breathing echoing off the stone walls of the tunnel. I quickened my pace towards the bright outline of the painting. When the tunnel expanded, I sprinted and slipped down the smooth corridor. Hurried footsteps followed me. Once I squeezed through the painting's surface and jumped off the tunnel's platform, Mrs. Crawly's happy face welcomed me.

"Help me!" I said as I tried to block the painting with my body.

"What on Earth are you doing?" She laughed. "We must wait for Mrs. Reed."

CHAPTER THIRTY-FOUR

Thai

A FORCE PUSHED THROUGH the painting. Mrs. Crawly approached the swirling paint and offered her hand to the emerging time traveler. Mrs. Reed gracefully hopped down.

"That was a close one." She grinned, brushing off the dust that had gathered on her black gown.

"Closer than Egypt?" asked Mrs. Crawly as she took Mrs. Reed's cloak.

"Even closer."

"I can't wait to hear all about it!"

"And so, you shall," promised Mrs. Reed. "Is everything in order?"

"The baths are drawn, and lunch is almost ready."

"Excellent ... Will you show Viola the way?"

"It would be an honor," said Mrs. Crawly, gently taking my hand. My mind blanked as she guided me past hundreds of art pieces. Every motion, sound, and smell was a vivid déjà vu. "Oh dear, you're shaking," she said squeezing my hand the way little Renzo had. Tears flowed steadily down my inked face. "The shock is normal, Viola. It will pass soon enough."

Warmth soothed my face as she opened a door off the wide carpeted hallway. She led me into the enormous bathroom. It had high ceilings and one large window that overlooked the miles of garden. Steam hovered over a bathtub propped up from the green marble floor by lion feet. Mrs. Crawly was about to leave me when she stopped short of the door.

"Shall I help you, Viola?"

I made no response. It was all so painful. My heart grieved for the hollow space where my friends had been. Every pore and muscle ached. I stared at my haggard reflection in the mirror. Ink had mixed with my tears leaving an indigo smear. Instead of hair, I had wild wire poking in all directions, but the worst of it was I didn't recognize myself.

Normally, in my lucid fifteen-year-old state, I would be too embarrassed to be naked in front of a woman I didn't know. But that afternoon, I was a limp lump. She helped me take off my clothes and get into the bath. If I had not been so dehydrated, I would probably still been crying. It felt glorious to submerge myself into the hot perfumed water. It had been so long since water encased me.

Wilted white petals spun around me as poor Mrs. Crawly washed my hair and spoke a constant stream of comforts. I let her motherly concern ease the ache while I looked absently over the white porcelain and into the garden's muddled grass below.

"You must be hungry, my dear ... Shall we get you to lunch while your clothes are being cleaned?" she asked, standing at the porcelain edge with a robe. I pushed myself out of the tub and slipped on the robe.

Barefoot, I followed Mrs. Crawly down the carpeted stairs and cold tiled atrium. Mrs. Reed was waiting for me at a humble table that faced the driveway.

"I thought we would eat here instead of the drafty dining room. We can also watch your father drive up." Mrs. Crawly came back with a cart laden with silver trays. "Let's start with the soup," said Mrs. Reed. The patient woman served the creamy coconut soup into bowls and left us to our meal. "I don't know about you, but I couldn't eat one more strand of spaghetti. Every time I come back, I have an incredible craving for Thai food." I could not help staring at her. She looked so calm whereas I felt like a wet dog. "You must have many questions." I took my spoon and dipped it into the creamy soup. *I didn't have many questions, I had thousands*, I thought, trying to pick one. "Well, I might not look it, but I'm quite tired so I can answer a few," she said.

"A few?" I scowled.

"Some things are better left for another time ... when emotions and memories are less fresh."

"I don't agree," I said over the scraping of spoons. "Let's start with why you tricked me in the first place."

"Tricked you?"

"Yes, you tricked me into going behind that painting."

"I did nothing of the sort! I merely pointed out Verrocchio's *Baptism of Christ* painting ... I didn't force you to go down the tunnel behind it," she said, serving herself some rice and curried vegetables. "You did that all on your own."

"With all due respect, Mrs. Reed, you are the one that put Idan in my satchel."

"Just in case."

"In case what?"

"Do you know anything about time travel theories?" She paused, looking out the window.

"No."

"Well, there are several. One is the 'Grandfather Paradox,' which says if you were to go back in time you could jeopardize the chances of your existence in the future. As we are still here, that is clearly not the case. At least to my knowledge." She filled my plate with the spicy green curry and pearly rice. "Another theory states that time is a fixed line. In other words, all your actions in 1469 Florence had already happened.

That is, it is a destiny that has already been written. I just put you in a situation that allowed you to go back, if, and only if you were meant to."

"So you are saying I was supposed to go to the past?"

"Correct ... I also believed you needed a push."

"Who asked you to push me?" I asked angrily.

"This might be hard for you to believe, but I care for you a great deal," she said, looking up from her plate.

"You hardly know me, and I could have died," I protested. "Several times!"

"I was there the entire time. No real harm would have come to you."

"What about when I was dangling off the tower?" I asked. She reddened.

"I confess to missing that episode. I had a mission to fulfill when I was there, and as Idan's time was running short, there was little time left."

"Did you have another Idan?"

"No, I was tagging along with you."

"What do you mean?" I asked, my head spinning.

"The same amount of people that go into the portal with Idan must come back ... So when I heard you unlock the latch, I was prepared to follow you through the tunnel."

"But how did you get back? I mean, Lorenzo could have followed me, and you would have been stuck in the past?"

"I was waiting for you at the mouth of the tunnel. You hurried right past me," she said, pouring herself some icy water. "I tried to protect you, but you kept ignoring my letters. So I decided to let you work it out your own way ... and look how well you did!"

"Pietro said you wouldn't come for me," I said, suddenly remembering his threats in the tower.

"Peter," she corrected.

"What?"

"His name is Peter."

"How do you know?"

"Because he's my son," she said, taking a large gulp of water. My eyes nearly rolled out into my curry. "It sounds like something Peter would say. He was just trying to scare you, darling. I have saved him plenty of times, although his pride will not allow him to admit it. Throughout his life, I made things far too easy for him. He never had to share or make sacrifices, like I did and still do. From a young age, I have lost so much—my daughter, John, and now my son. It is a great comfort to have you here with me, my dear Viola. I have so longed to meet you," she smiled but the corners of her mouth barely left their resting place. "Needless to say, I am sorry he took his anger out on you."

"He was angry about his missing statue."

"Not quite," she said, wiping the creases of her mouth with a cloth napkin. "We used to time travel together, my husband, Peter, and I. We used it more for educational purposes. We're not sure who invented it yet, but we think it might have started with Galileo. From an early age, it was clear that Peter was exceptionally talented. He learned from the best masters in history. Over the years, he became very solitary, proud, and resentful."

"Of who?"

"Everyone." She sighed. "My husband and I wanted to preserve the past, but my son wanted to play a grand trick on the world."

"What do you mean?"

"You saw it, no? Donatello's *David* ? " I nodded. "Well Peter wasn't just making a copy for fun. He was making a copy to replace it."

"Why?"

"I have come to two explanations for his behavior. The first is that he wants to keep the original for himself and to fool everyone else using his talent. Another reason is that he wants to make all those people who wait in line at the Louvre to take a picture of something like the *Mona Lisa* a fool."

"I still don't understand ... why would he want to do that?"

"Well, it is hard to put into one sentence. For starters, he was rejected from every art school he applied to."

"Why?"

"Each rejection letter said his technical skills were impressive but that he lacked creativity. As a result, he grew angry and contemptuous. He often said, 'Art died with the Impressionists,' meaning somewhere around the early twentieth century ... I'm not really sure what ultimately motivates his stealing and manipulation. He was extremely secretive growing up," she said, scraping her fork against the plate. "To get back to the point, people go to museums because they want to see the original artwork, so instead of seeing Donatello's David in a museum hundreds of years later, they would have been seeing Peter Reed's *David*."

"That's not right."

"I agree ... but you helped me with my mission. You provided enough of a distraction that he was caught off guard just enough for me to steal his copy and replace the original in the Palazzo Medici."

"What did you do with the copy?"

"I melted it." She frowned. "It broke my heart ... It was absolutely perfect."

"But how did you know where he was?"

"I told you I would answer a few questions," she said, ringing the bell. Mrs. Crawly came bustling in with crystal glasses brimming with rice pudding.

"Your clothes are good as new, Viola. They are in the bathroom just around the corner when you are ready. Your father should be here any minute," said Mrs. Crawly before rolling the cart away.

"Regarding the subject, I will say that my husband and I felt greatly responsible for Peter's vanity and disdain for others. First, we tried to reason with him, but he always eluded us. Then we made it our mission to stop him ... My John, Signore Reed that is, had a heart attack and since I have been unable to track Peter," she said, breaking the dessert's cinnamon crust. "I need someone to go back in time with me." Charlemagne's honk sounded from the driveway. "I suppose you'd better get dressed," she said, shaking her head.

The warm, pressed surface of my clothes truly looked new, apart from the rips in my jeans. I pulled my pants slowly over my fresh wounds. My green sweater smelled like roses as I slipped it over my head. When I emerged from the bathroom, Charlemagne was parked in the driveway. I ran outside to greet Dad, and Mrs. Reed followed close behind.

"We will see each other soon, sweet Viola," she said leaving an eerie imprint of her lipstick on my forehead.

To my unadjusted eyes, Charlemagne was the essence of technology. Once the car rolled to a stop, I hopped in. Mrs. Reed held the car door open, reaching over to shake hands with my dad. Her perfume clashed with my dad's familiar musky aftershave.

"Thank you so much for sharing Viola with me. I think we had a wonderful time."

"Thank you for having her." My dad smiled, letting go of her hand.

Mrs. Reed shut the car door and kept up a steady wave as we rolled back down the winding entrance. I sat savoring the comfort of just sitting down and not having to do anything for the next hour. I propped my head against the cold window as we drove past the dormant gardens and spider gate. The heat from the vents gave off a burnt smell, but the toasty car felt magnificent. My hands retreated into my knit sleeves as I sunk further into the car seat and let my eyes close.

"Missed you like crazy, Dad," I said, turning to squeeze him.

"Nonsense, Violet, I was only gone two hours!" He laughed, veering off onto the grass.

"Violet ... Violet Menet ..." I whispered to myself. It felt strange now to hear it. Who was Violet? She was a girl with no friends, no confidence, and scared of everything, including people, but especially of frogs. Was I Violet?

"Dad?"

"Hmm?"

"I don't think Violet suits me anymore."

"What do you mean?"

"I mean … I think Viola suits me better, not Violet."

"Is this about what I said to Mrs. Reed?" he asked as we braced a bump in the road. "I didn't mean to embarrass you. The words just flew out of my mouth. You have a term for that … what do you call it? Word vomit?"

"Wormit."

"Yes! Exactly … wormit."

"Don't worry, that isn't what this is about. I don't want to hide behind a name anymore. Viola is who I want to be."

"That's good enough for me. Your mom will be thrilled. How did you bang up your knees?" He winced.

"I fell down the stairs."

"So clumsy! Were your jeans torn when you left the house?"

"Yes, Dad."

"It's good I didn't notice until now, otherwise I would have asked you to change. I don't get this ripped jeans fashion statement. I hope I didn't pay for those," he rambled.

"Who won the game?"

"Manchester United, unfortunately," was the last thing I heard before I dozed off.

GLOSSARY

A

Aisle: a long pathway of an interior area, as in a church, separated from the main area by a structure like an arcade.

Allora: an Italian word that is used frequently as a filler or to express interest. It can mean "then," "really," "so," or to express surprise.

Arcade: a sequence of arches sustained by piers.

Arch: a structure (usually curved) that spans a distance and maintains the weight above it.

B

Baptistery: a Christian structure within a church or a separate building where the sacrament of baptism is administered.

Barrel Vault: also called tunnel vault; the extension of an arch's curve.

Basilica: this term was originally used to describe a public Roman building. It later became known as a large and important church that received special ceremonies from the Pope.

Bastard : the term bastard is often understood as an insult for children born to unmarried parents or children without legitimate fathers. During this period, an illegitimate child was relegated to second-class citizenry status and was unable to hold public office. Moreover, they were socially and professionally disadvantaged.

Botticelli, Sandro (b. 1445 – d. 1510): an early Renaissance painter whose major patron was Lorenzo de' Medici. He was born in Florence and given the name Alessandro di Mariano di Vanni Filipepi. It is noted that he was apprentice to Fra Filippo Lippi. He is well known for his beautiful allegorical paintings such as *The Birth of Venus* and *Primavera*. Some historians argue that he suffered from an unrequited love for Simonetta Vespucci. Prior to his death, Botticelli requested to be buried at her feet.

Brunelleschi, Filippio (b. 1377 – d. 1446) : was one of the most innovative architects and engineers of the Italian Renaissance. He is immortalized for engineering the dome of the Florence Cathedral or Basilica di Santa Maria del Fiore as well as for rediscovering architectural feats that had been lost in the Middle Ages.

C

Ceninni, Cennino d'Andrea (approx. b. 1370 –d. 1440) : a painter influenced by Giotto. He was the author of *Il Libro dell'Arte* (translated to *The Craftsman's Handbook*), which explains many of the complex procedures carried out in artists' workshops.

Charlemagne (approx. b. 747–d. 814 A.D.): also known as Charles the Great, or Charles I, the founder of the Carolingian Empire, reigning from 768 A.D. until his death.

Cloister: a rectangular building framed by open galleries with arcades running along its sidewalls. It is commonly attached to a cathedral or church to separate the life of the monks from that of the people.

Colonnades: a series of columns that can be open or joined by another form.

Creato: means little creature. It is what they often called young apprentices in workshops.

Credi, di Lorenzo (b. 1459 – d. 1537): an artist and sculptor that began his apprenticeship in Andrea del Verrocchio's workshop. After the Maestro's death, he inherited the direction of the workshop.

Crypt: a stone chamber built beneath the ground that can contain tombs, coffins, bones, or relics.

D

Dominican Order : a Roman Catholic religious order founded by Spanish priest Saint Domini de Guzman in the 13th century. This intellectual order preaches the gospel to fight heresy.

Dowry: the wealth given from the bride's family to the groom's family upon marriage.

Drum: the hollow space contained within the dome.

Duomo : Italian for dome. The Cathedral of Florence, also called Basilica di Santa Maria del Fiore, is nicknamed the *Duomo*. Its construction began in 1296. The base structure was crowned by its dome at the beginning of the 15th century.

F

Façade: a term that commonly refers to the front exterior of a building.

Fleur-de-lis: a heraldic device of three stylized petals or floral segments of an iris enclosed by a band.

Franciscan Order : similar to the Dominican order, a Roman Catholic order founded in 1209 by Saint Francis of Assisi. Followers of this order vow to live as Christ did, in that they are to have no worldly possession and to preach to the common people.

Fresco : a technique of wall painting that involves applying lime plaster and then painting directly on the surface while it is still wet. This locks the pigment into place.

G

Gables: part of the front or side of a building enclosed by a pitched roof: often includes a window.

Ginerva and Antonio: characters based on real people named Ginevra degli Amieri and Antonio Rondinelli, as well as related events from early 15th century Florence.

Grasso: upper or elite social class of Florence.

Guild: a group of merchants or artisans who strive to uphold standards and to defend the interests of its members.

H

Herculaneum: an ancient Roman port city that was destroyed along with Pompeii during the Eruption of Mt. Vesuvius in 79 A.D. Now, it is a rich archaeological site with thousands of petrified objects.

I

Incappucciati: a group of hooded men dedicated to the assistance of the sick and injured and the burial of abandoned corpses.

Inlay: a technique that is most often used with stone where separate pieces of stone are carved in an exact manner and then fused together by the precision of all the separate pieces.

L

Linear Perspective: a mathematical technique for illustrating three- dimensional objects and area on a two-dimensional surface by transecting lines vertically and horizontally that radiate from one point (one-point perspective), two points (two-point perspective), or several points on a horizon line.

Lost Wax Method: a method that involved carving a full-scale wax model and then covering it with a fire resistant material like clay. The wax and clay were then heated until the wax melted out, leaving a hollow mold.

Lapis lazuli : a blue stone known to be found only in what is now Afghanistan, hence its expensive price tag.

M

Malachite: a green mineral or basic copper carbonate. In history, it was often used to paint vivid green and blue hues.

Masaccio (b. 1401 –d. 1428): one of the great painters from the early Italian renaissance. His given name was Tommaso di Ser Giovanni di Simone. He inspired many artists in the Renaissance and is considered a painting pioneer in using linear perspective.

Medici, Giuliano (b. 1453 – d. 1478) : the younger brother of Lorenzo de' Medici and the second son of Piero the Gouty. It is said he was well loved and handsome. He fathered one illegitimate son, who would later become Pope Clement VII. Giuliano was assassinated at the Duomo during the Pazzi conspiracy.

Medici, Lorenzo (b. 1449 – d. 1492): also known as Lorenzo the Magnificent, was the eldest son and heir of the Medici fortune. He ruled the Florentine Republic for many years. He is noted for his academic and political prowess. In addition, his patronage of the arts and the humanist pursuits led Florence into its Golden Age.

Memento Mori : a Latin saying that means "remember that you will die." It is a symbolic reminder of the inevitability of death.

Mercato Vecchio : the old market built on the site of the ancient Roman Forum. It was in an area of Florence that was demolished, along with the old Ghetto, at the turn of the 20th century and led the way for the creation of the Piazza della Repubblica.

Minuto: lower class or "the people."

Monochromatic : a term to describe an object or painting made up of one color or shades of one color.

Moria : also called the Black Death, or the bubonic plague, was an epidemic that peaked in Europe from 1350 to 1400. During this period over a third of Europe's population was killed by the disease.

N

Nave : the main passageway of a church. It ranges from the main entrance or narthex to the altar. Aisles commonly flank its sides.

Niche : a decorative recess in a barrier. It is often used to hold statues or other ornamental objects.

Nonna: Italian for "grandmother."

Nonno: Italian for "grandfather."

O

Ocher : organic pigment obtained from the earth that ranges from yellow to orange in color.

Oculus: the circle at a dome's center.

Ospedale degli Innocenti : also called Hospital of the Innocents, was an orphanage designed by Filippo Brunelleschi, who received the commission in 1419.

P

Palazzo: Italian for palace.

Pediment : a low triangular gable that commonly forms a major division of a façade.

Perugino, Pietro (approx. b. 1450 – d. 1523) : a painter who was trained in Andrea de Verrocchio's workshop.

Piazza : a large open square. It is usually surrounded by buildings and has at its center a statue, monument, or fountain.

Pilaster: a rectangular structure jutting from a wall with a base and capital that mimics the form of a column.

Pillar : a shaft of masonry usually used as a building support but can also stand alone.

Popolo : an Italian word that refers to "the people."

Putti : cherub angels.

R

Relief : is an artistic method used when carving with stone. Scenes are etched in high or low relief into the stone. Low means a shallow carving and high refers to more modeling.

Rose Window : often refers to a principal circular window, but is often used to describe those found in church facades.

Renaissance : a time period of the renewal of art, literature, and human-ism in Europe beginning in the 14th century and lasting into the 17th century.

Renaissance Man : a term used to describe a person who shows talent or has an expertise over a wide variety of subjects.

S

Salai (b. 1480– d. 1520) : the only real person and artist whose character I transplanted into an earlier time. His given name was Gian Giacomo Caprotti da Oreno. He became an apprentice of Leonardo da Vinci in Milan and stayed under his workshop for many years. The nickname "Salai," means "little devil" and it was given to him by Leonardo for his mischievous nature.

Santa Croce : a Franciscan basilica in Florence consecrated in 1443. Its format is meant to imitate the Franciscan austere principles. It has long since been a popular center of patronage and contains the tombs of many famous individuals including Michelangelo and Galileo.

San Lorenzo : another basilica in Florence. Brunelleschi was commis-sioned to design the building, which was finished after his death in 1470. Its principle patrons were the Medici family. It is also where sev-eral prominent members of the family are buried, including Lorenzo il Magnifico and Giuliano.

Santa Maria Novella : a Dominican basilica consecrated in the year 1420. It was named *novella* (new) because it was built on the site of a 9th

century Dominican oratory. Several powerful Florentine families such
as the Strozzi or Gondi commissioned many of its pivotal frescoes.

Sarcophagus: a stone coffin that can bear inscriptions or sculpture.

Signoria : a noun signifying the government used by some Italian city
states throughout the Middle Ages and Renaissance.

T

Transept : a principal portion of the body of a church that often crosses
the nave.

V

Va bene: means "OK" or "all right" in Italian.

Vault : an architectural term describing an arched structure used to secure a space with a ceiling or roof.

Verrocchio, de Andrea (b. 1435 – d. 1488) : a sculptor and a painter, he
changed his given name from Andrea di Michele di Francesco de' Cioni to adopt the surname of the Master goldsmith under whom he was
an apprentice. Andrea de Verrocchio was also the Maestro of his own
workshop. His workshop is responsible for several pivotal sculptures of
the Golden Age and for pupils including Leonardo da Vinci and Lorenzo
di Credi.

Vespucci, Simonetta (b. 1453 – d. 1476) : was a young noblewoman from Ge-
noa and the wife of Marco Vespucci of Florence. It is hypothesized that
apart from being renowned as the greatest beauty of Florence, she was

the model for several of Botticelli's masterpieces, including *The Birth of Venus*.

Vinci, da Leonardo (b. 1377 – d. 1446) : One of the most famous artists of all time. He is the definition of what many call a Renaissance man. Not only is he renowned for his artwork but also for his ingenuity in the fields of engineering, science, music, and architecture. In his later years, he moved to Milan and offered his services to the Sforza family. In his life, he completed few paintings, but he left an invaluable legacy for generations in the form of studies and inventions.

Z

Zio: Italian for "uncle."

Zia: Italian for "aunt."

About the Author

MARIA CRISTINA TRUJILLO WAS born in the summer of 1987 at the Air Force Academy hospital in Colorado Springs, Colorado. As she grew up, she lived in several states and countries along with her parents, two sisters, and brother. In 2005, Maria moved from Santiago, Chile to Miami, Florida where she received her bachelor of arts in art history from Florida International University. While working towards her degree, she studied abroad in San Gemini, Italy. She went on to acquire her master's degree in art history, with a focus in Latin American textiles. Since graduating, she has worked towards bringing her passions of art and history to a broader audience by conserving them in the memories of the present. Apart from writing while consuming toxic quantities of coffee, she loves to read, paint, cook, and explore the world beyond her front door.

www.ingramcontent.com/pod-product-compliance
Lightning Source LLC
Chambersburg PA
CBHW080837250626
47160CB00009B/2962